A Twelfth Dan Master of ███████████ Illuminated order of the Cele████████████ has also had a total of thirty-n████████████ off-licence manager, market-stall trader, rock singer and garden gnome salesman. He lives in Sussex with his wife and family.

Robert Rankin is the author of *Snuff Fiction*, *Apocalypso*, *The Dance of the Voodoo Handbag*, *Sprout Mask Replica*, *Nostradamus Ate My Hamster*, *A Dog Called Demolition*, *The Garden of Unearthly Delights*, *The Most Amazing Man Who Ever Lived*, *The Greatest Show Off Earth*, *Raiders of the Lost Car Park*, *The Book of Ultimate Truths*, the *Armageddon* quartet (three books), and the *Brentford* trilogy (five books) which are all published by Corgi books. Robert Rankin's latest novel, *Sex and Drugs and Sausage Rolls*, is now available as a Doubleday hardback.

WHAT THEY SAY ABOUT ROBERT RANKIN

'One of the rare guys who can always make me laugh'
Terry Pratchett

'To the top-selling ranks of humorists such as Douglas Adams and Terry Pratchett, let us welcome Mr Rankin'
Tom Hutchinson, *The Times*

'A born writer with a taste for the occult. Robert Rankin is to Brentford what William Faulkner was to Yoknapatawpha County'
Time Out

'One of the finest living comic writers . . . a sort of drinking man's H.G. Wells'
Midweek

THE BOOK OF
ULTIMATE TRUTHS

Robert Rankin

CORGI BOOKS

THE BOOK OF ULTIMATE TRUTHS
A CORGI BOOK : 0 552 13922 X

Originally published in Great Britain by Doubleday,
a division of Transworld Publishers

PRINTING HISTORY
Doubleday edition published 1993
Corgi edition published 1994

7 9 10 8

Set in 10½ pt Linotype Sabon by
Phoenix Typesetting, Ilkley, West Yorkshire.

Corgi Books are published by Transworld Publishers,
61–63 Uxbridge Road, London W5 5SA,
a division of The Random House Group Ltd,
in Australia by Random House Australia (Pty) Ltd,
20 Alfred Street, Milsons Point, Sydney, NSW 2061, Australia,
in New Zealand by Random House New Zealand Ltd,
18 Poland Road, Glenfield, Auckland 10, New Zealand
and in South Africa by Random House (Pty) Ltd,
Endulini, 5a Jubilee Road, Parktown 2193, South Africa.

Printed and bound in Great Britain by
Cox & Wyman Ltd, Reading, Berkshire.

I dedicate this book to an old buddy from Ealing School of Art, Freddie Mercury.

You made the world a more fun place to be and died tragically still owing me that three quid from 1972.

We miss you, Fred.

Introduction

He had known many previous incarnations. And then some.

He had walked the Earth as Nostradamus, Uther Pendragon, Count Cagliostro and Rodrigo Borgia. Although probably not in that order.

He spoke seventeen languages, played darts with the Dalai Lama and shared his sleeping-bag with Rasputin, Albert Einstein, Lawrence of Arabia and George Formby.

He was worshipped as a god by an East Acton cargo cult and once scaled Everest in a smoking-jacket and plus-fours to win a bet with Oscar Wilde.

He travelled to Venus in the company of George Adamski, reinvented the ocarina and was burned in effigy by The Chiswick Townswomen's Guild.

He was an expert swordsman, a gourmet chef, a world traveller, poet, painter, stigmatist, guru to gurus and hater of Bud Abbott.

He could open a tin of sardines with his teeth, strike a Swan Vestas on his chin, rope steers, drive a steam locomotive and hum all the works of Gilbert and Sullivan without becoming confused or breaking down in tears.

He won a first at Oxford, squandered three fortunes, made love to a thousand women, imbibed strange drugs, sold his soul for Rock 'n' Roll, almost pipped Einstein for the Nobel Prize, was barred from every Chinese noodle parlour in West London and died penniless, at a Hastings boarding-house in his ninetieth year.

His name was Hugo Artemis Solon Saturnicus Reginald Arthur Rune. And he was never bored.

He penned more than eight million words. His autohagiography, *The Greatest Man Who Ever Lived*, chronicles the life of an individual who shunned the everyday, scorned the laws of ordinary man, laughed in the face of convention, reinvented the ocarina and hated Bud Abbott.

He was a character in an age of characters. An exaggerated shadow cast in the fashionable places of his day. The confidant of kings and criminals, popes and prizefighters, lighthouse keepers and lingerie salesmen, boffins and bikers.

Strangely enough, hardly anyone remembers him today.

His greatest work, *The Book Of Ultimate Truths*, has long ago vanished from the bookshelves. The British Library denies all knowledge of it. Smith's can't get it in and a recent privately printed edition turned out to be an elaborate hoax, perpetrated by a certain Sir John Rimmer, a bogus biographer of Rune, now living as a tax exile in California.

The Book Of Ultimate Truths was Rune's *magnum opus*. An encyclopaedia of his accumulated wisdom. Within it, the Master explains, in terms understandable to the layman, exactly what life is really all about.

Why there are always two small screws left over when you reassemble that broken toaster. Where all the yellow-handled screwdrivers go to. Why supermarket trolleys congregate beneath canal bridges. How the thermos flask knows what to keep hot and what to keep cold. Why the aspirin is only guessing. Where all the road cones come from and where they go to afterwards and why it's always right where you're driving. The myth of 'dry' cleaning. Dogturd geomancy. How Arran sweaters grow while you sleep. Why it is impossible to be first in a post office queue and much much more.

Throughout his colourful life the Forces of Darkness sought constantly to prevent Rune from revealing his *Ultimate Truths*. Satanic agencies plagued him in many human forms. Cuckolded husbands, the original inventor of the ocarina, The Chiswick Townswomen's Guild and The Bud Abbott Appreciation Society, to mention but a few.

Added to these were landlords and lodging-house keepers, the proprietors of West London Chinese noodle parlours, milkmen, tailors, shoemakers, manufacturers of magical accoutrements, travel agents and vintners. All labouring under what Rune referred to as, 'the curious misconception that a Master should pay his bills as do the humble folk'.

But, although under constant threat of assassination or litigation, Hugo Rune was never afraid to speak out, name names and point the finger of accusation. His modest aim was to increase mankind's knowledge and single-handedly bring about World Peace.

THE BOOK OF ULTIMATE TRUTHS MUST BE REPUBLISHED FOR ALL OUR SAKES

Peace Day Celebrations

Being too young to remember Peace Day, Cornelius Murphy asked his Uncle Brian to tell him all about it.

'Well, son,' said the uncle, settling himself on the box ottoman and sucking life into his pipe. 'What would you like to know?'

'Were there flags?' Cornelius asked.

'Flags?' The uncle puffed upon his ancient meerschaum. 'Flags there were, son. Flags of every shape and hue. The whole of Sprite Street was decked out like a stamp album. There were Union Jacks galore and your aunt and me made bunting from lengths of toilet roll and hung it out of the windows.'

'And were there cakes?' Cornelius asked.

'Cakes? I'll say there were cakes. Old Ma Riley made a cake like Buckingham Palace and the girls from the steam laundry baked buns like victory signs and battleships and lions and tigers. I even recall an unsliced brown, fashioned after the manner of Winston Churchill's cigar.'

'Gosh.' Cornelius hugged his knees. 'And dancing, Uncle Brian. Did people dance?'

'Dance?' The uncle waved his pipe in the air. 'Dance we did, son. We danced all night. Two brass bands came down from the colliery. Bands with horns and trumpets and big bass drums. We danced until our feet were sore and then we danced again.'

He sat back as if even the memory exhausted him.

'And were there toads, Uncle Brian?' For Cornelius had run out of questions and interest at exactly the same moment.

'*Toads?*' asked the uncle. 'I'll say there were toads. Toads as big as dogs. Dancing and singing and playing the bagpipes.'

It was the first time Cornelius had met with insanity and being only a small child he was favourably impressed.

1

The changing room smelt of stale plimsolls, young armpits and unwashed bottoms. Even now, when the boys responsible had become young men and gone off to make their ways in the world.

The August sunlight filtered through high panes with no particular enthusiasm. It touched upon empty lockers, unemployed clothes pegs and peely paintwork. It didn't make much of the singular individual draped upon the low bench beneath the window. But then why should it? The sun had far better things to be doing and far better places to be.

As did the sitter on the bench.

His name was Cornelius Murphy. And he was the stuff of epics.

Cornelius was a tall boy who had not as yet grown into his body. His limbs dangled and seemed forever uncertain what they should be doing with themselves. His dark hair, however, had made up its mind. It chose to defy all discipline, and form precarious waves. These broke in whatever direction the mood took them.

Cornelius had a noble brow in the making. A fine aquiline nose, sharp grey eyes and a wide mouth, which was, like as not, to be found smiling.

It wasn't smiling now.

Cornelius turned up his wristwatch and viewed the hour. A little after ten of the morning clock. The world awaited him.

The tall boy rose awkwardly, stretched and put his best foot forward. He opened the door and prepared to make good his escape.

The burly figure of the games master barred his way and shouted the words 'Science Room!' into his left ear.

The science-room windows were within easy reach of the schoolkeeper's shammy. They were clean. The August sun entered them with gusto.

The mahogany work tables, mottled by youthful misexperiment, shone with a rich dark patina. The Edwardian display cases containing apparatus whereby Boyle's Law could be proven beyond all reasonable doubt, veritably twinkled. Bunsen burners, Petri dishes, retorts and test tube holders winked enticingly. In a drawer the litmus paper mused upon which way to turn.

At a desk before the window sat a pale man in a dark suit.

He was a man 'driven'.

His name was Mr Yarrow and he was the youth employment officer.

To this pale and hollow man fell the enormous responsibility of placing every school-leaving boy in full-time employment before the end of his final term. And Mr Yarrow went about this task as one possessed. For indeed he was.

Under Mr Yarrow's guiding hand, the reputation of the school was untarnished, these five long years. He had seen to it that each and every boy found his way into a suitable occupation. And he did it through a method that was little less than divinely inspired.

It had come to him as a blinding revelation when he was but a small child. He had been playing *Happy Families* at the time and wondering why it was that

14

the families depicted on the cards should be so happy and his wasn't. And then it struck him. Bang! Right out of the blue. It was their names and the jobs they did. The two were magically linked! Mr Bun was a baker and Mr Thread a tailor. That was it. It was so obvious that he marvelled that none should have seen it before him. If you wanted to be happy in life, then you had to find an occupation that began with the same letter as your surname.

It was *that* simple!

At first it made him somewhat sad, because he dearly wished to become a train robber. And then it made him somewhat fearful, the thought that he alone should possess this knowledge. But possess it he did and there was no turning back. His future was mapped out for him. He would become Mr Yarrow the youth employment officer and bring happiness to thousands.

And for the last five years he had been doing just that.

Certainly many parents seemed genuinely bewildered upon learning the nature of the job he had lined up for their offspring. A few had even become downright hostile. These spoke openly of ropes being thrown over high beams and tar and feathers brought into play.

But he had skilfully pacified even the most vociferous of dissenters.

To those who did not respond to his sad soliloquies on the terrible social stigma which must naturally fall upon the parents who forbade their own child the opportunity of gainful employment and condemned him instead to a living purgatory of dole-queue misery, there was always the wall of shame, upon which their names must be forever writ in letters big, for destroying the glorious reputation of the school.

For the most part, however, parents seemed pathetically grateful that their wretched boys had any job to go to.

Mr Yarrow turned papers upon his desk. The papers came from a big fat file. Upon this the name of Cornelius Murphy was writ in letters big. Big and red.

Murphy's final year had come to an end and the loathsome boy remained without employment. It was the now legendary Nightmare Scenario.

With the final minutes of the term ticking away Mr Yarrow had called Murphy Senior and frantic talks had taken place. An agreement had hastily been arrived at, to the effect that Cornelius would be kept on at school for an indefinite period until matters could be expedited.

During this eleventh-hour telephonic summit, Murphy Senior had proved himself to be a tower of strength and a fortress of moral rectitude. He could not countenance, he said, the thought that his only son should besmirch the good name of his own old Alma Mater. But neither could his conscience allow him to enter into duplicity. He suggested an inspired compromise.

Cornelius would remain on at school until real work could be found for him. But during this period, in order that the school's reputation remain intact, he should be taken on in some capacity and paid a salary, that of a youth employment officer's assistant, for example. Mr Yarrow agreed willingly.

But a month had passed since then. A month which had seen less and less of Cornelius Murphy. Today, however, was Murphy's fourth payday. Mr Yarrow was determined that it should be his last.

The door opened and Cornelius Murphy was propelled into the science room.

'Sit down.' Mr Yarrow did not look up from his papers.

Cornelius chose a seat by the door.

'Over here.' A nicotined finger indicated the chair before the desk. Cornelius shambled over and sat down noisily. He smiled at Mr Yarrow. Mr Yarrow did not smile back. Three feet of desk top separated them. And about twelve million miles.

Mr Yarrow made a purposeful face and turned foolscap pages before him. It was a slow and deliberate process. There was no sense of urgency about it.

Cornelius studied the youth employment officer. He observed that his ears, made almost transparent by the sunlight, closely resembled a pair of human embryos. That the dandruff flecks on his left shoulder formed the configuration of Ursa Major. That the rich orange hue of the nicotined finger matched that obtained by the French painter Saint-Martin, who used ground fragments from the heart of Louis XIV to achieve the effect. That a bead of perspiration above Mr Yarrow's left eyebrow contained a microcosm of the visible universe.

Mr Yarrow continued to turn papers. At intervals he looked up at Cornelius and shook his head doubtfully. Cornelius found the habit mildly annoying, but as he prided himself that he could get through any interview with Mr Yarrow without uttering a single word, he refrained from comment.

At very great length Mr Yarrow leaned back in his chair, sighed deeply and gazed upon Cornelius Murphy.

'This is a fine pickle,' he said.

Cornelius nodded thoughtfully. A fine pickle and no mistake, he supposed.

'Do you know what I think when I see a lad like you?'

Cornelius shook his head. He didn't know. Neither did he care.

'I think, There but for the grace of God go I.'

Cornelius smiled warmly and rose to go with God's grace.

'Sit down!' Cornelius sat down. 'I think,' Mr Yarrow continued, squeezing his left earlobe and inflicting brain damage upon a metaphysical foetus, 'I think, What can I do for this graceless lad?'

Cornelius yawned.

'Sit up straight, lad.'

Cornelius made a vain attempt to do so. His hair made an unscheduled portside call. He forced it back to the starboard bow.

'Your school reports.' Mr Yarrow prodded the offenders. 'A tale of woe. Constant absenteeism. No team activities. Poor exam results. Chances thrown away. Advice ignored. No attempts made to knuckle down and smarten up. Have you filled in the application form I gave you?'

Cornelius recalled the form. It had become a paper dart. There had been mention of 'machine minding' on that form. And machine minding's star did not burn brightly in the Murphy firmament.

'You've lost it, I suppose.'

Cornelius nodded.

'Speak up.'

Cornelius nodded louder.

'How many interviews have I sent you to?'

Cornelius counted silently upon his fingers.

'Seven, that's how many.'

Cornelius thought seven seemed about right. He wasn't going to quibble.

Mr Yarrow read the list to himself. Mechanic, Merchant Seaman, Minicab Driver, Monumental

Mason, Motor Cycle Messenger, Marriage Counsellor, Male Model. Any one of these was surely right up Murphy's street. What was the matter with the boy? Didn't he want to be helped? Mr Yarrow shook his head. He'd never known a boy to fail *seven* interviews.

But curiously, as he perused once more the reasons given for Murphy's rejection, they hardly seemed to be the tall boy's fault.

He had been considered 'too well spoken' to be a minicab driver. 'Too sophisticated' to be a marriage counsellor. 'Too rugged' to be a male model, yet 'too delicate' to be a mechanic. And so on and so forth.

'I don't get it.' Mr Yarrow shook his head once more. 'I send you along to seven interviews. Clearly you do your best, the interviewers call me, praising you as an excellent chap. But then they abjectly apologize that due to some ludicrous technicality, they cannot employ you. How can anyone be "too tall" to be a monumental mason?'

Cornelius shrugged. Something to do with the average height of tombstones, he supposed.

'I just don't get it,' Mr Yarrow went on. 'Your school work is appalling, yet you shine at interviews. You shine at interviews, yet no-one is willing to employ you. It's a fine pickle and no mistake about it.'

Inwardly Cornelius agreed that it probably was.

Mr Yarrow tugged a long card-index box across the desk and set about it with a bespittled finger. Cornelius observed that the wooden bobbin dangling on a string from the window blind was the shape of an acorn. A relic of the belief that the oak, the sacred tree of the Thunder God, could protect you from lightning.

'Aha!' Mr Yarrow plucked a card from the box and waved it in the air. 'Gotcha!' He smiled at Cornelius.

Cornelius found the experience unsettling. 'I have it. Just the ticket.' His eyes narrowed upon Murphy. 'Do you know what I have here?'

Cornelius shook his head.

'Are you sure?'

Cornelius nodded.

Mr Yarrow chuckled. 'Are you sure you're sure?'

Cornelius nodded again.

Mr Yarrow chuckled again. 'Sure you're sure you're sure?'

Cornelius scratched his head inciting further wavy rebellions.

'Perfect, perfect.' The youth employment officer took a form from a folder. Filled it in with his fountain pen. Blotted it. Folded it into an envelope. Sealed this. Printed a name and address thereupon in big black capitals. Blotted this and handed the whole to Cornelius Murphy.

'There,' he said. 'Now be careful not to lose it. Go straight to the address and ask for Monsieur Messidor. And just be yourself. Do you understand? Don't try too hard. Just be yourself.'

Cornelius looked bemused.

'Perfect,' crowed Mr Yarrow. 'That's the stuff. Off you go now. I'll phone to say that you're on your way.'

Cornelius rose to his feet, knocking over his chair. Normally this was met with a stony stare. But not this time. This time Mr Yarrow roared with laughter and said 'perfect' once again.

Cornelius paused a moment to extend his right hand. Mr Yarrow paused a moment before placing a wage packet into it. Cornelius nodded his thanks. Mr Yarrow clapped his hands together.

By the time Cornelius had reached the door, the

youth employment officer was already tidying his desk.

And by the time Cornelius had left the playground and taken to the street, his feet were up and the cigarettes were out.

The sun shone in at the science-room window. Outside, on the coke heap, a retired tom-cat dreamed about Clara Bow.

The ashbowl was full and the fag packet empty when the telephone finally rang. Monsieur Messidor spoke in a thick French accent.

He had never met such a boy, he enthused. A boy whose future celebrity was assured by his sparkling personality, combined with a fearsome intellect. He could not thank Mr Yarrow enough for having introduced him. It would be a guerdon, second only to receiving the *Légion d'honneur*, to take and train this talented boy.

Mr Yarrow breathed a great and heartfelt sigh of relief. 'At last!'

'But alas,' continued the voice of Monsieur M, 'regretfully Master Murphy is "too well endowed" to be a MIME ARTISTE.'

Mr Yarrow buried his face in his hands and began to weep.

In a nearby telephone box Cornelius Murphy gently replaced the receiver. Much as he had done seven times before. Eight, if you counted the famous eleventh-hour summit.

'The world awaits,' said Mr Murphy the Mimic.

And so it did.

2

During the summer of 1967, Hugo Rune gave a series of lectures at The Rondo Hatton Memorial Hall in Brentford, West London.

These were all recorded on film, but sadly the present whereabouts of this historic footage is unknown. Transcripts of the lectures still remain, however, and these serve as fascinating documents. Demonstrating, as they do, not only Rune's undoubted genius, but his astonishing charisma and unfailing ability to hold an audience spellbound.

TRANSCRIPT FROM THE HUGO RUNE LECTURES.
LECTURE SEVEN. UNIVERSAL TRUTHS:
You want 'em. I got 'em.

Rune enters the crowded hall more than an hour late. He is carried slowly down the centre aisle upon a cushioned palanquin, borne upon the naked shoulders of four local May Queens. The acolyte Rizla walks before, swinging a lighted censer. The applause is deafening.

The palanquin is laid down before the stage. Rune is lifted carefully from it and placed upon a mound of plumped cushions.

The crowd chants, 'Hu-go Hu-go.'

After a five-minute standing ovation, Rune, who appears

to have been asleep throughout, raises a hand to still the multitude. The hall falls silent. The acolyte Rizla clears his throat to deliver the lecture.

Rune snores gently.

Peoples of the world. These are the words of Hugo Rune, delivered through the mouth of my amanuensis Rizla. Upon this day I bestow my wisdom upon you. That you might become as I. So be it. Let it be said.

Let me begin by explaining the universe.

The universe is a very quiet, very still, light and airy kind of a place. And in order to understand it and one's place in it, one must be *as* the universe. (Much nodding of heads.)

We have all endured for far too long, the blatherings of scientific greybeards regarding 'The Expanding Universe'. According to these learned fellows, the universe began with a violent explosion. A Big Bang.

Exactly who, or what, triggered this Titanic blast, or what exactly was going on half an hour before it went off, we are not told. (Laughter.)

But such matters do not concern friend greybeard. He has made up his mind that there was a Big Bang and that is that. And further he asserts, not only is the universe expanding, due to being flung in all directions by this genetic detonation, but that *space itself* is also expanding. (Wild laughter, hoots of derision.)

And do you know what I say to friend greybeard? I say, Tish and Tosh, and old wet fish! (Applause. Cries of, 'Bravo'.)

I say this. If space is expanding, then atoms and molecules, which contain space, must therefore be expanding also. Because if they didn't, then all solid matter would simply turn to vapour. And if everything is expanding, at the same time, then *relatively speaking* it must remain the same size. As there is nothing to judge the degree of its expansion against.

(Applause.)

Therefore the cosmos must be considered in a state of perpetual stasis. The same as it has always been. For ever and ever. The universe is going nowhere. *It is standing still!*

(Thunderous applause. Cries of, 'Nice one, Hugo,' and, 'Well spotted, that man.')

And standing still brings me to sitting still, which, the more observant amongst you will probably have noticed, I am doing now.

Because: *In order to be at one with the Static Cosmos, one must achieve a state of supreme stillness.*

This state is known as *Apathy*. (Gasps.)

The word APATHY derives from the Atlantean. A-PATH-Y. A meaning A. PATH meaning path. And Y being an abbreviation of WHY.

Quite literally A PATH TO THE MEANING WHY.

But it is a hard path to follow. And few are there with courage enough to try. The *Apathé*, i.e., 'seeker after truth', must maintain a strict regimen. He must discipline himself to rigorously avoid any form of activity, be this mental or physical. He must be prepared to sit, for years if needs be, until he is in tune and receives enlightenment. Others must selflessly administer to his needs. (Murmurs of disapproval from female members of the audience. Male cries of, 'Ssssh.')

The *Apathé* must guard against laziness.

Laziness is a vile and shallow thing, practised by wicked individuals who refuse to administer to the needs of the *Apathé*.

Come down hard on laziness. If detected in a wife or mother, the employment of a stout stick generally has the desired effect. (Cries of, 'Shame!' from members of The Chiswick Townswomen's Guild. Catcalls from the balcony.)

For one man to achieve the supreme state of Cosmic Consciousness, a state of absolute serenity, perfect peace and harmony, boundless knowledge and universal understanding, should this require the application of a thousand stout sticks, I would consider it a small price to pay.

(Screams of, 'String him up!' A woman's shoe is thrown.)

For such a man all things would be possible. Having reached the state of at-oneness with the universe, his wisdom would be utterly profound, his word divine law, his authority unassailable. So what if it calls for the stout-sticking of some idle spouse? (Townswomen's Guild members storm the stage. Fights break out. The acolyte Rizla is struck down by a handbag.)

TRANSCRIPT ENDS

Invisible lines form the network of our existence.

We move along them continually. Between home and school. Home and workplace. Home and social abode. And here and there and wherever. Some of us weave small tight webs. Others span the world. What it all means is anyone's guess.

Cornelius strolled along an invisible line which linked the secondary school with The Wife's Legs Café. It had become, of late, a quite well-trodden little line.

The Wife's Legs Café served a moderate spread at an affordable price and had an obvious attraction to recommend it.

It had become the regular haunt of hearty working men with fearsome bottom cleavage, who shared an appreciation of small newspapers with big headlines, a moderate spread at an affordable price and a well-turned ankle. In fact it had become such a moneyspinner that the proprietor, Mr Ridout the Restaurateur, had opened a small chain of similar eateries. These included The Sister's Legs, The Sister-in-law's Legs and The Mother's Legs (a meals-on-wheels service).

Sadly this expanding empire had fallen when he foolishly overstepped the boundary of good taste and opened The Girlfriend's Legs to a waiting world.

He hadn't come out of the divorce too well.

Cornelius found much to observe in the café. He had his own special seat by the window. The ex-wife, who had taken quite a shine to him, kept it reserved. When he returned to it from the telephone box outside, it was unoccupied.

Cornelius ordered another bacon sandwich and a cup of tea.

'Coming right up, precious,' crooned the wonderful woman. Cornelius observed that a beauty spot on her right thigh resembled the Isle of Lyonesse.

He wiped a peephole from the condensation on the window and viewed the world beyond. Something momentous was bound to happen soon. He just knew it.

The café door groaned open and Tuppe waddled in. He was carrying a brown paper bag.

Now Tuppe was squat. Even in the company of small people he was considered diminutive. Dwarves gazed upon Tuppe and asked, 'Who is the short bloke?'

Tuppe turned a fair coin impersonating babies for TV commercials, but his mind was ever upon higher things. Tuppe knew himself to be the stuff of epics. He was Cornelius Murphy's closest friend. Spying out the unevenly crossed legs, he steered his tiny shoe towards Murphy's table.

The ex-wife, bearing the tall boy's second breakfast, stepped over him, scooped up a stool and tucked it in beside Cornelius. Cornelius helped his companion on to it.

'Good-day, Tuppe,' said he.

'Good-day, Cornelius,' the other replied. 'Is that bacon within?'

Cornelius proffered his plate. 'It is. Eat your fill.'

Tuppe took advantage of his friend's largesse. 'A cup that cheers would not go amiss,' he remarked.

Cornelius ordered another tea. 'I can promise no applause.'

'Always the wag.' Tuppe tucked into his brekky.

'Might I enquire as to the contents of the enigmatic sack?' Cornelius indicated the bag on the table top.

'A hibernating fish. Held under test conditions.'

Cornelius steered the conversation towards another port of call. He had no love for fish.

'The loon Yarrow made another attempt to have me employed today.'

'A pox upon Yarrow and all his works.' Tuppe strained a bacon rind through the gap in his front teeth. 'You drew your salary of course?'

'Of course.'

'Then peace be unto you.' Tuppe munched on. Cornelius sipped his tea. Tuppe's arrived and he did likewise. 'Fab legs, the ex-wife,' he remarked. 'All the way up.'

Cornelius raised an eyebrow.

'Sorry-pardon. But you know how it is.'

Cornelius did. The two understood each other. Completely.

After a while Tuppe asked, 'How is the daddy?'

'Taken to his shed.'

'And the mother?'

'Under doctor's orders.'

'And what of yourself?'

'Sound in wind and limb. But having an itch I am unable to scratch.'

'The stuff of epics business? I feel it also.'

'I know that you do.'

'I think,' Tuppe pulled a converted shirt tail from

27

his trouser pocket and dabbed his mouth with it, 'that we had best finish up here and apply ourselves to adventures elsewhere.'

And so they did.

Above and beyond the secondary school and The Wife's Legs Café loomed Star Hill. Filling a substantial amount of skyline and covering six full squares of the Ordnance Survey map.

Star Hill was common land. And so its lower acres were given over to recreational pursuits. Footballs were kicked here, picnics and sports days held. Litter spread.

The wooded middle ground was reserved for track biking, bird nesting and youthful fornication. Here the men in the macs played hide and seek with the plain-clothed policewomen.

The peak, some three hundred feet above sea level, according to the bench mark, had a certain magic about it. The local Wiccans came up here on warm nights to dance around in their bare scuddies. Foxes fiddled in the thickets. Rare orchids bloomed unseen and the wind came always from the east.

A concrete plinth, erected by the town council in 1935, marked the spot where the earthly remains of the Reverend Matthew Kemp had been interred exactly three hundred years before. The Rev. had obtained the permission of the Archbishop of Canterbury to have himself buried there, at the highest point in the district, standing on his head. His reasoning being that when the clarion call is sounded on Resurrection Day and the whole world is turned upside down, he would be the first one out and standing on his feet.

The concrete plinth was surmounted by an engraved copper map of the district. Radiating spokes informed prospect-viewers of the distances and directions to such exotic destinations as Nepal, Tasmania, the Nile Delta, Portugal and Penge.

The copper map had evidently been fastened to the concrete plinth through the medium of some nineteen-thirties metallurgical technology which is sadly lost to us today, because it ruggedly defied even the most enterprising attempts to prise it free and bear it off to the smelting pot.

The concrete plinth exhibited similar stoicism, having withstood the best that several generations of secondary schoolboys could formulate and explode against it.

Both plinth and map remained inviolate.

Irreverent humorists chuckled in anticipation of the Reverend Kemp's unecclesiastical language when the clarion call was sounded and he tried to dig his way out.

Cornelius and Tuppe strolled up Star Hill. The invisible lines, which traced the patterns of their existence, merged into one. Became a geodesic spiral engirdling the hill. Terminated at the plinth and were never mentioned again.

Tuppe had travelled the latter part of the journey on the tall boy's shoulders. Cornelius lifted him down and set him upon the copper map. The burnished copper shone bravely, having only the previous night survived unscathed a particularly concerted attack upon its person. In a nearby bush a defunct oxyacetylene cutter attracted the attention of a passing stoat.

The young men of epic stuff took the air. Cornelius worried at his top knot and Tuppe kicked his tiny bootheels against the plinth and patted his brown paper bag.

The world as they knew it was displayed around and about.

To the north, the Grand Union Canal drew the line before the industrial estate.

To the west, the commoners' fields met the highway where the buses turned around and the shops went on parade.

To the south lay a vast area of redevelopment, relieved only by the remains of a Victorian terrace. Six houses, and one of these the Murphy residence.

To the east, well fenced and warning hung, a sheer drop of two hundred feet fell down to the golf course. Whilst being of no particular interest right now, this cliff would, nevertheless, have an exciting part to play somewhat later.

'How is the fish?' Cornelius asked, for its proximity troubled him.

Tuppe peeped into the bag. 'Ssssh,' said he.

'It's dead, that fish of yours, isn't it, Tuppe?'

Tuppe nodded. 'By the look of it I would think so.'

'Then what was all that talk of hibernation and test conditions?'

Tuppe winked. 'Did you ever hear tell of Polgar The Unprecedented?'

'He of Polgar's Porcine Circus?'

'The very same. My father worked the sideshow circuit with the man years back. Polgar exhibited a number of star turns. The Singing Sheep of Sudbury, Toby a Sapient Pig and The Extraordinary Exhibition of Industrious Fleas. Apparently the latter was a thing of great wonder. With trained insects reenacting the siege of Rorke's Drift to considerable effect.'

'But he is best remembered for his Porcine Circus.'

'Indeed. He toured the rural communities with it. The pigs were schooled to scale ladders, walk tightropes and perform feats of prestidigitation. At each venue he inevitably sold at least one of the pigs to an eager farming type.'

'That doesn't sound very practical.'

'Oh it was. The pigs were well trained. And as Polgar left town he rang the dinner bell and the sold pig climbed out of the farmer's pen and returned to him. It worked very well for a while. But eventually it cost him a term at Her Majesty's pleasure. By the time he got out, the performing pig had lost most of its charm for the paying customer.'

'But what about the fish?'

'Polgar's grandson is Peter Polgar. He of Peter's Pets in the high street.'

'I know of it.'

'And young Polgar is a gentleman of wild talent. Much given to the creation of the chimera.'

'I have passed his premises on many an occasion,' said Cornelius. 'Those beasts visible through the grimy window are all a shade too mythical for my particular taste.'

'Quite so and your reference to the window gives you the measure of the man.'

'He is careful with his pennies?'

'He is a tight-fisted bas—'

'Quite so.'

'And this fish in a bag is his latest accomplishment. An ungodly hybrid of squirrel and trout. His intention is the cuddly fish that feeds on acorns and sleeps through the winter when nobody wants to go outside and look in their fishpond anyway.'

'He is certainly a sharp one, this Polgar. But I do detect a slight flaw or two in his reasoning.'

'You do?'

'I do. For one thing, this is now high summer and not the hibernation season.'

'I did mention this to him. But he said he'd pay me a fiver if I took the fish out for a bit of fresh air in the hope that it might drop off to sleep. Fish never sleep, you see, so if this one does, then that's half the battle won as far as friend Polgar is concerned.'

'Which does rather bring me to flaw number two. Did you care to touch upon the fact that fish rarely flourish once they are removed from water?'

'No. I preferred to accept the fiver.'

'I would have done the same. Shall we bury the fish then?'

'What here? Hardly sporting to the Reverend Kemp.' Tuppe emptied the unnatural issue into his lap. Cornelius viewed it with distaste.

'Are those little feet?' he asked.

'Seems like. And it has really horrid teeth. Do you want to see?'

'No thank you.'

'As you please.' Tuppe took the furry fish by its tail and sniffed it. 'Would there be good eating in a fish like this, do you suppose?'

Cornelius held down his hair and shook his head. 'Not in the squirrel parts. Toss the thing away, Tuppe. I have no love for fish, furred, feathered, fried or farmed.'

'So be it. Sorry, little fishy.' Tuppe flung the aquatic anomaly over his shoulder, wiped his fingers on the paper bag and clambered to his feet on the copper map.

Cornelius put his arm around his friend's shoulder and the two gazed off towards the lands of the east, wondering once more what the fates held in store for them.

The sun cast their shadows behind them. And here occurred a curiosity. For although the two stood with their heads for once on a level pegging, the size of their shadows differed to no small degree.

That of Cornelius was its usual angular self topped off with a twirling banner. But the shadow of Tuppe extended to nearly double the length of his companion's. And even though the little fellow stood stock still, his shadow heaved and twisted as some living creature writhing in unimaginable torment.

And all the birds that saw it stopped singing upon the instant.

And the short hairs rose upon the neck of Cornelius Murphy and he felt suddenly afraid.

Cornelius turned with a jerk, nearly dislodging Tuppe from his precarious perch. But there was nothing for him to see.

'Oh ow,' cried Tuppe, struggling to keep his balance. 'What is happening?'

'I don't know.' Cornelius scratched at his chin. It was going to need a shave in a month or two. 'The birds . . .' He put a hand to his ear. The birds were singing once again.

Cornelius shivered, 'Let's go down, it's turning cold.'

'Cold? Cornelius?' Tuppe shinned down from the plinth.

The tall boy turned away and began to pace away down the hill.

'Cornelius, wait for me.' Tuppe limped off in hot pursuit.

In the long grass, where Tuppe's shadow had performed its curious gyrations, the furry fish awoke from its nap, snapped its horrid teeth and crept away in search of four-legged lunch.

3

Cornelius and Tuppe came down from the hill. At the place where the buses turn around they parted company. Tuppe returned to Peter's Pets, composing as he did an improbable yarn about animal rights activists and the forcible abduction of a furry fish, into a more than plausible truth. And one which would demand compensation.

Cornelius stopped off at the telephone box to call Mr Yarrow at his home. He spoke once more in the voice of Murphy Senior.

'My son is heartbroken,' he told the youth employment officer. 'He so wanted that job as a mime artiste. He is terribly distraught.'

'I'm so sorry,' replied the Yarrow, who most certainly was. 'But be assured of this. I will not rest until I have secured honest employment for your son.'

Cornelius feared that this would more than likely be the case.

He felt that he had seen more than enough of Mr Yarrow.

'I am sending the boy away,' he continued. 'A couple of weeks' rest, that's what he needs. Kindly have ten days' holiday money sent on.'

'Do what?'

'I am holding you directly responsible for the decline in his health. The constant disappointments. The building up and dashing down of his hopes. He is in no fit state to attend further interviews at this time.'

'I am sorry, but I can't sanction holiday money.'

'Then I will speak to the headmaster directly. We share the same lodge. Have no fear, he will sort the matter out.'

There was a bit of a silence at Mr Yarrow's end of the line.

'I hardly feel we need to trouble the head over such trifles.' Mr Yarrow's voice had that 'lost soul' quality about it. 'Do you want the cheque made out for cash?'

'That would be fine. I'll speak to you soon then.'

'Give Cornelius my best wishes and tell him I hope he gets well soon.'

'I will. Goodbye, Mr Yarrow.'

'Goodbye, Mr Murphy.'

Cornelius replaced the receiver. It was all too easy. It gave him no pleasure. But then the pointlessness of unemployment gave him no pleasure. He was bursting with grand schemes. Conning a few pounds from Mr Yarrow and walking the streets held little appeal.

Of course, he had no intention of becoming a nine-to-fiver. He was the stuff of epics after all. A young man of special gifts. Capable of changing the world.

But the world wasn't half taking its time to find this out.

The dustbin men were picking up outside The Wife's Legs.

'Morning, Cornelius,' they called gaily.

'Morning, dustbin men,' the youth replied.

'Don't forget to put your bin out today.'

'I won't.'

The bins were already out by the time Cornelius reached home.

Home was number twenty-three Moby Dick Terrace.

And number twenty-three was now the first house in the street. And number thirty-three the last. But more of that later.

Cornelius lifted the lid from the bin which stood before his front door. The bin was, as ever, empty. A weekly tribute to the mother's skills in conservation and the recycling of the Murphy waste. Whatever entered that house stayed there. If it could not be consumed or made to serve a useful purpose, then it didn't get through the front door. The mother was ecologically sound.

Her system was pretty straightforward. She only purchased unpackaged products, which she bore home in her ancient shopping bag. Fresh meat, fruit and veg. Whatever could not be purchased unpackaged she manufactured herself. Butter and jam and tea. What else did you need? The daddy's daily tabloid served as fire lighter and bottom wipe. Junk mail was readdressed to the sender and despatched stampless. Peelings fed the compost heap. Discarded clothing went to good causes.

Nothing slipped through the net.

Nothing went into the dustbin.

At Christmas the dustbin men always knocked to give Mrs Murphy a box of chocolates and a bunch of flowers.

Cornelius never failed to be unimpressed by the mother's ingenuity. He reasoned that at least half the population of the country was engaged in the production, marketing or disposal of totally useless articles. And should everyone act like his mother, society would grind to a halt.

Cornelius envisaged massive unemployment, anarchy and chaos. Pestilence and devastation would march across the land; and the four horsemen ride the sky. And all those nice dustbin men would be out of a job.

Cornelius dug in his pockets. He found the letter of introduction to Monsieur Messidor and tossed it into the dustbin. He was doing his bit to save the world.

Cornelius turned his key in the lock and quietly entered the ancestral home. He had not been altogether honest with the parents regarding the 'job situation' and considered it prudent to steal silently away to his room, rather than construct explanations for his early return from 'work'.

As he made to sneak up the corridor to the stairs, the sounds of heated debate reached his ears, issuing from the front parlour. Cornelius knelt and pressed an ear to the keyhole of the closed door.

'And I still say the boy should be told,' came the voice of the daddy.

'And I say that he shouldn't,' came the voice of the ecologically sound mama.

'But the rare mutant strain in his make-up could save the world.'

'A pension plan and prospects is all he needs.'

'You are missing the point, woman.'

'Don't call me woman. You're the one wearing the wig.'

'It's not a wig. It's a hair-enhancement accessory. And those aren't your own bosoms by the way.'

'My bosoms play no part in this discussion.'

'Nor does my bald spot.'

'Your bald spot is indicative.'

'Of what?'

'Of your bald outlook on life.'

'And who made it bald? You with the socks stuffed up your front.'

'They're matronly. They project a warm and caring

37

image. The boy needs that. And he needs a haircut also.'

'He can't cut his hair. It's big hair. Famous people always have big hair.'

'You don't.'

'I'm not famous.'

'I should never have married you. My mother was right.'

'You never had a mother.'

'Of course I had a mother. She was a pillar of the community.'

'She was a figment of your imagination. You never had a mother. I never had a mother. You know that.'

'But what about the boy?'

'He should be told.'

'We can't tell him. We took the oath. He must never be told. He will find out for himself when the time is right.'

'The stuff of epics,' said the daddy.

'About that . . .' Cornelius swung open the parlour door without knocking and strode into the room.

The daddy was snoring noisily beneath the daily tabloid. The mother was knitting something for seamen from coloured string.

'About *what*, dear?' she asked in a startled voice.

'About . . . oh . . .'

'You're home early. Did you have a nice evening?'

'Evening?'

The clock on the mantelpiece struck ten. Cornelius noticed that the lights were on and the curtains drawn. He glanced at his wristwatch. It agreed with the clock.

The daddy stirred from beneath his newspaper. 'What is it?'

'It's Cornelius, dear. What did you want, dear?'

'I wanted to know . . .' Cornelius could no longer remember what he wanted to know.

'Yes, dear?'

'Nothing, Mother.'

'Then good night, dear. And don't forget to put your light out.'

'I won't. Good night, Mother, Father.'

'Good night.'

4

Cornelius Murphy awoke in a cold sweat. It was very dark and a clock chimed three somewhere in the distance.

'Where am I?' Cornelius rubbed his eyes and squinted into the darkness. The darkness seemed somehow unfamiliar.

'What am I doing here?' He felt around for the bedside table and the box of matches. His hand found something warm and wet.

'What's that? That's not mine.'

'What's going on?' The voice was not his either.

'Who's that?'

Another voice said dreamily, 'Go back to sleep.'

'Who said that?'

The first voice asked, 'Who is there?'

Cornelius kept quiet. I am not alone, he thought, where are my damn matches?

'I haven't got them,' said a new voice. 'Go back to sleep, will you.'

Cornelius began to feel the seeds of panic taking root in his stomach. 'Help,' cried he. 'Let me out of here.'

'What's going on?' asked a voice Cornelius hadn't heard before.

The tall boy tried to rise, but something heavy was lying across his legs.

'Who's doing that?' asked a voice at his feet.

Cornelius wriggled free. He stumbled across the

room stepping on to grunting and squirming bodies.

'Get off there.'

'Who's kicking me?' Oaths and shouts broke the temporary silences.

Cornelius found himself at a door. He searched for the handle but found a light switch. He pressed his thumb down hard upon it.

He was standing in his pyjamas in his bedroom, which was empty but for the usual furniture.

Cornelius blinked. 'A dream. A bad dream.' He sighed deeply, switched off the light and returned to his bed.

'Watch where you're walking,' said a voice. 'That's my face you're stepping on.'

Cornelius woke again to find the world up and waiting for him.

The sun shone in at his window. The music of the everyday seemed louder than ever.

Milk bottles clinked in E sharp. Women's heels played taps upon the pavement. Heavy lorries did the big power chords and the postman whistled an old Rolling Stones number. It had to be Tuesday.

Cornelius gathered his hair and his thoughts together. Something very strange was going on. Something very strange indeed. An epic something perhaps? He certainly hoped so.

Having assured himself that he was all alone, he climbed from his bed, entered his dressing-gown and took himself down to the kitchen for the first breakfast of the day.

The Murphy kitchen was not something to dwell on. It was an uncompromising little den which, in keeping with the rest of the house, stoutly refused to make up for its lack of charm.

There were a couple of mismatched kitchen units, a butler's sink, an ancient gas oven of the enamel persuasion, a leaking radiator and an odd-legged table with a red Formica top.

Behind the table sat a large three-piece tweed suit. And inside the suit sat a large merry red-faced gentleman. He sported a wig composed from shredded J-Cloths, a present from his wife. His name was Jack Murphy and he was the daddy.

Jack had recently taken early retirement from the dole in order to spend more time with his family. And to devote himself more fully to his hobby.

Jack's hobby was model making and he was currently engaged in a vast and ambitious project. The construction of a model town.

At the end of the garden, in the shed of his own making, stood the fruit of his labour. It was a Utopian vision of Moby Dick Terrace and the surrounding area. Crafted with loving care, and precisely detailed, the model displayed a delightful semi-rural community. A harmonious blending of architectural styles, open spaces, shops and views and vistas.

It differed considerably from the big brash construction currently on display at the town hall, which stood beneath a sign which read NEW TOWN DEVELOPMENT.

Of course the word NEW was now something of a misnomer. The town hall's model was showing some signs of age and beginning to look a little dated. Although work on the NEW DEVELOPMENT had begun several years before, with much champagne bottle breaking and blue ribbon cutting, nothing very much had happened since. True the bulldozers had levelled the old town, but not a single foundation or main drain was, as yet, in place.

This came as a surprise to many. But not those

who knew Jack Murphy. And the borough planning committee had come to know Jack Murphy very well indeed.

All works in progress had ceased due to complicated legal technicalities. These centred around the discovery (by Jack Murphy) of numerous old charters, deeds, documents and papers pertaining to rights of way, common ground, bridle paths, wells, waterholes and Lord alone knows what else.

It was all going to take a good deal of sorting out. And while it did, the diggers stood idle and the construction crews drank tea in The Wife's Legs. And number twenty-three Moby Dick Terrace stayed exactly where it was.

Cornelius entered the kitchen, stubbing his toe on an upraised shard of lino and grazing his shin upon the door, which chose, this morning, to only open half of the way. The daddy smiled up from his copy of *MacKenzie's: Local Law and Lore 1655–1660*.

'Good-morning, revered author of my existence,' said Cornelius.

The oldster chuckled. 'Good-morning to you, respected seed of my loins. Your mother's gone out, but there's tea in the pot.'

'Glory be.' Cornelius poured himself a cup and topped up the daddy's.

'My thanks. Two letters for you.' A big hand indicated the pair of envelopes which lay on the unpolished table top.

Cornelius sat himself down and regarded the envelopes with suspicion. One looked safe enough, bearing, as it did, Mr Yarrow's distinctive scrawl. Cornelius tucked this, unopened, into a dressing gown pocket. Two weeks' holiday money, he assumed correctly.

The other envelope, however, was a different kettle

of fish. This one was big and smart and official looking. It had the words PRIVATE AND CONFIDENTIAL
printed in the top left-hand corner. The tall boy's name
and address were typed on. Dead centre. Cornelius did
not recognize the typeface. It had a slightly Gothic look
to it. He picked up the envelope and gave it a bit of a
shake. Something hard inside went to and fro.

'I did that,' said the daddy. 'Intriguing, isn't it?'

Cornelius replaced the envelope and sipped at his
tea. It was stone cold.

'This tea is cold,' he informed the daddy.

'I thought as much. The last cup was just the same.
Aren't you going to open your envelope?'

'I think not.'

'Let me do it then.'

'Certainly not. It says private and confidential.'

'Only the envelope.' The daddy finished his cold tea.
'I much prefer this hot, you know.' He waggled his cup
at Cornelius. 'Go on, open it up.'

'Oh all right then.' Cornelius picked up the envelope and tore it open. Out fell a sheet of typed
paper and a hard little something. Cornelius picked
up the something. He had never seen a credit card, and
indeed he was not looking at one now. What he was
looking at was something approximately the same size.
Cornelius turned it upon his palm. It was fashioned
from dark green plastic, wafer thin, yet of considerable
weight. A number of holes had been punched through
it. Cornelius observed that these corresponded in size
to the diameter of a number thirteen knitting needle.
He turned his attention to the typed paper. It was a
letter. It read:

Dear Cornelius Murphy
Arthur Kobold Publications are pleased to announce

a vacancy for an ambitious and enterprising young person.

A.K.P. are currently engaged in an epic work and require the services of an independently minded school-leaver prepared to work without supervision at hours of his own choosing.

High remuneration, excellent prospects and an immediate cash bonus await the successful applicant who will present himself at twelve noon today.

Good luck

Arthur Kobold

Cornelius read through the letter again and then whistled. And then he glanced down at his watch. And then he made a troubled face.

'Why do you make a troubled face, oh son of mine?' the daddy asked.

Cornelius handed him the letter. The daddy read through it once. Read through it twice. Glanced up at the kitchen clock. And then he too made a troubled face.

Cornelius observed that several strands of J-Cloth wig spelled out the words 'There is no God but Allah' in Arabic across the daddy's left temple.

'It is nearly ten of the morning clock,' said the elder Murphy.

'And the letter has no address upon it,' his son added.

'Show me the little something.'

Cornelius passed the something to his father, who examined it with great interest. 'What is it?' he asked at length. 'It has more weight than seems natural.'

Cornelius retrieved both letter and card and set them down before him. 'It is clearly a test of initiative. Locate the offices of Arthur Kobold Publications by twelve noon and win the big cash pay out.'

'Bravo, son. Please continue.'

'Well.' Cornelius scratched at his head. The daddy watched the big hair bob perilously. 'The card has a number of holes in it. My guess would be that if you were to place it over the letter and shuffle it about a bit, some sort of pattern might well emerge. Considering the limited time allowed, I doubt that a code, if such there should prove to be, would take too much cracking. Especially for someone ambitious, enterprising, young and independently minded.'

'Someone such as yourself, for example.'

'Precisely. Of course the secret might lie in the card alone.'

'Bravo once more. And so how will you deal with it?'

Cornelius smiled. 'In this fashion. I shall put the letter, the envelope and the little punctured card straight into the dustbin, wash, dress and repair to The Wife's Legs for a *hot* cup of tea.'

'Bravo once more,' chuckled the daddy. 'Exactly what I would have done. Put it in next door's bin though, don't want to upset your mother.'

'Of course.' Cornelius rose to take his leave.

'Just one thing before you go.' The daddy displayed another sheet of paper and handed it to him. 'A list of modelling supplies,' he explained. 'Balsa, glue, brass shimmings, things of that nature.'

'Oh yes?' Cornelius raised an eyebrow.

'Oh yes. I thought you might care to treat me.'

'You did?'

'Out of your "holiday money".' The daddy winked.

Cornelius smiled more broadly than ever. 'My pleasure,' he said.

Cornelius bathed, togged up in a faded Hawaiian shirt

and his favourite (only) summer suit. Slid his unsocked feet into a pair of canvas loafers and set out to test a certain hypothesis.

He breakfasted at The Wife's Legs. Cashed his cheque at the High Street bank. Left the daddy's list with Mr Moore (of Moore's Models) and then went off for a bit of a stroll around.

He passed the time of day with Two Coats the tramp. Waved to some strangers on a coach. Stroked a tom-cat under the chin and watched a steam train go under a bridge.

His strolling took no fixed route. On the contrary, he wandered where the spirit led him. As the town hall clock struck twelve he found himself in an untidy cul-de-sac beneath the railway arches. And as the final chime rang out, before a dark green door.

Cornelius stepped sharply up and rapped upon it with his knuckle.

The door flew open and a small whiskered face peeped up at him.

'Mr Kobold?' Cornelius asked. 'Mr Arthur Kobold?'

'Cornelius Murphy,' said Arthur Kobold. 'I have been expecting you.'

5

'Please be seated.'

Cornelius found himself in the uncluttered office of Mister Arthur Kobold. It was furnished in a style which was new to the tall boy.

The furniture was of antique design and superior craftsmanship, yet appeared fresh from the showroom. Reproduction then? Cornelius thought not. There was more the feeling of a museum about the place. As if the office, its panelled walls and rich dark furnishings had been preserved from the rigours of time.

As had Mr Kobold.

He was dressed in a Victorian morning suit, high starched collar, watered-silk cravat. A diamond tie pin glittered at his throat. He was short and rotund, his face was broad and flat, his hair a high dark ruff. His side whiskers were magnificent.

Cornelius seated himself in an exquisite chair before a mahogany partners' desk. Mr Kobold seated himself behind it. He plucked at the fob chain on his waistcoat and produced a ring of tiny brass keys. With one of these he unlocked an ornately decorated tantalus.

'I think this calls for a small port,' he said merrily as he decanted rich red liquid into a pair of minuscule glasses.

'Here you are.' Mr Kobold passed a glass to Cornelius who raised it in salute.

'To success,' said Arthur Kobold.

'To success.' Cornelius raised his glass but did not drink from it. 'About the cash bonus?' he asked.

'All in good time.' Arthur Kobold delved into a desk drawer and produced an enormous fruit cake. 'Would you care for a slice of this?'

'It looks a magnificent cake, but I've just eaten.'

'As you will.' Arthur Kobold cut himself a generous wedge and thrust the better part of it into his mouth. 'Have any trouble getting here?' he enquired between munchings.

'Apparently not.' Cornelius had noted that famous men and women generally claimed to have fallen into their famous careers through sheer chance. They just happened to be in the right place at the right time. Whether this was simply false modesty on their part, or something of a more cosmic nature, Cornelius had always been eager to discover.

And so here he was.

'Well, here I am,' said Cornelius.

'Indeed you are. And you're the man for me. Would you like to know all about the job?'

'I would prefer first to accept the cash bonus.'

'Have you ever heard of Hugo Rune?' Mr Kobold brushed cakey fragments from his side whiskers.

Cornelius held his hair and nodded. 'A local man by all accounts. Wasn't he burned in effigy by the women of Chiswick?'

'That's the fellow.'

'My father has one of his books.'

'Which one?' Mr Kobold dug into the cake once more.

'*The Book of Ultimate Truths*. I have not read it as yet.'

'Then you should. Carry it with you at all times from now on.'

'Well. I'm reading my way through all the daddy's books. But that one is still many shelves away. Lodged, if I rightly recall, between volumes eighty-nine and ninety of *Local County Bylaws Through The Ages*. The daddy has a great interest in that kind of thing.'

'Well, be that as it may. My company is seeking to republish Rune's work. But in its entirety. Rune was a man of erudite learning. A genius and visionary. *The Book of Ultimate Truths* was his masterwork. But when it was published, years after his death, it was incomplete. Whole sections had been removed.'

'And you are seeking to recover this lost material?'

'Exactly. More port?'

'I haven't finished this one yet.'

'No you haven't. Drink up.'

Cornelius moved the glass towards his lips. 'And where do you suppose this lost material to be? Have you contacted the original publishers?'

'Good boy.' Mr Kobold sucked his fingers. 'Long ago gone into liquidation. No trace. But possibly here.' He dug a wad of papers from another drawer and passed them across the desk to Cornelius.

'There is an auction sale tomorrow. Amongst the lots are the personal effects of the late Victor Zenobia.'

'Zenobia?' Cornelius asked. 'Wasn't she the third-century queen of Palmyra, who was captured by the Roman emperor Aurelian?'

'That's the one. But this Victor Zenobia was one of Rune's former acolytes. He was Rune's secretary. And so, amongst his personal effects are a number of papers. They may be those that I seek, they may be not. They may, however, furnish some clues. I have also a list of names. People I should like traced. Someone has the missing papers. Of this I am certain.'

Cornelius was currently working his way through the

seedy section of the daddy's library. He was at present enjoying *Bodies On The Backlot*. A Lazlo Woodbine thriller.

'What you need is a private detective,' said Cornelius Murphy.

'In as many words, or fewer, yes.' Arthur Kobold smiled.

'You've cake in your teeth,' said Cornelius. 'Might I see your list?'

Kobold dug it out and passed it over. So much paper passing to and fro in a single day, thought the tall boy. He examined the list. There were five names. Victor Zenobia's was right at the top. It had a tick against it.

'And the whereabouts of the other four are unknown?'

'Unknown. I spotted Victor's name in an obituary column. I phoned the paper and learned about the auction. Sheer chance.'

Sheer chance, thought Cornelius. 'And where is the auction to be held?'

'Edinburgh. Tomorrow at 1 p.m.'

'Edinburgh?' Cornelius liked the sound of that.

'All your expenses will be paid. First-class travel and accommodation.'

Cornelius liked the sound of that also.

'More port?' asked Arthur Kobold.

'No thank you.' Cornelius laid down the unsipped glass. 'I should be happy to accept the position. I will need an advance, however. I am currently without funds.'

'The cash bonus is five hundred pounds.' Arthur Kobold rammed the last of the fruit cake into his mouth. 'You really should try this.'

'I think you've finished it.'

'Oh yes, indeed. Well. Go to Edinburgh. Purchase the

effects of the late Victor Zenobia. Report your findings to me. Follow up whatever clues you can glean. Open a bank account for yourself. Phone in your expenses. They will be covered without question.'

'Without question?'

'Naturally. I am employing you because I believe you will do a first-class job. If I provide you with second-class expenses you would be justified in cheating me. If I offer you first-class treatment, what possible reason would you have to play me false?'

'None whatever, but for basic dishonesty.'

'And do you consider yourself basically dishonest?'

'No. In all honesty, I do not.'

'Neither do I. Then we have a deal. Just one more thing you should know. Time is of the essence. I am not the only one searching for these papers, there is a rival publisher. The stakes, as they say, are high. If you are successful there will be much work for you in the future.'

'Have no fear. If the papers exist, I will find them.'

'I am quite certain that you will. Now, here is five hundred pounds to get you started. Shall we say a weekly wage of five hundred also?'

'That seems good enough to me.' Cornelius Murphy grinned from ear to ear.

6

Cornelius returned home via Moore's Models.

The daddy had, no doubt through some oversight, neglected to mention the matter of his long overdue account with Mr Moore and the tall boy was forced to pay this before the shopkeeper would part with the goods.

'Charge all future bills directly to me,' Cornelius said with a smile. The Moore came over all giddy at this and had to have a sit down.

Once back at Moby Dick Terrace, Cornelius explained matters to the parents. Borrowed *The Book of Ultimate Truths*. Had his bags packed for him, and took his leave.

He bade his farewells to Tuppe at The Wife's Legs. His pleas to Mr Kobold for an assistant, even one paid for at his own expense, had fallen upon deaf ears. Mr Kobold was adamant. Cornelius must go it alone.

'And so it is farewell, I'm afraid,' he told the short person.

'Send me a postcard then.' Tuppe raised his teacup in both hands. 'And if you could see your way clear to buy me one of those little Scottish drummer-girl dolls in the transparent plastic cartons.' Cornelius put a thumb up. 'Then you'd probably see your way clear to getting me a bottle of Scotch instead.'

'I'll buy you a case.'

'My thanks. I see that you're all packed up.' Tuppe indicated the suitcase and rucksack beneath the table.

'I have to start right away. Catch the train tonight.'

'So what's in the rucksack?'

'Winter woollies, a thermos of coffee and a pack of the daddy's ex-T.A. field rations. The parents would not let me leave home without them.'

'Very wise. And you'd best go to the toilet before you leave. You don't want to get caught short.' Tuppe grinned foolishly.

'Too true.' When Cornelius returned from the gents, Tuppe was nowhere to be seen.

At precisely the stroke of six the mighty Leviathan Class locomotive, gushing steam and panting dramatically, left King's Cross Station behind and set off for Scotland.

In the first-class dining-car Cornelius Murphy spooned Brown Windsor into his mouth and leafed through *The Book of Ultimate Truths*. He folded back a page at random and read the chapter heading.

WONDERS OF THE ANIMAL KINGDOM

And what lay beneath it.

Throughout history many 'learned' men have studied the animal kingdom and spoiled countless reams of perfectly good paper with their observations.

Pliny the Elder was a great man for this kind of thing. In his *Natural History*, first published in AD77, he devotes a chapter to the humble goldfish.

Here are his 'Seven Wondros Verities' on the subject.

1. The goldfish is the only creature which does not displace its own weight in water.
2. In order to survive, the goldfish must consume at least four times its body weight every hour.
3. Under a new moon a goldfish always points due north. (Marco Polo is known to have carried a number of goldfish with him in case his lodestone ever broke down. H.R.)
4. In Upper Sumatra goldfish are used as currency.
5. In Egypt goldfish skins are used as condoms.
6. Powdered goldfish is a popular aphrodisiac.
7. The goldfish is the rarely used thirteenth sign of the zodiac.

Well, we've certainly come a long way since Pliny's day. Goldfish skins are now in common use as condoms the whole world over.

But do we really know any more about the animal kingdom now than Pliny thought he knew then? I wonder.

Take, for example, the phenomenon of 'fish falls'. Rains of tiny fish cascading down on the planet. Observed by many, disbelieved by most, understood by none. And what about hedgehog falls? So much solid evidence and no research carried out whatever.

Take a drive in the country during the hedgehog season and you will see the remains of thousands of them splattered across the roads. And observe just how flat they are. They must have fallen from a very great height to end up like that!

The popular 'explanation' for these pitiful remains is that the hedgehogs have been run over by motor cars. Oh dear, oh dear. It is quite clear to me that the hedgehog, or hedge-hopping hog, as it was originally known, is a dweller of the upper atmosphere. It feeds upon flying insects and the tiny fish that inhabit the *Aquasphere*.

The Aquasphere, as all who have read my monograph

Noah's Flood: Where all that water actually came from
will know, is the mile-thick outer layer of water which
prevents our atmosphere from drifting away into space.
Hedgehogs, which fish in this region, float about up there,
remaining aloft due to the inflated sacs of natural methane
which surround their bodies. When they die, often due to
punctures received during the rutting season, they deflate
and plunge down to earth, exploding as they strike the
Tarmac. The fact that you never see a flat hedgehog upon
a soft grassy field, bears this out and proves my point
somewhat conclusively, I so believe.

Another case of popular explanation falling well wide of
the mark is that of the so called 'extinct' woolly mammoth.

During my travels across the Siberian Steppes, some years
ago, I chanced upon a team of Russian palaeontologists, who
were clearly in a state of heightened exuberance.

Apparently, an unseasonable deluge had washed away
a section of river bank, exposing the perfectly preserved
carcass of a woolly mammoth. The beast was frozen in a running posture and looked as fresh as the proverbial daisy.

The Russian greybeards were quite beside themselves with
glee, considering this to be the find of the century. Somehow
they had got it into their heads that the specimen was at
least fifteen thousand years old.

I introduced myself and upon learning my identity they
naturally begged me to examine their treasure and offer an
authoritative opinion.

I was pleased to do so, having nothing else planned for
the morning. I perused the beast and proclaimed that it
was indeed a woolly mammoth, of the genus *Mammuthus
primigenius*. And that it had been dead for at least half an
hour!

The woolly mammoth, I explained to them, is a burrowing
animal, which lives exclusively beneath the ground and is
very common in these parts. It tunnels with its enormous

tusks and dies instantly upon exposure to sunlight.

'You have a nice fresh one here,' I told them, 'and it would be a shame to waste it.'

Without further ado I had my servants haul the carcass back to the village where I was staying and get the fire stoked up.

The greybeards made a quite unnecessary fuss about this and I was forced to employ my stout stick. With typical bad grace they did not attend the barbecue.

'Is sir ready to order his main course now?' Cornelius looked up from his reading to view the spiffingly clad dining-car attendant.

'Yes,' said he.

'We have fillet of goldfish, poached in white wine; châteaubriand of hedgehog, garnished with tiny fish; or entrecôte of woolly mam—'

'I'll take a salad please,' said Cornelius Murphy.

At seven-thirty of the next morning clock the mighty Leviathan gasped its way into Edinburgh Central without any fanfare whatsoever.

Cornelius stuck his head out of the window of the first-class sleeping compartment and breathed in Scotland. His hair took to the forming of dreadlocks. It looked like another beautiful day out there.

The tall boy washed, cleaned his teeth, fought bravely with his comb and then dressed in a faded Hawaiian shirt and his summer suit. He considered leaving the rucksack on the train, but as it contained several of his favourite Fair Isle jumpers, and this was bonny Scotland after all, he thought better of it and shouldered the thing. Then clutching his suitcase, he tottered down on to the platform. A stranger in a strange land. And all alone by the looks of it.

His first thought was to phone in his expenses to Arthur Kobold. His second, to take breakfast.

His first disappointment was the lack of a porter to carry his bags. His second came at the ticket booth, where there was no-one for him to show his first-class ticket to.

Cornelius dragged his suitcase across the deserted concourse of the grand Victorian station. Ahead a kiosk, fashioned in the manner of a tartan fairground booth, offered up the tantalizing fragrances of fried bacon and freshly brewed coffee. Cornelius found a spring creeping into his step.

Behind the counter a gaunt-looking woman in an apron was standing with her hands on her head.

'Good-morning, madam.' Cornelius lowered his suitcase, took off his rucksack and climbed on to a stool before the counter.

The gaunt woman did not return the merry smile he offered in greeting.

'We're closed,' she announced in a frosty tone. Cornelius observed that a small blue vein, snaking down the bridge of her nose, reproduced the course of the Euphrates.

'No you're not,' said the undaunted lad. 'You're open. I'll take coffee and the full breakfast please.'

'The coffee's off.'

'No it's not. It's bubbling away on the hob there.'

'It's off.'

'Might I just sample it?'

'The coffee's off. Sling your hook.'

'You didn't move your lips when you said that.' Cornelius wondered whether he had stumbled into the rehearsal for some fringe event of the now legendary Edinburgh Festival.

'How did you do that?' he asked.

58

'*I* did it!' A head rose from behind the counter. It was a perfectly spherical head and it wore a tartan tam-o'-shanter. It also wore a youthful face, the greater part of which lurked behind the thick pebbled spectacles of the seriously myopic. Beneath a nubbin of a nose, a mouth, not unlike that of a goldfish, stuck out its bottom lip in a menacing manner. Cornelius worried most about the nose. How could it support the weight of the spectacles?

'Campbell,' said Cornelius.

'I don't know you, do I?' The young man squinted at Cornelius and then generally about the place.

'The tartan. On your tam. That's the clan cloth of Callum the Great. Dates back to the fourteenth century.'

'Shove off,' said the Campbell.

'I want my breakfast.' Cornelius rubbed his hands together.

'Listen, friend,' the Campbell produced a pistol and pointed it at the tall boy, 'do you see this?'

Cornelius nodded. 'That's an Ozi nine-millimetre machine pistol. Fully automatic, twenty-five round clip. Detachable stock.'

'And it's loaded, by the way.'

'Possibly with plasticine. It's an Airfix kit, I've got one like it at home. The sight on the barrel is too long. I wrote to Airfix about that, but they never answered my letter.'

A look of horror appeared on the Campbell's clock face. He held the gun close to his spectacles and worried at the trigger. It came away in his hand and tinkled to the counter.

Cornelius picked it up. 'I mentioned that too. Look out,' he added. But he was not quick enough.

The gaunt woman head-butted the Campbell and

he vanished beneath the counter. His howls echoed around the empty station as she began kicking him.

'I'll wait until you're done then.' Cornelius made himself comfy on the stool and sniffed at the coffee pot.

'And don't come back!' The gaunt woman lifted a counter flap, swung open a section beneath it and hurled the Campbell across the concourse. He bowled over several times before rising in a confusion of camouflage, clutching his spectacles to his face and taking to his heels. The gaunt woman hurled his plastic pistol after him.

'A pox on all the bloody Campbells,' she cried, echoing the sentiments of many a fine art lover at an Andy Warhol retrospective. 'So, what about you then?'

'Breakfast for me,' smiled Cornelius. 'Eggs if you have them.'

The gaunt woman turned away.

'And bacon.'

The gaunt woman glared round at him. 'And?'

'And everything you've got really.'

'Everything I've got.' Muttering beneath her breath she set to the preparation of the tall boy's breakfast.

Back in Moby Dick Terrace, the street's only telephone began to ring. The daddy swayed from the kitchen, teacup in hand and picked up the receiver.

After a few moments a voice said, 'Hello, is there anybody there?' It was the voice of the youth employment officer.

'What is it, Yarrow?' The daddy raised his teacup to his lips.

'Cold again.' He shook his head.

'Mr Murphy, I want to speak to your son. It's very urgent.'

'My son is presently in Scotland.'

'Your son is a very wicked boy, Mr Murphy. He has played me false. This letter . . .'

'Letter?' The daddy finished his tea.

'From your son. Demanding money.'

'Surely not. My son would never do a thing like that.'

'He would and he has. He claims to have found employment for himself.'

'That doesn't sound very demanding to me.'

'He claims that I employed him as an assistant in order to find him a real job.'

'Which you did.'

'But now he claims that as he has found work independently, I can no longer employ him in this capacity.'

'Which you can't.'

'So he is therefore claiming that, as I have no further work for him, then I must make him redundant.'

'Which I suppose you must.'

'But he wants redundancy money! A month's pay!'

'Seems a reasonable enough request to me.' The daddy held the receiver at arm's length, to spare his ears the inevitable assault.

'Reasonable?' screamed Mr Yarrow. 'Reasonable? It is outrageous.'

'Well, technically speaking,' the phone was back at Jack Murphy's ear, 'you are no longer in a position to provide him with employment. And, of course, you had no written contract. I can cite several legal precedents. Industrial relations is something of a speciality with me. For instance, there was the case of John Vincent O'Mally versus Arthur Doveston, Purveyor of Steam Velocipedes to the Gentry.'

'Arthur who?'

'Doveston. Bankrupt now, of course. It wasn't a particularly big case, but it attracted a lot of attention from the local Press. You know how they like crusading for the cause of the underdog.'

'I won't have it, Mr Murphy. Bankrupt, case, Press, underdog?' he continued in a lesser voice.

'You stand your corner,' the daddy advised. 'Have your day in court.'

'My day in court?'

'I'll have to go now,' said the daddy. 'I think the cat wants to be let out.' He replaced the receiver and collapsed into fits of laughter.

His wife appeared at the top of the stairs wearing a dressing-gown of many colours. 'Who was that?' she asked.

Her husband did his best to sober up. 'Mr Yarrow,' he replied between convulsions. 'Apparently Cornelius wrote to him demanding redundancy money.'

'Nonsense,' said the mother. 'My son would never do a thing like that.'

'That's just what I said to Mr Yarrow. My son would never do a thing like that.' The daddy returned to the kitchen and poured himself another cup of tea. 'That's why *I* did.' He chuckled.

Quite unaware that he had a month's redundancy money coming, Cornelius finished his breakfast. He passed a nice new five-pound note across the counter.

'First class,' said he. 'Could I trouble you for a receipt?'

The gaunt woman did not reply.

As there was still no sign of a porter, or anyone else for that matter, Cornelius shouldered his rucksack, took up his case and walked. He went in search of a taxi.

He didn't find one though. But he did find the rank. And sitting on the ground, with his back against the sign which told travellers which side they should be queuing on, he found the Campbell.

The erstwhile bandido wore a bloody nose which he was dabbing at with an oversized tartan handkerchief. He gazed up at Cornelius through the unfractured lens of his spectacles.

Cornelius wondered whether the Festival might be staging a production of *Lord of the Flies* this year.

'Thanks a lot,' said the Campbell.

Cornelius shrugged. 'You started it. I hope you didn't pay too much for the toy gun. The gaunt woman broke it.'

'The bastards said it was a real one. They'll never let me join their gang now.'

'Bastards?' Cornelius had heard tell of bastards and how, if you ever met any, you should be careful not to let them grind you down. He couldn't recall actually having met any himself, as yet. A good many fools certainly, but no real bastards.

'Of which bastards do you speak?' he asked the Campbell.

'The Wild Warriors of West Lothian. They get all the best lasses. And have adventures and stuff. I wanted to join their gang.'

'And you had to rob the kiosk, is that it?'

'Rob the kiosk and then blow it up.'

'Blow it up? With what?'

'They gave me a hand grenade.'

'You're certain it's a real hand grenade. Not a cigarette lighter?'

The Campbell yanked a Mills bomb from a camouflaged pocket and flung it up at Cornelius.

The tall boy caught it. It was a cigarette lighter. He returned it to the failed initiate without comment. A taxi was approaching.

63

'You're probably not really cut out for the life of brigandry and terrorism,' said Cornelius kindly. 'Can I offer you a lift home?'

'You wouldn't let me take you hostage by any chance?' the Campbell asked hopefully. 'They might make do with that.'

'I really don't have the time, I'm afraid. I have an appointment at one. Perhaps later, if I come back this way.'

'It wouldn't take long. An hour maybe. Listen, I'd really appreciate it. They wouldn't actually want to keep you, of course. But it would show them that I'm ambitious, enterprising, young and independently minded.'

'I suppose it would. Are you sure that you want to join this gang?'

'It's either that or take the job the youth employment officer has set up for me.'

'And what's that?'

'Carpet salesman,' said the Campbell in a low, doomed tone.

The taxi drove the Campbell and his hostage through the historic streets of Edinburgh. Cornelius enjoyed every moment of it. He kept an eye out for fierce-looking highlanders with red beards, kilts and claymores. But he didn't see any.

'Where are all the sporrans and the dirks in the socks?' he asked the Campbell.

'Where's your bowler hat?' the Campbell replied. And the two sat a while in silence.

'Here on the corner do you, Jimmy?' the taxi driver asked.

'Jimmy?' Cornelius turned to his kidnapper. 'The taxi driver knows you by name?'

'All Scotsmen are called Jimmy.' The Campbell straightened his tam. 'Everyone knows that. It's a tradition or an old charter or something.'

'I thought all Scotsmen were called Jock.'

'Och away. That's Irishmen.'

'Irishmen are called Mick and Londoners are called John.'

'Jack,' said the taxi driver. 'Londoners are called Jack. Or at least Jack London was. *Call of the Wild*.'

'Wilde was called Oscar,' said the Campbell.

'Jack Nicholson won an Oscar,' said the taxi driver. 'And he's called Jack. But I think he's an American. I wonder what the rest of them are called.'

'Bastards,' said the Campbell.

'Well, you learn something new every day. That'll be two pounds please, Cornelius.'

Cornelius fished out the money. 'Could I have a receipt for that?' he asked. 'And I never told you *my* name.'

The taxi driver scribbled something indecipherable upon the back of a Woodbine packet and handed it to Cornelius.

'Only winding you up. I saw your picture in the paper.'

'My what?'

The taxi driver held up a copy of the day's *Edinburgh Mercury*. Its banner headline read EPIC TRAVELLER FOILS STATION KIOSK HEIST.

Beneath this was a photograph of the hero taking breakfast.

Cornelius snatched the newspaper and gawped at it in disbelief.

'Come on,' said Jim Campbell. 'I thought you were in a hurry.'

7

'First house along here.' The Campbell gestured to the remains of a terraced street which rose from a wasteland of redevelopment.

'Number twenty-three. This rucksack is well heavy,' he added. 'And the handle's coming off your case. Is it real crocodile skin, by the way?'

Cornelius was stumbling along behind, marvelling at the *Edinburgh Mercury*. He shook his head in wonder and his hair went every which way.

The newspaper spoke of hidden station security cameras, faxed photographs, network identification computers, instant Press access to newsworthy material and the *Edinburgh Mercury* always being first with the news.

Cornelius leafed through the remaining pages. These were singularly dry of any news. But they were heavily bathed in advertising for first-class accommodation, eating houses, menswear salons, car rental firms, bordellos, camping equipment.

Everything, in fact, that an epic traveller might, reasonably or otherwise, require.

'Jim?' Cornelius caught up with the Campbell. 'Hold on there.'

'What's your problem?' Jim put down the suitcase and unshouldered the rucksack.

'You were holding up the kiosk when I got off the train, weren't you?'

'And making a good job of it.'

'Did anyone else get off?'

The Campbell shook his head. Then he fumbled around on the ground for his glasses. Cornelius stooped and returned them to him.

'Thanks.'

'No-one at all got off that train except me?'

'Of course not. The taxi driver wouldn't have turned up if he hadn't read about you in the paper. You'd be walking if it wasn't for me. Don't show the boys that paper by the way.'

Cornelius folded the *Mercury* into his pocket.

'And I think you'd better carry your own bags from here. It wouldn't look good if they saw me carrying them.'

Cornelius shrugged and took up his luggage. 'Just along here, you say?'

'Number twenty-three. Aye.'

It looked just like home sweet home. There was even a dustbin outside. Cornelius chose not to lift the lid. The potential Wild Warrior knocked upon the door.

An eye appeared at an eyehole, which was appropriate enough.

'Identify yourself,' said a voice.

'Let us in, Sawney. It's me, Jimmy, and I've busted my specs.'

'Identify yourself and use the password.'

'You didn't tell us a password.'

'It's a new rule. If you don't know the password you can't come in.'

'But I live here. Let us in. I've got a hostage with me and he can't stay long, he has an appointment.'

'Does he know the password?'

The Campbell turned to his captive. 'Do you know the password?'

'Just say the first thing that comes into your head.'

'Brassière,' said the Campbell.

'Enter, friend.' The door opened and Cornelius was ushered inside.

'Oh,' said he. Beyond lay rubble. The house was nothing more than a front wall. A small campfire billowed smoke and around this crouched . . .

'Yes,' said Cornelius Murphy. 'This is more like it.'

Around the campfire crouched three red-bearded highlanders, clad in considerable quantities of musty-looking tartan and armed to the yellow teeth. Tall eagle feathers quivered in their war bonnets.

'You asked about the dirks,' said Jim.

'And who is this?' A fearsome warlike apparition flung a horn beaker aside and rose to his feet, making motions towards his sword belt.

'A hostage,' said the Campbell proudly. 'Cornelius Murphy, this is Angus, he's the leader. And over by the fire is Hamish, and Sawney let us in, of course.'

'Hi there,' said Sawney.

'Hello,' Cornelius waved at Sawney.

'Hostage?' Angus, or Black Angus as he preferred to be called, eyed Cornelius with contempt. 'We send you out to buy sandwiches and you come back with a hostage?'

'Buy sandwiches?' Cornelius turned to the Campbell. 'But you said . . .'

'And where's my bloody cigarette lighter?' roared Hamish. 'You know I cannot abide to light my Woodbine from the campfire.'

'Sorry.' The Campbell dug out the bogus grenade and handed it back to its rightful owner.

'I don't think you've been altogether honest with me.' Cornelius made a stern face at the Campbell.

The Campbell took off his spectacles and tucked them into his pocket. 'Shut your mouth,' he snarled, 'if you know what's good for you. And sit down, Angus!'

Angus slunk back to the campfire. Cornelius viewed the Campbell. All trace of the short-sighted incompetent had vanished. The clear blue eyes glittered with menace. The face wore an undeniably evil expression. The Campbell leered at him. 'An overly complicated piece of subterfuge perhaps. I am subject to whimsicality in these matters. You are now my hostage.'

'I'm too thin to be a hostage,' said Cornelius. 'What is all this about?'

'Hand over all your money please.'

'I certainly will not.'

'Then it will be all the worse for you.' The Campbell snapped his fingers. The three warriors climbed to their feet, drawing murderous-looking blades.

'I bags his jacket,' said Sawney.

'And I'll take his flowery blouse, it will look well on my lassie.' Angus ran his thumb along a knife lined with crocodile teeth.

'What size are your boots?' Hamish asked.

'Eight and a half.'

'They'll do for me right enough then.'

'I would prefer to keep them if it's all the same with you.'

Cornelius struck out with the right one catching Hamish an agonizing blow to the sporran. The highlander doubled up, eyes crossed and streaming. His companions made a rush at Cornelius. The tall and cornered boy swung his suitcase. He managed to catch Angus a half-decent clip across the right ear, but the sinister Campbell grabbed him from behind and clung to his neck. Cornelius elbowed him where he could, but the camouflaged figure appeared quite impervious to that kind of thing. Sawney raised his claymore in both hands and prepared to bring down the hilt.

'Hold it right there!' The voice did not come from Cornelius, although those were the words he had in mind to use. They came from a police loud hailer. 'Lay down your weapons and let the hostage go.'

'Aye what?' The Campbell glared about him. He didn't loosen his grip on Cornelius though.

'You are surrounded,' continued the police voice. 'Put down your swords. And let the lad go, Campbell.'

'Er?' said the Campbell.

'Best do what he says,' said the tall boy.

'No. I don't see any police. Listen!' he shouted. 'We've got the hostage and we're keeping him.'

'Our marksmen have you in their sights. Right at the big pimple on your forehead.'

'Pimple?' The Campbell released Cornelius and took to fingering his forehead. 'That's a birthmark, by the way.'

'It's a bloody big bubo,' swore Hamish, clutching at his kilt. 'A proper target, so you are.'

'Where are you?' shouted the Campbell, spinning about in small circles.

'All around. We've had you under surveillance since you set up camp here. Now let the lad go or we open fire.'

Angus and Sawney flung down their weapons. Hamish sat nursing his loins. The Campbell clenched and unclenched his fists.

'Well, I'll be off then.' Cornelius backed towards the door.

'Don't forget your luggage, you fool,' called the police voice.

Cornelius hastily snatched up his bags. 'Of course not. Thank you.'

'And come out alone.'

'I certainly will.'

'The rest of you back behind the campfire.'

The Wild Warriors of West Lothian made a surly and grumbling retreat.

Cornelius Murphy left the building.

He ducked out of number twenty-three and slammed shut the door. And then he turned to thank his rescuers.

The street was deserted.

'Well don't just stand there. Run for your life.' The voice came close at his ear. Cornelius ran for his life.

He dived away at the double and took himself as far as his long legs would carry him. When finally they would carry him no more, he ducked into a doorway and sank on to his bottom, breathing heavily.

'Now open your rucksack.' It was that voice again.

'Is this God?' Cornelius searched the heavens for shafts of golden light.

'No. It's me.' The voice belonged to Tuppe.

Cornelius pulled open the rucksack.

'Tuppe! This is something of a surprise.'

The small fellow climbed from the rucksack and stretched what there was of himself to stretch. 'I'll bet you're glad I hitched a ride.'

Cornelius embraced the small fellow. 'Tuppe!' was all that he could say.

'That's enough hugging thank you.'

'Sorry. But it's so good to see you. How . . . ?'

'I hitched a ride. I could hardly let you go off on an epic journey all by yourself. There's no telling what kind of trouble you might get yourself into. So I climbed into the rucksack while you were taking a pee back at The Wife's Legs. Been living on the daddy's field rations. Can't say much for the mother's coffee though. And I could really use the toilet about now.'

'Well,' said Cornelius. 'Just fancy that. You hitch-hiking in my rucksack all the way up here without me knowing and then doing a perfect impression of a police loud hailer.'

Tuppe held his nose and barked into the empty thermos flask. 'Throw down your weapon and come out with your hands up, you are surrounded.'

Several nearby windows came up and a number of guns flew down into the street. 'Don't shoot, G-man,' called someone.

'I wouldn't have believed it if I hadn't heard it myself,' said Cornelius. 'Thanks very much indeed.'

'Don't mention it. You would have done the same for me.'

'Naturally. And I would have bested those blighters eventually, you know.'

'I have absolutely no doubt of that. I just wanted the fight to stop before you began wading in with the rucksack.'

'Quite so. Then, as my breath has now returned to me and I find myself in the company of my bestest friend, it is my considered opinion that we proceed together upon the epic journey and face as one whatever adventures lie before.'

'Well said. And wherefore art we headed?'

'The auction room, Sheila na gigh.'

'And how might we get there, do you think?'

Across the road a bus drew up at a stop. It was a big bright green bus and the sign on the front read, SHEILA NA GIGH.

'We'll take the bus,' said Cornelius Murphy, smiling merrily.

8

His name was Felix Henderson McMurdo. But they called him the un-canny Scot.

The old grizzled grannies cursed him as he passed them by. Doggies bared their fangs and babbies filled their nappies. Small boys spat down on him from the safety of high windows and their mothers clenched their buttocks and turned away their glowing cheeks.

All that knew McMurdo agreed that he'd end his days on a hangman's rope.

Felix, who always thought of himself as a bit of a lad and an all-round popular fellow, took it in good part.

'The folk in these parts have a funny sense of humour,' he told strangers to the parts of which he spoke. And the strangers smiled back at him and shook their heads.

But once he was safely out of sight, these same strangers unclenched their buttocks and declared that 'there goes a wrong'n if ever there was, who'll end in a gallows dance.'

Now, on the corner of Agamemnon Street there was a tobacconist shop owned by a Scotsman named Patel. And outside that shop was the last outdoor cigarette machine in Scotland.

And approaching that very machine, his last pound coin clutched in his fist, was Felix Henderson McMurdo.

And just across the street was an auction room.

It was one of those memorial halls or Methodist Congregationals, or Wesleyan chapels or whatever they were. They all look pretty much the same and you see them everywhere. They were raised in the middle years of the last century from sturdy stocks and grey slate, with glorious tiled floors and superb vaulted ceilings. And they are a perfect testament to the canny Victorians' sense of foresight.

Because their interiors perfectly reflect the fine re-production pine furniture that you find for sale in them today.

There was scaffolding up outside this particular one and a pair of rugged, manly types were bolting a large sign into place. This sign announced that The Victorian Fitted Kitchen Company would soon be opening there for business.

But today was auction day and the hall looked very well inside, stacked up with all that bygone bric-à-bracery.

Cornelius and Tuppe entered the hall.

'Nice ceiling,' said Cornelius.

'Nice tiled floor,' said Tuppe.

'Shall we peruse Mr Kobold's intended purchase?'

'Why don't we do that very thing.'

There were ranks of trestle tables. And these were piled high with items which had probably been all very well in their day. There was a good deal of ropey old furniture. Some duff oil paintings and the inevitable far-too-good-to-be-true Cadbury's shop cabinets. Then there were the armchairs and sofas that travel around the country from auction to auction to auction. Why they do it and for how long they have, are anyone's guesses.

Tuppe examined a row of spittoons and an elephant's

74

foot commode. Above him Cornelius ran his eye over a box of ancient cane carpet beaters. He consulted the catalogue Mr Kobold had given him. 'Lot forty-two. A collection of early French tennis racquets.' That didn't bode particularly well.

'Tell me what I'm looking for again, I've forgotten,' said Tuppe. 'Ye gods!' he added hastily dropping the lid of the commode.

Cornelius read once more from the catalogue. 'Lot one hundred. Large green canvas portmanteau containing personal effects of the late Victor Zenobia. Brush-and-comb set in calfskin case. Various papers. Duffle-coat (lacking toggles) some wear on elbows. No reserve.'

'And all Kobold wants is the papers?'

'That's what he said.'

Tuppe rubbed his tiny hands together. 'Splendid. Then I bags the portmanteau. It will provide spacious accommodation for the journey home and spare you the expense of my fare.'

'What a well-considered choice. Then I shall go for the brush-and-comb set in the calfskin case.'

'No less than you deserve. Which leaves us with the matter of the duffle-coat.'

'Lacking toggles.' Cornelius made a face.

'And some wear on the elbows.' Tuppe made one to match.

'We had best hold the duffle-coat in reserve.'

'Perfect. As I notice that no reserve has been included in the lot, it should fit the bill precisely.'

Pleased with the celestial harmony thus achieved, Cornelius and Tuppe set out in earnest to locate Lot 100.

'Lot one hundred?' Cornelius asked a tall porter in a brown overall.

'Lot one hundred?' Tuppe asked his shorter counterpart.

'Over there.' The tall porter pointed.

'Over there.' The shorter did likewise.

Tuppe and Cornelius followed the pointing fingers and set off in different directions.

Felix Henderson McMurdo pushed his last pound coin into the cigarette machine and mused upon the pleasures of the Wild Woodbine he was shortly to enjoy. Felix whistled 'Cigareets and wuskey and wild wild women' and wondered why the latter never made his acquaintance.

And then he wondered why it was that he hadn't heard that satisfying little clunk the coin usually made as it dropped inside the machine.

On a distant corner two small boys tittered into their unwashed hands and one slipped a tube of Superglue into the back pocket of his ragged pantaloons.

'Come on now.' Felix gave the machine a playful tap. 'Let's be having you.'

The machine did not reply.

The hall was filling up. The auction was set to begin at one and it was nearing that time when Cornelius finally met up once more with Tuppe.

'Any luck?' The small fellow pulled at the tall boy's trouser leg.

'None whatever. I couldn't find it.'

'Give me a hoist up on to your shoulders then. Maybe it's tucked away on a high shelf somewhere.'

Cornelius shouldered his companion.

'Oh golly. Put me down and join me there.'

'What is this?'

'Do as I say. Quickly.'

Cornelius lowered Tuppe to the floor and knelt down beside him. 'What is it?'

'It's the Campbell and his cronies. They're down at the front.'

'I never saw them come in.'

'Then let's trust that they didn't see you. How come they're here?'

'Coincidence?' Cornelius suggested.

Felix Henderson McMurdo struck the machine a slightly less playful tap. 'Pay up with my Woodies,' he told it. 'And sharp.'

Mr Patel issued from his shop. 'Away from my machine, accursed one,' he told McMurdo.

'My coin is stuck.' The un-canny Scot smote the machine once more.

'I'll fetch my stout stick to you,' warned the tobacconist.

A suave-looking gent, with a dapper moustache, tweedy cap and sheepskin car coat climbed the steps of the Gothic pulpit and addressed the congregation of bargain hunters.

'Ladies and gentlemen . . .' Feedback shrieked about the vaulting and the congregation cowered beneath it, sheltering their ears.

'Sorry,' came a small voice from the rear of the pulpit. 'Try again.'

'   ,' said the auctioneer.

'Once again.'

'Ladies and gentlemen.'

'That's it.'

'Ladies and gentlemen. Welcome to the weekly auction here at The Anabaptist Reform Church. I see a lot of familiar faces, but as there are a few new ones,

I'll just run through the procedures. As there're a good many lots to get through this afternoon I'll keep it plain and simple.'

'Good,' said a familiar face.

'We accept all major credit cards. Personal cheques will also be accepted if accompanied by a valid cheque card. No personal cheques above fifty pounds please. Lots secured by deposits must have their balances paid off within twenty-four hours. Items under twenty-five pounds must be paid for in cash and no deposits will be accepted on these. So, with that understood, let us proceed to lot number one.'

A lady in a straw hat put up her hand.

'A little quick off the mark there, madam,' smiled the auctioneer. 'Please wait until I start the bidding.'

'I wanted to ask a question,' said the lady.

'The toilets are by the door, madam.' The auctioneer increased the magnitude of his smile.

'I don't want the toilet. I want to ask a question.'

'Go on then.'

'Can lots over twenty-five pounds be paid for in cash?'

'Of course. Now, lot number one.'

'But not lots under twenty-five?'

'No, madam.'

'Well, what if I purchased two lots which added up to less than fifty pounds, could I pay for them with a personal cheque, assuming, of course, that I had a valid cheque card?'

'Yes, madam. If the overall figure is more than the twenty-five pounds minimum. Now can we please get on?'

'Well, what if I decided to put one of the lots back into the next auction, could I postpone payment on that until after it was sold?'

'No. Certainly not.' The auctioneer was still smiling. Just.

'So I'd have to pay for both lots when I bought them, even if I put one straight back into the next auction?'

'Yes.'

'Well, what if the lot I put back didn't reach the reserve price I decided to put on it?'

'I suppose you'd just have to take it home, madam.' The auctioneer's smile was naught but a memory.

'I don't want a thing like that in my house,' said the lady. 'What kind of a person do you take me for?'

Outside and across the street a small crowd was gathering.

'All I want is my Woodbine,' said McMurdo. 'Paste me again with that stick of yours and you're a dead Scotsman, Patel.'

'At the end of a rope, that's how he'll end,' said an ancient granny.

'Surely I recognize you, madam,' said the unsmiling auctioneer. 'Weren't you here last week?'

The lady in the straw hat nodded. 'I purchased two lots. I've put one of them back into the sale this week. I'm going to bid for it myself.'

'Why?'

'Well, I paid far too much for it the first time, so I've put a really low reserve on it now. If I can pick it up this week it should be a real bargain.'

'But I thought you said you wouldn't have a thing like that in your house.'

'I did, but you can't pass up a bargain, can you? And if I get it really really cheap I might put it back into next week's auction.'

'Oh I do hope so,' said the auctioneer. 'Now, lot number one.'

'This is my lot,' said the lady, 'so no-one else bid.'

'What's going on here?' A smart young police officer pushed his way through the crowd. 'Stop hitting that man, Patel. Oh, it's you, is it, McMurdo? What villainy are you up to this time?'

'It's not my fault,' wailed Felix, as Mr Patel struck him a blow to the shin. 'My money's stuck in this machine, that's all.'

'I saw everything,' said a young mother with clenched buttocks. 'McMurdo started it. The fiend.'

'I did not. All I want is some cigarettes.'

Mr Patel took another swing at the un-canny Scot and hit the young police officer.

'This could be a long afternoon,' said Tuppe. 'Should we pop out for an hour or so and take a late breakfast?'

Cornelius shook his head and vanished under his hair. 'Not likely. I've seen that one before. We slip out for five minutes and the lot will be sold before we get back.'

'You are wise beyond your years.'

'Don't mention it.'

'Sold to the lady in the straw hat,' said the auctioneer. 'Lot ninety-seven.'

'Told you,' said Cornelius. 'You've got to have your wits about you in this game.'

'Stand back, the lot of you.' The young police officer fished out a twenty-two-function Swiss Police knife and selected a worthy blade. 'I'll soon deal with this.'

He worked the blade into the slot and waggled it about.

'Don't you damage that machine,' said Mr Patel.

'Sir, I know what I'm doing. We're trained to deal with situations like this.' He gave the knife a violent twist.

The blade snapped off.

The police officer gaped at his Swiss Police knife. Its functioning power had just been reduced by a factor of one.

'My best knife.' The police officer burst into a flood of tears.

'Look what you've done now, McMurdo.' The tobacconist raised his stout stick. The crowd cheered him on.

'Lot ninety-seven. Leonardo Da Vinci's missing work-book. Containing his designs for the perpetual-motion helicopter. Mathematical principles appertaining to the five-sided cube and the formula for the transmutation of base metal into gold. Who'll start me off with a fiver?'

'Four,' said a fellow in a green cagoule.

'Five over here,' said a big fat man in a shameless wig.

'I have five,' the auctioneer waved his gavel around. 'Do I hear six? I'd like to hear six.'

'Six,' said someone.

'I have six,' said the auctioneer.

'No, you don't have six,' said the someone. 'You wanted to hear six. And now you've heard it.'

'It's you again, isn't it, madam?'

'Only kidding,' said the lady in the straw hat.

'This is a very peculiar auction,' said Tuppe.

'My penknife,' wailed the officer of the law.

Several young, and reasonably wild wild women

stepped forward to comfort him. A man in a uniform was a good catch in these parts.

A bus drew up at the lights and the driver, an excitable Puerto Rican, climbed down from his cab to see what all the fuss was about.

Up on the scaffolding, the two rugged manly types whistled at the womenfolk.

The lights changed to green and the traffic began to back up.

'Six,' said the big fat man in the shameless wig.

'But you said five,' said the auctioneer.

'I can change my mind if I want to.'

'No. That's not what I meant.'

'I'll bid seven,' said the cagoule. 'Can I bid seven with a major credit card, by the way? I'm not sure whether the lady asked about that.'

'Eight down here,' cried Tuppe, just for the hell of it.

'Eight somewhere down the back,' said the auctioneer.

'Who said eight?' the fat gentleman asked. 'I'll go to nine.'

'Who said nine?' Tuppe asked.

'Chap in the wig,' said Cornelius, giving his chum a leg up. 'Shall I bid ten?'

'Move your bus!' shouted a travelling salesman with places to be.

'Your mother!' cried the Puerto Rican, making a gesture with thumb and front teeth.

'See you, Jimmy!' The travelling salesman climbed from his car, rolling up his sleeves as he did so.

'It was a birthday present from my old white-haired mother,' blubbered the officer of the law.

'Would you like to come back to my place for some oral sex?' a young woman asked.

'I have ten.' The auctioneer waved his gavel in the air.

'Who said ten?' Tuppe asked.

'Chap in the cagoule.'

'What's a cagoule?'

'Eleven? Do I hear eleven? Big fat man with the shameless wig? No? Still with the chap in the light-weight, knee-length anorak of French origin, very popular with bearded prannies who wear ethnic shoes, get off on Olde English folk music and have girlfriends called Ros who run encounter groups where you can find your true self and be at one with the cosmos. Eleven still with you, sir.'

'*Well!*' said the chap in the cagoule. 'I don't know if I want it now.'

'Oh go on,' said Ros, his girlfriend.

'Twelve,' said a new voice.

'Twelve.' The auctioneer was all smiles once more. 'Twelve I have.'

'Who said twelve?' Tuppe asked.

'Who cares?' Cornelius replied.

'Twelve I have. All finished at twelve then? Twelve million once . . . twelve million twice . . .'

'Twelve *million*?' Tuppe asked.

'There's wee lads robbing your shop,' a granny told Mr Patel. 'If you'll give us a lend of your stout stick I'll deal with McMurdo while you see to them.'

'Thank you, madam.' The tobacconist parted with his stick and fought his way through the noisy crowd that now spilled into the road.

'All I want is my bloody Woodbine.'

83

'I know you, McMurdo, child eater so you are.' The granny swung the stout stick.

Peep peep peep barp barp and honk, went the traffic.

'Who you calling a wetback, *homes*?' The bus driver kicked the travelling salesman where Cornelius had kicked Hamish.

A group of shaven-headed yobbos, with tattooed cheeks and nationalistic leanings, observed this from the upper deck and came swarming down from the bus.

The rugged manly types on the scaffolding flung nuts and bolts at them.

The comforting young woman led the sniffing police officer up the stairs to her bedroom.

'And sold to the Sultan of Brunei, for twelve million pounds. Thank you, Your Majesty.'

'Will you take an IOU?' the sultan asked.

'How much money do you have about your person?' Tuppe asked Cornelius.

'A little over four hundred pounds. In cash.'

'Lot ninety-eight. Garish print, "The Crying Child", with Artexed frame and piece of knotted string for hanging purposes to rear. Some small area of fire damage. What do I hear for this little beauty? Pound anywhere?'

'Pound over here,' said the lady in the straw hat. 'Could we have a window shut, do you think? There's a terrible rumpus going on outside.'

'Crash' went a brick through the window of a nearby television shop and things took a new, but not entirely unexpected, turn for the worse.

A circling police traffic helicopter radioed in to base.

'Yours for a pound then,' said the auctioneer.

'I'd like to put it back into the auction for next week,'

said the lady. 'It hasn't reached the reserve price.'

'Lot ninety-nine. Three mulatto slaves. One answering to the name of Henry. Good house-boy. City and Guilds certificates in business management, light engineering and macramé. Enjoys windsurfing, working out at the gym and strutting his funky stuff on the dance floor. Who'll start me off then?'

'Twenty-five pounds,' said the lady in the straw hat.

'Twenty-six,' said the Sultan of Brunei.

'Thirty,' said Ros.

'Pass out those C.D. players,' said the bus driver. 'Load them into my cab.'

'Uncle Wolf!' cried Mr Patel into his telephone. 'Big race riot going on here. Get the boys together. Bring many guns. Bring Clicki Ba!'

'And sold to the young woman who runs the encounter group.'

'Huh,' said the chap in the cagoule, making a huffy face.

'Lot one hundred,' said the auctioneer.

'We're on,' said Tuppe.

'Lot one hundred. Large green canvas portmanteau containing the personal effects of the late Victor Zenobia. Brush-and-comb set in calfskin case. Various papers, duffle-coat (lacking toggles) some wear on elbows. No reserve.'

'Can you see it?' Tuppe asked.

Cornelius craned his neck. 'It's on a table by the pulpit. The Campbell is leaning on it.'

'All right now, ladies and gentlemen. Who's going to start me off on this one? Very chic brush-and-comb set. Tenner anyone?'

'Ten,' said the Campbell, glowering around the place.

Cornelius stuck his hand up, caught the eye of the auctioneer and ducked down again.

'Eleven I have at the back there.'

'Who said eleven?' growled the Campbell.

'Do I hear twelve?'

'Twelve.' The Campbell curled his lip.

Cornelius stuck his hand up again.

'Thirteen at the back of the hall.'

'Fourteen!' The Campbell raised his voice.

Cornelius raised his hand.

The sound of an explosion issued from the street. And the distant wail of police sirens.

'Twenty-five pounds!' stormed the Campbell. 'And the devil take the man who offers more.'

'Thirty!' Cornelius had to shout. There was a rat-at-tat of machine-gun fire and several windows shattered. The auctioneer took the dive for cover. He took his microphone with him.

'Do I hear forty?' he called. 'And you'll have to speak up.'

'Forty.' The Campbell drew out a pistol which had no hint whatsoever of the Airfix factory about it.

'Fifty!' called Cornelius.

'Uh-oh.' Tuppe spied the lower portions of Angus and Sawney approaching through the forest of legs. 'They're on to us.'

Cornelius scooped up his chum and scrambled on to the nearest table, scattering antique French tennis racquets.

'One hundred pounds,' he shouted.

'One hundred.' The auctioneer waved his gavel above the pulpit. 'Do I hear one-fifty?'

The Campbell rooted in his combat jacket. 'I don't

know if I have that much on me,' he said. 'Could you just hold up the bidding while my boys settle with the opposition?'

'Going once at one hundred,' called the auctioneer, assuming the foetal position.

'Look out!' Tuppe clung to the tall boy's neck. Cornelius leapt nimbly as crocodile teeth fanned the air beneath them.

Outside in the war-torn street, Special Forces vehicles drew up in an uncompromising line. Steel doors rose at their rear ends and heavily armed men dropped to the ground.

'Have at you, spalpeen!' Angus took another swipe. Cornelius took another leap.

'Gas masks on,' ordered the commander of Special Services. 'Fire on my command.'

The mob, now several hundred strong, and going at it hammer and tongs, took time out to boo and jeer at the military presence. Some began to hurl stones. Shaven-headed Nationalists rolled a car on to its side and took up positions behind it.

'Going twice,' said the auctioneer. 'Twice at one hundred pounds.'

'One hundred and five,' called the lady in the straw hat. 'What the heck eh? It's only money.'

'Fire!' Tear gas canisters broke into the mob. The Nationalists replied with Molotov cocktails and foul language. Petrol from the upturned car flooded across the street and took fire beneath the bus, which erupted in a gush of flame.

'You did that, you peeg!' The bus driver drew out a Saturday-night special and shot the travelling salesman.

Above the war cries and the screams and the order to 'fire at will', came the thunder of approaching hoofbeats.

Down Agamemnon Street, leaping motor cars and fleeing rioters, came a horde of Afghani horsemen. And to the van of them, high upon a pure-bred white Arab stallion, the Wolf of Kabul.

Mr Patel waved from his shop doorway. 'Hi, Uncle,' he called.

'Two hundred pounds.' Cornelius leapt from table to table, Tuppe held high. 'All cash.'

'Two hundred pounds I hear.' The auctioneer stuck his head up above the pulpit and the Campbell took a shot at it.

'Everybody down.' The Campbell fired into the air, taking a chip out of the magnificent fan vaulting. 'On your knees, heads to the floor, or you're dead.'

'Controlled bursts. Choose your targets.' The Special Forces commander raised his hand. The Wolf of Kabul bore down upon him. The now legendary Clicki Ba whirling above his turbaned head.

'Destroy the infidels,' cried the Wolf of Kabul.

'Bloody hell,' cried the Special Forces commander. 'Take cover.'

Firing wildly in all directions, his men did just that.

A ricocheting bullet chanced to take the front from the cigarette machine. And Felix Henderson McMurdo, who was cowering beneath it, suddenly found Woodbine raining down upon him.

'This must be my lucky day,' said the un-canny Scot.

Special Forces men burst through the front door of The Anabaptist Reform Church, and gaped in horror at the unholy tableau spread out before them. They had stumbled in upon what was quite clearly nothing less than a pagan sacrifice.

The ungodly congregation knelt with their faces bowed to the floor. Above them, in the pulpit, a black magician in a tweed cap held his hands high in blasphemous benediction.

And before him, upon an altar table, flanked by sword bearers, stood a tall wild-eyed figure. Surely he wore the mane of a lion upon his head and clutched in his upraised claws, the lifeless body of a small child!

'Holy stations of the cross.' A Special Forces man made the sign over his chest with a gun-free hand. 'Devil worshippers.'

His comrade at arms caught sight of the Campbell, who was struggling with Hamish to shift the green canvas portmanteau. 'I know these bastards, sarge,' said he. 'They're the Wild Warriors of West Lothian. Cannibals to a man Jack of them.'

'Jack?' asked the sergeant. 'As in Jack London?'

9

REGARDING AN ULTIMATE TRUTH
OF NO SMALL MAGNITUDE

People often ask me, 'Hugo, why is it that when dining with royalty, you always keep your hat on?'

I explain that this is due to an old charter, dating back to the time of Sir Hugo de Courcy Rune, third earl of Penge. And then go on to tell this tale.

Apparently, King John and Philippe II of France were in dispute over the duchy of Normandy, and agreed to settle the matter by single combat. Sir Hugo de Courcy Rune was King John's champion, and big with it. And, as legend has it, no sooner had he put spur to his mount and raised his stout stick, than the French champion fled the field of honour. King John, being rightly chuffed, asked Sir Hugo what reward he would care for.

The third earl replied, 'Sire, I have titles, lands and wealth enough. But I would crave a boon for myself and my successors. To remain covered about the head regions in the presence of your highness and all future sovereigns of the sceptred isle.'

King John, knowing full well Sir Hugo's 'thing about his bald spot' and considering this pretty cheap at the price, gave the request the Royal thumbs up.

And so, whenever I am called to dine at the palace, I always sport an old straw boater or knitted bobble hat, to exercise my hereditary privilege.

I am born of noble stock and I am not too proud to admit it. When it comes to deeds of great valour performed in the cause of king and country, the name of Rune is up there with the best of them. And then some.

Which brings me to the matter of my heroic cousin, Lord Victor Rune VC, and the most singular circumstances surrounding his tragic and untimely demise. It began in this fashion.

After several years of rank rising, deed doing and medal winning, 1945 found Cousin Vic leading an armoured battalion into Berlin.

Considering this an ideal opportunity to notch up a final few medals for the family collection (now housed in a vault beneath Windsor Castle), it was Cousin Vic's plan to round up all the Nazi war criminals and march them off to prison.

Imagine his surprise, therefore, when he discovered that not a single German he met had ever been in the Nazi Party, let alone had even heard of a concentration camp.

Cousin Vic was frankly baffled.

'Where did all the Nazis go?' he asked a Berliner who was waving a Union Jack.

'What is a Nazi?' the other replied.

And wherever he went in the city he found it to be the same. Everyone was a civilian. None of them had ever supported Mr Hitler and most were shocked to hear that anything like that had been going on.

'And who's going to pay for all this damage?' the Mayor of Berlin asked my cousin.

Vic returned to England without further medals, pondering on the mystery. Where did the Nazis go?

One minute there had apparently been an entire nation, set upon racial purity and world domination, and then the next . . .

As the years passed, my cousin came to encounter this phenomenon again and again.

There were Peace Rallies in the 1960s, with stone-throwing anarchists running amok. But, the next day in court, these same stone-throwing anarchists complained that they were nothing more than innocent bystanders, who had been brutalized by policemen and thrown into Black Marias.

And the policemen themselves, when accused of baton charging peacefully protesting women and children, denied that they had ever done any such thing. Not us, they swore under oath.

Curiouser and curiouser.

And then there were the free pop concerts which attracted as many as a quarter of a million hippies. They were there and then they weren't. Where did they go to? When did you ever see even four hippies anywhere else?

And the annual Wembley Country and Western festivals. Thousands and thousands of fans, all wearing full western regalia. Cousin Vic could not recall ever once having bumped into a cowboy in the street.

And those football supporters, storming the terraces. When the football season ended, these warrior bands literally vanished. They were never seen waving their scarves, chanting and kicking people with their Doc Martens at any other time of the year.

Where did they all come from and where did they go? That was the question.

It was the day of the first London Marathon that Cousin Vic knocked upon my door. He was carrying a battery-driven television set and shaking terribly.

'Look at them, Hugo,' he pointed to the tiny screen. 'Where did they all come from? If they behaved like that every day, the city would grind to a halt. And I'll wager that if you go down there tomorrow there will be no trace of them. What does it all mean?'

He sank into a fireside chair and I poured him a small medicinal quart of Absinthe to steady his nerves.

'I can tell you,' said I. 'But I don't know if I dare. The truth, when it is revealed, will rock this world upon its axis. It is better that I alone bear the burden. In fact the secret must remain with me until the day I die. I am sorry, Victor.'

'Hugo,' said Cousin Vic, 'you have my word as an officer and a gentleman, that what ever you tell me will not go beyond the walls of this room.'

'Cross your heart and hope to die?'

'In a cellar full of sex-crazed Turkish truckers.' He solemnly crossed his heart.

'Then so be it.' I refreshed his glass and told him the terrible truth.

'I have studied this manifestation for many years and have devoted considerable thought to it. I have given it a name. *Spontaneously Generated Crowd Phenomenon.*

'Have you ever wondered why it is always hot and dry in the Sahara Desert and cold and raining in Wales?'

He shook his head.

'The alchemists believed in the principle "as above so below", that everything is linked. The Sahara is hot, dry and golden. So it attracts the sun. Wales is grey, dull and closed on Sundays. Therefore, weatherwise, it gets what it jolly well deserves.

'S.G.C.P. is a bit like that. At a certain place, at a certain time, under certain conditions, things will occur.

'The crowds, of which you speak, are not truly crowds at all. They are not composed of real people. These "crowds" are vast living organisms, formed from thousands of single human-like cells. They flourish when the perfect conditions occur for them to do so. Theirs is a brief Mayfly existence. When the event, whatever it may be, finishes, the cell structure decays, the cells divide, fade away and die.

'Certainly a few misguided humans will attend football matches and Country and Western festivals. But one look at the uniform blankness of expression on the faces of the "crowd" should tell you all you need to know. The crowd is not human.

'I contend that these crowds spontaneously generate from microscopic spores which constantly drift about in our atmosphere, awaiting the perfect conditions in which to briefly flourish. Your vanishing Nazis, for instance. The climate which spawned them, what is referred to as a "social climate", ceased to exist when the war ended. Thus your Nazis simply faded away.

'I further assert that these spores have been with us since the birth of mankind. Ever growing in number. And I fear that they are evolving. Reaching sentience.

'Victor, I have evidence to suggest that they are now actually capable of creating the conditions suitable for generation on a global scale. If they cannot be stopped in time, mankind will surely be doomed.

'The entire planet will eventually consist of one vast chanting inhuman crowd.'

'By all the gods,' cried Cousin Vic, 'it all makes sense now. This explains crowd mentality. The following of false messiahs. Why charismatic leaders come to power. The whole shebang. Hugo, this rewrites human history! You must publish these facts at once. You must warn the world.'

'And who should I tell?' I asked. 'A crowd of politicians perhaps? The assembled multitude at The United Nations? Should I ask first for all non-humans to leave the room?

'Victor, all about us the spores float in the air. I picture them as neurons, part of a great mass mind. Exchanging information, plotting the replacement of man. Do you think they would allow me to pass on this ultimate truth?'

'Then if *you* will not, *I* must!' cried my noble cousin, flinging down his television set and plunging for the door.

'No, Victor,' I called after him. 'You will not succeed. You cannot. *They* will not let you.' But my words were to no avail.

I heard his footfalls upon the stairs. The sound of the front door slamming. Then a squeal of brakes and a deadly concussion.

Before I reached my window I knew full well the terrible sight which surely awaited me.

Victor lay dead in the middle of the road.

A crowd had already formed around him!

The Book of Ultimate Truths
Hugo Rune

There were many arrests made that day. But there would be no successful prosecutions. Order was restored around four o'clock in the afternoon, when the tanks encircling the town removed the covers from their guns and Mr Patel heard on his wireless set that the British prime minister had sanctioned the use of carpet bombing.

Happily there had been no actual loss of life. The only real hospital case was a travelling salesman who had been shot through the foot.

Many upstanding townsfolk of Sheila na gigh were, however, now crowded into police cells at the Edinburgh nick, loudly protesting their innocence and awaiting the arrival of their solicitors to prepare charges of police brutality and wrongful arrest.

One married couple in particular expected to do very well out of it. They had come home during the height of the disturbances to discover their teenage daughter being ravished by a young police officer. Exhibit A was expected to be a twenty-one-function Swiss Police knife.

Then there were the fifty-five auction bidders who were filing a mass suit for slander and defamation of character against a sergeant in the Special Forces.

The Sheila na gigh bus company was suing for the

loss of its only bus and Mr Patel for his Woodbine machine.

More than one hundred smartly dressed American solicitors had already chartered a plane and were even now heading across the Atlantic.

Police Chief Sam McAggott was having a 'rough one'. He sat at his desk rooting through a tower of statements.

'Do we have anyone in our cells who does not claim to be an innocent bystander?' he asked his sergeant.

The sergeant pushed back his cap and scratched his head, the way some of them do. 'McMurdo,' he said.

'McMurdo? That name seems to ring a bell. Does he have any "previous"?'

'Well, no sir. He doesn't actually have a record. But he's a wrong'n right enough. We've got him banged up in a high-security cell. I've had him put in a strait-jacket and one of those leather masks with the little bars over the mouth hole. He won't be biting anyone's face off while he's in our custody. Have no fear of that, chief.'

'I'm very glad to hear it. And what did we arrest him for?'

The sergeant flourished McMurdo's statement. 'He coughed up, sir. Came clean.'

Sam read through the statement. 'He confessed to being in illegal possession of two packets of Woodbine? Is that it?'

'Yes, sir.' The sergeant winked. 'But I can pencil in a few other little misdemeanours. Clear up a few unsolveds, eh sir?'

'No no no!' McAggott ripped up McMurdo's statement and flung the pieces into the air.

'But, sir. I'm sure we could tie him into a couple of

torso cases and a bullion robbery. Just give us time. I'll beat the truth out of the maniac.'

'No,' said McAggott. He turned further sheets of paper. 'What about these two tourists? Murphy and Tuppe? What kind of name is that, Tuppe?'

'I believe it's Welsh, sir, or Danish.'

'So, what about them?'

'They're witnesses, sir. Against the Campbell.'

'Then why are they locked in a cell?'

'For their own protection, sir.'

'From who?'

'The Campbell, sir.'

'And where's he?'

'Locked in the next cell, sir.'

McAggott sighed. 'Let them out, sergeant. Get full statements from them and send them on their way.'

'Yes sir.'

'Sergeant, I can't seem to find any shaven-headed Scottish Nationalists here.'

'We didn't arrest any, sir.'

'And what about this Wolf of Kabul fellow?'

'Fictional character, sir. Out of *The Hotspur*.'

'Out of *The Hotspur*. I see.' McAggott rose wearily from his desk and smote the sergeant a blow to the skull. 'Put the kettle on, sergeant,' he said.

At a little after six of the early evening clock, Cornelius and Tuppe were once more in Sheila na gigh. A Sheila na gigh which now resembled Beirut on a bad day. Their taxi pulled up outside The Anabaptist Reform Church and Felix Henderson McMurdo climbed out.

'Thanks very much for the lift,' said he. 'And may God go with you on your epic journey.'

'A pleasure,' said Cornelius. 'And good luck to you.'

Tuppe waved. 'Be lucky,' he called.

'Bye.'

'Nice chap,' said Cornelius to Tuppe,

'One of the best,' said Tuppe to Cornelius.

'He'll finish his days at the end of a rope,' said the taxi driver, unclenching his buttocks. 'Do you want me to wait, by the way?'

'Oh yes.' Cornelius climbed from the cab and stood amidst the rubble. 'We have to pick up some belongings and then we'd like you to drive us.'

'Where to?'

'The south. A long way to the south.'

'No problem there. It's cash only for all trips costing less than twenty-five pounds, of course. But I will accept personal cheques up to fifty pounds if they are accompanied by a valid cheque card. And any major credit card . . .'

Cornelius left two hundred pounds in cash in an envelope pinned to the pulpit. He also left his address, with a request that a receipt be sent on to him.

'First class,' said Cornelius, once the green canvas portmanteau and his personal baggage were all in the boot of the taxi.

'South?' asked the taxi driver.

'South,' said Cornelius Murphy, grinning like a good'n.

10

It was a beautiful evening.

Even out there, in the middle of nowhere, it was a beautiful evening.

The taxi rattled to the side of the road, steam issuing from its bonnet regions. The driver got out of the car. Lifted the bonnet. Dropped the bonnet. Blew on to his scalded fingers. Cursed the bonnet. Lifted the bonnet again with his elbows. Peered into the engine area. Cursed the engine area. Kicked the radiator and screamed as the bonnet fell shut on his fingers.

He was cursing still as Cornelius bandaged him up.

'I'm sorry we broke off the bonnet,' the tall boy said. 'But we got you free and that's all that really matters. I don't think anything's broken, by the way.'

'Apart from the bonnet, of course,' said Tuppe. 'And the fan belt. You don't happen to carry a spare, I suppose.'

The driver looked him daggers.

'No, I thought not.'

Cornelius glanced over his shoulder and then stuck his head out of the window and squinted into the distance. The road before looked much like the road behind. It was long and straight and surrounded by bleak-looking moor.

'You'd better set off now before it gets dark,' he told the driver.

'I'd better what?'

'Go for help. We'll wait here for you.'

'And if you find a café, could you bring back a couple of bacon sandwiches?' Tuppe asked.

'No no no,' said the taxi driver. 'One of you can go.'

Cornelius shook his head. 'I am too frail to be a moors walker. And I can hardly be expected to leave my three-year-old brother here in the care of a strange man.'

'Three years old?' The driver viewed Tuppe with suspicion.

'Waaaaaaaah,' went Tuppe. 'Don't let the nasty man touch me.'

'All right. I'll go. But you pay me now. I don't want to get back here and find you've legged it. I'm no fool you know.'

'No, I'm sure you're not.' Cornelius paid up. 'I'll need a receipt for that, if you don't mind.'

The driver displayed his bandaged fingers. 'Sorry,' said he in a tone which suggested that he was anything but.

'You'd better take a coat,' said Tuppe helpfully. 'You never know.'

The driver made a gesture with his bandaged fingers. Gazed up at the clear evening sky and slouched away without his coat.

He was a mere dot on the horizon when the sky clouded over and the storm broke.

'He's no fool you know, that driver,' said Tuppe.

'So I've heard.' Cornelius stretched a long arm to the dashboard and unclipped the driver's radio mike. 'Mayday Mayday,' he called into it.

'I wondered about that also,' said Tuppe. 'But as the driver was being so grumpy I decided not to mention it to him.'

*　　*　　*

Cornelius spoke to many interesting people on the radio set.

He spoke to a motor cycle messenger who had once been a roadie for King Crimson. A trucker named Keith who was delivering coal to Newcastle. A radio ham called Tony and an ambulance driver who had just picked up a man with bandaged fingers who was suffering from exposure. Cornelius would have liked to have spoken more with the ambulance driver but the signal faded away.

'I think the car battery has just gone flat,' said Tuppe.

Cornelius replaced the radio mike. 'I think we are well and truly marooned,' said he. 'I spoke to three different minicab firms, but none of them wanted to come out and fetch us. I wonder why.'

'I think to hear the baying of a monstrous hound,' said Tuppe.

The storm worsened. Lightning dipped and veered in a manner which was far too close for comfort. The howling wind blew the broken bonnet away and rain began to flood in under the dashboard.

'My feet are getting wet,' said Cornelius.

'Mine aren't,' said Tuppe. 'But I know what you mean.'

It was getting on for ten of the storm-lashed grim night clock when the headlights appeared. They moved slowly and steadily towards the stranded taxi and then they stopped.

'There,' said Cornelius. 'The day is yet saved.'

'The day is yet saved!' Tuppe sat gloomily upon the

tall boy's rucksack. His back against the portmanteau. Cornelius had his suitcase on his lap. He was leaning against the coffin.

'A hearse,' whispered Tuppe. 'We are in the back of a hearse. The back of a hearse which is already occupied. We should have stuck it out in the taxi.'

Back along the road, a forked tongue of lightning struck the taxi. The explosion was quite dramatic, but the rain eventually put out the fire.

Cornelius called forwards to the driver. 'If you could just drop us off at the first five-star hotel you come to.'

The driver said nothing, and the hearse, one of those really spiffing nineteen-forties jobs, with the scrolled ironwork around the roof and the etched glass windows, continued soundlessly through the storm-tossed night. And then suddenly it stopped.

'Fan belt, do you think?' Tuppe asked. 'We've only travelled about half a mile.'

The driver turned to face them. A long, pale face beneath a long, dark hat. 'The village of Milcom Moloch,' he announced, in a funereal tone. 'There is an inn here. We go no further.'

He left the driving seat, went around to the rear and swung up the door. Cornelius peered out through the rain.

Across the street warm lights showed through pebbled glass. An inn sign swung to and fro in the wind. Faint sounds of revelry issued into the night.

Cornelius and Tuppe dragged the luggage from the hearse and thanked the driver.

Tuppe waved. 'Be lucky,' he called.

'Come on,' said Cornelius. 'Let's get out of this rain.'

There was a 'Hah-up!' A crack of a whip. And a

whinny of horses. The epic duo turned and thought to see a Victorian high-wheeled hearse vanish into the storm.

'Trick of the light,' said Tuppe.

'Undoubtedly,' Cornelius agreed.

A dash of lightning lit up the inn sign. The words THE HANGMAN'S ARMS showed up just long enough to be read.

'Come on.' Cornelius dragged the portmanteau towards the inn door. Tuppe struggled manfully with the rucksack and suitcase.

Cornelius raised the rough iron catch and the storm caught the inn door, blasting it forwards.

All sounds of revelry ceased. Cornelius fought with his hair.

'Good-evening,' he called, smiling invisibly for all he was worth.

'Bye now.' The police sergeant waved to Mr Patel. Mr Patel did not wave back. The sergeant shrugged, put the bolt on the front door and returned to the office of Police Chief Sam McAggott. 'That's about the last of them, sir,' he said.

Sam sat with his head in his hands. 'Ruination,' was all he had to say.

'Come now, sir, it's never as bad as you think.' Behind his back the sergeant rolled the copy of tomorrow morning's *Edinburgh Mercury* between his hands. The front-page banner headline read DIS-GRACED POLICE CHIEF TO STAND TRIAL.

'I know we had to let them all walk free. But we do still have the Campbell.'

'Ah,' said Sam. 'The Campbell.'

'The Wild Warrior of West Lothian, sir. We have him bang to rights on the kiosk heist and Special

Forces caught him redhanded holding up the auction room and trying to make off with a green canvas portmanteau.'

'A guilty man? And actually in our custody? Can this be right?'

'Locked up neat and nice, sir. Of course, we'll have to let him go in the morning.'

'And just for why?'

'Well, sir. Apparently someone recorded over the station security video by mistake, the gaunt woman who runs the kiosk is not prepared to testify. The portmanteau can't be found. Murphy has left town. The other auction bidders are all tied up with litigation against the Special Forces. And the Special Forces guy's solicitor has advised him not to make any statements.'

'So the Campbell is not bang to rights at all.'

'But he doesn't know that, sir. We'd get a confession out of him easy as blinking. Possibly even tie him into a couple of torso cases and a bullion robbery.'

Sam shrugged. 'I like the way you think, sergeant. Pull this one off and there could be a promotion in it for you.'

'Thanks, sir.' The sergeant rammed the rolled copy of the *Edinburgh Mercury* into his back pocket and fished down the ring of cell keys from its hook by the door. 'Shall I bring my big truncheon?' he asked Sam.

The cells were, as they say, hewn into the living rock. Water oozed from their ceilings and plip-plopped into rank pools. Rats scuttled. Strange cries echoed.

'Here we are, sir.' The sergeant turned a key in a cell door.

The door went EEEEEEEAAAAAAAAW as he pushed it open.

'The Campbell,' said the sergeant.

'Get up, Campbell,' said Sam McAggott.

The Campbell drew a deep breath. Then he got to his feet and glared at Sam McAggott. 'I'll be on my way now,' he said.

'Not yet, my lad,' said Sam.

'Oh yes.' The Campbell lifted one foot in the air. Then he lifted the other. He hovered a moment in complete contempt for the law of gravity and then he left the cell. At impossible speed.

He swept past McAggott, bowling him from his feet. Soared over the ducking head of the sergeant. Flew along the corridor. Burst through door after police door and was gone into the night.

McAggott climbed over the sergeant, who had assumed the foetal position, and staggered back to his office. He picked up his telephone and dialled out a number. Somewhere a phone began to ring.

'Hello,' said a voice. 'Who is it?'

'McAggott,' gasped McAggott.

'Ah. What news? Did all go according to plan?'

'Yes, sir. Well, no sir. The one you're looking for . . .'

'You caught it?'

'It escaped, sir. We didn't know it was . . . an *it*. We couldn't stop it. It moved so fast.'

'You fool. Did it change? Did you see it change?'

'No, sir. It glared and it floated and it flew like the Devil. But it didn't change.'

'What about Murphy? Is Murphy all right?'

'He's fine, sir. We sent him off on his way.'

'He'd better be fine. Now get your men out after the it. Tell them to shoot on sight. If it can be shot. Who is following Murphy?'

'No-one, sir. I thought you . . .'

'Buffoon. You are a buffoon, McAggott.'

'Sorry, sir. Goodbye, sir.'

'Goodbye.' Arthur Kobold replaced the receiver.

'And good luck, Murphy. You're going to need it.'

'Hello,' called Cornelius Murphy. 'Good-evening to you.'

It was a snug little bar. Blackened beams ribbed it all around and about. A fine log fire crackled in the inglenook. The floor was of mellow golden stone. The tables and benches burnished bog oak. There were copper kettles and warming pans and horse brasses. Very snug indeed.

'Aiiiieeeee!' went the patrons of this snug little bar, cowering in their seats. 'The Lord preserve us.'

Cornelius looked at Tuppe.

Tuppe looked at Cornelius.

'A Special Forces pub, do you think?' Tuppe asked.

'Away, thou spawn of the pit!' cried the landlord, flourishing a string of garlic and making the sign of the cross. 'Back to the depths of Hell with you.'

'Would there be any chance of a room for the night?' Tuppe called.

'The Devil's familiar!' The landlord pointed to the small fellow. 'Back, ungodly issue!' The cowering patrons were pulling silver crucifixes from their pockets and holding them between trembling fingers. 'Out, demons, out . . .' they began to chant.

'Stuff this,' said Cornelius. 'Let's try up the road.'

'Out, demons!' shrieked the landlord.

'All right. We're going.' The tall boy turned towards the storm.

'Oh come on in and shut the bloody door,' said the landlord and the bar erupted into gales of laughter.

'Ah,' said Cornelius, fighting down his hair, hauling in the portmanteau and forcing shut the door. 'This would be some of that famous north-country humour I have read so much about.'

'Lost on me I'm afraid,' muttered Tuppe.

He and Cornelius approached the landlord, who was clutching at his mid regions and laughing like the drain of proverb.

'Take no notice of them, lads. They do it to every-one.' An extremely attractive young barmaid appeared on the scene. She was pale and willowy, with a large mouth and the most amazing violet eyes that you ever did see. Cornelius observed that freckles on her left cheek mapped out the Tuamotu archipelago of south-west Polynesia. She smiled upon Cornelius and Cornelius smiled mightily upon her.

'My name is Cornelius Murphy,' he told her. 'And I would be honoured if you would bear my children.'

The landlord smacked the counter and fell into further hilarity.

'Get away with you.' The barmaid fluttered exotic eyelashes at the tall boy. 'What'll it be?'

'I'll take a short,' said Tuppe.

'The little'n'll take a short.' The landlord sank beneath the counter and lay on his back kicking his legs in the air.

'Smashed out of their bloody boxes as usual.' The beautiful barmaid shook her beautiful head. 'Scotch will it be, love?'

'Two,' said Cornelius. 'No ice.'

'I missed that,' croaked the landlord. 'What did he say?'

'He said, no ice.' The landlord thrashed about help-lessly. The barmaid drew off two measures and passed them across the counter. Cornelius helped Tuppe on to a stool and found one for himself. 'Would you care to join us in a drink?' he asked the barmaid.

'I'll take the money, if you don't mind. Someone has to stay sober around here.'

'As you wish.' Cornelius handed her a five-pound note. The barmaid rang up the drinks on the till and then pocketed all of the change.

'Could I have a receipt for that?' Cornelius asked.

'What you got in this big trunk, mister?' A big, ruddy-faced farming type tapped the portmanteau with the steely toecap of his sturdy work boot. 'Dismembered body, is it?'

His drinking buddies cheered and hooted.

Cornelius made a distraught face and chewed upon his knuckle. 'It's my hideously deformed brother,' he said in a hoarse whisper. 'We are taking him back to the institution. Don't awaken him. If he was to get free again . . .' The tall boy covered his face. 'The blood, all the blood . . . all those chewed-up limbs . . .'

The patrons collapsed into further mirth.

'Do you have a vacant room for the night?' Cornelius asked the barmaid.

'There's only the one. Your friend and you will have to share.'

The pub door swung open.

'Aiiiieeeee!' went the patrons. 'Save our souls.'

'Leave it out, you silly buggers.' A local in a waxy anorak entered, shaking rain from his hat. He shut the door, turned and tripped straight over the portmanteau. The patrons rose to new heights of glee. Laughter rattled the horse brasses and echoed in the warming pans.

The ruddy-faced fellow fingered his joke crucifix. 'Pray that you have not awakened the mad brother,' said he, helping the fallen anorakster to his feet.

'Do they always carry on in this fashion?' Cornelius asked.

The barmaid nodded. Cornelius caught the fragrance

of *L'Air du Temps*. 'They didn't used to be like this. They used to all sit glowering into their beer. Then the mill closed down. And the crops failed. And the brickworks went out of business. And the processing plant moved to Solihull. And now they're all on the dole with no prospect of ever working again.'

'I see,' said Cornelius.

'I don't,' said Tuppe.

'Then,' continued the barmaid, as Cornelius sniffed on appreciatively, 'this meteor came down in old Jack Spar's field, least as how they thought it were a meteor. But it weren't. It were a kind of metal cylinder. The men dug it out of the ground where it fell and hauled it back to the village. The old boys said it were a gift from the elder gods and they built a special shrine for it in the square.'

Cornelius looked at Tuppe.

Tuppe looked at Cornelius.

They finished their drinks.

'Might we see our room now?' Cornelius asked.

'Certainly. I'll show you the way.'

Tuppe and Cornelius hastened to collect the luggage. The barmaid led them from the bar and up some rickety steps. The patrons cheered their departure and raised glasses in salute.

'There were this big storm, see. Just like tonight. And lightning struck the shrine and the cylinder cracked open and out came this thing.'

Cornelius bumped the portmanteau up the stairs behind the barmaid. 'White stockings,' he sighed.

'You'll have to duck your head here, love.'

Clunk went the head of Cornelius Murphy. 'Ouch,' he said. 'Out came what thing?' he asked.

The barmaid swung open a door and switched on the light. It was a snug little bedroom. Oak-framed bed. Chintzy bed cover. Plump goose-feather pillows. A cozy little fire burned in the hearth.

'Fell out.' The barmaid turned down the chintzy bed cover. 'It were a machine inside. A sort of box with dials on and a little television screen. And a microphone.'

'Probably an interositor,' said Tuppe, who had seen *This Island Earth* three times.

'No, it weren't an interositor, them has triangular screens and positronic wave cross-band modulators which operate on the principle of ionized beta photons bombarding the nucleus of an alpha particle. Same as a linear accelerator.'

'Not one of those then?'

'No.' The barmaid tossed her head. A swirl of soft brown hair. 'It were a karaoke machine.'

Cornelius sighed once more. But this time it had nothing to do with white stockings. 'Is that it?' he asked. 'Or is there more?'

'There's more. Let me give you a hand with that suitcase, little manny.'

'Thanks,' said Tuppe.

The barmaid humped the suitcase on to the bed. 'Is this real crocodile skin?' she asked.

'No.' Cornelius shook his head. The barmaid tittered. 'That time when you shook your head, your hair just stayed still.'

'It does that. Go on then. The karaoke machine?'

'Well see. They brought it into the bar. It were a bit charred by the lightning, but they plugged it in and music came out and the words to the music came up on the little television screen.'

'That's what they do.' Tuppe put down the rucksack and kicked it under the bed. 'Or so I've been told.'

'Well maybe they do. But this machine played music

no-one had ever heard before. Catchy tunes, though, and everyone had a singalong. Cheered them up no end it did.'

'And so that's why they're all so jolly?'

'No, that's not it at all. Just you listen. It were a month after they first started playing with the machine that someone hears one of the tunes they were singing on the wireless set.'

'That's what the machines do,' Tuppe explained. 'They play popular tunes of the day.'

'No,' said the barmaid. 'I'm not explaining myself right. The karaoke machine had played the tune a month before the tune turned up on the wireless set. It played music from the future. Next month's top ten, to be precise.'

'Next month's top ten?' Cornelius sat down on the portmanteau. 'You are making fun of us, surely.'

'I am not. The machine played music from the future.'

'I see,' said Cornelius, who was beginning to. 'So the folk of the village capitalized on this gift from the gods, that had come to them in their darkest hour. Let me guess, they placed bets with bookmakers about who would be top of the charts at Christmas. They took out copyright on lyrics that had not even been written yet. In short they are all now fabulously wealthy. That's why they laugh all the time.'

The barmaid shook her head. More brown swirlings, more *L'Air du Temps*. 'No. That's not it at all. Though the other fellow did say all the kind of things you just did say.'

'Other fellow. What other fellow?'

'He was from London. His name was Jack, I think. There was this storm see, just like tonight. And he were a taxi driver and he'd got lost. And when he come into the pub he hears the village lads singing along with the machine and he has a go himself and gets to talking with everyone. A real friendly fellow he were by all accounts, bought 'em all drinks.'

Cornelius did not possess a machine that could predict the future, but he felt certain he knew just how this tale was going to end. 'He took the machine away with him, didn't he?'

'How did you guess? That's just what he did. He said he had connections with the music industry and how he was always having famous musicians and producers sitting in the back of his cab. And how he could make all the village wealthy.'

'And the villagers let a complete stranger drive off with a machine that could play music from the future . . .'

'Course they didn't. Do you think we're all daft? No, they sent a big strong farmer's lad down to London with this Jack, to make sure there were no funny business.'

'I'm sure I'm missing something here. How long ago did this happen?'

'Oh, before my time. About thirty years back. And do you know what?'

'What?'

'They never heard from either of them again. So . . .'

'So?'

'So, you have to laugh, don't you?' The barmaid slapped her knees and did just that. Cornelius set free another sigh.

'This big farmer's lad?' Tuppe asked. 'I travel about a bit. You don't happen to recall his name, by any chance?'

'Brian.' The barmaid dabbed at her eyes. 'Brian somet or other.'

'Epstein?' Tuppe enquired.

'That's it. Brian Epstein. Do you know him then?'

Tuppe shook his head. 'Just a lucky guess,' said he.

'Brian Epstein!' The barmaid had departed and Cornelius was unpacking his suitcase. 'Brian Epstein indeed.'

Tuppe was toasting his feet by the fire. 'I've travelled, like I say. And I've heard that story before.'

'Not true then?' Cornelius unfolded his pyjamas. Tuppe caught sight of them. Cornelius stuffed them hastily back into the suitcase.

'I'm not saying it's not true. Only that I've heard it before. Perhaps if you hear a thing told often enough, it makes it true. What nasty pyjamas, by the way.'

'They are rather vile, aren't they?' Cornelius closed his suitcase. 'I suggest we have a look in the portmanteau. That is why we're here after all.'

'What a good idea.'

They dragged the portmanteau into the middle of the room. Cornelius prised open the locks and lifted the lid. A stale musty old smell filled the air.

'That's a dirty old duffle-coat, if ever there was one.' Tuppe leaned into the portmanteau, scooped out the duffle-coat and tossed it into a far corner. 'But see, here is your brush-and-comb set.'

Cornelius took it up. 'This case is never calfskin. Plastic.'

'Perhaps you might put it back into next week's auction.'

'I think not. Now, what papers do we have?'

They didn't have many. And what they did were mostly bills of the unpaid variety. These covered a wide range of goods. Expensive cigars. Brandies and liquors. Rare books. Exclusive clothing. The bills were all made out to Hugo Rune. Demands for payment and court summonses were pinned to most of them.

'He certainly knew how to live, this Rune.' Tuppe flicked through the bills. 'Big-game rifles. Hand-tailored shirts. Imported toiletries.'

'What is this?' Cornelius brought to light an ancient photograph. Curly at the edges and mottled with age.

It was a group shot of four men. Three were young, smiling. The fourth, who stood head and shoulders above them, was older. He wasn't smiling. He wore a plaid plus-fours suit over a more than ample frame. His head was a great shaven dome. His eyes dark and piercing. Across the photograph was scrawled in blue ink, US WITH THE MASTER. HIS BIRTHDAY, JULY 1936. Beneath this was an arrow pointing down and the words, TO MOLLY.

'I have a Molly on my list.' Cornelius handed the photograph to Tuppe. 'Pity she's not in the picture.'

'Who's that fat bastard?' Tuppe asked.

'The lad himself, as they say.' Cornelius took back the picture and tucked it into his top pocket. 'Anything else?'

Tuppe climbed into the portmanteau and dug about. 'Some letters. No lost manuscripts though.'

'Check to see if the trunk has a false bottom.'

Tuppe stuck his head up. 'That's what I *am* doing.'

Cornelius examined the letters. They were all from Rune, addressed to Victor Zenobia, requesting funds for one project or another. Maps. The purchase of a London taxi. Ropes and climbing tackle. Gunpowder.

'I think we have the measure of Mr Rune.' Cornelius tucked the letters into his pocket. 'Barking mad and always on the ear'ole.'

'He didn't seem to care what he spent, as long as

he didn't have to pay for it. I wonder what your Mr Kobold sees in him.'

'Or the rival publishers. The Campbell must surely be in their pay.'

'You think that?'

'What other explanation can there be? He was waiting for me when I arrived. He knew I was coming. He planned to get me out of the way so he could bid for the portmanteau. Nab the papers.'

'All seems a bit drastic. But it's epic stuff right enough. Ah, what's this? Oh, nothing, just an old paper bag.' Tuppe screwed it up and flung it on to the carpet.

'Oh good,' said Cornelius. 'A vital clue.'

'A vital what?'

'Clue. Whenever a piece of paper gets screwed up and thrown away like that it's always a vital clue.'

'Oh yes, so it is. Quick, give it the once over.'

Cornelius picked up the old paper bag and carefully uncreased it. 'Molly's Wholefoods.' Cornelius read aloud. 'Number one, Marduk Parade, High Street, Milcom Moloch.'

'Well, how about that?'

'How indeed.'

They had a bottle of the best port sent up. And they sat and they plotted what they should do next. Presently the port was gone and the fire gone and Tuppe had gone to sleep in the portmanteau. So Cornelius crept off to the bathroom, performed fastidious ablutions, togged up in the vile pyjamas and returned to the bedroom.

He tucked the chintzy bed cover over his sleeping friend and switched off the light. In the unfamiliar darkness he wondered over the peculiarities of the day. But being able to make nothing of them he finally drifted off to sleep.

In the far corner of the room, the duffle-coat stirred. A black rat crept out of the left sleeve and scuttled away in search of cheese.

11

THE MYSTERIES OF TIME

Most of us like to celebrate our birthdays.

My own, for example, is a national holiday in Tibet, a 'Day of Gladness and Rejoicing' in Upper Sumatra, and, no doubt, many other parts of the world.

But how many have ever stopped to consider this particular riddle?

If you are born on a Monday, then the next year your birthday will fall on a Tuesday. The next on a Wednesday and so on and so forth. Therefore, by the time you are seven, although your birth*date* remains the same, you must actually be celebrating your birthday one week later in the year.

By the time you are thirty, an entire lunar month later. Therefore, a man born in the spring must surely celebrate his ninetieth birthday in the middle of the summer.

This is what you call a Cosmic Mystery. And I will return to it.

There is a great deal more to time than meets the eye, or has, in fact, ever been 'explained' by that unprincipled scoundrel, A. Einstein, Esq.

For instance, who amongst us has not said at one time or another:

Doesn't time fly when you're enjoying yourself?

Time really drags in this job.

Not bloody Christmas again already!

My wife says I'm a bad lover. How can any woman tell that in thirty seconds?[1]

Isn't that window-cleaner coming more often than he did last year?

Now, I am the last man on Earth to cry, CONSPIRACY! But I think to detect the acrid stench of its breath in this one.

Allow me to explain.

Time, as you will agree, is the most valuable commodity that we possess. And, as we know only too well, every really valuable commodity falls, sooner or later, into the hands of some unscrupulous individual, who then exploits it for their own ends. It is my contention that 'time' is now under the control of such an individual, who manipulates it in order to do down the working man.

Allow me to explain further.

The average working man spends roughly half of his life working. This involves a lot of clock watching. The working part of the working man's life seems to last 'for ever'. Then, if he survives this and retires, one of two things happens. Either, he finds 'time dragging terribly' and returns to work, or, he resists this urge, takes off to the seaside, wakes up one morning, says 'Twenty years retired, it seems like only five minutes,' and drops dead.

There is no escape for the working man!

His 'time' is being controlled!

Let me cite the example of Shakespeare. How could he have completed so many plays, as well as formulating the beer which bears his name and opening so many tea rooms? Remember, there were no typewriters or photocopier machines in those days.

If Shakespeare wrote a play with a cast of twenty-five, then he must have had to write a separate copy for each of the cast. I estimate that he must therefore have penned

[1] Humour

118

no less than five thousand words per minute, ten hours a day, for twenty years. No mean feat!

There are two possibilities here. Either, that time was substantially different in those days, let us say that a minute then, would be equivalent to an hour and a half now; or that somehow Shakespeare had 'time on his side'. Under his control, in fact. Oh yes? I contend that it was all down to Shakespeare's employer. *He* had control of Shakespeare's 'time' and was determined to milk it for every ounce of potential profit.

So, I hear you cry, tell us how it's done, Hugo. And tell us who is doing it.

And so I shall.

THE POPE CONTROLS 'TIME' ON THIS PLANET!

Come come, I hear you cry. Surely this is sour grapes, Hugo. Because your application to become Pope has been turned down yet again. Not so, my friends, not so.

I will now explain everything.

A BRIEF HISTORY OF TIME
by HUGO RUNE

No-one knows exactly who originally discovered the existence of time. But it was certainly the Romans who first thought of splitting it up into units of measurement.

The Roman senate started off with seconds and decided that sixty of them should equal one minute. Being extremely fond of naming things, especially after themselves, the sixty-man senate arrived at this particular figure without much in the way of heated debate. And each had a second named after themselves.

They did not, however, agree upon a uniform length for the second. And since some senators had much longer names than others, jealousies soon arose. In no time senators were renaming themselves with longer and longer titles so that their seconds should be bigger than everyone else's.

We have the sixty-first senator to thank for the length of the second. Arriving back, as he did from his holidays, to discover that his honourable companions hadn't given him a second to call his own, he took umbrage (somewhere near Troy)[1].

And being a conniving little toady with an eye for the main chance, he proclaimed that the second should equal exactly the time it took to say 'praise Caesar'. And that they shouldn't have names at all, but simply be numbered from one to sixty.

This didn't go down very well with the rest of the senate, but found great favour with Caesar, who allowed the sixty-first senator to keep umbrage.

The Caesar in question was the almost forgotten Flavius the Noseless. And it was he who originally decreed that all Roman sculptures should be fashioned without noses. A fact which seems to have slipped by the greybeards of the art world. The same greybeards, in fact, who still refer to Henry Moore as an 'abstract' sculptor. I knew Moore for many years and can testify that he was a master of lifelike representation. He just knocked around with some very funny-looking women. But I digress.

Now, the senate, having got time divided up, named and tamed, were not happy. They had already invented The Class System (we have much to thank the Romans for). And they were saying to themselves, 'Why should time be the same for everyone? Surely *we*, as the ruling intelligentsia, should have posher time than the slaves and plebs?'

A whole lot of serious debating went on about this.

Many suggestions were put forward. That the plebs should have less seconds in their minutes. That they should have the same number of seconds but be taxed for using them.

[1] Humour

That somehow their seconds should be made longer, so that they could do more work in a day.

It was the latter suggestion, and how it was put into practice, that has enslaved the working man to this day.

Now, there was this Greek fellow called Archimedes, who had built up quite a reputation for himself. He had invented this word called EUREKA! which, if shouted under certain conditions in the bathroom, enabled him to solve any manner of obtuse conundrums.

Flavius the Noseless had booked two weeks in Greece for his holidays, so whilst there he dropped in on Archimedes and asked if he could come up with anything.

Archimedes stroked his beard and retired to cogitate.

Eventually he emerged from his bath, somewhat prunelike about the toe regions, but with the E–word once more on his lips.

'The answer lies in the soap,' he told Caesar.

'Kaendly eggsplene,' said the noseless one.

'Certainly. Now the way I see it, you want more upmarket time than the plebs. Now, I must make this quite clear to you, you can't actually mess around with time. But, you can mess around with the perception of time. What you need is a special drug, which, when administered to the plebs, will alter the way they perceive time. It will make time appear to travel slower. Thus, whilst in this state, they will get much more work done than they would normally. Do you know anything about chemistry?'

Caesar nodded sagely.

Thought not, thought Archimedes. 'Well, I happen to know of such a drug. It has a very complicated chemical formula ($C_{11}H_{17}NO_3$). And I alone can manufacture it. All you have to do is introduce it into the plebs' soap. They wash with the soap and ingest the drug. And away they go.'

'Bet whet abeet thee greet unweshed?' Caesar asked.

'Stick it in their tea. Agreed the working masses may not

121

bath as regularly as might be wished, but they all drink tea. Listen, I'll distil you a batch. You take it back to Rome. If you're happy with the results, put in a regular order and we're in business.'

Palms were spat upon and smacked together. And the rest, as they say, is history.

Caesar returned to Rome. Tested the drug. Found that it worked magically. Rome thrived. Caesar, being an astute businessman, if not a terribly nice person, sacked Greece, arrested Archimedes and tortured the formula out of him.

The Caesars eventually turned to Christianity and became Popes. And the Vatican has held the secret to this very day.

Hang about, I hear you cry, doubting Toms that you are. This doesn't ring true. Surely we all use soap and drink tea. We can't all be permanently drugged.

No, say I. Not *all*.

Because not all tea and soap is infected. And, if only the Vatican were in on the conspiracy, it could never operate. The manufacturers of tea and soap are in collusion. The distributors are in collusion. Higher management is in collusion. All those who drink exotic tea and smell differently from the rest of us are probably in collusion.

It is an international conspiracy. Huge and insidious and the Pope is behind it all.

I detect that some doubts still remain. That you really believe that *you* could not possibly be a victim of this terrible conspiracy.

But consider this, 'Time really flies when you're enjoying yourself.' This is because alcohol negates the effects of the drug. Ever found time flying when you're taking a bath or drinking a cup of tea? Aha!

And let me mention this. The drug is addictive. Ever found yourself 'dying for a cuppa'? Aha!

Ever wondered why the Catholic Church was so keen to convert the natives of South America? You know South

America. Where all that *coffee* comes from. Aha!

Ever wondered why the formula for Coca-Cola is such a closely guarded secret? Aha!

I could continue at great length. But I will not. I opened this piece by stating that your birthday falls upon a different day each year. But that logically, it could not.

Ever heard the expression, 'He's so stoned he doesn't know what day of the week it is'?

Aha!

In concluding, I would just like to say that it has been a very great honour to be invited here tonight to The William of Orange Memorial Hall, Belfast, as guest speaker at *The Independent Shopkeeper of the Year Awards*.

To find myself in the company of so many eminent, discerning and open-minded independent shopkeepers, affords me pleasure beyond expression.

I trust that my revelations have amused you. I know that they will draw considerable interest from the buying public when they are revealed upon the front pages of certain newspapers this coming Sunday. Considerable interest.

You will notice that I have before me a selection of RUNE BRAND products. For instance, EARL RUNE. Now, this particular tea is guaranteed one hundred per cent $C_{11}H_{17}NO_3$ free. Organically grown, packed in an ozone-friendly biodegradable carton and marketed at a price to please both shopkeeper and purchaser alike. As with CAFE RUNE GOLDEN BLEND, HUGO-COLA and RUNELIGHT SOAP. Now, I have to knock these out by the case, so who'll be the first one up? You, sir? The tall distinguished gentleman. Twelve cases of EARL RUNE? Certainly. Rizla, fetch twelve down from the back of the van . . .

> Offered as exhibit A for the prosecution
> in the case of *Nearly Everyone versus
> Hugo Rune*.

The smell of frying bacon awoke Cornelius Murphy from an erotic dream about a barmaid with violet eyes. He climbed from the bed and shambled over to the dressing-table mirror. There were no signs of a five-o'clock shadow. His hair had formed itself into an interesting anthill kind of a shape though.

Cornelius drew the curtains and gazed out upon the day. The village below looked pretty charming. If you liked that sort of thing. Cornelius wondered whether he did.

'No I don't,' he decided.

Tuppe awoke with a shout and leapt from the portmanteau.

'Something wrong, Tuppe?'

Tuppe shook his head. 'Bad dream, that's all, get it now and then, dream there's this big black bag full of horrible squirming things and it's tied to my heels. I can't get away. Horrible.'

'Sounds it.'

'No, horrible. Really horrible.'

'Horrible, yes.'

'Your pyjamas,' said Tuppe. 'Really horrible.'

In the back kitchen of The Hangman's Arms, Milcom Moloch, a young man's dream stood over the frying pan.

'Hello,' she said, making eyes at Cornelius. 'I thought you might have stopped by my room last night. I were real lonely.'

Cornelius groaned and bit his lip.

'You win some, you lose some,' whispered Tuppe. 'You missed all the excitement.'

'Evidently.' Cornelius hung his head. His head hung its hair.

'No. Down in the bar. We had a spontaneous human combustion.'

'Pooh,' said Tuppe. 'I've always wanted to see one of those.'

'Third one this week.' The barmaid broke eggs into the pan.

'Do you have any mushrooms?' Tuppe asked.

'Surely do, little manny. I'll stir them in. Charred to a crisp he were. Had to scrape him off the flag stones with this here spatula.' She raised the utensil in question from the frying pan.

'Toast and marmalade for me, I think,' said Cornelius. 'A light eater, me.'

An ancient black Volkswagen, covered with vicious spikes and fitted with all-black windows, slipped out from a back street lock-up in Sheila na gigh. At the wheel sat Hamish. In the back seats, Angus and Sawney. In the front passenger seat, the Campbell.

The Campbell's all-black window swished down and evil Jim stuck his head out. He sniffed the air.

'South,' he said.

Cornelius chewed upon cold dry toast and watched in disgust as Tuppe tucked into a fry-up of suitably epic proportions.

'Have you got muesli?' Cornelius asked the barmaid.

'How dare you.' The barmaid took a swing at him with the dreaded spatula.

'It's a breakfast cereal,' the tall and ducking boy explained. 'It's full of nuts and bran and raisins and healthy things like that.'

'Well no.' The barmaid returned to her cooking. 'No call for stuff like that round here.'

'Surely there must be somewhere I could buy some. A present for my mum.'

'Well, there'd be Molly's. She sells healthy things and that.'

'Local family business?' Cornelius chewed upon his toast.

'No. She's from the south. No-one ever goes into her shop. That fancy food. For the swells, that is. Tourists.'

'And you get a lot of those?'

'No. None.' The barmaid raised the spatula and brought it down upon a bluebottle. Tuppe flinched, but continued to fill his face.

'Is Molly's far from here?' Cornelius watched as the barmaid scooped up the bluebottle with the spatula, flipped it into the air and batted it out of the window.

'Out the front. Turn left and first on your left. More bacon, little manny?'

'Yes please,' said Tuppe.

'Out the front. Turn left and first on the left.' Cornelius gazed in through the front window of Molly's Wholefoods.

Tuppe gazed up at the crumbling façade. 'Looks somewhat gone to seed.'

'She must know something. Shall we investigate?'

'Lead on, Mr Murphy.'

Cornelius pushed open the door. The door went creak and groan and a little cracked bell went clink.

'It smells in here,' Tuppe remarked.

Cornelius perused the premises. Cobwebs clung to every corner. Dust put the shelved stock out of focus. What light struggled through the unwashed front window soon gave up the ghost in the air that seemed almost palpably grey.

Cornelius plucked an apple from a basket on the low counter. He stroked the dust away with his thumb. The apple crumbled away to dust in his hand.

'Hello,' called Cornelius. 'Is there anybody there?'

Something rustled at the rear of the shop. The sound as of dry leaves being crushed together. A thin, reedy little voice asked, 'Who is it?'

'A customer,' Cornelius replied. 'Good-morning to you.'

'I don't want any customers. Bugger off.'

Cornelius peered into the gloom. A patch of darkness in a far corner seemed somewhat darker than the less dark darkness that surrounded it. So to speak.

'Are you Molly Hartog?'

'Who knows my name?' The little dark patch of slightly darker darkness shrank back to merge quite convincingly with the less dark darkness and form an overall dark sort of an area. All in the one place. As it were.

'My name is Murphy.'

'Audie Murphy? America's most decorated hero of the Second World War? Star of *Hell Guns of Glory Beach*?' The little dark patch sank deeper into the surrounding darkness. Visually, the change was too subtle to attract much notice. Or any, in fact.

'His name is Cornelius Murphy,' Tuppe said. 'And he is the stuff of epics.'

The little, now indistinguishable dark patch gave a jump and then moved slowly forward into the uncertain light. Here it became an uncertainly illuminated little dark patch. A very little uncertainly illuminated little dark patch. It reached out a tiny hand, encased in black silk. Tuppe took the hand between his own and kissed it.

'Little manny,' said Molly Hartog. 'What is Tiphareth to Kether?'

'He is the son and not the servant.'

'And whither comes the wind?'

'From the east and we with all.'

'Good good. You may walk with me then.' The tiny woman took Tuppe by the hand and led him into the darkness at the rear of the shop. Cornelius stared on in wonder.

'Don't lag,' called Tuppe. 'And best mind yourself.'

Clunk went the head of Cornelius Murphy.

Cornelius sat, uncomfortably doubled up, in a sitting room of meagre dimensions. The ceiling was scarcely four feet above a floor, which was, for the most part, occupied by his legs.

The little woman was brewing tea at a toy stove by the window. She appeared as a Victorian doll, curiously animated. Her tiny pinched face of sculpted wax.

'What is all this wind from the east business?' Cornelius whispered.

'Kin folk.' Tuppe shushed him to silence. 'Let me speak to her. Give me the photograph.' Cornelius gave Tuppe the photograph.

'Travelling stock, your people?' The Victorian doll filled a teapot and covered it with an egg cosy.

Tuppe nodded. 'Before times fell away. My grandfather was with Toomey for a spell and with Wombwell and Tom Norman.'

'The Silver King? I knew them. Knew them all. And I'll know you too. Let me have a squint.' She perched a pair of ivory-framed pince-nez on to her sparrow's beak of a nose and peered through them.

'Ha ha,' she crowed. 'You're a Tuppe.'

'I am that. But I don't know the Hartog clan.'

'But I knew your pa well enough. Him and his porker pigs. He skipped out when they sent old Polgar to the chokey, eh?'

'That was him, right enough. And that was him done with the travelling life.'

'All gone now.' Molly turned away to pour tea. She stepped on to the tall boy's left ankle. Cornelius bit his lip. 'What do you want from me, Tuppe?'

'Hugo Rune,' said Tuppe. 'You knew him.'

'Poor dear Hugo. I knew him well. He reinvented the ocarina, you know. And, oh how he hated Bud Abbott.'

'He left some papers, I believe.'

'Papers? Piles and piles of them. He was a genius, a master. Years before his time. Decades. This world wasn't big enough to hold Hugo Rune.'

'These papers? Were they part of a manuscript?' Tuppe accepted a tea cup the size of a shrunken thimble. 'Thanks,' said he.

'Part of a book.' Molly passed a cup to Cornelius, who perched it on the palm of his hand and gaped at it in awe. 'The book. *The Book of Ultimate Truths*. Such knowledge the Master had. Such wisdom. Such genius. Such an appetite. Barred from every Chinese noodle parlour in West London, he was.'

'Why was that?'

'Due to his allergy.' The miniature woman seated herself on Murphy's left foot. Cornelius marvelled anew. She was apparently without weight.

'He was allergic to noodles?' Tuppe sipped his tea.

'No. Money. Couldn't bear to have it anywhere near him. Broke out in a sweat at the very sight of it. Or the mention. So there was always trouble when someone presented him with a bill. He offered the world his great wisdom. All he asked in return was that the world should cover his expenses. Meagre as they were.'

Tuppe raised an eyebrow to Cornelius, who was raising one of his own.

'And the world wasn't keen?'

'Conspiracies. All around. Petty men seeking to do him down. To steal his knowledge and use it for their own wicked ends.'

'About the papers. Do you have them?' Tuppe finished his tea.

'No.' Molly shook her head. Golden motes drifted from it and hung in the air. 'Not I. Perhaps Victor.'

'Victor Zenobia?'

'Poor dear Victor.'

'Victor is dead I'm afraid.'

'Oh.' Molly bowed her head. 'Then there are few enough of us left to the cause.'

'These men?' Tuppe handed the photograph to Molly.

The little woman gazed at it through her pince-nez. 'So long ago. There is Victor and the Master, of course. That silly bastard that took the photo didn't get me in. He made a right fuss about not getting his fee, if I recall.'

'The others in the picture. Who are they?'

Molly pointed. 'That is Rizla and the other, Joseph.'

'Might one of them have the papers?'

'One of them must. Victor was the Master's accountant. Joseph, his chauffeur. And Rizla, his magical son.'

'Do you know where Joseph or Rizla might be now?'

'Why do you want the Master's papers, young Tuppe?'

'To publish them in their entirety.'

'Publish them?' Molly toppled from the tall boy's foot and collapsed on to the floor. Tuppe hastened to help her up.

'Publish them?' Molly cackled to herself. 'You can't publish them. No publisher would dare to publish them. Or even if they did . . . no, no. It couldn't be done.'

'Why not?'

'If you had read the papers, then you would know.'

'Tell me, Molly. Joseph and Rizla. Where are they now?'

'Won't do you any good. Even if they have the papers, they won't show them to you.'

'I could at least ask them.'

'As you will. All right. Perhaps and perhaps. You have come to ask and so I must tell you. Rizla took holy orders. You will find him at the monastery of Saint Sacco Benedetto.'

'And Joseph?'

'Joseph.' The small woman spat. 'He's in London. Calls himself Jack something or other. A big noise in the record industry, whatever that is.'

Cornelius stuffed things into his suitcase. He and Tuppe were now back in their bedroom at The Hangman's Arms.

'Well,' said Tuppe. 'What did you make of Molly?'

'I think I'll give her muesli a miss.'

'So,' Tuppe sat on the portmanteau, kicking his heels. 'What do you propose we do next?'

'We shall visit brother Rizla at the monastery. But before we do, I must call Mr Kobold, tell him what I have found out and have him send some more money.'

'You nip off then. I'll finish packing.'

'Thank you, Tuppe. Stick all the papers in the rucksack. We'll leave the portmanteau behind. I'll go downstairs and call Mr Kobold. They're bound to have a phone in the bar.'

They didn't. In fact they didn't have a phone any-where in the village.

'Never needed one,' the beautiful barmaid explained, as Cornelius settled up for the bread and board. Tuppe struggled down the stairs with the luggage.

'Tell you what though,' the barmaid went on, 'I've been thinking about what you were saying. And I'd quite like to bear your children.'

Cornelius looked at Tuppe.

Tuppe looked at Cornelius.

'I'll go and see if I can arrange some transport,' said Tuppe. 'I might be some time.'

Milcom Moloch didn't boast a taxi service. But a nice undertaker with a very smart 1950s hearse agreed to take them to the next town.

Cornelius waved through the back window. The beautiful barmaid waved down from an upstairs win-dow. The hearse drove away.

'Did you get a receipt?' Tuppe asked.

'Yes thank you.' Cornelius was grinning in a manner which was quite difficult to describe.

An hour and a bit later the hearse stopped in a town called Cromcruach. Which is just off the main Hebon under Pertunda bypass, twenty miles north of Triglaf.

'Thanks very much.' Cornelius waved to the depart-ing hearse.

'Be lucky.' Tuppe waved also.

The hearse went back along the road for a bit, then rose into the sky and vanished into the clouds.

'There is something very suspicious about that hearse,' said Cornelius.

'There certainly is,' Tuppe agreed. 'It drove off with your suitcase.'

Cromcruach wasn't much of a town to speak about. It lacked the bypass of Hebon under Pertunda, and Triglaf certainly had the edge on it when it came to a southerly location.

But it did have a garage and it did have a telephone box. And both of these were to come in handy.

Cornelius took himself off to the telephone box.

Tuppe hung around the garage.

Presently Cornelius returned.

'How did you get on?' Tuppe asked.

'I spoke with Mr Kobold. He seemed very agitated. Kept saying to be careful.'

'And what did you tell him?'

'What I knew. About the papers in the portmanteau and Molly and how I'm going on to the monastery next.'

'What about Karaoke Jack?'

'I didn't mention *him*. Anyway Mr Kobold suggested that I press on to Manchester tonight.'

'Manchester? Where is that, do you think?'

'We can look it up on the map. It's just outside Manchester, the place we want. The Holiday Inn, North Ameshet. First-class accommodation, I am assured. A room will be waiting and money will be in the post, to arrive first thing tomorrow.'

'Hats off to Arthur Kobold,' said Tuppe, rubbing his hands together. 'By the by, Cornelius. Do you know how to drive a car?'

'Of course. The daddy taught me.'

'But your daddy doesn't own a car.'

'No. Not as such. But a great lover of the automobile, the daddy. Every time some new one comes out on the market he always calls up the maker and tells them about the small pools win he's just had.'

'But your daddy doesn't do the pools.'

Cornelius raised an eyebrow.

'Quite so,' said Tuppe. 'So you got to try out a few of these nice new cars yourself.'

'Exactly. I got the hang of it in the end.'

'And do you have a licence?'

'Certainly. The daddy gave me his old one.' Cornelius delved into a pocket and pulled it out. 'He said it would come in handy one of these days.'

'Indeed.' Tuppe smiled up at Cornelius. 'I'd like you to meet my new friend Mike. He's a mechanic.'

DA DA DA DA . . . GIT YA MOTER RUNNIN . . .

The 1958 Cadillac Eldorado swept out from the garage and set off down the road from Cromcruach.

GIT OWT ONNA HIGHWAAAE . . .

'Do you know what I'm looking for?' Cornelius asked.

'Adventure,' Tuppe suggested.

'And?'

'Whatever comes your way, would be my guess.'

'And what am I born to be?'

'*Wild*, Cornelius. That is what you're born to be.'

'Correct, dear friend. Correct. Tuppe, this a splendid car. I can't believe that Mike just let us drive it away.'

'I think it was you telling him about all those posh cars you test drive that really swung it.'

'And we actually get paid for delivering it to his rich client in London.' Cornelius stuck his elbow out of the window. 'Imagine that.'

'Right place at the right time. Let's face it. You have to have an epic car if you're going on an epic journey.'

'You surely do. And this is one epic car. Electric-blue paint job. Electric-blue upholstery.'

'Electric windows,' said Tuppe. 'Electric sunroof . . .'

'Electric lights,' Cornelius suggested.

'Electric wireless set.' Tuppe switched it on.

'You're a pink toothbrush, I'm a blue toothbrush,' sang Max Bygraves.

'Electric toothbrush?' Tuppe asked.

The spikey black Volkswagen growled to a halt before The Hangman's Arms. The Campbell stepped from the car and sniffed the air.

'They've been here,' he said.

Hamish got out and speared a map on to a couple of bonnet spikes. 'And where is *here*, by the way?'

The Campbell examined the map. 'Right here. Milcom Moloch.'

'Milcom Moloch?' Hamish gazed about the place. 'Did someone nuke it, or what?'

Little remained of Milcom Moloch. The Hangman's Arms was naught but a roofless ruin. The shells of shops and houses rose from scrubby grasslands. The road was gone into pot holes. All was desolation and decay.

'There was a big storm,' said the Campbell. 'Like the one last night. Thirty years ago. The village was cut off by floods. Then some Londoner drove in here. And they'd gone. The village was deserted. No trace. Food still on the tables. Vanished off the face of the earth. Pop!' The Campbell snapped his fingers.

Hamish took off his war bonnet and scratched his head. 'I've never heard that story before. A whole village vanishes?'

'Pop,' said the Campbell. 'Gone. Now go and search around. See what you can find. *And* you two! Hurry up about it.'

Angus and Sawney slouched from the car.

In the ruins of The Hangman's Arms they would find a green canvas portmanteau, a brush-and-comb set in a plastic case and a duffle-coat (lacking toggles), some wear on elbows.

Hamish would take a shine to the duffle-coat.

Not half a mile along the road from the ruins of Milcom Moloch they would find the ruins of a burned-out taxi-cab. And a man with bandaged fingers and a blue complexion weeping over it. Hamish would take pity upon this sorry figure and give him the duffle-coat to keep himself warm.

Later in the day the taxi driver would be readmitted to the nearby hospital, this time in a state of shock and suffering from suspected rabies. He would insist to his dying day that an arctic wolf had savaged him. He would also give up taxi driving and become a monk.

'I wouldn't fancy being a monk.' Tuppe put his hands behind his head and smiled up at the passing sky. 'You go bald too quickly.'

Cornelius smiled and drummed his fingers on the steering wheel. 'They shave their heads. It's called a tonsure. From the latin *tonsura:* a shaving.'

'Why?' Tuppe made the electric window go up and down. 'Why do they do that?'

'To signify their renunciation of the world and all its vanities. Do leave the window alone, Tuppe.'

Tuppe left the window alone. His hand strayed to the cigarette lighter. 'Speak to me of tonsures,' he said.

'Certainly. There are three types. Firstly there's the 'tonsure of St Paul'. That's the entire head. Mostly practised by the eastern church . . . Then there's the 'tonsure of St Peter'. That's the most common one. A circular patch on the crown of the head. And finally, there's the 'tonsure of St John'. The front of the head is shaved on a line drawn from ear to ear. That was the ancient Celtic method. So it's sometimes called the Scottish or Irish tonsure. Do leave the cigarette lighter alone, Tuppe.'

Tuppe left the lighter alone. 'I wonder which method they favour at Saint Sacco Benedetto's?' he wondered.

'Eyebrows and all, I expect. I understand that it is considered the most austere order in the country. Really medieval.'

Tuppe twiddled the wireless dial. 'Fings ain't what they used to be,' sang Max Bygraves.

The electric-blue motor car, with the high fins and the open top, sailed over the crest of a hill and down the other side. The driver's hair followed close behind. The sun shone brightly down upon the epic travellers. Tuppe found a pair of really spiffing sun-glasses in the glove compartment and Cornelius put them on.

And at precisely twelve o'clock the fan belt broke.

And at precisely five minutes past twelve, they were on their way again.

'Large kudos to you, dear friend,' Cornelius told Tuppe. 'To have Mike the mechanic pack three spare fan belts, that is foresight indeed.'

'Once bitten and things of that nature,' smiled Tuppe.

Cornelius slipped one of the spare fan belts on as a headband. 'I'll be able to see where I'm going a lot better now,' he said. 'Much of it has been guesswork up 'til now.'

'What?'

At a little after one of the sunny afternoon clock they

stopped at a vast motorway services area thingy. Here Cornelius fed the motor car with the best petrol that money could buy and then took himself up to the restaurant to join Tuppe.

The restaurant was a great long refectory of a place. A wall of windows overlooked the motorway. Ranks of Formica-topped tables were besieged by steel chairs, which did not encourage a long stay. Tuppe sat dejectedly at a table by the door. No food lay spread before him.

'Whither lunch?' Cornelius asked.

'It's a self service. I can't reach.'

'How thoughtless of me. My apologies.' Cornelius got in double rations. And much ice-cream.

Tuppe set about the meal. 'You know,' said he, between great chewings, 'I've never been in one of these places before. But I've seen them on the pictures. There's usually a heavy-metal band sitting in one corner, their van's broken down, you see, and they're on their way to an important gig. And there's also this couple, deeply in love, well, she is, he's going to go back to his wife . . .'

'Cad!' said Cornelius.

'Quite so. And there's a spy. He often gets shot dead in the toilet.'

'What, he gets shot dead more than once?'

Tuppe scooped beans into his mouth.

'Sorry,' said Cornelius. 'Anyone else?'

'There's us, of course. Two young heroes on an epic journey.'

'Anyone else?'

Tuppe glanced about the place. Apart from the two young heroes, the remaining cast of *Vast Motorway Services Area: The Movie* had yet to turn up. Tuppe did, however, spy out a lone figure at a distant table.

138

'There's him,' said Tuppe, pointing past the tall boy's elbow. Cornelius turned and squinted. The sun blazed in and lit upon a large, broad-shouldered, shaven-headed man. He wore a plaid plus-fours suit and a silk cravat.

Whilst his companion's back was turned, Tuppe swiped one of his sausages and thrust it into his mouth.

Cornelius turned back. 'He looks familiar. Perhaps he's the spy. Where's my sausage gone?'

Tuppe suddenly spat stolen sausage all over Cornelius.

'Steady on!' Cornelius flapped at himself. 'No need for that. It's only a sausage. I don't mind.'

'No, no.' Tuppe was coughing away like a good'n. 'It's him. It's him.'

'Who him?'

'In the photo. Get out the photo.'

Cornelius pulled the late Victor Zenobia's snapshot from his top pocket. 'What?' He made to have another look at the distant diner. 'It can't be.'

'Don't look. Let me see the photo.'

Cornelius turned it to Tuppe. Tuppe gave it a squint and then took a peep past the tall boy's elbow. 'It *is* him,' he whispered. 'Cornelius, it's Hugo Rune.'

'The bloke you're talking about,' said Mike the mechanic, 'long tall bloke? Hair all over the place?'

He was speaking to a bald-headed man. A bald-headed man who favoured a camouflaged combat jacket to a plus-fours suit.

'What do you want with him then?'

'It's a private matter,' said the Campbell.

'None of my business then.' Mike turned away, wiping his hands on an oily rag, the way only a real mechanic can.

'I could make it your business.' The Campbell's hand fell upon Mike's left shoulder. It was a heavy hand, with a good firm grip.

'Oh yes?' Mike turned and looked the Campbell up and down. He didn't very much like what he saw. And as for the three highlanders lounging around the spikey Volkswagen. He prised away the hand, which still gripped his shoulder.

'I need to know where he's travelling to. It's very important.'

'He didn't say.' Mike shrugged easily, but his right hand crept around to the rear pocket of his overall, where he kept the big Stilson spanner. 'Sorry I can't help you.'

'I really must insist.' The Campbell removed his broken spectacles and slipped them into his pocket.

'Look, piss off, will you?' The spanner was out.

The Campbell smiled at it. Then he smiled at Mike and stared deeply into his eyes. Then he leaned forward and whispered something into his left ear.

The colour drained from the mechanic's face. His body began to tremble. The big spanner fell from his hand.

'Where?' asked the Campbell.

'London,' answered Mike, in a cold dead voice.

'Somewhere else on the way, I think.'

'He bought a map from me . . .'

'And?'

'A monastery. Saint sack of Benny Detours.'

'Saint Sacco Benedetto's. There, that was easy, wasn't it? I generally take pleasure in a more subtle approach. But I really don't have the time right now. Thank you so much for your co-operation. You've been such a help.' The Campbell leaned forwards once again and kissed Mike deeply upon the mouth.

The mechanic wet his pants.

Cornelius shuddered.

'Are you all right?' Tuppe asked. 'You were miles away. You're white as death.'

'Something just happened. Not here. Somewhere. Something bad.'

'This is very often the case. But what about him?' Tuppe made furtive pointings. 'It *is* him. Just like the photograph.'

'It can't be.' Cornelius gulped his coffee. 'That picture was taken more than half a century ago.'

'Same suit,' said Tuppe. 'Same man, I'm telling you. Take a look. Go on.'

'You leave my last sausage alone then.'

'I swear.' Tuppe crossed his heart.

Cornelius turned and took a good long look. The bald-headed man caught his stare and waggled his fingers in a friendly fashion. Cornelius smiled and turned back to Tuppe.

Tuppe held up the photograph. He didn't speak. His mouth was full of stolen egg.

The tall boy's head sank deeply into his chest. 'Tuppe,' he whispered through clenched teeth. 'It's Hugo Rune. What are we going to do?'

'We?' Tuppe swallowed. 'You'd best go over and pass the time of day. Ask him where he left his papers. I'll mind your lunch.'

'Oh no. We go together. You're in this epic too.'

'Okey doke.' Tuppe shinned down from his chair.

Cornelius rose from his. 'Come on then.'

The bald-headed man stared placidly towards them as they approached.

And as he drew nearer, Cornelius became painfully aware of a curious buzzing sound in his ears. And of the fact that Hugo Rune appeared a mite indistinct about the edges. His great be-ringed fingers seemed to waver sometimes above and sometimes into the tabletop. There was something altogether untoward about the reinventor of the ocarina.

Suddenly there was a whole lot of noise, commotion and hubbub. And a number of long-haired young men, with leather jackets, tight trousers and snakeskin boots, bustled into the restaurant. One of them carried a guitar case.

Behind these came a weeping woman and a comforting man. And behind them, a furtive-looking fellow with a briefcase.

And suddenly Tuppe and Cornelius were in the thick of them.

And when they no longer were, Hugo Rune had gone.

12

They didn't speak much during the afternoon drive. And they didn't stop to pick up any hitchers either. So all the exciting young women, serial killers and wild-eyed prophets of doom, who raised their hopeful thumbs to the passing Cadillac, had to walk.

And they didn't even switch off Max Bygraves when he sang about the need for hands. Cornelius and Tuppe were troubled.

They perked up a bit when they finally reached the car park before the North Ameshet Holiday Inn though.

'My, my.' Tuppe craned up his head to the mighty hotel. 'And isn't that tall?'

'Even from where I'm sitting.' Cornelius observed that of the twenty-seven windows on the first floor, eight were open, with their blinds up, eight were closed with their blinds down, nine were closed, with their blinds up, one was open with its blind down and one was closed, had its blind halfway up and the light on. Two eights, one nine and two ones. Or, a pair of eights, a nine and a pair of aces. The last poker hand dealt to Wild Bill Hickok, just before he was shot in the back by Jack McCall in Deadwood City, South Dakota.

'Now in a place like this,' Tuppe began, 'there's bound to be a heavy-metal band breaking up the room. Two lovers rooming under the name of Smith, a spy with a roll of microfilm in—'

'Let's book in,' said Cornelius.

'Can we use false names? I've always wanted to do that.'

'You can. I have to use my own. Mr Kobold's money in the morning, remember?'

'Quite so.' Cornelius parked the car. And let Tuppe make the roof go up, down and up again several times.

'Thanks,' said Tuppe. 'I did enjoy that.'

There is something strangely comforting about a Holiday Inn. No matter which part of the world you might be travelling in, if you enter a Holiday Inn, you can always be assured of two things. One, that it will be exactly the same as every other. And two, that Status Quo have stayed in it.

Coincidentally, Status Quo were just leaving this one as Tuppe and Cornelius entered it.

'Hi, Tuppe,' called the drummer. 'How's it going?'

'Fine. Anniversary tour?'

'As ever.' Status Quo left the building.

'You actually know The Quo?' Cornelius was impressed.

'Of course. I've travelled. I told you.'

'What's the drummer's name then?'

'Search me,' said Tuppe.

Cornelius announced himself to a desk clerk who wore a badge saying, 'Hello my name is Danny'. Danny confirmed that a room had already been booked and soon a porter, who wore a badge saying, 'Hello my name is Peter' conveyed the rucksack of Mr Cornelius Murphy and his companion, Mr Howard Hughes, up to their room.

Cornelius tipped the porter. 'Could I have a receipt for that please, Peter?' he asked.

Peter did not reply.

Now, a Holiday Inn room is a Holiday Inn room. It is always very clean. It has twin beds. A little writing table and chair. A television set with all kinds of channels and a Bible written by someone called Gideon. It also has an ensuite bathroom facility, with all sorts of things in little sealed packets for you to take home for your children. And, of course, it has a telephone, on which you can make a right nuisance of yourself. Especially if you're not paying the bill.

'Can I call room service?' Tuppe asked. 'Have them send something up?'

'Absolutely. I shall make much of unpacking my rucksack. As I no longer possess a suitcase.'

Tuppe climbed on to the bed by the window. 'Bags this one's mine.' He picked up the telephone. 'Yo, room service,' said he.

Cornelius unzipped his rucksack.

'Please can you send up a bottle of Jim Beam, two glasses, a plate of steak sandwiches . . .'

Cornelius shook out his rucksack.

'Bags of crisps, assorted . . . twenty small cigars . . .'

'Where have my pyjamas gone? I know I packed them in here.'

'And a pair of pyjamas, size large, pattern plain. Thank you.'

'Another spot of Jim?' Tuppe lounged upon his bed. A small cigar in his mouth. The bottle at his elbow.

Cornelius made a bitter face over his steak sandwich. 'You might have had the decency to order us some drink that wasn't called *Jim*.'

'Jim? Oh, I see. Sorry, my friend.'

'Never mind. Pass the bottle.'

Tuppe passed the bottle. 'So what are we going to

do tonight, Cornelius? Take in the night spots? Bop till we drop? Things of that nature? Pass the crisps.'

Cornelius passed the crisps. 'I am going to sit here, on my bed, clad in these very large pyjamas, study the daddy's copy of Rune. Sift through the letters and bills and whatnot and see if I can make any sense of it all.'

'Sounds rather dull.'

'Tuppe, please help yourself to what cash you think you'll need. Go forth and bop till you drop. But . . .' Cornelius held up a cautionary finger. 'Do not return here at three in the morning with a bunch of new-found friends who are looking to "party".'

'What if there're only two new-found friends and they are both young and female?'

'Then phone up from reception and give me time to comb my hair and hide my pyjamas.'

Cornelius waved off his companion. Put the DO NOT DISTURB sign on the door. Made a vain attempt to tidy up the room, which was already looking like a heavy-metal combat zone, and took himself off for a shower.

Later, he donned the vast pyjamas, switched on the television for a bit of background and settled down on the bed with the half-bottle of Jim Beam and *The Book of Ultimate Truths*.

I have penned many profound words upon the subject of 'inanimate objects'. A good many of these have been produced with the aid of a Biro.

During the course of a single year I will use upwards of one thousand Biros, yet I have never actually worn one out. Why should this be?

My studies lead me to the conclusion that the Biro, as with many other forms of 'inanimate object', hates its role in life.

The Biro is by nature a celibate creature which resents spilling its virile essence upon paper. I do not arrive at this conclusion lightly, but through years of painstaking research and at no small cost to my health.

My findings may be summed up thus:

1. The Biro does not serve man willingly.
2. The Biro is a wily beast, which, if given the least opportunity to make good its escape, will do so.

TWO SIMPLE EXPERIMENTS WITH BIROS

1. Purchase fifteen Biros. Hold them tightly all the way home to prevent escape. Place five in the pencil pot in the kitchen. Five in the decorative mug next to the telephone in the hall. Five in a jar on your writing desk. Pointedly ignore the Biros and allow one week to pass. Try and find a Biro.
2. Bend down and tie your shoelace. Try and find a Biro.

SUICIDAL TENDENCIES AMONGST BONDAGE BIROS

Many attempts have been made to tame the Biro, or at least bring it to heel. All have been doomed to failure. One inspired notion was the creation of a Biro which was worn on a thong about the neck clipped into a plastic harness.

This unnatural practice is rarely seen today. The severe psychological damage inflicted upon the captive Biros led them to tear themselves from their shackles and plunge into toilet bowls, become suicidally entangled about gear sticks or wrap themselves around handlebars.

It is also understood that these Biros were capable of

telepathically transmitting their cries for freedom to companions of their tormentors, with the result that these would remark, for no logical reason, 'You look a right prat with that thing hanging round your neck, throw it away.'

PARKER? GORN, M'LADY!

There exists a school of thought, that an expensive Biro, wrought from gold or silver and branded with the potential owner's name, will become a cherished possession. Perhaps the principle is that if the owner loves the Biro, the Biro will return the affection and become a loyal companion. Sadly no. In fact, due to the precious metals employed in the manufacture of these items, they are truly a cut above the average when it comes to evasiveness.

These Biros are most popularly given as Christmas presents. But exalted be the man who can use such a creation to pen a thank-you note come Boxing Day. Most potential owners will spend the morning emptying dustbins and uncrumpling wrapping paper in the vain hope of unearthing the cherished-possession-to-be.

I contend that such Biros employ an advanced form of camouflage. Also that they are capable of dematerialization. It is to be observed that many such Biros arrive in hermetically sealed gift boxes which are a right bugger to get open.

These boxes ensure that the Biros remain safely entrapped whilst at the shop. But *caveat emptor,* once you're home, you're on your own.

The Irish maintain that there exists, somewhere upon the planet, a treasure trove of Croesusian magnitude, where these gold and silver fellows hobnob with single earrings beyond number and a million gemstones from engagement rings.

It is situated at the end of a rainbow. Or so I have been led to understand.

HOMICIDAL BIROS

Man has never been slow to mould the world to his whim. But in doing so he has conceived many a dangerous folly. Nuclear Power, CFCs (Chelsea Football Club supporters)[1], toxic chemicals and Bud Abbott. But none more potentially disastrous than the Whimsical Novelty Biro, or W.N.B.

This is, to all intents and purposes, a normal Biro, but affixed to it is the head of some currently marketable 'character'. Snoopy, Garfield, Bart Simpson, Barry The Sprout, or what-have-you.

It is to be noticed that such 'characters' generally emanate from America. *Home of the Serial Killer*.

The victim-to-be purchases, or is given, the W.N.B. and places it unsuspectingly in the top pocket of his or her jacket, with the humorous head protruding. Then at some time during the day, he or she has cause to turn their head sharply to the left, or attempt to take off the jacket.

Either way the result is inevitably the same. A severed jugular! And does the Government insist that health warnings be printed upon W.N.B.s? Does it 'eck as like! The needless slaughter has been going on for more than a century. But the conspiracy of silence prevails to this day.

Note this: it is a significant fact that all the victims of the so-called *Jack The Ripper* murders died within walking distance of The East London Patent Pen Works. This factory specialized in the manufacture of dip pens capped with silver facsimiles of Queen Victoria's crowned head.

Only one such pen survives. It is kept under lock and key in Scotland Yard's Black Museum.

[1] Humour

It was found at the bedside of Mary Kelly, the last of *Jack*'s victims!

Before concluding this section it is worth drawing the reader's attention to the so-called suicide, by hara-kiri, of the Japanese writer, Yukio Mishima.

He wrote with a Biro.

He that liveth by the sword shall perish by the sword.

The pen is mightier than the sword. Nuff said.

THE MYSTERY BIRO

I must, before concluding this erudite monograph, dwell upon a curious anomaly. The black sheep of Birodom. THE MYSTERY BIRO. This, unlike the rest of the species, craves the company of man.

It will appear suddenly in the pocket of a jacket you haven't worn since it came back from the cleaners. In the glove compartment or boot of the car. At the bottom of a handbag or raffia shopper. In the kitchen drawer or tool chest.

And once it has found you, it is yours for life.

It is, inevitably, a shoddy, plastic, giveaway affair, with a spring arrangement housed within, purportedly to bring down the ballpoint.

It can be instantly recognized by its bright plumage. Bold primary colours and embossed lines of print, which spell out things like: NICKED FROM THE ARCHDUKE FERDINAND AERATED BREAD CO., or WANDERING BISHOPS WORLD CON 79.

Of course it doesn't actually work. But it's always there when you need it. And just you try and get rid of it. Leave it where you will. Folk will pursue you down the street crying, 'You forgot your Biro.' THE MYSTERY BIRO has come to stay.

As to its origins. These remain shrouded in mystery also.

Often a telephone number will be printed upon the Biro. But spare yourself a florin. Either the number has been discontinued, or the premises named upon it simply do not, and have never, existed.

The employment of a stout stick is recommended. Followed by the incineration of the pieces.

ANOTHER MYSTERY SOLVED

I am often asked how, with Biros vanishing as often as they do, is it possible for some writers to get so much down on paper in a single lifetime?

Shakespeare, for example.

Shakespeare wrote 100,000,000 words in twenty years. No small feat. I am happy to reveal here a little known fact about the 'Immortal Bard'.

Shakespeare was, in fact, a retired pirate, who, after losing his right hand to a round of chain-shot on the Spanish Main, gave up the life of brigandry on the high seas and took up writing as a hobby to pass the time.

Intimates knew him as Stumpy Will and remarked upon the craftsmanship and lifelike nature of his carved elm prosthesis.

The forefinger of this was capped with a golden nib!

It is said that the impossibly prolific Master of Macabrery, Stephen King, has a Biro surgically grafted to his right hand.

The Book of Ultimate Truths
Hugo Rune

Cornelius closed the book without comment. The television was going hiss and the tall boy looked at his watch. Nearly three in the morning. That seemed a bit sudden. He took up the remote controller and did the ever-popular 'Channel Hop'.

'Don't mess with this guy,' said an on-screen extra. 'He knows karate.'

'Goes with the sickle,' replied Mr Elvis Presley.

'Seen it,' said Cornelius. 'Twenty-three times.'

Hop

'. . . furry, but with the head of a fish,' said a man in an anorak. 'Up on the hill. And it ate my dog, Prince.'

Hop

'In answer to your question,' said the large American author to the late-night chat-show host, 'the Biro is surgically implanted into the forefinger of my right hand.'

Hop

'The Sasquianna Hat Company,' said Lou Costello, in black and white.

'Hold on,' said Cornelius Murphy.

Hop back

The imaginative chat-show host was now asking the large American author where he got his ideas from. The author seemed somewhat stumped for a reply to such an unusual question and stared into the camera, as if in search of inspiration. And then a huge smile formed on his face.

As Cornelius looked on, the author's features appeared to swim. The hair faded. Heavy jowls formed and blue, piercing eyes glittered beneath a great beetling brow. The eyes gazed out from the screen. 'Any other questions?' asked Hugo Rune.

There was silence. Onscreen and off. Cornelius caught his breath.

'What about you, Mr Murphy?' asked Hugo Rune. 'Nothing you'd like to ask?'

Cornelius clutched at his hair. 'What?' went he.

'Good question.' Rune nodded his shaven dome of a head. 'If you knew the *what*, then you would learn the *why*. And if you knew the *why* you should soon know the *who*.'

The bedside telephone began to ring. Cornelius snatched it up. 'Who . . . ?'

'Tuppe,' answered Tuppe. 'I've got a pair of new-found friends with me. Female ones. I don't like the look of your one much though.'

Cornelius slammed down the phone. 'Mr Rune? Mr Hugo Rune?'

The big face filled the screen. 'Find the papers. Find the map. Find me.'

'Who has the papers? Do you know?'

The phone began to ring again. Cornelius snatched it up again.

'Not now!' he shouted.

'I was only joking about yours. She's a real cracker.'

'Tuppe, not now.'

Interference crackled across the screen. Rune's face began to fade.

'No, wait.' Cornelius fought with the remote controller, but the picture was breaking up. Static fizzed and popped. For a fleeting moment the Master reappeared. He was playing an ocarina.

And then he was gone.

'Hey, Abbott,' said Lou Costello, in black and white. 'Who's on first?'

13

His name was still Felix Henderson McMurdo. But now he was Scot (un-canny) many leagues from home.

He'd never hankered after the travelling life. In fact it had always been the last thing on his mind. Him having so many dear friends and everything. But circumstances had pressed, of late, most sorely upon him.

It was, he'd considered, the product of sheer happy chance, that his house alone in the street had escaped the conflagration during what the Press were now calling THE BLOODBATH OF SHEILA NA GIGH. And he was toasting this self-same happy chance in home-made elderflower wine when he first heard the chanting. And, turning back the net curtain in his wee front parlour, caught sight of what he took to be a torchlight procession.

McMurdo was touched to the very soul. That the people of Sheila na gigh could rise from the ashes of their homes and join together in a celebration, a unity in the face of such adversity, made him proud to be a Celt.

And so he slipped on his anorak and scurried outside, bottle in hand to join in the festivities.

It was only once he got outside that he became aware of what the good people were chanting. They were actually chanting his name.

It was with tears of joy in his eyes, that Felix went forward to meet the torchbearers, who by their chants were evidently proclaiming him the hero of the hour.

Much of what happened next was still hazy to him. He remembered shouts, 'There's the bastard now,' was one, and, 'He's carrying a Molotov cocktail,' was another. Then there was much scuffling and grabbing and a lot of talk regarding which lamppost the rope should be thrown over.

And there was the strong smell of hot tar. He could smell that even now. And all those feathers. And there was being thrown from the railway bridge and landing on top of the moving carriage. Then some hours later there was falling off the carriage into the cow field.

Then it all went black for quite a while. The next thing he recalled after that was waking up in hospital and this man with bandaged fingers in the next bed rambling on about a duffle-coat and how he'd been bitten by a wolf.

They'd all been kind enough to Felix in the hospital. Well, as kind as they had time to be. Doctors and nurses, he supposed, were very busy people. And hospital beds, precious things. He was heaved out of his almost as soon as he regained consciousness. The doctor said he had a cousin in Sheila na gigh. Felix said he'd pass on his best wishes.

It seemed a little drastic the way they frog-marched him through Casualty and tossed him into the street. But it was very kind of the fellow in the next bed to give him a duffle-coat for a present.

From then on it had been a funny old kind of a day. He'd hitched a ride from a 1950s hearse. This had dropped him at a garage in Cromcruach and had then mysteriously vanished before he could offer his thanks. At Cromcruach he'd met a mechanic named Mike, who seemed in a terrible state. He kept mumbling that he'd met 'the very Devil himself' and was shivering terribly. Felix wrapped him up in the duffle-coat.

And then Mike ran off screaming about snakes. With the coat still on.

Felix was forced to conclude that the English were a very eccentric people. Friendly though. The heavy-metal band that picked him up were very friendly. They were on their way to a really important gig. And the driver wanted to get even more friendly with some exciting young women they'd picked up earlier. And so Felix offered to take over the wheel and drive for a while.

And it wasn't really his fault. All those cars bumping into one another. He'd been adjusting the driving mirror and he'd only taken his eyes off the road for a moment. It was lucky that the twenty-seven-car pile up occurred within walking distance of one of those vast motorway service areas.

He'd had to walk on for quite a bit after that and it was quite late in the day when it occurred to him that the villagers had probably been just having a joke with him and that they would no doubt be feeling anxious by then and starting to worry. And he was just crossing over the dual carriageway to reach the northbound lane when the Status Quo tour bus ran over him.

He'd only sustained minor injuries and the drummer had patched him up and given him a pair of free tickets for an anniversary concert in Tierra del Fuego.

After that things became hazy once more. He thought he must have passed out on the grass verge. And the next thing he remembered was the minibus stopping and the monks helping him into it. Then it all went black again.

*   *   *

They sat over breakfast. They weren't smiling.

'It was Rune.' Cornelius poured milk over his cornflakes.

'Real crackers,' muttered Tuppe. 'Except for yours, that is. Locking us out of the room like that. Poor show, Cornelius. I had to make love to both of them in the lift. It was the least I could do.'

'Tuppe, I saw him on the television set. He spoke to me. He's still alive. He needs our help.'

'You were drunk. You finished that bottle of J . . . Mr Beam.'

'I finished that later. And I came out to look for you.'

'I kipped down in the broom cupboard. I don't think they should charge you full-board for me.'

'Mr Kobold's money arrived.' Cornelius patted a bulging envelope. 'Another five hundred pounds.'

'Then you can make it up by purchasing me a change of clothes.'

Tuppe hailed a passing waitress. 'We'll go on to the full first-class breakfast now please, miss.'

The waitress smiled, winked and wiggled away.

'Fine-looking woman,' said Cornelius, admiringly.

Tuppe shrugged. 'She was your one,' he said.

The summer sun shone warmly on the Cadillac Eldorado. It was drifting through the suburbs of outer Manchester.

They went every which way and there seemed no end to them.

Max Bygraves was singing 'The Diabolical Twist'.

Tuppe was wearing a very smart tartan shirt and a pair of Osh Kosh dungarees. Several carrier bags with the *Mothercare* logo upon them lay on the back seat.

'So,' said Tuppe. 'How do you intend to deal with this monastery business?'

'I have given the matter much thought. It is not the easiest thing in the world to enter a closed order and have a chit-chat with a monk, who has most probably taken a vow of silence.'

'So?'

'So, I propose first to employ implicit honesty. And if that fails, to resort to other means.'

'Which would be?'

'Low cunning,' said Cornelius Murphy.

'Oh good. Low cunning has always been a favourite with me. Anything low, in fact.'

'Do turn off Max Bygraves. The man fair gives me gip.'

There were all sorts of busy monkish things going on in the courtyard of the monastery of Saint Sacco Benedetto. But upstairs, in the guest cell, Felix Henderson McMurdo slept on right through them.

'How far now?' Cornelius asked. It was now mid morning and Manchester was far behind.

Tuppe consulted the map. 'It's sort of in North Wales. Almost. A bit on yet, I feel.'

'Sing us a song then. Just to pass the time.'

'I don't do songs.' Tuppe didn't do songs. 'I'll give you a poem, if you want.'

'Oh yes please.'

'Which one would you like then?'

Cornelius almost scratched his head. But, as today he had taken the precaution of restraining his crowning glory within a *Mothercare* bag, he scratched his nose instead.

'Give me "Billy O'Rourke". That's my favourite.'

'"Billy O'Rourke" it is then.' Tuppe did little coughings and clearings of the throat. The way one does. And began his recitation.

'"There used to be totters," said Billy O'Rourke,
With big smelly horses and that
And my dad knew gypsies who smile when they talk
And live by the tip of the hat."

But nobody cared for the stories he told
And he sat all alone of a night
Until one day a traveller came in from the cold
A sorry and miserable sight.

To the traveller, said Bill,
"It would give you a thrill
To hear all the tales of my youth
Of days dead and gone
But the memory lives on
And I swear every word is the truth."

Well the traveller grinned
And Billy beginned
To tell the most marvellous tales
Of earthquakes and crimes
And fabulous times
And whole families swallowed by whales.

And he spoke for three hours
About ivory towers
And warlords in armoury suit
And the traveller sat
And stared into his hat
Because he was a deaf and dumb mute.

Thank you.'

*   *   *

'Bravo.' Cornelius made cheering noises and drummed his hands on the steering wheel.

'Care for another?' Tuppe asked.

'I don't think so. One poem is pushing things. Even on an epic journey. Two would be nothing short of gratuitous.'

'Quite so. Shall we have Max on again?'

'Why not.'

They followed the map. Presently it led them from the main highway to minor roads and country lanes. Hedges rose to either side and the Cadillac's wing mirrors clipped against them. The trees locked hands overhead. And eventually Cornelius had to put the headlights on. The wireless set hissed and crackled and Max Bygraves faded all away.

Tuppe fiddled with the knobs. 'White noise,' he exclaimed. 'It shouldn't be making that.'

'Hills all around, do you think?' Cornelius switched on the windscreen wipers. The screen was starting to fog up.

'Hills wouldn't do that.' Tuppe shivered. 'Could we have the roof back on? It's growing a smidgen chilly.'

Cornelius flicked the switch. But nothing happened. 'Now, that's odd. It was working perfectly back in Manchester, when you had it going up and down at the traffic lights to impress those schoolgirls.' He flicked the switch up and down a few more times. 'Dead. Are you sure we're going the right way?'

'Best check at the next crossroads. See a signpost or something.'

'Or something.' Cornelius drove slowly on. Branches clattered against the car. 'This isn't going to do the paint job any good. Oh damn.'

A branch whipped across the screen and tore off one of the wipers.

'Oh dear,' sighed Tuppe. 'Do you think we'd better back up?'

'Back up, or walk.'

'We can't leave the car blocking this lane, can we?'

'No.' Cornelius put the Cadillac into reverse. The gearbox made terrible cries of complaint. Cornelius tried again, but to no avail.

'We seem to be right out of reverse gears at the present,' he said, in a gloomy sort of a voice.

'Shall we press on then?' Tuppe looked up at Cornelius.

'Press on.'

They pressed on. And on.

Tuppe donned two nice new jumpers, but was still cold.

Cornelius switched on the heater. The heater did not work.

'Cornelius,' Tuppe hugged his elbows. 'Cornelius, I am growing afraid.'

'Fear not, little friend.' The tall boy patted his small chum on the shoulder. 'We'll soon be out of here.'

But they weren't. The headlights cut into the growing murk. The car bumped in and out of potholes. Both their watches stopped. And suddenly Cornelius stopped the car. Tuppe tumbled forwards from his seat. 'What is happening?' he asked.

'Up ahead. In the road.'

'What? What?'

'We didn't pass any turnings, did we?'

'Not a one. What do you see?'

'Wait here.' Cornelius climbed over the windscreen. Across the bonnet. And dropped down in front of the car. He walked on for a few yards, stooped and picked something up.

'What do you have there?' called Tuppe.

'Oh dear. Oh dear,' said Cornelius.

'What is it?'

Cornelius held up the object. It sparkled in the headlight's beam.

'Our windscreen wiper,' said Cornelius Murphy.

'It isn't very good in the dark, dark wood.' Tuppe's teeth were chattering.

'We definitely didn't pass a turning, did we?'

Tuppe shook his shaking head.

'And I don't see how we could have just driven around in a circle. I've hardly turned the wheel. So, where does that leave us?'

'It leaves me in a state of considerable nervousness. Let's walk back. If we're no further on than we were half an hour ago, then we'll have no further to walk back.'

'There is wisdom in your words. But I don't think we should leave the car. Although,' he tapped at the dashboard, 'it would appear that we are almost out of petrol.'

'How about if we *ran* back?' Tuppe suggested.

'No. That is not what we will do. Put your safety-belt on, Tuppe.'

Tuppe clipped himself up. 'I'm not going to like this, am I?'

Cornelius revved the engine. 'Probably not. Perhaps you should close your eyes.'

'Why is that?'

'Because I am going to close mine.' Cornelius gave the accelerator pedal full wellie and slammed the car into gear.

He let out the clutch.

The wheels spun. The engine screamed and the car shot forwards.

Cornelius gripped the steering wheel with both hands and kept his head well down. Branches snapped and crackled. The windscreen shattered. The headlights did likewise. Cornelius kept his foot right down on the floor.

'Oooooooooooooooooh!' shrieked Tuppe.

'Hold tight!' Cornelius swung the steering wheel hard to the right. The Cadillac swerved. Tore into the hedge. Crashed through it.

There was a great fireball of light. The car seemed to hang a moment in space. And then it plunged down and down and down.

Cornelius held his breath.

Tuppe held his breath.

Crash, bang and wallop, went the Cadillac and finally . . .

Tuppe's eyes remained tightly shut. 'Cornelius,' he whispered. 'Cornelius, are you there?'

'I'm somewhere.' The tall boy had his hands over his head. 'What do you see?'

'I don't see anything. I'm not looking.'

Mmmmmmmmmmmmmmmmmmm. Clunk.

'What was that?'

'I think it was the roof closing. Do you smell something, Tuppe?'

Tuppe sniffed. 'I smell flowers. Oh Cornelius, I smell flowers.'

'I smell flowers too.'

'Cornelius. I think we're dead.'

'Then we've gone to the good place. Flowers have to be the good place.'

'. . . Tulips from Amsterdam,' sang Max Bygraves, all of a sudden.

'Or possibly not,' groaned Cornelius Murphy.

'Oooh and ouch!' Cornelius Murphy's trousers began to burn. 'We've gone to hell.'

'I don't think so.' Tuppe floundered about blindly and turned off the heater. Cornelius fanned at his trouser bottoms and slowly drew himself back into the vertical plane. 'Gosh,' said he. 'Would you look at that?'

Tuppe crept up beside him and took a peep. 'Ooh,' went Tuppe.

The Cadillac was standing in the middle of a small grassy field. Not twenty yards from the open gateway it had apparently just driven through. On the road beyond cars went by.

Birds twittered. Flowers bloomed. The sun shone.

Cornelius stood up, drew back his hair and scanned the horizon. No hedgerows. No overhanging trees. He climbed from the car and examined it with interest. The windscreen was intact. Both wipers were there. The headlights were on. The paintwork was immaculate.

Tuppe scrambled out to join him. 'Not a scratch. Nothing. What happened? Were we dreaming?'

'Not dreaming. Come on. Help me search the car.'

'For what?'

'I'll know when we find it.'

They searched the car. They were very thorough.

Tuppe found a pair of knickers down behind the back seat.

Cornelius rummaged through the contents of the boot and found them to be very oily indeed.

Suddenly Tuppe said, 'What's this?'

'What do you have there?' Cornelius slammed shut the boot.

'A little black package, sealed with wax. It was under the driving seat. It feels very cold.'

Cornelius came around the car and took it from him. He weighed the thing on his palm and turned it with his thumb. 'Would you care to hazard a guess at the contents?'

'I don't think it's a bar of chocolate. It's not a bomb, is it?' Tuppe ducked back into the car.

'Not a bomb. I would suspect that it's a model car. Probably a Cadillac Eldorado, with the windscreen painted black.'

Cornelius tore open the little package. It *was* a model car. It *was* a Cadillac Eldorado. A piece of black gaffer tape had been secured across the windscreen.

Tuppe looked at Cornelius.

Cornelius looked at Tuppe.

'Lucky guess?' Tuppe asked.

The Cadillac was now parked in a lay-by. Tuppe sat in the front passenger seat brrrming the toy car up and down the dashboard.

Cornelius was in a telephone box. Tuppe couldn't hear what he was saying. But he could understand his friend's body language. Things weren't going well.

Cornelius slammed down the receiver and stalked back to the car. He flung himself into the driving seat. Tuppe thought it best not to ask.

'I'm sacked.' Cornelius threw up his hands and brought them down amidst a torrent of hair. 'Sacked.'

'Why?' Tuppe asked.

'For my own safety. Mr Kobold says I am in grave danger. He says I should forget about the monastery. Come back home at once.'

'What did you tell him?'

'I told him no.' Cornelius fought to free his fingers from his hair.

'Good for you. No, what am I saying? We're out of our league here.' Tuppe waggled the toy car beneath the tall boy's nose. 'This is witchcraft. We were hexed, or hoodooed, or something. We can't mess around with stuff like this.'

'I'm not quitting.' Cornelius folded his arms. 'I'm not.'

'I understood that you'd been sacked.'

'Tuppe, whatever we've got ourselves into is something really big. The epic something. We can't quit now. Not at least until we know exactly what we *have* got ourselves into.'

'Could we quit *then*?' Tuppe made a hopeful face.

'You can quit now if you want to. I'm going on to the monastery. And I'm going to find the papers. What do you say?'

Tuppe stroked his pointed chin. 'They would seem to be most valuable papers. And as you are now unemployed, I see no reason why you shouldn't search for them in a freelance capacity. And then perhaps, sell them to the highest bidder.'

'These thoughts have crossed my mind. So, will you join me, or should I drop you off at the nearest station?'

Tuppe gave his chin another little stroke. 'As you may have noticed, Cornelius, I am only a small person. And I greatly fear magic. Especially magic that actually works. I feel that I might prove a hindrance rather than a help.'

Cornelius nodded carefully. 'I understand. I'll drop you off at the first station we come to.'

'You must be joking. I wouldn't miss this for the world.'

'Then you'll stay?'

'Of course I'll stay.' Tuppe tinkered with the wireless.

'Born to be wild,' sang Steppenwolf.

'That's more like it,' cried Tuppe. 'Let's Rock and Roll.'

'Let's do that very thing,' Cornelius agreed. And the big grin was back with a vengeance.

14

THE SMALL SCREW PHENOMENON

Have you ever dismantled a malfunctioning electric toaster in order to effect a repair?

Have you then located the cause of the problem, generally something trivial, a disconnected wire or whatnot, made the repair, reassembled the toaster, tested it and found everything once again working properly?

And then discovered you had *two small screws left over*?

Then heed the words of Rune.

Open the nearest window.

Take the screws in your right hand.

(Or your left, if this interferes with your Biro implant.)

Defenestrate the screws.

That is THROW THEM OUT OF THE WINDOW!

Because if you do not, then all that lies before you is madness, misery and the ruination of your health.

If you again dismantle the toaster and search for places to refit the screws, you will very shortly become aware of two things.

    1. Once reassembled, the toaster will no longer work.

    2. You are now the proud possessor of *three* small screws!

That the mystery of the small screw phenomenon, S.S.P., has baffled the scientific greybeards of our age is hardly surprising. The greybeards lean naturally towards bafflement.

However, I Rune, understanding, as I do, all things, reveal this truth unto you.

SMALL SCREWS BREED INSIDE ELECTRICAL APPARATUS.

The small screw, as may be observed through a very powerful lens, resembles the spiral of D.N.A. It is a living body.

The fact that toasters, as with all electric appliances, possess self-healing screw holes, has long been recognized as fact. All screw holes have the tendency to shrink once the screw has been removed from them. This is natural. Nothing enjoys having a foreign object forcibly inserted into it. With the notable exception of certain members of The Chiswick Townswomen's Guild. But this does not have any particular bearing upon the subject of S.S.P.

The small screw is the demon spawn of modern technology. It has driven many good men to early graves, cost industry countless billions of pounds each day, crippled innovation and lost us The Empire.

I have recently been made privy to certain 'leaked' Ministry of Defence documents.

These refer in great detail to S.S.P. in regard to the construction and maintenance of so called 'Nuclear Submarines'[1].

These submersibles are literally bulging with electronic hokus pokus, which, having been constructed to the very highest standards of technological perfection, is in constant need of repair.

During a recent overhaul, the multiplicity of small screws became so pronounced and the incidences of madness amongst the service teams so apparent, that the M.o.D. was forced to seek a socially acceptable excuse. They chose *Radiation Leaks*!

The S.S.S. (Special Screw Service) were called in to descrew the submarines and removed nearly three tons of small

[1] See *Nuclear Power. The Myth Exploded*, Hugo Rune.

screws, all of which had apparently come out of something or other, but nobody knew what.

The small screws were packed into containers, labelled TOXIC WASTE to avoid suspicion, driven to the south coast of England and dumped into the sea.

My own interest in the subject of S.S.P. began in the late 1940s. I was in India, acting as Gandhi's spiritual adviser. At the time I write about, he and I were travelling on a steam packet out of Bombay. We had decided to get away from it all for a couple of weeks and 'do the nightlife' in Calcutta. As usual we went incognito, adopting our favourite guise of 'man and wife'.

Gandhi had a natural bent for female impersonation. Had he chosen to take it up professionally, it might well have made his fortune. His Widow Twanky was formidable. And how well I remember his rendition of 'I'm Just a Girl Who Can't Say No', performed in blond wig and ball gown, to the appreciation of the British Trade Delegation outside the Taj Mahal (by moonlight).

Although we had begged the captain to see to it that we remained undisturbed, word soon got out that one of the world's greatest spiritual leaders was on board the ship.

In no time, passengers and crew alike were beating on our door and begging *me* to bless their children, cure their baldness, restore their youth, and double the length of their 'old chaps'. All of which I did, simply in the hope of getting a bit of peace during the rest of the voyage.

When all were satisfied I prepared to turn in for the night. But noticed that a single figure yet remained, cowering in the corner of the cabin.

Having done my bit that day for the good of mankind, I told him to clear off at the double, or know my wrath. But he flung himself down before me and kissed the hem of my raiment.

He was as ragged a wretch as ever I saw. And I've

seen some. Stained a deep chestnut by the subcontinental sun, white of hair and mad of eye.

It was only when he spoke that I realized he had once been an Englishman. And a gentleman to boot.

He told me that he had a terrible confession to make and knew of no other man on earth to whom he could make it. His name was Lord N— (I withhold his name because his family are prominent members of the ruling class, and to reveal it would bring shame upon a noble house and in all probability bring down the present Government).

The tale below is told in his own words.

During the early 1930s, I spent a period passing the time as a news reader for the BBC. In those days the BBC was staffed exclusively by members of the English aristocracy. It had very much the atmosphere of an exclusive gentleman's club.

The news was supplied to the readers by a team of back-room Johnnies whose job it was to think up items of news suitably cheerful and patriotic to broadcast. This was generally done by recycling whatever news had proved the most popular the previous year, or taking passages from the pages of *Old Moore's Almanac*. During the depression, the BBC Northern Service broadcast 'live coverage' of the King's coronation every three or four weeks, to great spirit-raising effect. And you will no doubt recall how the summers were so much better before the war. This was due to the BBC's policy of always adding a few degrees to the temperature on all weather forecasts. A little wrinkle picked up from the Russians, who used it to ensure good turnouts on May Day.

Anyway. Each morning, when I arrived at Broadcasting House, I would leave my top hat and cane with the porter and collect my daily supply of news from my special pigeonhole. It was always there in a large, crisp, buff-coloured envelope.

Once in a while, if I felt in the mood, I would flick through it in advance, to see what the Johnnies had dreamed up for the Empire to be doing. But mostly I did not, considering it unsporting for a news reader to know the news before the listener.

However, one particular morning, I noticed that the buff-coloured envelope presented a somewhat shabby appearance. There was evidence of a finger-mark and what looked to be a ring made by the damp underside of a coffee cup. You can imagine my surprise, as the BBC was always scrupulous about providing saucers.

I complained at once to the Director General, an Etonian uncle of mine, and he agreed that the culprit should be given a stern ticking off and that I should be the one to do it.

Now, I did all my news readings from a comfortable drawing room on the third floor and had never ventured down into the labyrinth of sub basements beneath Broadcasting House. It took me nearly an hour to locate the back-room Johnnies' room. The sign on the door said, BACK ROOM KEEP OUT.

I knocked loudly. But illiciting no response, turned the handle and went in. What I saw upset me not a little. I had expected a number of learnèd bookish types, being terribly earnest and responsible, seated at great desks, studying mighty leather-bound tomes. But no. The room contained but a single cove, clad in an overall and worrying at a complicated-looking electrical contrivance about the size of a portmanteau. This was all covered in dials and valves and little lights and mounted on a sturdy work bench.

'You, sir,' I hailed the cove and waved the grubby envelope in his direction. 'I demand to know the meaning of this.'

'Oh, you've read it, have you?' he replied. 'Well sorry, guvnor, you'll just have to wait.'

I did not like his tone, nor did I understand the meaning of his words. So I opened the envelope and acquainted myself with the contents. On a sheet of paper, torn from a cheap copybook, were scrawled the words NORMAL SERVICE WILL BE RESUMED AS SOON AS POSSIBLE.

'I demand to know the meaning of this also,' said I, striking a martial pose.

'It means what it says,' said the overalled cove, in what I now came to realize was a working-class accent. 'Until I get this fixed there ain't going to be no news. So you'd best go back upstairs and apologize to the listeners.'

I shook my head. 'That is not the way things are done at the BBC,' I told him.

'Well, it's how they are today,' came his insolent reply. 'Until I have this here gadget all tickety-boo, there'll be no news today.'

'And what, pray tell me, exactly is this gadget of yours then?' I enquired.

'A radio receiver.'

'You mean a wireless set,' I corrected him.

'I mean a radio receiver. It picks up news reports from all over the world.'

'What? Foreign news?' I was flabbergasted. 'The listeners don't want to hear news about a bunch of damned foreigners. They want English news. Made up by Englishmen for Englishmen.'

'Progress,' said he.

'Progress?' Well, I was rattled at this, I can tell you. Progress is not a word a gentleman uses. But then, this cove was evidently no gentleman.

'I wish to speak to your master,' I told him.

'Bugger off,' quoth the lout, and then, 'Strike me pink, another of the little perishers.' And with this he flung a tiny screw in my direction.

By now I had heard quite enough and stepped forward to give the blighter a sound thrashing. But I lost my footing upon numerous similar little screws which covered the floor and fell heavily. Striking my bowling arm on the table and my forehead on his infernal machine.

'Have a care,' he cried, with no concern for what damage my person had received. 'I've nearly got it fixed.'

'Sir,' said I, rising with difficulty and dusting down my tweeds. 'Sir. Where are the back-room Johnnies who make up the news?'

'Gorn,' said he. 'All sacked last Friday. New policy, what with the war coming up and all.'

'War? What war?' I was astounded.

'No-one's supposed to know about it yet. But I suppose it can't do no harm to tell you . . .'

And then he went on to tell me that a Second World War had been arranged. Something to do with solving unemployment and getting full use from allotments. And that there was to be a 'war effort' and a 'Blitz spirit' and lots of songs from Vera Lynn. And how this radio receiver was to play a vital part in the running of it all. And how it was all very hush hush and top secret.

'And so,' he continued, 'I am doing work of national importance here. And if you care about King and country, you should muck in and give us a hand.'

And so I did. Poor fool that I was. And that is how I came to be as you see me now.'

He sank to his knees weeping bitterly. Gandhi came mincing in. Full drag, a sailor on each arm.

I sent him packing and ordered Lord N— to finish his tale.

'It was the small screws,' he wailed. 'The more we tried to fix the radio receiver, the more small screws we were left with. We worked at it day and night. The back-room Johnnies had to be called back in the mean time, while we worked on and on and on.'

'But you must have got it fixed eventually,' I said to him, 'because the Second World War did go ahead on schedule.'

'No it didn't. It was supposed to start in 1936. By 1939 Hitler said he couldn't wait any longer for the BBC and he was going to start without them. The whole thing was a complete shambles and it was all my fault.'

'Well, not *all* your fault. The cove in the overalls was really to blame.'

'No,' wept N—. 'He was a genius. He finally swept away all the small screws. Obtained a wiring diagram. Stripped down the receiver completely and rebuilt it from the ground up. It worked perfectly first time.'

'But I thought you said—'

'I did. He got so excited that he rushed upstairs to tell the Director General. And while he was gone I twiddled the dials and listened to the news coming in from all over the world. It was wonderful, I can tell you. But then I noticed that one of the dials was a bit loose. So I took it off to have a look at it and a small screw dropped out. So I removed the dust cover from the front to see where it had come from. And you'll never guess what happened then . . .'

But I allowed Lord N—'s tale to go no further. I brought out the stout stick that I always carry with me when travelling in the east and smote him fiercely upon the head with it. Called up the captain and had Lord N— promptly bundled into an open boat and set adrift.

Having waved him my goodbyes, I returned to my cabin and chanced to notice several small screws lying upon the floor where he had fallen. In the spirit of devilment I placed two next to Gandhi's hairdryer.

I would draw his attention to them the following day.

The Book of Ultimate Truths
Hugo Rune

The monastery of Saint Sacco Benedetto was not a pretty sight.

All the world over there are beautiful monasteries.

They nestle into hillsides or ride high upon craggy peaks. They grow up from the landscape. They are at one with it. At peace and in harmony with it. Which is partly what monasteries are all about really.

But not this one. This one was an irregular eyesore.

And it had always been so. Since the first stones were laid, folk looked up at that monastery and went 'blurgh'.

It was difficult to say exactly what was wrong with it. Well, actually it wasn't. Everything was wrong with it. The overall design. The colour of the stones. The angle of the rooftops. The shape of the windows. Et cetera and et cetera.

The blame lay with the original architect. Norris the Nomark. Well, actually it didn't. It lay with his dad, Mergus the Mighty, and a little thing called nepotism.

Mergus was one of those Dark-Age Celtic warlord kind of bodies, who knocked around with King Arthur and slew on a regular basis.

He was considered a doer of mighty deeds even amongst those who did mighty deeds for a living. And there were a lot of them about back then.

Everything about Mergus was mighty. His helm was heroic. His hauberk Herculean. His vambraces were valorous and his greaves grandiose. It took four strong men to buckle on his cuirass. And it was said that he once left his codpiece out in the rain and a cow fell into it and drowned.

Naturally his horse was pretty big also. And as for his sword!

Well!

The Venerable Bede writes thusly of it:

And the sword of Mergus was a mighty sword. Forged in the fires of Argsnargh the Armourer from the blades of an hundred warriors that Mergus did slay before breakfast.

And so mighty was this sword of Mergus that none but he could wield it. And him sometimes with difficulty. But wield it he did. And often. And no man could stand before that mighty sword when he was a wielding of it. And once he had done with the wielding of it, those that still bore heads upon their shoulders did give thanks, and say verily here is a bad man to get the wrong side of. And things of that nature.

All in all, then, the kind of fellow who probably wouldn't have taken too kindly to remarks about his son's ineptitude as an architect.

High upon a not too distant hillside, a patch of blue sky took on another shade of blue as a Cadillac Eldorado purred to a standstill.

Tuppe climbed up in his seat and stared down at the monastery.

'Blurgh,' said Tuppe. 'What a horrid building.'

'It does lack a certain something,' Cornelius agreed.

Tuppe turned to his friend. 'Now,' said he, in a serious tone, 'I have given this matter much thought and I truly believe that I should be the one to go down there and acquire the papers.'

'Absolutely not. I wouldn't hear of such a thing.'

'It would be for the best. Please let me do it.'

'My job.' Cornelius put a thumb to his chest. 'I will go. If you see anything suspicious, meep the horn.'

'Meep the horn? Cornelius, you are making a mistake. I can get in there. Let me do it.'

'No.' Cornelius stepped from the car and slammed shut the door. A slight breeze caught his hair and tossed it back in a romantic fashion. Cornelius affected a manly pose and stared down at the monastery.

'Stay here and read this.' He pulled the daddy's dog-eared copy of Rune from his pocket and handed it to the small fellow with the shaking head. 'It might help.'

'I certainly doubt that. Cornelius, please.'

'Tuppe, no. I am in complete command of the situation. Farewell.' Cornelius turned away to take his leave and in doing so left behind a goodly portion of his right trouser leg, which was trapped in the car door.

One change of trousers and a long hike down the hillside later and Cornelius found himself standing before the monastery of Saint Sacco Benedetto. Its walls overhung in a precarious fashion with iron spikes depending. The great door was bound with beaten hasps. A thing of formidable construction. Hundreds of rivet heads testified to its fortitude. This was a door which made a statement. It said, 'KEEP OUT.'

Cornelius flattened down his hair, which during the hike had composed itself into a passable facsimile of the Pisa tower, straightened his lapels, threw back his shoulders and squared up to the challenge.

He sought out the bell-pull.

There was no bell-pull.

Undaunted, he reached for the knocker.

This also was notable only for its absence.

As was the letter flap.

Cornelius made little whistling noises, gave the matter a moment or two's thought and then set out to test a certain proposition.

He thrust his hands into his pockets. Turned casually and leaned upon the great door. It swung open and he toppled backwards into the monastery.

Cornelius climbed to his feet, dusted himself down and

178

gently closed the door. He now stood in a horrible-looking vestibule, lined with irregularly spaced columns. The walls were painted in gloss green, the ceiling was far too high and the uneven flagstones lay in wait.

Cornelius observed the unmistakable face of Max Bygraves in a damp patch on the right-hand wall, divided by a long white crack which traced the route of the sixty-five bus from Ealing Broadway to Richmond. Cornelius stepped warily.

'And what have we here?' he asked himself.

A blue plume of smoke drifted from behind an ir-regularly spaced column. The sounds of smothered coughing followed it.

Cornelius stifled a smirk. His kind of monk. He called out in a strident voice, 'Hello there. Anybody home?'

The coughing ceased. There was the sound of a foot stamping and a hand became visible. It flapped at the air.

'Who goes there?' asked a tortured voice.

'Papal emissary,' Cornelius replied. 'Here to see the abbot.'

'Papal bloody what?' A monk appeared from behind the column. His cowl was drawn down over his face and his hands were tucked, each into the sleeve of its opposite number. 'Who let you in?' he demanded to know.

'No-one. I used my pass key.' Cornelius stepped forward and put out his hand for a shake. 'Murphy's the name. Of the papal nunciature. Grants department. Here on special assignment. And you are?'

'I'm a monk,' said the monk, declining the offer of Murphy's hand. 'Don't they teach you anything?'

'I meant your name. You do have a name, I suppose.'

'We have no names here. We renounce all such worldly affectations. Here we have only numbers.'

'And so yours is?'

'I am number Six.'

Cornelius fought back the snappy rejoinder with the greatest of difficulty. But he managed it nonetheless.

'I would like to see the abbot. Kindly take me to him.'

'No-one can *see* the abbot.'

Cornelius stuck his hands into his trouser pockets and blew a rogue strand of hair from his face. 'The abbot is expecting me. I phoned earlier.'

'We don't have a phone,' said Brother Six.

Cornelius made the sign of the cross on the floor with his left toecap. 'The Pope isn't going to like this,' he said. 'Like as not he'll make me bring back all the money.'

'Money?' The monk made a small involuntary step forwards. 'What money?'

'The grant. For the rebuilding of the monastery. A not inconsiderable sum. All in cash. Apparently the holy father is so impressed with the privations of his children here that he has felt fit to award a bursary. And institute a new experimental regime. From what I've heard it sounds like a real papal bull of a plan.'

'Go on?' said Brother Six. 'Tell me more.'

'Well. Apparently he feels that the brothers here should know more about the pleasures of the flesh. He thinks it would be good for them to have a greater knowledge of the outside world. Therefore he plans the installation of satellite TV. A bar with a holy hour. French chef. Oh yes, and he is quite insistent that tobacco and soft drugs be readily available.'

'Get away,' said the monk. 'You're pulling my plonker.'

'I am doing no such thing. But . . .' Cornelius turned away. 'If the abbot cannot be spoken to, so be it. I do have other monasteries to visit today. There is a Jesuit sanctuary not far from here, I believe. Perhaps you would be so kind as to direct me.'

'Not so fast.' Brother Six forced out a 'my son' to go on the end. 'I never said we weren't interested.'

Cornelius turned back.

'What kind of soft drugs?' asked Brother Six.

Arthur Kobold stuffed a large piece of cake into his mouth and munched upon it. The telephone on his desk began to ring.

Arthur wiped a sleeve across his face and picked up the receiver.

'Kobold,' he said, spraying crumbs into the already crumbed-up mouthpiece.

'What progress?' asked the voice at his ear.

Arthur Kobold stiffened to attention. 'Matters are in hand.'

'And what of Murphy?'

'I dismissed him.'

'You did *what*?' The voice was high and piping.

'I dismissed him. I thought it best under the circumstances.'

'And so where is Murphy now?'

'At the monastery, I should imagine. Proving himself to be the stuff of epics.' Arthur's fingers strayed towards another helping of cake. 'He'll get the papers. Have no fear.'

'He better had. Or you know what will happen to you.'

Arthur's fingers withdrew, cakeless. 'I'm doing the best that I can,' he complained. 'These things take time.'

'Too much time. Two more days, Kobold. That's all the time you have. If the papers are not delivered by then, the project will be cancelled and you recalled. And more direct measures will be taken.'

'More direct? How direct might that be exactly?'

'Very direct. Totally, in fact. I will set in motion *The Train of Trismegistus*!'

'Not *The Train of Trismegistus*?' gasped Arthur Kobold.

'*The Train of Trismegistus*. And you know what that means.'

'No more cake,' sighed Arthur Kobold. 'Not none at all.'

'Two days or else!' The line went dead and Arthur Kobold replaced the receiver.

'No more cake.' Arthur's bottom lip began to quiver. 'Not none. At all.' He pulled the half-finished Black Forest Gâteau towards him and buried his face in it.

'Bhang,' said Cornelius, as Brother Six led him along a truly horrendous gallery. 'Angel dust, Acid, amphetamines . . .' The wonky walls were made gay with many paintings, each depicting violent martyrdom. Cornelius had often wondered why it was that so many saints went off to glory bereft of their clothes. And such fine physical specimens they all were. Each a veritable Adonis. Here was Saint Sebastian, his superbly muscled torso cruelly pierced by all those arrows.

Cornelius stopped to consider his expression. He looked quite cheerful really. Almost as if he was . . .

Brother Six turned to hurry Cornelius along. He followed the direction of the tall boy's gaze.

'That would make your eyes water, eh?'

'I'm sorry?'

'Never mind. Go on with what you were saying.'

Cornelius continued with his narcotic litany. 'Amyl nitrate, barbs, benes, *Cannabis Sativa*, cocaine . . .' He followed the monk with the spring in his step. 'Dagga, dwale, Ecstasy, Frisco speedball, fly agaric, ganja . . .'

'Stick on 'G',' said Brother Six. 'We're here.'

They had come to a narrow doorway, that framed an even narrower door. It was painted bright yellow.

'I'll just pop in and tell the holy father that you've arrived. I'm sure he won't wish to keep you waiting. What did you say your name was again?'

'Murphy,' said Murphy. 'Cornelius Murphy. Perhaps it would be better if I was to . . .' But he got no further. Brother Six had knocked, opened and gone inside. The door slammed shut behind him.

'Possibly run.' Cornelius prepared to make away on his toes. And so he would have done, had not the yellow door suddenly re-opened and Brother Six come bowling through the doorway.

He struck the tall boy with considerable force. Lifting him from his feet and carrying him across the gallery, where the two came to rest in some confusion.

Cornelius struggled to his feet. Prepared to make a fight of it. He raised his fists. 'Come on then,' he said.

The monk looked up at him. A puzzled expression on a face that seemed scarcely older than the Murphy's. 'Do what?' he asked.

'I don't want to fight with you.'

'I don't want you to either.'

'But you attacked me.'

'No I didn't.' Brother Six rose with as much dignity as he could muster. 'I tripped coming out of the door. The holy father told me to hurry up. I'm sorry. You can go straight in.'

'I can? What did you tell the holy father about me?'

'Just your name. That's all. He said he was expecting you.'

'Yes. Well. I told you he was.'

'Right. Come on then.' Brother Six urged Cornelius over to the little yellow door. 'We mustn't keep the holy father waiting, must we?'

'We must not.'

Brother Six knocked and announced. 'Mr Cornelius Murphy.' Then he opened the door and pushed Cornelius forwards. 'Mind the step,' he advised.

Cornelius didn't mind the step. Possibly, had he been able to see the step, he would have minded it. But he couldn't so he didn't. He tumbled into utter impenetrable darkness. The door slammed shut behind him and he slammed heavily to the invisible floor.

He blinked his eyes and fumbled around and wondered, very reasonably enough, whether he had just walked into a very big trap.

'Hello,' he called lamely. 'Is there anybody there?'

'Welcome, my son,' came a hoarse whisper. 'I trust you have not injured yourself. I really must do something about that step.'

Cornelius felt that, other than for his pride, he had sustained no lasting injury. 'I don't seem to be able to see anything. Might we have the light on?'

'No light,' whispered the abbot. 'I have taken a vow of darkness.'

'Oh. I see. Or rather I don't. But I understand what you mean.' Cornelius rose once more to his feet and dusted himself down. He could see absolutely nothing. But he could smell a great deal.

A dozen years before this moment, Cornelius had been brought low with scarlet fever. The doctor didn't understand quite how, because, as an illness, scarlet fever was no longer fashionable.

The current craze was for hyperactivity brought on by food additives or dairy products or whatever. Scarlet fever had gone the way of rickets and ringworm. But Cornelius had managed to contract it nevertheless and the upshot of this was that the tall boy, in fact quite a small boy at the time, although tall for his age, had been confined in a dark bedroom for six weeks on a diet of poached white fish.

Whether this was the correct treatment or not, no-one seemed certain. But it obviously did the trick, because he fully recovered. But there had been a curious side effect. Lying there in the darkness day after day, Cornelius became aware that, deprived of his sight, his other senses were compensating for the loss. Quite wonderfully. His hearing became intensely acute. But it was his sense of smell that really came into its own.

After a week Cornelius found that he could distinguish between the various visitors to the house, even before he could hear their footsteps or they entered the sickroom. And soon he was able to sniff out what they had in their pockets. Folded linen handkerchiefs, bags of sweeties, the ink in their fountain pens. He would lie in his bed and build up an olfactory image of the visitor. From whatever they had on the soles of their shoes to the brand of hair cream they favoured.

He could smell the breakfast on their breath and certain more personal things, which he was, at that time, too young to understand.

The daddy, who spent many long hours in the sickroom, entertaining his son with tall tales of his youth, encouraged this new-found talent and brought Cornelius boxes of unrelated objects for him to test himself upon. Animal, vegetable, mineral. Whatever came to hand. And once smelt and identified, Cornelius was rarely wrong the second time.

Naturally the daddy was not slow to spy out the sunlit window of financial opportunity in the night-dark sickroom. And many visitors arrived, eager to ask Cornelius what they were holding behind their backs or had stuffed deeply into their pockets. It passed the time, and as soon as Cornelius had managed to distinguish between the scent of a one-pound note and that of a fiver, even beyond the closed door, the daddy split the takings fifty-fifty.

It was a very satisfactory arrangement, while it lasted. It certainly made the six weeks go fast. It was a terrible shame though about the epidemic of scarlet fever which subsequently spread across the surrounding neighbourhood.

The daddy had taken the family away on a good long holiday as soon as Cornelius was well enough to travel.

And so now, here stood Cornelius in another dark room and the memory of that illness, so long ago, returned to him. With a vengeance.

He sniffed tentatively and tried to make what sense he could of his surroundings. He felt himself to be in a room of considerable size. A room which contained many ancient books. The distinctive odour of their leather spines, a rich sweet musk, was heavy in the air and formed a deep background to what else lay within.

There were many woods in the room. Cornelius recognized the light scent of polished ash, the rosey perfume of mahogany and the sombre incense of oak drifting up from the floorboards on which he had just fallen. Along with these came other essences. Burnished brass, black ink, old paper, red wine, lavender. And something less pleasant.

Cornelius flexed his nostrils and sought the location of the abbot. But his teenage nose had lost much of its childhood cunning. The woollen cloth of the holy father's scapula was apparent. The tunic, girdle, belt and hood. Even the sandals.

But the habit's inhabitant exhaled nothing that Cornelius could identify. He could tell where he was, several feet away, seated behind a walnut desk. But that was about it.

Cornelius took a few more sniffs. But to no avail.

'Do you have a cold, my son?' the abbot asked in another whisper.

'No, I'm fine really.'

'Then if you will feel your way forwards there is a chair just in front of you.'

Cornelius knew that there was. But he blundered into it anyway. 'I can manage.' He righted the chair and sat down upon it.

'Good. Then I should like to know why you have come to Saint Sacco Benedetto.'

'Well, sir.' Cornelius shifted uneasily. The truth seemed a good enough reason. 'Well, sir, I . . .'

'Sir me no sirs, my son. I have also taken a vow of humility. Speak to me as you would a friend. You may call me by my Christian name.'

'And that is?'

'Bud,' whispered the abbot.

Cornelius felt that had the light been on he would have seen that one coming.

'Well . . . Bud. I wish to speak to one of the brothers.'

'I regret that it is not permitted.'

'The circumstances are somewhat exceptional. It is a matter of great importance.'

'Matters which appear important beyond the cloister have little relevance within it. I am sorry I cannot help you.'

Cornelius had hoped that his eyes might have become accustomed to the dark by now. They hadn't. 'Bud,' said he, 'the brother I wish to speak to is in considerable danger.'

'Danger?' The whisper was without tone. 'And why should this be?'

'I believe that he has certain papers in his possession. I do not understand fully their significance. But there are those who will go to almost any length to acquire them.'

'Papers brought in from the outside world?'

'Yes.'

'Then you need have no fear for the brother's safety.'

'Why not?'

'Because all the brothers give up all their worldly goods when they take their vows and enter the monastery.'

'Give them up? Leave them behind, do you mean?'

'No. I mean give them up. To me.'

'Then if the papers are here, you will have them?'

'No.' The voice was as soft and measured as ever. 'They would all have been destroyed.'

'Destroyed?' Cornelius made a bitter face in the darkness.

'By fire.' The abbot's whisper echoed in the void. 'Everything. All burned.'

'*Auto-da-fé*,' mumbled Cornelius.

'No. We sell the cars off at auction. Tell me, my son, the brother whom you seek, what is his name?'

'His name?' Cornelius paused. And then he said breezily, 'That hardly matters now. If the papers have all been burned.'

'But you said he was in danger. It would be best if you told me his name.'

'I think that it would not. If anyone comes asking, you can simply tell them what you just told me. These are evil people and if you knew the brother's name,

188

there is no telling what they might do to extract it from you.'

'Hold on.' The whisper had a tremulous quality to it now. 'A minute ago you would have told me his name. You would have put me in danger then.'

'Oh no. If you *had* allowed me to speak to the brother. And he *had* got the papers, and he *had* passed them on to me, then you could have told the evil people this fact. They would have gone off in pursuit of myself and no harm would have come to yourself or the monastery. I doubt whether they would even have troubled to set it ablaze.'

'Ablaze?' There was definite alarm now in the whisper.

'As they did with the town of Sheila na gigh. Perhaps you heard about that.'

'Burn down the monastery?'

'Much in the same way as you burned the papers. Assuming that there *were* any papers, of course. You would certainly have burned them, I suppose. Not perhaps put them in a vault somewhere. If, say, the brother in question had told you that they were of considerable importance and had been placed in his trust. I am only hypothesizing here, of course.'

'Of course.' There was a bit of a silence. Cornelius twiddled his thumbs in the darkness.

'I do think that I now recall certain papers,' whispered the abbot. 'But it is so long ago. Would they have been the work of some scholar?'

'They would indeed.'

'I dimly recall a name. The scholar's name. Prune, would it be?'

'Rune,' said Cornelius. 'Hugo Rune.'

'Hugo Rune. Yes, that was it. So long ago. So very long ago.'

In the darkness Cornelius Murphy had a very large grin on the go. 'Perhaps I might see these papers,' he suggested.

'Out of the question, I'm afraid.'

'But the monastery? The flames? The loss of innocent life?'

'I might speak to the brother on your behalf. If only I could remember his name. Which I cannot.'

'Tell me, Bud,' asked Cornelius, 'is it true that the sacred bones of Saint Sacco Benedetto are interred here at the monastery?'

'Whatever has that to do with anything?'

'Would they be in the vault? I still fear for the sacking of the monastery. That sacrilege might occur.'

'Happily the sacred bones are in Rome. Now if you will just refresh my memory as to the brother's name, I will speak to him. And if he wishes to speak to you, then I will grant my permission. How might you be reached?'

'I could just hover about in the gallery for convenience,' Cornelius suggested.

'No,' whispered the abbot. 'The gallery is a very dull place. You would grow bored with it in no time.'

'I could take a little nap.'

'Sleeping in the daytime is an unhealthy thing. You might find yourself sleep walking. Possibly you would wander to the vault and perhaps trip on the stairs. I would not wish to be responsible for any injury you might cause yourself.'

'Quite so.' Cornelius bit his lip. 'Perhaps I might wait outside the monastery.'

'I think that would be best. Now, let us hasten matters. The brother's name. What is it?'

'I think I'd better whisper it to you,' replied the Murphy. 'You never know who might be listening.'

'Wake up, Tuppe.' Cornelius gave his friend an urgent shake.

'Ooh! Ah! Get off there! Cornelius, hello.'

'Bad dream?' Cornelius asked. 'You were pulling at your heels.'

'Something's going on with me.' Tuppe rubbed at his eyes and sat up.

Cornelius scooped up the daddy's book from the front seat. 'I suppose you finished this before you dropped off to sleep.'

'Naturally. And a right load of old codswallop it is. How did you get on at the monastery? Couldn't get in, eh?' Tuppe made a smug little face. Cornelius ignored it.

'I got in all right. But I smell deep trouble.'

'You mean *deeper* trouble. What happened?'

Cornelius swung into the driving seat. 'I spoke with "the abbot". He inhabits a pitch-black room. I smelt fresh blood on the floor.'

'Oh dear,' said Tuppe.

'And this abbot thinks an *auto-da-fé* is a burning car and that Saint Sacco Benedetto was a person.'

'Oh dear, oh dear.'

'But all isn't quite lost yet. The phoney abbot may not know his *auto-da-fé* from his elbow, but he doesn't know the name of the monk who has the papers either.'

'And you didn't tell him, I'll bet.'

'I certainly did not. Although he really wanted to know.'

'So what did you tell him?'

'I gave him a false name to be going on with, while we plot what to do now.'

'You cunning dog, Cornelius.'

'Yes, I am, aren't I?' Cornelius made foolish collar

preenings. 'Tuppe. You'll really laugh when you hear the name I gave to the false abbot.'

'I will?'

'You will, go on have a guess.'

'I'm not really in a guessing sort of a mood at present.'

'Oh well, please yourself. I told him it was . . . wait for it . . . ta-raaa Brother Tuppe!'

'Brother *what*?' Tuppe fell back in alarm.

'Tuppe. Some hoot, eh?' Cornelius collapsed in laughter.

'That's not funny. Cornelius, that is anything *but* funny.'

'Oh come on.' Cornelius dug his small friend in the ribs with a jolly elbow. 'It is quite funny.'

'No it's not.' Tuppe flapped his hands about. 'Blood on the floor you said. Fake abbot you say. What's happened to the real one then? Eh? Eh?' Tuppe drew a finger across his throat in a horrific manner. 'And you tell this . . . this . . . whoever this is . . . that Brother *Tuppe* has the papers.'

'To throw him off the scent. What harm did it do?'

'What harm? What harm?' Cornelius had never seen Tuppe so animated. 'I told you I could get us into the monastery. I said let me do it. But no, in you go. Cornelius, you have really fouled up this time.'

'Why?' Cornelius was now in some confusion. 'Why?'

'Because,' said Tuppe, 'I could have got us into the monastery. Because my uncle is in that monastery. I was keeping it a secret. I wanted to impress you. To make you proud of me.'

'Your uncle?'

'My uncle. Brother Tuppe.'

15

All the shouting woke up Felix Henderson McMurdo.

He yawned. Stretched. Wondered where he was. Vaguely remembered. And stumbled from his bed to peer out of the window.

There was a right old fuss going on down in the courtyard. Monks were running all over the place, hitching up their habits and looking most distraught. Felix suddenly caught sight of a man in highland garb. He was waving a claymore. He was also shouting things such as: 'Where is he?' and 'Hand him over or else!'

Felix sank down beneath the window. He'd seen that man before. Where was it? Back at the police station, that was where. He was one of the Wild Warriors of West Lothian!

Felix began to chew on his knuckles. What could this mean? Clearly it could mean only one thing. There could be no other logical explanation. The Wild Warrior was looking for *him*. The townsfolk of Sheila na gigh had obviously gone completely insane. They had sent a mercenary, a hired killer, to track him down. This was no laughing matter.

'I shall have to get out of here,' said Felix. 'But how?'

And then, as chance would have it, he just happened to espy nothing less than a monk's habit (his very size) hanging on the back of the cell door.

'Now,' said Felix Henderson McMurdo. 'That's handy.'

'How was I supposed to know?' Cornelius threw his hands high. 'You should have told me.'

'We'll have to go down there at once.' Tuppe drummed his fists on the dashboard. 'Put the car in gear. We'll smash the door down.'

'That is somewhat drastic, don't you think?'

'Drastic? Who is down there, do *you* think? Eh, Cornelius? About to take it out of my uncle? Come on, take a little guess.'

'It's the Campbell,' said Cornelius in a low tone. 'Even though he was whispering, there was no mistaking that voice.'

'How come this Campbell is always one step ahead of you, Cornelius?'

The tall boy shrugged. 'I don't honestly know.'

'Put the car in gear, Mr Murphy.'

Mr Murphy put the car in gear.

Felix Henderson McMurdo pulled down his cowl to shelter his face, tucked his hands into their opposite sleeves and hurried along a corridor which would have been all the better for redecoration, or demolition.

He hadn't gone more than a few yards, before the sound of marching feet reached his ears. There was a door to the right and one to the left. Felix chose the one to the right, turned the handle and slipped quietly away. He pressed shut the door and pressed his ear to it. The marching marched up, marched past and marched off.

'Phew,' said Felix Henderson McMurdo. 'That was close.'

'What was close?' asked a voice.

Felix turned in horror to view the speaker. He was a very small speaker. A miniature monk. Felix recalled a toby jug his mum once kept on the mantelshelf. He recalled also how he'd broken it.

The monk stood upon a high stool. He had a large screwdriver in his hand and before him on a work table there was a lot of complicated electrical gubbinry. There was an awful lot of other gubbinry about the room. Stacked up on shelves. Piled into corners. It was all very broken-looking gubbinry.

'Are you the repair-man from Saint Greaves?' asked the tiny monk.

'Er, yes. That's right,' Felix replied. 'What needs fixing?'

The Cadillac rolled down the hill towards Saint Sacco Benedetto.

'Faster, faster,' cried Tuppe.

'No no no,' replied Murphy.

'Yes yes yes. We have to get inside.'

'I know we do. That's why I left the door on the latch when I came out.'

'It's a karaoke machine,' the small monk explained.

'It certainly is.' Felix approached the work table, rolling up his sleeves as he did so.

'I'm so glad you've come.' The small monk made a large and joyful face. 'Saint Greaves promised they'd send their best man over. You're him then, are you?'

'Well actually, no.' Felix rooted around on the work table.

The small monk's large and joyful face shrank away. 'Who are you then?'

'I'm a victim of circumstance.'

'Ah.' The small monk nodded thoughtfully. 'I'm one of those also.' He reached up to Felix and shook his hand. 'Hello anyway,' he sighed. 'I'm Brother Eight.'

'Wotcha,' said Felix. 'I'm Felix.'

'And I suppose you know nothing about karaoke machines.'

'On the contrary.' Felix twiddled his fingers over the bench-top confusion. 'I know all there is to know. Hand me your screwdriver.'

The car was parked out of sight and the epic twosome came forwards through the long grass, commando fashion.

'I don't really need to crawl.' Tuppe plucked a daisy from his teeth. 'I could simply walk and be about the same height.'

'There might be lookouts.' Cornelius put his hand in something nasty. 'Lookouts with guns.'

'I can crawl.' Tuppe continued to crawl. 'What's that funny smell?' he asked.

The abbot's study was no longer in darkness. The heavy curtains had been biblically rent asunder to reveal an enormous stained-glass window of bowel-moving vulgarity.

This depicted another saintly muscle boy. This one wore the standard wistful expression and regulation gossamer posing pouch. He was being torn between two stallions, which were in every detail anatomically correct. All about spectators looked on with appropriately glazed expressions, hands joined either in prayer or appreciation, it was hard to tell. One appeared to be reading a newspaper. Another fondled a penguin, which possibly had some masonic significance.

What light struggled through this travesty, lit upon a room of singular hideousness. In fact, so singularly hideous was it, that it will receive no mention here whatsoever.

At its centre sat a man of middle years. He was bound and gagged. His body was finely muscled. He wore nothing but a gossamer posing pouch.

The abbot, for it was he, glared daggers at the fellow seated upon his desk. The fellow who wore the abbot's own robes of office and who was even now lighting up one of his best post-Lent cigars.

The Campbell, for it was he, grinned evilly. A shaft of sunlight, entering by the formerly mentioned stained-glass posing pouch, haloed his baldy head.

'I won't keep you long,' spake the Campbell, puffing on the panatella. 'All I want is the papers.'

'Mmmmmph,' the abbot replied, struggling heroically and bringing areas of muscle definition into dramatic prominence.

'Sorry, I didn't quite catch that.' The Campbell leaned forward and tore off the abbot's gag.

'I said you're a fat-assed baldy-headed little toerag,' quoth the abbot.

Monks were being herded into the courtyard. There seemed to be a lot of confusion and Hamish was in the thick of it. He was demanding to know the whereabouts of a certain Brother Tuppe.

The monks, for their part, were trying to be helpful. They were saying things mostly to the effect of: 'Brother *who*?'

'I have this contract,' Brother Eight told Felix. 'It brings in a bit of revenue for the monastery. I used to be an electrical engineer, you see. So I can fix things. Well, some things. Small things. Sometimes. But this,' he pointed to the dismembered karaoke machine. 'This has me completely baffled. It was sent up from London. The note said that it had a small screw loose.'

Felix gazed about the floor. 'You seem to have rather a lot of small screws loose now,' he observed.

'They keep coming out.' Brother Eight twiddled at a dial. A small screw dropped out. 'There's another,' he sighed.

McMurdo gave his head a thoughtful nod. 'You have to defenestrate them,' he said.

'Come again?'

'Throw them all out of the window.'

'What? All of them? That can't be right, surely.'

'Oh yes. It's right all right. I read this book once. Trust me, I'll soon get this blighter going again.'

'Now now now.' The Campbell blew cigar smoke into the abbot's face. 'Let's have no rudeness from you. I need to talk to Brother Tuppe and I need to talk to him now.'

'What is *your* name?' the abbot enquired.

'Campbell,' said the Campbell.

'A Campbell.' The abbot flexed his pectorals. 'I might have known it. Sheep shaggers and well poisoners to a man. A pox on all—'

The Campbell kicked him from his chair. Leaped down from the desk and stood over him. He pulled out his pistol and glared down the long barrel. 'You are unwontedly outspoken for a bound man in a Spandex codpiece. How would you like it if I took my gun and . . .' He bent down and whispered specific details into the abbot's ear.

'Well,' said the abbot wistfully. 'I'm game if you are.'

Cornelius flattened himself against the monastery door in the generally approved manner. 'You cover me,' he told Tuppe. 'I'm going in.'

'Cover you? With what?'

'I think this valve is supposed to go somewhere.' Brother Eight looked all forlorn. 'But I've never seen a layout like this before. I'm beginning to wonder if it's some kind of practical joke. The karaoke machine seems to be full of rubbish. Old tennis balls with nails sticking in them, drinking straws, and look at this.' He pointed to a clockwork mouse in a tiny treadmill. 'I don't see how any of this could work at all.'

'I do,' smiled Felix. Who actually did.

Hamish had his pistol out and he waved it in the air as he marched up and down before the line of captured monks in the courtyard.

The monks watched him at it. Beneath their habits each was a potential *Chippendale*.

Hamish ceased his marching and waggled his pistol at the nearest monk. 'How many of you should there be?' he demanded to know.

Brother Five grinned at the gunman. 'Twenty-three,' said he.

'And how many are here?' Hamish wasn't much of a numbers man when he ran out of fingers.

Brother Five did countings up. 'Twenty-one,' he announced.

'Then there's,' Hamish set about the subtraction, 'two missing.'

'I'm not missing.' Brother Two raised a hand upon a finely muscled arm. 'I'm here.'

'What?' Hamish hastened in his direction. 'What did you say?'

'I'm Two,' said Two.

'Don't get funny with me, laddie.' Hamish made a menacing expression.

'No, no.' Brother Five rose to Brother Two's defence. 'Two is quite correct.'

'Two, yes, two.' Hamish glared.

'Yes, Two. It's Six that's missing.'

'Six? What do you mean six? You said two.'

'And Eight,' added a muscular monk. 'Eight isn't here either.'

'Who said that?' Hamish swung around.

'Seven.' Brother Seven put up his hand.

'Seven? You just said eight.'

'Six and Eight,' said Brother Two and all the monks began to nod in agreement. Six and Eight it was.

'Six and eight. That makes ... that makes ...' Hamish worried at his fingers. 'That makes fifteen.'

'Fourteen,' Brother Two corrected him. '*Fourteen!*'

'Does somebody want me?' asked Brother Fourteen. 'You'll have to speak up if you do. I'm a bit deaf.'

'I don't think,' the Campbell straightened up from certain unmentionable acts, 'that I am quite getting my point across to you.'

'Oh you are, you are.'

'I want Brother Tuppe.'

'I don't see what he's got that I haven't.'

'Possibly a lifespan extending beyond the next five seconds.' The Campbell cocked his weapon and pressed the muzzle to the abbot's forehead. 'Listen,' he continued, 'while you were locked up in your cupboard ...'

'Which I quite liked . . .'

'Shut up! While you were locked up in your cupboard, you no doubt heard what Mr Murphy had to say. He was telling the truth when it came to the matter of pyrotechnics. I wouldn't think twice.'

The Campbell snapped his fingers and fire branched between them.

'How do you do that?' The abbot looked on in no small awe.

'Never you mind. Deliver Brother Tuppe to me immediately, or I will shoot you in the head and burn the monastery to the ground.'

'You wouldn't prefer to torture it out of me a bit more?'

'No I bloody well wouldn't.' The Campbell shook his baldy head. Strange nubbins and bumps now protruded from it and his face had become curiously elongated. 'It's Brother Tuppe or a quick end to you. That's about the size of it.'

The abbot mulled it over. 'Oh all right,' he said sulkily. 'Brother Tuppe is probably in his workshop. Up the stairs in the courtyard and first door on the left. But listen, if you want to come back later, we could crack a bottle of Beaujolais and . . .'

Up the stairs from the courtyard and beyond the first door on the left, Brother Eight watched Felix at work.

'Are you sure you know what you're doing?' he asked.

'Of course I do. I've realigned the transponders and the inductance coils. Cleaned the master cylinder and the circuit breakers in the forward manifold. The particle accelerator should be good for another thousand miles as long as no-one tries to push the electrostatic potential beyond the fifteen-million-volt ceiling. Oh, and I've given the clockwork mouse a bit of a wind. So all we need now is a new fuse in the plug.'

'Gosh,' said Brother Eight. 'You certainly know your karaoke machines, friend.'

'I know this one well enough,' said Felix. 'My dad built it.'

*   *   *

Cornelius crept along the nasty gallery towards the abbot's study. Tuppe crept along behind Cornelius.

'This is a very horrid gallery,' Tuppe peered up at the paintings. 'Why is it that so many martyrs get martyred in their underwear?' he wondered.

'I wish I had a stout stick about my person.' Cornelius crept on.

'Pssst.'

'What do you mean, pssst?'

'I don't mean anything,' Tuppe replied. 'Because I never said it.'

The Campbell struggled to open the hinged portion of the abbot's stained-glass window.

'You have to waggle its bottom about.' The abbot waggled his. 'It always jams.'

The Campbell stepped back from the window. Raised his pistol and did the world of ecclesiastical art a big, big favour.

Stained glass rained into the courtyard.

A bitter argument of a numerological nature ceased and all eyes turned to the breaker of the sacred panes.

'Hamish!' screamed the Campbell. 'Up the stairs. First door on the left.'

'Who?' Hamish asked.

'First door on the left?' Brother Two thought about it. 'Ah,' said he. 'That's where Eight will be.'

'If there's eight of them dug in there, I want back-up,' snarled Hamish.

'What do you mean, your dad built it?' Brother Eight watched as Felix skilfully replaced the faceplate of the karaoke machine.

'Thirty years ago, almost to the day.' Felix scooped up a few small screws and secured the faceplate. He cast those left over over his left shoulder. Which was easier to do than to say. 'Long before I was born, of course. But I've still got all his plans. Here, have a look at this.' He spat on to his finger and applied it to a grimey little plaque on the base of the machine. Bringing up a name.

Brother Eight squinted. 'The Singalonga McMurdo,' he read. 'Pat Pending. Who was Pat Pending then? Your dad's partner?'

Felix wondered whether that was supposed to be funny. 'Were you any good as an electrical engineer?' he asked.

'Not really.' Brother Eight hung his tiny head. 'I'm colour-blind, you see. I was all right with the stripey wires. But the other two, well . . .'

Felix grimaced. 'Yes, I can imagine. Anyway, my dad built this machine. It was the prototype. I can't imagine how it ended up here though. I always thought it must have been destroyed in the explosion.'

'Please!' Brother Eight covered his ears. 'Not *that* word.'

'Sorry. You had one or two of those yourself then?'

'And then some. That's why I became a monk. But I'd rather not talk about it, if you don't mind.'

Felix didn't mind. 'It was his shed,' he said.

'His shed?'

'Where, you know, that word, happened. Mum had got him to build the shed as far away from the house as possible. Things occasionally went wrong with his inventions.'

'How wrong?' Brother Eight wondered whether he really wanted to know.

'The newspaper men blew it up out of all proportion.'

'The newspaper men blew up his shed?'

'No. It was the reactor in the spaceship that blew up the shed.'

'Spaceship? What spaceship?'

'The one he was building so that Scotland would be the first country to put a man on the moon. The Scots are always the first to invent everything. Renowned the world over for it. It's a tradition, or an old charter, or something. The Scots invented television and the hovercraft and the steam engine. The first man to reach the South Pole was a Scot.'

'*Scott*,' said Brother Eight. '*Scott*.'

'That's what I said.'

'No, you said . . . no never mind. Just let me get this straight. Your dad built a nuclear reactor in his shed to power a spaceship—'

'To put a Scotsman on the moon, yes. Surely you remember the "space race"?'

'Yes, but that was between Russia and America.'

Felix shook his head. 'Not a bit of it. It was between my dad and Mr Patel who runs the corner shop.'

'Mr Patel? Who runs the corner shop?'

'Oh, do you know him then?'

'No.' Brother Eight was becoming more than a little confused. 'I've never heard of him before.'

'You'd like him.' Felix gave the top of the karaoke machine a dust over with his sleeve. 'Very nice chap.'

'And he was building a spaceship also?'

'Yes, I told you. So you can understand why my dad wanted to get his to the moon first.'

'Well, I, er, yes . . .'

'Dad was a *Rangers* supporter to his dying day.'

'Eh?'

'*Rangers*. You know. Mr Patel is a *Celtic* fan.'

'*I* said pssst.'

'He said pssst.' Tuppe clung to the tall boy's knee. 'Pssst, that's what he said.'

'Who is saying pssst?' Cornelius asked.

'Over here.' A puff of cigarette smoke issued from behind an irregularly spaced column.

'Number Six, it's you.'

'Number Six?' Tuppe looked up at Cornelius.

Cornelius looked down at Tuppe, 'Don't say it,' he said.

'Over here, papal nunciat Murphy. Something terrible is going on.'

'Papal nunciat?'

'Silence, Tuppe. He's one of the good guys.'

'Tuppe?' Brother Six peeped around the column. 'Is that Brother Tuppe?'

'It's his nephew.' Cornelius made the introductions. 'Brother Six, meet *Cardinal* Tuppe. Fellow of the Holy See. He's come to supervise things.'

Brother Six curtseyed. 'Pleased to meet you, Your Eminence.'

'Bless you, my son.' Tuppe made a peace sign. 'Now what's this I hear about a spot of bother?'

'Terrorists. I've seen their pictures in the paper. The Wild Warriors of West Lothian.'

Cornelius and Tuppe shared first prize in the dismal-face competition.

Brother Six went on. 'One's holding the abbot captive. I peeped in. It's your uncle they're after, Eminence. I heard them talking. Then a gun went off. I took cover.'

'Very wise, my son.' Tuppe inclined his head. 'Where do you keep your stout sticks?'

'Down in the armoury,' the brother replied. 'With all the serious weaponry.'

'I'm sorry.' Brother Eight scratched his tonsure (it was a St Michael's, close crop with a chevron razored out at the back in the form of stylized Y-fronts). 'I don't seem to be able to follow any of this.'

'Allow me to explain.' Felix slotted a new fuse into the plug, screwed back its cover and pressed it into a wall socket. 'My dad was a follower of a certain Hugo Rune. Scientific genius, Rune was. Reinvented the ocarina. Hated Bud Abbott. He taught Einstein everything he knew.'

'Bud Abbott taught Einstein?'

'Rune! Rune taught Einstein.'

'Oh!'

'Except Einstein got everything wrong. He thought the universe was a really complicated place.'

'And isn't it?'

'Nope.' Felix shook his head. 'Not according to Rune. Rune said that people just try to make out it's complicated to prove how clever they are. Have you ever had the back off a transistor radio?'

'Of course. I was an electrical engineer.'

'But do you understand how it actually works?'

'Not entirely.'

'That's because it doesn't. Not in the way people think it does. Not really.'

'I see.' Brother Eight was beginning to regret that he'd never had a lock fitted.

'Ever heard of the crystal set?' Felix went on.

'Is all this going to take very long? I heard footsteps in the corridor. I think there's someone at the door.'

'Rune invented the crystal set to win a bet with Marconi. Another Scot, you notice.'

'Marconi? A Scot?'

'McOni. That's how it's really spelt. McOni was obsessed with big valves and coils and stuff. Rune said it was all just dressing. He bet McOni that *he* could knock up a working wireless set with nothing more than contents of the nearest waste-paper basket.'

'Which just happened to contain a cat's whisker, a piece of crystal and . . .'

'Oh, you've heard the story? Well you know the outcome then. Rune certainly left that famous Scotsman with egg on his old grey beard.'

'Funny how you don't see a lot of crystal sets around today.'

'But you do. Except now they're called transistor radios. Allow me to explain.'

'Look. Just explain about the nuclear reactor. The one that . . . you know.' Eight mimed a mushroom cloud.

'I was coming to that. Cold fusion. Rune made it work. It can power anything, spaceship, you name it. All you need is a couple of tennis balls, a few nails, some drinking straws, a clockwork mouse and a little treadmill. Well, I'm all finished here. Let's switch her on and see what happens.'

Felix reached towards the switch.

Tuppe, Cornelius and Brother Six stood before a large shining steel door. Brother Six tapped out the combination on one of those digital panel sort of arrangements that strongrooms and vaults always seem to have. Each little number had its own separate note. The sequence Brother Six tapped out played 'Now is the hour'.

The door swished aside and Brother Six led the way in.

Cornelius stopped short in the doorway. Tuppe stopped shorter.

'Guns!' Cornelius gasped.

'Guns,' Brother Six agreed. 'All standard Vatican issue. Every monastery is kitted out. Always has been. We're only lightweight tactical here. The Jesuits hold the nuclear stockpile. But you'd know all about that, of course.'

'Of course.' Cornelius held his amazement in check.

'They're all in mint condition. We do "naming of parts" every Monday. Anything in particular take your fancy?'

Cornelius perused the hoard. 'Ozi 9mm. Forty-five longslide with a lazer sight. EX-34 chain gun. Five point five six M249 Squad Automatic. Pump-action Winchester.'

'You sure know your weapons, buddy. Which do you want to take?'

'All,' said Cornelius Murphy.

'Any Derringers?' Tuppe asked.

The explosion tore off the workroom door.

Shards of manky wood burst *into* the workroom.

Felix and Brother Eight gaped, white-faced in horror, as the grenade smoke slowly cleared to reveal Hamish and Sawney.

They were both carrying guns.

Hamish stepped forward and brandished his. 'Brother Tuppe?' he demanded. 'Which one of you is Brother Tuppe?'

Felix hastily concealed his face beneath his cowl. 'That's me,' he said, cunningly. 'I'm Brother Tuppe.'

Cornelius slung bullet belts over his high shoulders and snapped a clip of shells into an AK-47.

Tuppe regarded the performance with some bewilderment. 'What ever do you think you're doing?' he enquired.

'Saving the day, of course.'

'Cornelius, you don't know how to handle weapons like these. You don't know how to handle any weapons.'

'There has to be a first time for everything.' Cornelius fed cartridges to the 45 longslide and tucked it into his belt.

'Leave it to Number Six here. If he's trained and everything.'

'My job.'

'My job? This isn't funny any more.'

'Phase plasma rifle in a forty-watt range,' said Brother Six. 'These are new in. They really get the job done.' He pushed a shell the size of a baked-bean can into the breach, slammed it shut and handed the outlandish demi-cannon to Cornelius.

'Oh get real please.' Tuppe began to jump up and down.

'Let's go.' Cornelius cocked the phase plasma rifle.

'We're all gonna die.'

The tall boy turned to his lesser chum. 'Listen,' he said. 'I am going to save your uncle, if it's not already too late. If you don't feel up to it, I quite understand. You can wait down here until it's all over.'

'What?' Tuppe shook his head with vigour. 'And give you the opportunity to say *"I'll be back"*? No chance. Where are those Derringers?'

Felix had been marched from the workroom. Booted down the stairs. Dragged across the courtyard. Manhandled along the gallery. And slung through the narrow doorway into the abbot's study. Now he lay in a heap on the floor. Bruised and bemused.

Some mysterious sixth sense told him that he had possibly chosen the wrong brother to impersonate. I wonder where all this is leading? he wondered.

The Campbell suddenly snatched up Felix. Lifted him high into the air and flung him down into the abbot's vacant chair.

Felix kept his face covered as best he could.

'Brother Tuppe.' The Campbell bopped Felix on the head with his pistol. 'We meet at last.'

'Ouch,' said Felix.

'The papers. I want them and I want them now.'

The mysterious sixth sense informed Felix that to answer, 'What papers?' would probably be to court another bop on the head.

'Yes,' said Felix. 'The papers. Yes indeed.'

'Well then?'

Well then and then some, thought Felix. 'You couldn't be a little more specific, I suppose? I have so many papers.' He flinched in expectation, but curiously the blow didn't come.

'The Hugo Rune papers.' The Campbell's voice came close at his ear.

'Ah,' said Felix brightly. 'Then I can help you there.'

'Excellent. Excellent.' The Campbell gave the abbot a perfunctory kick. 'Hear that?'

Felix peeped down at the abbot. And who is this bondage freak in the gossamer posing pouch? he wondered.

The abbot peered up at Felix. And who is this strange monk sitting in my chair? he wondered.

Brother Six led the way up from the armoury. He now sported Los Angeles police-issue body armour and travelled, like John Wesley Harding, 'with a gun in every hand'.

Behind him and somewhat overburdened in the hardware department, Cornelius yomped unsteadily.

Two steps down from Cornelius, Tuppe followed on. He felt a certain concern for the way his friend tottered from side to side.

And behind Tuppe came his enigmatic shadow. It

bumped noiselessly up the stairs, but it squirmed and writhed in a manner which was not pleasing to gaze upon.

'Now,' said the Campbell, sucking upon his cigar and blowing smoke up at a ceiling which vaulted downwards rather than up. 'The papers.'

'The papers,' said Felix. 'Yes.'

'Where are they?'

'In the suitcase,' said Felix helpfully.

'Which is where?'

'On top of the wardrobe.'

'And where is the wardrobe?'

'At my mum's house.'

'*And where is your bloody mum's house?*'

The mysterious sixth sense warned Felix that it might be well to answer this question with extreme precision.

'Twenty-three Ragnarok Terrace, Sheila na gigh,' he blurted out.

'*Sheila na gigh? Sheila na bloody gigh?*'

Felix shielded his head as best he could. 'It's true. All the plans and stuff. My dad's stuff. Please don't hit me again.'

'*Sheila na bloody gigh!*' The Campbell was ranting around the room. He kicked the abbot's desk. He kicked the abbot's bookshelves. He kicked the abbot for good measure. Finally he turned upon Felix. 'Right, you.' He hauled the cowering McMurdo from the abbot's chair. 'You're coming with me. Hamish!'

Hamish, who had been quietly picking his nose in a corner, stiffened to attention. 'Yes, sir?'

'Hamish, go out to the courtyard and tell Angus he can stop holding the monks hostage.'

'Yes, sir.'

'Tell him to shoot them all instead.'

'Hang about,' said the abbot.

'Shut up, you.' The Campbell aimed a mighty kick. 'Then, Hamish, you and Angus can feel free to burn down the monastery.'

'Oh thanks,' said Hamish, 'I will enjoy that.'

'Where's Sawney?'

'I'm here.'

'Oh so you are. Sawney, you go out the front and put a couple of rounds through Cornelius Murphy. We won't be needing him any more.'

Hamish and Sawney squeezed through the abbot's narrow yellow doorway and out into the gallery. Here they became cleanly cut and colourful images in the high-tech macroscopic 40-watt laser sight of Murphy's phase plasma rifle.

'Would you put your hands up please?' Cornelius asked from the shadow of an irregularly spaced column.

'Who said that?' Hamish cocked his pistol.

'*Drop your weapons. You are surrounded.*' Even without the benefit of the thermos flask, Tuppe's police-chief-through-loudhailer voice was still very convincing.

'Who said *that*?' Sawney pulled out his pistol and cocked it in a likewise fashion.

'Tell them again,' whispered Cornelius.

'*Come out with your hands held high,*' went Tuppe.

'No I won't.' Hamish fired his gun at the hidden policeman. The small fellow ducked even closer to the floor, as a bullet whistled by, ricocheted off the column and struck one of the great paintings. St Sebastian took it like a man.

Hamish glanced up at the punctured posing pouch. 'Gotcha,' he chuckled.

'C-C-Cornelius. That maniac just shot at me.'

'That does it.' Cornelius flipped the cover from the firing button. 'Stay behind the column and leave this to me.'

'Your job. Yes indeed.'

'Throw down your weapons,' Cornelius shouted. 'This is your final warning.'

The two Wild Warriors blew raspberries and waggled their bums about.

'All right then, you asked for it.' Cornelius stepped boldly from the shadow. A single shaft of sunlight caught him to heroic perfection as he angled up the mighty gun and squeezed the trigger.

A gout of blue flame roared from the barrel. The recoil from the demi-cannon threw Cornelius from his feet. The discharge vaporized a three-foot circle of wall above the abbot's little yellow doorway.

Within the study a bookcase exploded hurling blistered tomes of an antique nature down upon Felix, the abbot and the Campbell.

'What the . . . ? Oh damn!' The Campbell hopped about amidst the smoke and chaos. Queer guttural sounds rose from his throat and his already distorted head began to bulge and pulse. Weird tendrils sprouted from his eyebrows and thrashed violently.

Burning books smashed into the curtains setting them ablaze.

The abbot rolled around trying to break free. Felix assumed the foetal position.

'Blimey.' The two Wild Warriors in the gallery gawped at the smoking hole. 'What kind of gun is that?' Hamish asked.

'Get up. Get up.' Tuppe tugged at Cornelius. 'You've definitely got them worried.'

'I think my shoulder's broken.'

Brother Six, who had been keeping something of a

low profile, stamped out his cigarette. 'Shall I have a pop at them?' he asked, reaching down for the demi-cannon.

'I can manage thank you.' Cornelius struggled to his feet. 'Stick up your hands!' he shouted. 'Where did they go?' he asked.

Tuppe squinted along the gallery. It was rapidly filling with smoke. 'I think they're hiding. The cowardy custards.'

'Come out now, or I'll . . .' Cornelius mimed a gun thrust and trigger squeeze. It was a hair trigger, very sensitive. As blue flame gouted again, Cornelius toppled back into Brother Six.

There was a further explosion. More brickwork reduced to its sub-atomic components.

'We're all gonna die.' Tuppe crossed himself.

'Not a bit of it. We have superior firepower. Help me up please.'

Tuppe helped him up.

'I'm winded here,' Brother Six complained.

A strange and eldritch Campbell tore down the blazing curtains and stamped out the flames.

'What is going on here?' he fumed. 'Who did that?'

From his earliest years Felix had learned that it was always prudent to respond to the latter question with the words 'it wasn't me'.

'It wasn't me,' he whimpered.

'I know it wasn't *you*.' The Campbell caught the cowering Felix by the scruff of the habit and dragged him to his feet. The cowl fell away and the two found themselves staring face to face.

'*You!*' The Campbell stepped back in amazement. '*You*, I know *you*!'

'Blurgh!' went Felix, recoiling in no small horror. 'You've got tentacles growing out of your bonce.'

In the courtyard, monks were flexing their hidden talents and muttering amongst themselves. What were those bangs? they wanted to know. And what about all this smoke?

Angus, for his part, averred passivity and aloof detachment. Stressing the inadvisability of positive involvement and the potentially insalubrious consequences appertaining thereto.

'Stay out of it or I shoot you dead,' was the way he put it.

Cornelius marched forward, big gun at the ready. Brother Six was close behind Cornelius and Tuppe was quite close behind Brother Six. And he did have his Derringer out. Not that he had any intention of using it, of course.

Hamish still had a bit of fight left in him. He fired his gun again.

So Cornelius fired his.

Two of the irregularly spaced columns supporting the floor above came down. And then a lot of poorly plastered ceiling.

Up in his workroom Brother Eight said, 'Oh my goodness,' as the floor sank beneath him. He clung to his stool with one hand whilst clawing at the work table with the other. And his clawing fingers just happened to draw down the on switch of The Singalonga McMurdo.

'Mmmmmmmmmmmmmmmmmmmmmmmmmmm,' went the karaoke machine, warming up.

'Ohnooooooooooooooooooooooooooo,' went Brother Eight, going down.

The Campbell rose above the terrified Felix. All semblance of humanity had dropped away from the erstwhile Wild Warrior.

Extraordinary metamorphoses were on the go.

The Campbell's eyes expanded. Became spherical. Became two small globes of the Earth which began to revolve in different directions.

The Campbell's nostrils spread. Became twin tunnels. A tiny blue train issued from the left one, went 'too-too' and vanished into the right.

The Campbell's mouth grew wide. A paper-thin tongue unrolled. It had a feather on the end. The feather tickled McMurdo's nose. A concealed hooter went, 'Paaarp'.

Terror became entrancement. Felix stared in wonder.

The tentacles, thrashing from the eyebrow areas of whatever this was, wound themselves together into a tight cone. Became a little silver hat. A pink pom-pom appeared upon the top.

The Campbell held up what might have been his right hand. It appeared now to be a bunch of bananas. He held it towards Felix. From the palm, the skin extruded an ectoplasmic foam. This congealed into a slim disc. The disc became a paper plate.

The plate wavered. On to it a pastry base materialized. Within this base substances bubbled and frothed. Became an amalgam of eggs, milk, sugar, cornflour, salt, natural flavouring, stabilizer (E415) and anti-caking agent (E341).

Became custard.

The Campbell held the custard pie at arm's length. Drew it back and then smacked Felix right in the face with it.

'Ohnoooooooooooooooooooooooooooo!' Brother Eight continued.

'Agggggggggggggggggggggggggggggh!' went Hamish and Sawney as a goodly amount of lath and plaster, wormy floorboards, brickdust and rubble descended upon them. With this came an added bonus of broken pop-up toasters, transistor radios, kitchen blenders, bedside teasmade machines (whatever happened to them, eh?), half a million small screws and one small monk.

'Gotcha!' cried Cornelius, invisibly in the dust.

'Mmmmmmmmmmmmmmmmmmmmmmmmmm,' went the karaoke machine upstairs, growing nice and hot.

It was all too much for Angus. He was a man of action. Being lumbered with standing out here in the courtyard holding a gun on a lot of boring monks wasn't his scene at all. He swung his pistol in the direction of the latest brouhaha.

Seizing the opportunity, three muscular monks brought him down and sat upon him.

Cornelius coughed and gagged. He shook dust from his hair. Swatted laths from his shoulders. Flung aside the demi-cannon. Pulled the forty-five longslide from his belt. Cocked it dramatically and kicked fallen debris aside.

'Dig them out and arrest them,' he told Brother Six. 'Tuppe, where are you? Are you all right?'

'I think so,' answered two identical voices.

'Clever.' Cornelius nodded appreciatively. 'Even better than the police-chief-through-loudhailer. Okey doke, let's go.'

Cornelius put his foot to the abbot's narrow yellow door. Kicked it open and leapt into the room with the gun in both hands, shouting, 'Don't anybody move!'

'Gracious,' he continued, drawing to a halt.

Although smoke still wreathed the devastated study, the sunlight, streaming through the ruins of the stained-glass window, illuminated a scene which was not altogether without interest.

Especially for the aspiring student of fine art, encapsulating, as it did, three textbook examples of separate and contradictory schools, juxtaposed in a manner which said 'now discuss'.

Cornelius viewed the abbot with an uncensorious eye. Savouring the sensitive chiaroscuro which the mottled sunlight played upon the smoothly muscled torso of the reclining nude. Reminiscent of the now legendary Michelangelo da Caravaggio at his most tenderly exquisite.

Contrasted to this, there was Felix Henderson McMurdo.

He stood, utterly motionless, clad in his monkish attire. The custard pie still firmly in place across his laughing gear.

One for all lovers of surrealism here and no mistake.

Cornelius thought to discern the influence of Max Ernst and Salvador Dali, along with the rollicking heretical humour of Clovis Trouille.

The third piece of work was not to the Murphy's taste at all.

It was one of those pretentious disposable affairs, wrought, apparently, from foodstuffs now well past their sell-by dates. Composed into a gross parody of the human form. A mildewed melon for the head and the leftovers from the Portobello Road fruit market making up the rest.

A slight breeze brought its taint to the nose of Cornelius Murphy. Causing him to clutch at his nostrils and ruefully conclude that its creator had obviously done a great deal too much acid back in the sixties.

'Blurgh!' went Cornelius.

'Don't just stand there going blurgh, young man,'

said the Caravaggio, suddenly rolling in his direction. 'Shoot it!'

'Waaaaaaaaaaaaaaaaaaaaaaaaaaaah!' went the pretentious disposable affair, taking life in an alarming fashion. It split into its component parts and these flew at Cornelius. A torrent of mouldy fruit, stale pies and pasties, festering cheese, maggot-ridden vegetables and general horridness swept across the study.

Cornelius ducked beneath it, too startled to let fly with his gun. The festering foodstuffs hurtled over his head and swung through the narrow doorway.

'Don't let it escape,' cried the struggling abbot. 'Get after it. Shoot it. Shoot it.'

Cornelius leapt to his feet. Flung himself through the doorway. Tripped straight over Tuppe and fell flat on his face.

He would recall, once he regained consciousness, that the last thing he glimpsed was a stream of soupy non-consumables flowing down the gallery to vanish through the open monastery door. And the last thing he heard was the distinctive three-chord riffing of Status Quo, blasting down through the hole in the gallery ceiling, singing something about thirty-five happy years together.

16

Those fates that decree what is going to happen and to whom, had evidently been applying themselves with such vigour to Cornelius Murphy, that they had quite forgotten all about his father.

Murphy Senior had been sitting outside his garden shed for the better part of this particular day and nothing out of the ordinary had happened to him.

'I can't understand this,' said the daddy. 'I was quite certain that the fates had something up their collective sleeve for me today. But it seems I was mistaken.'

'That looks about the size of it,' said Charlie, the daddy's close friend. 'Though I had a sort of a feeling myself.'

'You can't always trust a hunch and there's a fact for you.' The daddy sighed a heartfelt sigh and scratched in the dust with his dibber.

'Some days are just plain dull.' The voice came from an old watering-can, known to the daddy as Boris.

The daddy yawned and scratched his tweedy trouser legs. 'Nice day though.'

The watering-can kept its own counsel. Charlie the trowel said, 'Perhaps something will happen.'

But nothing did.

As it was now approaching 7 p.m. and beginning to turn cold, the daddy gathered up his pals and put them back on their shelves in the shed. 'I'll see you boys tomorrow,' he said.

During the night that followed, certain persons surreptitiously prised the padlock from the daddy's shed door, gained unlawful entry and tampered with his doings. The model town was vandalized.

The watering-can, of which he was so proud, received second-degree denting and several of his best trowels were spirited away. Including Charlie.

With the coming of a troubled dawn, the full horror of the previous night's happenings became manifest.

The daddy was quite disheartened by the sight of the up-turned hoe and the displaced shears. In fact he was taken somewhat poorly, which was the cause of no small concern to his wife, considering his normally robust constitution. She had to rush into the house and bring him out a chair.

'Would you like a cup of tea?' she asked. 'I think there's still some left in the pot from last night.'

'My trowels,' moaned the daddy. 'My *Rygo and Westerley* brass-tipped, cedar-handled trenching trowels. Gone and never called me mother.'

'Typical of trowels, that is.' Mrs Murphy folded her arms under her prosthetic bosoms. 'Off without a word of goodbye. Not that they ever had much to say for themselves. Very uncommunicative.'

The daddy offered her a cold fish eye.

'No thanks, dear, I've just put one out.'

'Eh?' said the daddy.

'Tools,' his wife went on. 'Few of them there are that will answer to their names. And fewer that can solve even the most rudimentary algebraic problems. The humble dibber, for example, rarely knows more than the most basic form of communication. Namely, that of mime.'

'Eh?' said the daddy, again.

'However,' his wife went on, again, 'I once observed a pair of secateurs perform the final act of Gilbert and Sullivan's *HMS Pinafore,* without music, or vocal rendition, to the appreciation of an entire shed full of implements.'

'Have you been sniffing glue again, woman?'

'Certainly not. I was just trying to cheer you up.'

'Well don't bother. I will weather out this particular storm by myself.'

'Stuff you then.' His wife departed, taking the kitchen chair with her.

The daddy viewed his dishevelled shed. 'What a mess,' he muttered. 'Who ever could have done such a thing?'

'It was that Harry Thompson from the Borough Planning Committee,' said a five-pound bag of fertiliser.

'Councillor Winthrop was with him,' an eighteen-inch garden sieve added helpfully.

Inside the house Mrs Murphy poured herself a cup of cold tea. 'I shall have to have my husband taken away,' she said. 'Any man who talks to his tools is clearly mad. But any man who talks to them and gets an answer could well be dangerous.'

'You'll need a doctor's note,' said the teapot.

'Doctor Jameson down at the clinic is always good for one of them,' the coal-scuttle added.

Cornelius Murphy awoke with a bit of a headache. He was all tucked up in the abbot's bed, although he wasn't to know this yet, as he hadn't opened his eyes.

'Are you feeling better now?'

Cornelius blinked, focused and rapidly shut. 'Not

altogether good. I appear to have . . .' he squinted at the pair of Tuppes, '. . . double vision.'

'He'll be as right as rain,' said Brother The Uncle Eight.

'The stuff of epics.' His nephew grinned. 'He'll be fine.'

'And double hearing.' Cornelius groaned.

The abbot, now restored to dignity, dabbed the Murphy's forehead with a cold sponge. 'You are the hero of the hour,' he told Cornelius. 'You risked your life to save the monastery.'

The tall boy smiled up at the abbot. 'I hope I didn't cause too much damage.'

'Have no worries on that score.'

'Good,' said Cornelius. 'I won't then.'

'No, of course not. Brother Six has told me all about your mission here and the cash you've brought. The damage can be paid for out of that. It shouldn't be more than twenty thousand or so.'

Cornelius groaned once more.

'So tell me,' the abbot went on, 'about the soft drugs and the satellite television? When can we get started on that? And what's the Pope really like, by the way? Is it true he has his own gymnasium? Have you ever seen him working out?'

Cornelius groaned once more, once more.

The abbot collapsed in a fit of irreverent laughter.

'Eh?' went Cornelius.

'I'm sorry,' the abbot dabbed at his eyes. 'You should have seen your face. A picture.'

'Eh?'

'Don't worry. The young Tuppe here has told me everything. Why you are here. With whom you wish to speak. So, when you feel up to it, I will introduce you to Brother Rizla.'

Cornelius Murphy grinned from ear to ear. 'Now that would be just the job.' He paused and sniffed the air.

The abbot saw his expression change. 'What is it?' he asked. 'What do you smell?'

'Bacon,' said Cornelius Murphy.

The abbot and the Two of Tuppes left the tall boy to wash and dress. Cornelius was more than pleased to find that his clothes had been laundered and his shoes shined.

He took his breakfast with the abbot in an ill-lit refectory.

The tiny windows were set so high in the bulging walls that they scarcely offered any illumination whatsoever. Thus, large pewter candelabra stood upon each dining table, weeping wax into everyone's meals.

While the Murphy filled his face with food, his ears were filled by the abbot's speculations regarding the enigmatic Mr Campbell.

'A demonic agency,' the abbot assured Cornelius. 'Captured me. Locked me in my cupboard. Stole my robes. And finally, I saw it change before my very eyes. Then, whoosh, straight out of the door. You saw that yourself.'

'I certainly did.' Cornelius pushed a fried mushroom to the side of his plate. The image of that mouldy fruit and veg parading out through the abbot's door was going to haunt him for a good long time.

'That would be Satan's work right enough.' The abbot swigged herb tea.

'Satan?'

'He of the cloven hoof, no other. Something of an occupational hazard in this profession. I shall have to atone. I will get one of the brothers to give me a sound birching. Come to think of it, I'll get all the brothers to give me a sound birching. Better to be safe than sorry. Don't you agree?'

'Far better.' Cornelius pushed his skinless sausage to the side of the plate. This Campbell was clearly something less than human. But a Satanic agency? That took a lot of coming to terms with. Of course, there had been the matter of the toy Cadillac. Some kind of voodoo was certainly involved there. But real demons? A man that could turn into a carton of festering fruit? Worrying stuff. Whatever was in Rune's papers had to be pretty important if Satan himself was after it. *Satan himself?*

Cornelius toyed nervously with his prunes. They had been wrapped in sliced bacon and served upon individual portions of toast. And very toothsome they looked too. But Cornelius felt no longer hungry. He pushed his plate aside.

The abbot took it and swept its contents on to his plate. 'Devils on Horseback,' he said. 'My favourite.'

Whilst the abbot ate mightily, Cornelius sipped his herb tea and settled down to listen, as the abbot told him, between mouthfuls, of all the comings and goings Cornelius had missed.

Angus, Hamish and Sawney had been rounded up and were currently under lock and key in the monastery dungeon. The abbot had decided that it would be best for their souls if they indulged in a little community service. He planned to have them repair all the damage. Under heavily armed supervision, of course.

There was also the matter of the vanishing hitch-hiker. Originally discovered wandering in a confused state, by brothers Ten and Twelve, who were returning in the staff van from a Status Quo Anniversary Gig. This strange fellow had apparently risen from his bed of delirium, donned a habit, then magically mended the karaoke machine Brother Eight had been labouring away at for weeks. Then he had nobly impersonated Brother Eight to protect him from the Wild Warriors. He had undergone torment at the hands of the Satanic Campbell, and received the metaphysical pie in the face. And then, during all the confusion that followed, he had slipped silently away, never to be seen again.

All about the monastery monks were a muttering about the hitcher's possible identity. Scriptural verses of the 'I was a stranger and you took me in' variety were being quoted. The word was out that Saint Sacco's had received a 'visitation'. That the mystery man was none other than Our Lord himself.

And what with the Miracle of The Mended Machine, there seemed good grounds to support the theory. Added to this, brothers Ten and Twelve, lifting the sheet from the hitchhiker's sick bed, on the off chance that any Turin Shroud-style laundry-soiling may have occurred, happened upon nothing more nor less than . . .

Two free tickets for the Status Quo Anniversary Gig in Tierra del Fuego. And if *that* wasn't a gift from the Lord . . . well.

The abbot was weighing up the pros and cons of all this, before he took the very large step of writing to Rome and putting in for a pay rise.

'But now,' said the abbot, 'I am sure that you are anxious to meet Brother Rizla. Shall I lead the way?'

Tuppe and his uncle were seated on the floor outside the refectory, discussing the sad decline in the popularity of the Porcine Circus and how tall young women were getting nowadays.

They both rose as the abbot appeared with Cornelius. Not that it made any significant difference, height wise. But it was polite.

'Brother Eight,' the abbot smiled down upon that body. 'I was just telling Mr Murphy here about the karaoke machine. He would very much like to speak to you about it. But for now I am taking him down to meet the Secret Brother. So perhaps you should stop the small talk and bugger off back to your work-room. Get some work done, eh?'

'Yes, Holy Father. Yes indeed.' Brother Eight bowed. Not that it made any significant difference, height wise. But just to be polite.

'This way then,' said the abbot.

The abbot led Cornelius and Tuppe through a maze of corridors and down many flights of steps. Tuppe stepped very warily.

Cornelius asked the abbot, 'Why is Rizla referred to as the Secret Brother?'

'Brother Rizla suffers from a terrible affliction which makes it impossible to join in the everyday life of the monastery.'

Tuppe made a troubled face. 'Terrible affliction? Would that be as in hideously disfigured or highly contagious?'

'No,' the abbot smiled wanly. 'Nothing like that. You will understand when you meet him. His cell is just along here. Follow me.'

They turned the corner into yet another corridor. Cornelius eyed it with amazement. There seemed to be no perspective.

'Distracting, isn't it? The far end of the corridor is

six times larger than this. Doors, everything. Watch.'

He strode forward. The effect was striking. The abbot appeared to shrink.

'I'm not going down there.' Tuppe shook his head fiercely. 'I shall vanish for certain.'

'Come on, Tuppe.' Cornelius followed the abbot. Tuppe followed Cornelius.

The abbot stopped before a door some thirty feet in height. Into this a six-foot door had been cut and fitted. And into this, a little peephole. The abbot put his fingers to his lips and urged Cornelius to take a peep through it.

Cornelius did so and a startled cry rose from his lips.

Beyond the peephole lay a large and brightly lit room. It was sparsely furnished. There were many books. At the centre of the room stood a writing desk. At it sat a monk.

There was nothing particularly remarkable about him. He was tall, thin, whitely bearded and late in years. It was the thing floating over his head which had given Cornelius cause for concern.

It was approximately twelve inches in diameter. Glowing brightly. It was a halo!

At the sound of Murphy's cry, the old monk looked up. The halo vanished, to be replaced by a large, free-floating, red question mark.

Cornelius drew back from the peephole and gaped at the abbot.

'Brother Rizla,' the abbot told him, 'suffers from a unique condition. We don't know the actual name of it, so we have tentatively given it one of our own. We came up with Bloke-what-has-all-them-little-lines-and-stuff-coming-out-of-his-bonce-like-what-they-do-in-cartoon-strips Syndrome.

'*This* I have to see,' said Tuppe.

The abbot knocked.

'Come,' called Brother Rizla.

The abbot swung open the door within a door and entered the big room. Tuppe and Cornelius followed.

And Tuppe saw the big red question mark.

'Good Gawd!' went he.

Brother Rizla's face clouded and tiny daggers sped from his eyes toward the small blasphemer.

'Oh no!' Tuppe took shelter behind Cornelius.

'Brother Rizla,' the abbot nodded to the tall old monk, 'I am sorry to trouble you at your devotions, but an urgent matter has arisen.'

The daggers were gone. The question mark swam once more above the brother's head. 'How might I help you?'

'This is Mr Cornelius Murphy and his companion Tuppe.'

Tuppe peeped out and made a brave face. 'Sorry,' said he.

'No, I am sorry.' The old monk smiled serenely. The halo was back.

'Brother Rizla, Mr Murphy here saved the monastery from destruction. A Satanic agency entered the cloister. It sought something. Something that you may have in your possession.'

'Ah.' Brother Rizla ran his rosary through his long slim fingers. 'So it has come to that. I knew that one day it must.'

'You have some papers, sir. Papers which once belonged to Hugo Rune.'

'*Rune!*' As Cornelius spoke the name a small dark thundercloud materialized above Brother Rizla.

Cornelius pointed to it. 'Is this his doing?'

'Not his directly. But he was ultimately responsible.

229

If I had not gone with him. Gazed in *there* . . .' Red letters spelt the word GLOOM across the thundercloud.

'Would it trouble you greatly to speak of it?' Cornelius asked.

'No. Not any longer. But firstly you must tell me, why do you wish to see Rune's papers?'

'In order to have them published.'

'*Published!*' Several exclamation marks appeared. The monk shook his head. 'They will never be published.'

'I intend to see that they will.'

'And who might you be to do such a thing?'

'He is Cornelius Murphy and he is the stuff of epics,' said Tuppe. 'If anyone can do it, he can.'

Brother Rizla stared into the air above the Murphy's head.

Cornelius turned up his eyes. He could see only hair. 'What are you looking at?'

The old monk stroked his beard. 'Interesting. Very interesting. Your small friend appears to be telling the truth.'

'What are you doing? You're doing something.' Cornelius felt suddenly very uncomfortable.

'He's reading your thought bubble,' the abbot explained. 'We all have them, all the time. Except when we're sleeping, then all we have is little rows of Zeds. Of course, they are generally invisible to the naked eye. Brother Rizla is probably the only man on Earth who can see them.'

'What a gift.'

'Not a gift, Mr Murphy. A curse.' The monk gazed down at Tuppe, who was now feeling the air above his head. 'All in good time,' said he.

'I never said anything.'

'No, but you were thinking it. *"Grab the papers,*

Cornelius, and let's get out of this loonie bin." That's what your little bubble had written in it. Loony is spelt with a "y", by the way.'

Cornelius spoke up. 'If our thoughts are made plain to you, you will know that we speak the truth. Might I see the papers?'

'As I told your friend, all in good time. I will give you the papers. But there is much we must speak of first.'

'Then I'll take my leave for now,' spake the abbot. 'I have a pressing matter which must be taken in hand.'

'So I see.' Brother Rizla smiled broadly. 'Such atonement. You won't be able to ride your bike for a week.'

'Quite so.' The abbot blushed. 'Then farewell, Brother Rizla. And I will speak to you later, gentlemen.'

'Farewell, Holy Father. And don't forget to turn the other cheek.'

'Goodbye and thanks,' said Cornelius.

'Be lucky,' said Tuppe.

The abbot left in haste, closing the door behind him.

Tuppe looked at Cornelius.

Cornelius looked at Tuppe.

And both gazed up at the air above their respective heads.

Brother Rizla laughed. 'You don't know what to think. If you would prefer it, I shall stand in the inglenook with my head up the chimney.'

'No please. We have nothing to hide.'

'As you will then.' Brother Rizla fanned out his long fingers on his desk. 'I have Rune's papers. Some, but not all. And I do not have the ocarina.'

'The ocarina?' Cornelius asked.

'The reinvented ocarina. When you have read the papers, you will understand why they can never be published. Also why you will need the ocarina.'

'Tell me about Hugo Rune. You knew him for many years, did you not?'

'Many years. I was his acolyte. His Boswell. His amanuensis. I travelled the world with him. Never was there such a man as Rune. Such a thinker. Such a genius. Such a hater of Bud Abbott.'

'But he was a nutter, surely?' Tuppe put in. 'I flicked through his book. Hedgehogs falling out of the sky. Biros with minds of their own. Small screws breeding inside pop-up toasters.'

Brother Rizla smiled again. 'You don't believe a word.'

Tuppe shook his head.

'Yet you believe other things. You believe that the Earth revolves around the Sun, for instance.'

'That's because it does,' Tuppe protested.

'But who would have believed you if you'd said that five hundred years ago? Copernicus was given a pretty rough ride by the Inquisition. Would you have been prepared then to back him up?'

'Well . . .' went Tuppe.

'Probably *not* is my guess. But now we accept the Copernican system as a scientific fact. But there are no ultimate facts. What is believed to be a fact is only a fact until another fact supersedes it. Science is only a fashion. Nothing more.'

'But some of Rune's facts are pretty fanciful,' said Cornelius.

'You have read them. Can you actually prove them wrong?'

Cornelius scratched his chin. 'Not as such.'

'How many primary colours are there?' the old monk asked.

Cornelius thought about it. 'As I recall, the *psychological primaries* number six. Red, yellow, blue, green, black and white. Any colour can be regarded as formed from a mixture of two or more of these.'

'He knows all kinds of stuff like that,' said Tuppe. 'You should try him on tonsures.'

'I am sure your friend is a mine of esoteric information. He is wrong about the primary colours though. There are in fact nine. Rune discovered the other three.'

'Now that is nonsense,' said Cornelius.

'Indeed?' Rizla rooted in the lap pocket of his habit and pulled out a crumpled piece of paper. He presented it to Cornelius.

The tall boy stared at it. The paper had been printed with a colour. It was a reddy yellowy bluey greeny blackish sort of white. Except that it was not. It was an entirely new colour.

Cornelius found his eyes beginning to water. He pinched at them.

'You can't look at it for more than a moment.' Rizla plucked the paper from the Murphy's fingers. 'The other two are much worse. One of them makes you break out in hives. The other will put you in a coma. Care to see?' Rizla offered the slip to the doubting Tuppe.

The small fellow turned his face away. 'No thank you.'

'Did you know that pigs can see the wind?' asked Brother Rizla.

'Actually I did,' Tuppe replied.

'And that on Christmas Day all sheep bow three times to the east in reverence to their ancestors who attended the birth of Christ?'

'Pigs I know all about. Not sheep.'

Cornelius began to feel that a lot of valuable time was perhaps being wasted. 'Why can't Rune's papers be published?' he asked.

'Because *they* would never allow it.'

'*They?*' Tuppe made a patronising face. 'This would no doubt be the *they* who suppressed Rune's work throughout his lifetime. The dreaded greybeards of the scientific fraternity.'

'No. This is another *they* entirely. And you look very foolish with the word SMUG printed across your forehead.'

'Who are they?' Cornelius demanded. 'You know. Tell us.'

The old monk sighed. 'All right. They are beings of an order halfway between man and the angels. Another race. They have always been here. Hugo Rune discovered them. They ruined him for it.'

'Is Hugo Rune really dead?' The eyes of Cornelius Murphy focused above the old monk's head. 'He isn't, is he?'

Brother Rizla fell back in his chair. Extraordinary little lights fizzed and popped around him. 'Rune died in Hastings. In a cheap boarding-house. I have the death certificate.'

'He never died. I have spoken with him. Where is he?'

'No. This interview is ended. I have told you enough. You may take the papers. Read them and you will understand. Seek out the rest. Find the ocarina.'

Cornelius watched the pyrotechnic display die down. The ancient ex-acolyte reached into the drawer of his desk and took out a green leather volume. 'These are his papers. I had them bound together in chronological order. Take them and go.'

Cornelius accepted the volume and hugged it to his chest.

'If I can solve this, perhaps you might be cured of your affliction.'

'It cannot be solved. All is lost to me now. I am cursed for my folly. I stepped inside. I saw them. Rune never returned. I came back alone and this is what I became.'

'I'll solve it,' said Cornelius.

'He will,' Tuppe agreed. 'Trust him, he'll solve it. Whatever it is. What is it, by the way, Cornelius?'

The tall boy managed a wink and a reasonably sized grin. 'I think I know. I think I've always known. You'll have your cure, Brother Rizla. Keep watching the sky.'

The old monk gazed back at him. 'You have a huge lightbulb flashing above your head,' he observed.

17

Many years ago I conducted an interesting scientific experiment in the company of my dear friend, Mr H. G. Wells. The nature of this was to prove once and for all the real shape and size of the planet Earth.

Had I realized then that my experiment would come to change the face of twentieth-century art, I would surely never have begun it.

Wells, as most will be aware, was a man of erudite learning and great scientific knowledge. He was also, and this is not perhaps so generally known, a master of disguise, who lived a complicated double life. Writing, as he did, not only under his own name, but also that of Sir Arthur Conan Doyle. A fictitious personality, invented by Wells as a prank early in his student years.

Wells passed from Oxford with a doctorate in English Literature. His thesis was *The Life and Works of Sir Arthur Conan Doyle*. Ho ho!

I first met Herbert Wells, or Herbie as he preferred to be called, at a Masonic Luncheon, held at the Savoy, to honour me on the occasion of my first successful three-way Channel swim in 1929. I shared the high table with both he and 'Sir Arthur' and how well I remember the great amount of toing and froing about the gentlemen's toilets. And how they were never actually seen together.

My suspicions became aroused during the prunes and custard when Herbie returned from the gents, where 'Sir

Arthur' had gone in search of him, wearing the latter's now legendary straw boater.

I quizzed him on the matter later on in the privacy of my private suite and he broke down and confessed everything.

What had begun as a high-spirited jape, he explained, had turned into a living hell. His two wives were beginning to suspect something and the burden of work was intolerable.

I swore to keep his secret, but imposed one condition.

One year later Sir Arthur Conan Doyle plunged to his death over the Reichenbach Falls.

His obituary in *The Times* was written by H.G. Wells.

Looking at their photographs today, with the obvious trick spectacles and false moustaches, it is hard to imagine how Wells succeeded with his deception for so long. But those were the days before television and few people ever met authors in the flesh.

I once asked Herbie why he chose to run the terrible risk of exposure by attending my honorary do in both personae. He replied that his two wives had pressured him into it. Both ladies being understandably anxious to make the acquaintance of the fêted three-way Channel swimmer, who was at that time being lionized throughout Europe.

Our scientific experiment began one evening in 1931. Herbie had coerced me into adding the considerable weight of my celebrity to a charity darts match he had got up with some chums to raise money for a worthy cause. I later discovered this to be the erection of a statue of Sir Arthur Conan Doyle on the vacant plinth in Trafalgar Square. The very plinth the late King had reserved for me!

The match itself was an informal affair, a group of aspiring young writers and some arty types from the local polytechnic. We naturally split the teams up into writers versus artists.

Our team, as far as I can remember, consisted of

Wells, myself, Ernie Hemingway, George Orwell and the ever-youthful 'Boy' Betjeman. Our worthy opponents being Max Ernst, Salvador Dali, Man Ray, René Magritte and their guest celeb', the greatest artistic genius of the day, Hieronymus Tucker, who was at this time preparing for his first London exhibition.

The writers won the match with very little trouble. The opposing team choosing either to throw fish instead of darts, or simply to stand around with paper bags on their heads for art.

Those were the days, my friends!

It was during the post-match festivities that Herbie chanced to remark that ale always tasted better from a straight glass than a beer mug. Boy added that this was also the way with tea. Which was infinitely finer when sipped from a Sèvres bone-china cup than a chipped enamel workman's mug. And in no time at all, as we'd all had a few, the talk turned towards the cosmology and metaphysics of shape.

Herbie was soon propounding his theories about the universe in general and the shape of the planet in particular.

'And what shape do you believe this to be?' I asked him.

'Oh, spherical, of course,' he laughed, spraying me with half-munched potato crisps.

'And about what size?'

He named a figure. I forget what it was. But it was the one which is still in use today.

'A fashionable notion,' I told him. 'But wildly incorrect.'

'You have some other theory then?' He laughed again, but this time I had covered my drink in readiness. 'You are perhaps going to tell us that the world is flat.'

Dali, who was hovering nearby (I never did find out how he did that), suggested that the world was the shape of a giraffe.

'Take a little water with it, Dali,' said Wells.

'The world is not flat,' said I. 'For if it were there would be no horizon. The world is indeed spherical. But it is somewhat larger than you or your greybeard cronies think it to be.'

'Oh yes? Oh yes?' Wells whacked down his empty glass.

'Do you have about your person a world map?' I asked.

'Of course.' Wells produced his *Collins Sportsman's Pocket Diary* and flashed it around the table. In those days the *Pocket Sportsman's* was considered *de rigueur*. This progenitor of the Filofax contained not only photographs of Stanley Matthews and Bobby Charlton, the lighting-up times, high tides at Tower Bridge, the line of the British Monarchy, national holidays throughout the Empire, the precise number of bushels in a peck and when to celebrate the feast of the circumcision of St Paul, but also a traditionally out-of-register two-page map of the world.

I examined the map. 'And is this the world as you perceive it?'

'You know that it is.'

'And this also?' I displayed a small tin-plate globe of the world which had fallen into my pocket as I walked through Woolworth's that very morning.

'It's your *round*, I think,' spluttered Wells, giggling foolishly.

I ignored his feeble jest. 'Would you say that the map in your diary is approximately to the same scale as this toy globe?'

'As near as dammit,' said a huffy Herbie.

'Then while I get the drinks in, you try and fold your map around my globe. I bet you a guinea piece that you cannot do it convincingly.'

'Elementary, my dear Rune,' said the creator of Sherlock Holmes, collapsing once more into drunken paroxysms.

I took my time at the bar and watched Wells with great amusement. He and Dali had detatched the map from the diary and were labouring in vain to fold it around the globe. There was a good deal of paper crumpling and no shortage of advice. In no time most of our company had become noisily and argumentatively engaged in the project.

Hemingway suggested that success could be achieved by simply chopping off the north and south poles where most of the surplus paper seemed to be, on the principle of 'who would miss them?' Dali had now become convinced that the world was quite probably the shape of a doughnut.

I left them to it for a while. But when the voices became too overly raised and Hemingway head-butted George Orwell and called him a 'know-nothing lout', I felt that I should intervene.

'How are we doing?' I asked, returning to the table with a tray of drinks. 'Who ordered the packet of bird seed by the way?'

'Me,' said Max Ernst.

'You'll have to make do with pork scratchings, I'm afraid. Now, how is the map fitting coming along?'

'Wells has muffed it up,' seemed to be the general opinion.

'And who is responsible for all those little snippings in the ashtray?' René Magritte tucked away his Swiss Army knife.

'Would you like me to explain?'

Heads nodded gloomily. Herbie said, 'Go on then.'

'It is an evil business,' I said in a low and leaden tone. 'And a conspiracy of epic proportion. Neither the globe, nor the map, offer a true representation of the world's geography or its true size. The flat map will not fit the globe, because there is, quite simply, too much map. In order to make the map fit you must increase the size of the globe by at least one third again. I contend that the world is a good deal larger than we are being told. And that there are portions of it which are not printed upon the map. Portions that are hidden from us.'

'Oh come off it,' sighed Wells. 'The world is charted. There are no spare bits.'

'Charted yes. But the charts lie. Do we have any world travellers with us tonight?'

Hemingway stuck up his hand. 'I've been around a bit,' he boasted. 'And then some.'

'And on your travels, have you found maps to be reliable, distance wise?'

Hemingway shook his beard. 'Anything but.'

'And in our own fair land. Boy Betjeman, you favour a country bike ride. Speak to us of the English signpost.'

'The signpost does tend towards modesty when it comes to the matter of miles,' said Boy. 'Although I understand this to be tradition, or an old charter, or something.'

'Or something. And what say you all regarding this?' I pulled a London A–Z Street Directory from my pocket and placed it on the table.

'Er . . . ah . . . hm,' went the assembled company.

'I am sure that each of you has at some time attempted to navigate across the metropolis with the aid of this.'

Heads went nod nod nod.

'With any success?'

'Not much,' Wells conceded. 'In fact I threw mine away a long time ago and always travel by—'

'Taxi?'

'Indeed.'

'Indeed. In fact I'll wager we all came here tonight by cab.'

All heads nodded except for Dali's. The word giraffe was again upon his lips.

'Then ponder this. You take a cab from home. The cab takes a certain route. Covers a certain distance in a certain time, you are charged a certain fare. Later the same night you engage another cab to take you home. This time you find yourself travelling by a route which is utterly strange to you. The journey takes half the time, yet the fare is almost double.'

'Yeah, well, but—' went Wells.

'But me no yeah-well-buts and kindly put a sock in it until I've finished.'

Wells hung his head.

'What you have here is a conspiracy. It exists in every great city. It is a conspiracy of cab drivers to keep their customers always confused about their exact whereabouts. So that they can never get their bearings. They do this to conceal the huge areas of uncharted metropolis from the public. These areas are disguised by intricate one-way systems, pedestrian precincts, no-through roads and diversions. These are the areas which never appear on any map.

'Let me reveal to you a closely guarded secret. Before a London black cab driver can officially don his sacred blue cap and receive his mystical number, he must first take something which is called THE KNOWLEDGE.

'This is a rigorous test of his courage, stamina, endurance and dedication. He must debase himself by riding around London for months on end, mounted upon a moped with a wooden board fastened before his eyes, memorizing the name of every London street. Few survive. Those who do then sit before a Secret Council of Elders. If they are deemed worthy, they receive THE KNOWLEDGE and are formally initiated into the Black Order. London's Legion Of Cab Knights. BOLLOCKS for short. THE KNOWLEDGE is a secret so terrible that they are sworn upon pain of terrible death never to reveal it. They are told what lurks within the concealed areas and why no man must ever enter them. And they learn the true meaning of the A–Z.

'A–Z, gentlemen, means Allocated Zones. The zones allocated for mortal man to inhabit.'

I gazed from face to shocked face. Gauging the effect of my words. It has always been the way with me, that when I speak, others crave to listen.

All of a sudden George Orwell burst out laughing.

He could never keep a straight face for long and was always the first to see the funny side of any situation.

'Hugo,' he howled, 'you outrageous liar. You really had us going that time.'

The genius Tucker cast Orwell a disparaging glance before turning back to me. 'Mr Rune,' said he, for we had not been formally introduced, 'these hidden areas of land . . .'

'The Forbidden Zones.'

'These Forbidden Zones yes. What lies within them?'

'Some dark and brooding force,' I told him. 'Perhaps some ancient intelligence which is not of man. The old maps labelled such areas with the words 'and here be dragons'. I believe the Forbidden Zones contain strange beasts and stranger people, who sometimes spill across the borders and enter our world. Who has not heard reports of curious flying machines, out-of-place animals, abominable snowmen, ghosts, fairies and bogey men? And what of all those people who vanish without trace every year? Could they have wandered unawares into a Forbidden Zone?'

Tucker's jaw hung open. George was giving me a very stern look. And it was then that I remembered he had once earned a living as a London taxi driver.

'Enough,' said I. 'A joke and nothing more. I hear the barman calling last orders and I believe it is George's round.'

George got them in and we made merry. But all was not well with Tucker. I had aroused in the genius a terrible curiosity. And I wish for all the world that I had not.

I did my best to cheer him up and he eventually came around and joined in the singing.

We left the bar that night somewhat legless and made

our separate ways homeward, promising to meet up the following week at a café where George was working.

But the meal we took there was a joyless affair. My worst fears were founded. Tucker had vanished from the face of the earth.

Max told us that the genius had refused to share a cab home with him on the night of the darts match. Determined to cross London on foot, in a straight line.

An eye witness later reported to a newspaper that he had seen a young man of Tucker's description, arguing with the driver of a black cab. But this witness did not come forward to the police.

What actually became of the genius may never be known. Only that he was lost for ever to this world. I left for a polar expedition on the day following our sad meal and did not return to London for over a year.

When I did so it was to learn of a further tragedy.

Apparently a mysterious fire had broken out in Tucker's studio and destroyed all the work that was destined for his first major exhibition. The police suspected arson, several empty Spanish brandy bottles being found amongst the rubble. But nothing could be proved.

The exhibition, however, had gone ahead. But it had displayed work credited to Tucker's assistant. A shadey and untalented individual of foreign extraction, whom Tucker kept on out of the goodness of his heart.

The exhibition had been the hit of the year. And when I availed myself of a catalogue it was obvious to see why.

The paintings were all the ones from Tucker's studio. The work he referred to as his 'Blue Period'.

It is not for me to name the scoundrel who erased Tucker's signature from the pictures and substituted his own. The greybeards of the artistic Establishment must do this. One wonders why, noting the obvious lack of quality in the scoundrel's later efforts, that they choose not to do so. Do I detect some kind of conspiracy at work?

To this day two things still haunt me. Firstly that I was responsible for the disappearance and probable death of the century's greatest artist. A disappearance which allowed a charlatan to hoodwink the world.

And secondly, that I forgot to ask Wells for the guinea piece he owed me.

Tuppe had been reading the passage aloud to Cornelius. But now he fell suddenly back upon the Cadillac's rear seat and cried in a piteous voice, 'Oh my God! They got Tucker!'

Cornelius offered the small man a stern face in the driving mirror. 'Put a sock in it,' he said.

'Well *really*.' Tuppe made a face back. 'As with the now legendary curate's egg. This takes a lot of swallowing.'

'Do we still have Victor Zenobia's papers?'

'They're in the rucksack. On the floor here.'

'Well have a root around in them. I seem to recall there being some letters, the mention of purchasing a London cab, maps and gunpowder. See if you can find them.'

Tuppe shrugged. Reached over to scoop up the rucksack and fell into it.

The Cadillac sped away towards the lands of the South.

Cornelius and Tuppe had bade their farewells an hour earlier to the monks of Saint Sacco Benedetto and were now bound upon what was possibly the final leg of their moderately, if not altogether, epic journey. They were bound, in fact, for the domicile of a certain Mr 'Jack London'.

Because, of course, on the rear seat, next to Tuppe, was a large packing case. And in this was a miraculously mended karaoke machine. And dangling from the packing case was a label, with Mr London's name and address in big black print.

Brother Eight had been profuse in his gratitude when Cornelius had offered to drop the machine off.

Cornelius had told the small monk to think nothing of it, because he was going that way anyhow. And indeed he probably would have been, had he troubled to examine the delivery note for the Cadillac Eldorado, which Tuppe had received from Mike the mechanic and stuffed into the glove compartment without a second glance.

For on this was also the self-same name and address!

Coincidence is a queer old business. But then without it where would a yarn like this, or any other, be?

A queer old business indeed, coincidence.

'I wonder what the folks back home are doing,' Cornelius wondered.

And at the exact moment of this wondering . . .

The front-door bell of twenty-three Moby Dick Terrace went *bing bong* and the mother rose from the sofa, teacup in hand, to answer it.

On the doorstep stood a personable young man. He wore a dove-grey, double-breasted suit. White shirt, black tie. His shoes were highly polished. So was his head. His eyeglasses lacked a lens.

'Good-morning,' smiled the Campbell, flourishing the brown envelope which Cornelius had left pinned to the pulpit in the auction room at Sheila na gigh. 'I assume that the beautiful young woman I am addressing must be the sister of Cornelius Murphy. This is the right address, isn't it? I have some money here for your brother. Has he returned home yet? I wonder if I might just step inside and wait for him? What a very charming housecoat, did you knit it yourself? Just through here, is it? Thank you.'

18

It's a fair old haul, from what might have been some-where in North Wales to somewhere else entirely in the London area. And an expensive one, if you happen to be driving a 1958 Cadillac Eldorado, which does about twelve miles to the gallon.

There are numerous routes you can take. And any one of them might well lead to adventure. In fact, on an epic journey, and with such a distance to travel, the possibilities are endless.

Tuppe consulted the map. 'Motorways all the motor-ing way,' he affirmed brightly. 'M54, M40, London.'

'Good,' Cornelius grinned. 'We don't need any further complications.'

'Exactly. I've got those letters from the rucksack. Shall I read them out to you?'

'Please do. The more we know about all this before we confront Mr London, the better.'

'Are you sitting comfortably?'

'I am.'

'Then I will begin.'

The Cadillac sped on down the middle lane of the M54.

Coming up behind, and evidently enjoying life in the fast lane, was an ancient black Volkswagen. It was all covered in spikes.

'*Mrs* Murphy?' The Campbell smiled sweetly. He was

now seated on the family sofa, sipping tea. It was cold, but he didn't seem to notice. 'You have a lovely home here, Mrs Murphy. But I see there's so much redevelopment going on in this area.'

'There was. But it's all stopped now.' The mother straightened a wandering bosom.

'It must be a worry to you. Being in such an isolated and dare I say vulnerable position here.'

'We get by. Would you care for a top up, Mr . . . ?'

'Kobold,' the Campbell replied. 'Arthur Kobold.'

'He's lying,' murmured the teapot. 'Don't trust him, Bridie.'

My dear Victor, (Tuppe read)
Regarding our most recent telecommunication.
I require the following items.
One black London taxi-cab (new and in mint
      condition).
One taxi driver's uniform (you know my size).
One miner's helmet (also my size, full working
      condition).
Two hundred yards of climbing rope.
Two hundred yards of slow fuse.
Ten cases of gunpowder.
One box of matches.
Spare no expense and purchase only the best.
I shall expect delivery first thing tomorrow.
Everything depends upon this.
Yours omnipotently,
H. Rune (perfect master).

'Is that it?' Cornelius asked.

Tuppe turned over the letter. 'There's something scribbled on the back. In Victor Zenobia's handwriting, I think.'

'Go on then.'

'It says, *"Up yours, fat boy!"*'

'A sentiment you no doubt share.'

'Well . . .' Tuppe shrugged. 'Blimey!' he continued. 'Look out, Cornelius!'

The spikey Volkswagen roared by at speed, slowed suddenly and swerved in front of the Cadillac. Cornelius dragged the steering wheel to the left and applied the brake. Spikes glanced across the chrome bumperwork, raising showers of sparks. The Cadillac screeched to a halt in the slow lane. The Volkswagen sped away.

'Don't stop here. This is a motorway. Put your foot down. Keep going.'

'That car tried to run us off the road.'

Tuppe's head appeared above the front seat. He glanced over his shoulder. 'Get a move on. There're three lanes full of lorries all coming this way.'

Cornelius tried to restart the car, which had, somewhat inconveniently, stalled. 'Bother,' said he.

The oncoming lorries made dramatic full-bore cruiseliner hootings.

'Get out! Push it on to the hard shoulder. Hurry up!'

'I can't do that. It's too heavy. Let me have another go at starting it.'

'No, Cornelius! Get out! Jump!'

Three lanes of lorries thundered forward, hooting mightily, but showing no sign of applying a little brake.

Tuppe climbed on to the tall boy's head and tugged at his hair.

'Jump, Cornelius!'

Cornelius turned his head, with Tuppe clinging to it. The wall of lorries rushed at him. He could see the faces of drivers and their hands flapping. 'Save yourself,

Tuppe.' Cornelius plucked the weeny man from his hair and hurled him towards a grassy knoll beyond the hard shoulder. 'Start, you bastard!' he told the car.

It didn't.

'Stuff you then.' Cornelius made for the last-minute leap. His left trouser cuff caught upon the brake pedal and held him fast.

The lorries were almost upon him. Cornelius fought to free himself.

'Help!' cried Cornelius Murphy. 'Somebody help!'

'Baaaaaaaaaaaaaaaaaaaaaaaaaaaaaaaaarp!' went the lorries. Slowing not one jot.

Tuppe struggled to his feet on the grassy knoll. 'Cornelius!' he screamed, as the lorries filled his vision.

'Baaaaaaaaaaaaaaaaaaaaaaaaaaaaaaaaarp!' went the lorries.

In the front room of number twenty-three Moby Dick Terrace, Mrs Murphy suddenly clutched at her heart and sank into an armchair.

'Ooh dear,' she went. 'Do excuse me, Mr Kobold. I've had a bit of a twinge.'

'Can I help you, dear lady?' The Campbell set aside his teacup.

'I'll be all right in a minute. Could you call my husband?'

'Your husband? Where is he?' The Campbell got to his feet.

'Out in the back yard. Ooh I do feel queer.'

'Leave it to me. I'll take care of everything.' The Campbell patted Mrs Murphy on the arm and left the front room. He closed the door gently upon her and slipped along the short corridor to the kitchen.

Certain household items watched him with suspicion, but said nothing.

251

*　　*　　*

'Baaaaaaaaaaaaaaaaaaaaaaaaaaaaaaaaaaaaaaarp!' Three
lanes of lorries continued on their way, as if the mashing
to pulp of a beautifully restored 1958 electric-blue
Cadillac Eldorado was absolutely nothing at all.

Tuppe watched the lorries recede into the distance,
still meeping their horns. He scrambled down from
the grassy knoll and stumbled to the now deserted
motorway.

The lorries were gone. And so was the Cadillac. No
trace of it remained. No mangled metal, shredded seat,
or crumpled chrome. There was not even the hint of a
broken body, automotive or human.

There was nothing.

Well, not altogether nothing.

There *was* something. But it was a something of very
curious aspect. And not the sort of something you see
every day. Leading to this something were skid marks.
Now, these you do see every day. Although rarely
so crisp and sharp and at such an exact right-angle
to the carriageway. It was the something into which
these skid marks vanished that was really worthy of
consideration.

This something was big and black and vaguely
coffin-shaped. It stood upon the hard shoulder like
a great three-dimensional shadow.

Tuppe approached it with trepidation. He shuffled
around it. He gave it a sniff. He dared a prodding
finger. He backed away, baffled and bewildered.
And finally he sat down on his bum and glared
at the thing. It was big and black and vaguely
coffin-shaped and it stood upon the hard shoulder
like a great three-dimensional shadow. And that was
really all you could say about it.

The weeny man put his elbows on his knees and

cupped his chin in his hands. His bottom lip began to quiver and a big tear welled up in his small right eye.

'Cornelius,' Tuppe began to blubber. 'Cornelius, where are you?'

'Mr Murphy? Where are you?' The Campbell pushed open the back door and perused the garden. Birdies twittered from the washing line. A retired tom-cat lazed upon the coal bunker dreaming of Gloria Swanson. Runner beans crept imperceptibly up the trellis. And in an upturned flowerpot on the top of a bamboo cane an earwig wondered what it was really all about.

'Mr Murphy,' called the Campbell.

Sounds issued from the daddy's shed. Singing. The Campbell cocked an ear. The final act from Gilbert and Sullivan's *HMS Pinafore*, surely?

'Mr Murphy,' called the Campbell. 'Helloee.'

The singing ceased and Murphy the elder stuck his head out of the shed window. 'Who's that?' he wanted to know.

'Mr Murphy.' The Campbell stepped into the garden, closing the back door behind him. 'I have some money here for your son.'

'Money?' The daddy's head vanished from the window. It reappeared in the company of his body at the shed door. 'Cornelius told me you might call by. He said I was to accept the money on his behalf.'

'Indeed?' The Campbell inched along the garden path. Beneath his feet the crazy paving shifted uneasily. And above his head the birdies ceased to twitter. The daddy sensed a sudden chill in the air.

The Campbell sidled past the coal bunker. In his feline dream, the retired tom shrank in horror as Gloria Swanson pulled a gelding knife from her swimsuit and sprang upon him.

'When exactly are you expecting your son back, Mr Murphy?'

The retired tom awoke with a shriek. The Campbell glanced around at it. 'Nice wee pussy,' he said, reaching a hand. The cat arched its back and hissed at him.

'We've a wrong'n here, right enough,' the wheelbarrow whispered.

The Campbell gave an easy shrug as the retired tom backed away.

'Now, Mr Murphy. Mr Murphy? Where have you gone?' The Campbell squinted about the garden. The daddy was nowhere to be seen. The shed door was now firmly shut.

'Mr Murphy, where are you?'

'Cornelius, where are you?' Tuppe blubbered at the roadside.

'I'm in here.' The daddy called through the keyhole. 'I'm very busy for now. Kindly leave the money on the coal bunker. I'll pass it on to my son.'

'I think not.' The Campbell approached the shed. The birdies winged it off to perches new. The runner beans took a turn for the worse. 'Mr Murphy, please come out.'

'Sorry. Too busy. My shed is in disarray. I have clearing up to do.'

'Now!' The Campbell stamped a foot. The earwig in the flowerpot had a heart attack. 'At once!'

'Sorry. Goodbye.'

'Mr Murphy, I really must insist.'

'Oh well, if you really must insist, then I suppose I have no choice.' The shed door swung open and the daddy emerged, large, red-faced and tweedily suited. He now wore an ARP helmet on his hairless head and carried a stick of the stout variety. 'Get off my land,' he said.

The Campbell eyed both stick and helmet. His piggy peepers narrowed. Sunlight glinted on the single lens of his spectacles. He raised his left hand. 'Thus and so,' said the Campbell.

Skin extruded. The paper plate grew. The metaphysical pie took form.

And the daddy watched it do so.

'Well?' asked the Campbell.

'Well what?' The daddy studied the smiting end of his stout stick.

'Well, *this*, of course.' The Campbell made menace with the pie.

'Oh that.' The daddy shrugged.

'What do you mean, *oh that*? I have just conjured forth this pie and all you have to say is, *oh that*?'

'Well, it's not a very big pie, is it?'

'*Not very big?*' The Campbell was appalled. 'But I con—'

'Conjured forth. Yes I heard you. Somewhat archaic expression and hardly accurate. Listen, if conjuring forth is your *métier*, you want to get yourself a wand. Or a stick. Get a stout one. Like mine.'

The Campbell growled a horrible growl. Drew back his hand and hurled his pie at the daddy.

Murphy the elder gripped his stick in both hands and swung it cricket-bat fashion. He struck the hurtling pie a mighty blow and sent it sailing over the roof of the house. The Campbell turned to watch it go. His mouth fell open.

'Six!' cried the daddy. 'A lovely piece of batting there from the England captain. Straight over the pavilion roof.'

'Well done, that man,' went the wheelbarrow.

The Campbell turned upon the daddy. He wasn't smiling. 'You really shouldn't have done that,' he snarled.

'I'm afraid I really must ask you to leave now,' said the daddy. 'Or I will be forced to strike you on the head with my stick. Repeatedly, if needs be.' He raised the stick in question, that the Campbell might gauge its fighting weight.

But, impressive though this was, the Campbell stood his ground. He knotted his fists and the knuckles became deathly white. Veins rose and throbbed upon his forehead. And had Cornelius been present, he would no doubt have observed that they reproduced a scale map of the Mortlake sewerage system, with an accuracy which was little less than fearsome. 'I'll . . . I'll . . .' The Campbell's baldy head began to bob up and down. His stocky frame shook violently.

The daddy took a tightened hold on his stout stick. A passing sixth sense, which just chanced to be in the neighbourhood, informed him that something very unpleasant was about to occur.

'No!' shouted the Campbell, in a voice so loud that it rattled the chimney pots and quite put the fear of God into the otherwise atheistic watering-can. 'No. No. No.' The Campbell got a grip of himself and regained his composure, such as it was, in a quite astounding fashion. He straightened his spectacles upon his nose and adjusted the cuffs of his dove-grey jacket. 'Not now,' he whispered. 'Not now, I cannot spare myself on you. Perhaps later, when I have all that I require.'

'Excuse me?' went the daddy.

'Stuff you,' said the Campbell. He lifted his hands and flung them wide. *'Shazam!'*

'Pardon?'

'See you later.' The Campbell turned away. 'You just stay put.'

'Stay put? Now just you see here . . .' The daddy took a step forward and struck his head on an invisible barrier. 'Ow!' he went on.

The Campbell was making back to the house.

'Hold on! Wait!' The daddy put his hands to the unseeable barricade. The resistance was cold and glassy. Unyielding.

'Stop! Let me pass.' But the Campbell didn't hear him. The Campbell was entering number twenty-three Moby Dick Terrace. The Campbell closed the back door and the daddy was left all alone.

'He stitched you up like a kipper there,' said the hoe. 'You really should have seen that one coming.'

The daddy struck the invisible wall with his stout stick. It rang like a great church bell.

'Bother,' said the daddy. 'Cornelius, where are you?'

'I'm here,' called the voice of Cornelius Murphy,

'Cornelius? What? Where?' Tuppe jumped to his feet. And as he did so, he noticed something rather alarming. Here he was, on this bright August day. But . . .

'I don't have a shadow.' Tuppe turned in circles like a dog chasing its own tail. 'My shadow's gone. Where's it gone?' He danced about foolishly on the hard shoulder. But his shadow did not dance with him.

'Tuppe, help. I'm all in the dark here.'

'Cornelius, where are you?' Tuppe ceased his dervish impersonations. 'You sound miles away.'

'In here.'

'In where?' It was a very silly question really. Because it was surely obvious where Cornelius was.

'You're in there.' Tuppe gaped at the big black

coffin-shaped blot on the landscape. 'Come out.'

The words were scarcely spoken before the deed was done. The big dark coffinish thing began to dissolve. Trailers, as of greasy black liquid, slid from it. Became twisted streaks of moving darkness, which rolled like mercury. Then swept with a sudden lemming-like dash at Tuppe.

'Ooh help, no . . .' The small fellow leapt about as the blackness engulfed him. Then slipped like silk from his shoulders, dropped to the ground and congealed. Became once more his own little shadow. Tuppe stared down at it. 'Gosh,' said he.

Cornelius blinked at him from the front seat of the Cadillac Eldorado which had now emerged from the big black whatever it was.

The car was unscathed. The skid marks led directly to its tyres. Some mighty force had dragged the Cadillac from the path of the oncoming lorries. Had saved the bacon of Cornelius Murphy.

'Tuppe,' Cornelius rubbed his eyes, 'I don't know how you did that. But I know that you did. Thanks very much indeed.'

Tuppe smiled. 'Nice to see you back,' he replied. 'Give us a grin then . . .'

The telephone rang and Arthur Kobold answered it.

'Put down that cake, Kobold,' said the voice on the line.

Arthur Kobold put down the cake.

'What have you to report?'

'As I predicted, Cornelius Murphy went to the monastery. I am reliably informed that he now has certain of the papers in his possession.'

'And do you think he will bring these papers to you?'

'No, I do not. He will surely go straight on to

find the last man on my list. Once he has all the papers, then he will come to me.'

'What makes you so sure of that?'

'When he knows the truth, he will come here, to the one person he can trust.'

'All well and good in theory. But our number-one priority is the recapture of the deviant. He must stand trial for his crimes. If he remains at large in the outer world and discovers the whereabouts of the ocarina, we are all doomed.'

'Cornelius will lead him here. We will recapture him. Never fear.'

'That is good to know,' said the voice on the line. 'Because I have to inform you that you only have until eight o'clock this evening to achieve this.'

'Eight o'clock? But you said . . .'

'Eight this evening. The Train of Trismegistus stands ready in the station. The boiler is stoked. The deviant must be recaptured today.'

'Yes but . . .'

Slam! went the phone at the end of the line.

'Bugger,' said Arthur Kobold. 'Bugger the time and bugger the train and bugger the deviant too.'

The deviant was washing his hands in the Murphys' kitchen sink.

He dried them upon a patchwork tea towel. Drew a glass of water from the tap and returned with it to the front parlour.

'How are you feeling now?' he asked the mother.

'Much better now, thank you. Everything seems to have righted itself.' She accepted the glass of water.

'I'm glad to hear you're feeling better.' The Campbell reseated himself on the family sofa. 'It pains me greatly to see a beautiful woman in distress.'

259

'Flatterer.' The mother sipped her water. It tasted dreadful. She put the glass aside. 'Where is my husband?'

'Out in his shed. Said he was too busy to bother with you.'

'Typical.' The mother smiled coyly at the Campbell. 'He's somewhat past his sell-by date, that one. But let's talk about you, Mr Kobold. Publishing must be an interesting business. Have you ever met Jeffrey Archer?'

The Campbell shook his head. 'His wife, Doris. I bumped into her once at a Young Farmers' do in Borchester. Fascinating woman, she used to do this act where she stood on her head and put a bottle of *Crème de Menthe* . . .' The Campbell leaned towards the mother and whispered gross details into her ear.

'Go on?' the mother nodded. 'A bottle of *Crème de Menthe*? I've seen it done with a skinned rabbit and a colostomy bag, of course.'

'Eh?' went the Campbell.

'And one time when I was in Tunisia I went to this bar where the castrati used to perform and there was this fellow who . . .'

'Cornelius, you are driving rather fast.' Tuppe clung to his seat.

'We have to get to London. If this Campbell, whatever he is, is always one step ahead of us, he could well be at Jack's place by now.'

'Nah.' Tuppe shook his head. 'I've been thinking. He can't know where we're going next.'

'He has done before.'

'But that's because we've let him. Listen to me. It must have been the Campbell who put the voodoo model under your seat, mustn't it?'

'I can't think who else it could have been.'

260

'And how did he know we'd be staying at the Holiday Inn?'

Cornelius shrugged.

'Because you let on to Mike the mechanic that we were going there. Just like you told him we were going to the monastery.'

'I did not.'

'You did too. Mike sold you the map. You asked directions.'

'And you think the Campbell followed us to Mike's?'

'And probably duffed him up. Mike spills the beans. The Campbell hoodoos the motor car and gets to the monastery first.'

'The evil sod.'

'Agreed. But we foiled him back at the monastery. He doesn't know Jack's address. We wouldn't have known it, if my uncle hadn't just happened to have been working on Jack's karaoke machine.'

'You're right.' Cornelius bounced up and down in the driving seat. 'The Campbell can't possibly know.'

'So slow down a bit, will you?'

'Of course.' Cornelius slowed down a bit.

'Thank you.' Tuppe lay back and watched the sky slide past. He felt reasonably certain that the Campbell didn't know Jack's address. But he felt equally sure that, by fair means or foul, he had probably gleaned that of Cornelius from the auctioneer in Sheila na gigh.

And so they travelled south. They passed through Birmingham. A city notable only, in Tuppe's opinion, for the excellence of its science fiction book shop, hit the M40 and headed on down.

The journey was without further incident, which might have been the product of happy chance, but was more likely something to do with urging on the plot.

And at a little after four-thirty of the sunny afternoon clock, they found themselves on the outskirts of Penge. Which as those in the know, know, is a very nice place, although Tuppe and Cornelius had never been there before.

Sunnyside Road was living up to its name. A row of pleasantly appointed 1930s villas, divided by well-tended hedges and sheltered beneath redly tiled roofs. Lawn sprinklers sprinkled, pigeons cooed. A small girl skipped. All was normality and reason.

At the end of the road, the Cadillac Eldorado stood out like a great sore electric-blue thumb.

'It's not what I expected,' said Cornelius Murphy. 'It's all so . . .'

'I think *safe* is the word you're looking for.'

'Which house do you think belongs to Jack?'

Tuppe turned up the label on the karaoke's crate. 'Number eleven, The Laurels. Drive on a bit.'

Cornelius drove on a bit and stopped outside number eleven.

It was just the same as all the rest. Lawn, flowers, a stone gnome or two. Peaceful, normal, *safe*.

'Are you feeling as uncomfortable as I am?' Tuppe asked.

Cornelius nodded. 'It's as if we're trespassing. We don't belong in a place like this.'

'Go and knock on the door. Let's get this over with.'

Cornelius flattened down his hair. Net curtains were twitching around and about. The small girl had taken her skipping-rope inside.

'All right. Let's get it done.' Cornelius climbed from the car. He closed the door quietly and picked up the crate from the back seat. He sniffed the air. It smelt wholesome. It smelt *safe*.

Cornelius Murphy approached The Laurels.

He opened the sun-ray gate. Walked up a short gravel path and stood before the front door. Its upper portion displayed a stained-glass representation of a laurel tree. Cornelius pressed the doorbell. Bing-bong, it went.

Cornelius waited. But no-one came. So he waited again. A ladybird tottered about the rim of a polished milk bottle which stood on the doorstep. Cornelius observed that it had five spots on its back and that these formed the configuration of Cassiopeia.

Cornelius pressed the doorbell again. Bing-bong went the bell once more. But still no-one came. He glanced around at Tuppe, who made an encouraging face.

The finger of Murphy was just snaking out for a third time when the door opened a crack. 'Not today thank you,' came a voice from within.

'Delivery,' Cornelius replied, pointing to the crate.

'Not here. You want next door.'

'No. It's here I want.' Cornelius peeped in. The pinched face of an anxious-looking woman peeped out.

Cornelius caught the fragrance of sandalwood talcum powder. And a glimpse of leopard-skin leotard.

He put his foot firmly in the door. 'Good-morning again,' he said, smiling bravely. 'I assume that the beautiful young woman I am addressing must be the daughter of Jack London, Esquire. This is the right address, isn't it? I have a crate here for your father. Are you expecting him home soon? I wonder if I might just step inside and wait for him? What a very charming leotard you're almost wearing. Did you bag it yourself?'

'Take your foot from my door, or I'll set my dog on you.'

Cornelius turned to offer Tuppe another shrug and saw to his astonishment, that a crowd had gathered, as if by magic, around the Cadillac. 'Ouch!' he cried, as the front door slammed violently against his foot.

'No, please let me explain. I have to speak to Jack London.'

'I don't want you to explain. He's moved. Go away.'

'Oh come on.' Cornelius bing-bonged the bell. His shoulder was now against the door.

'Princey,' called a voice from within. 'Bad man at the door, Princey. Rip his foot off, there's my good boy.'

Cornelius withdrew his foot in haste and the door banged shut.

The tall boy laid down the karaoke crate. Paused a moment to compose his thoughts. Then knelt low and pushed open the letter flap. 'Will you please give me Jack London's new address?'

'No I will not!'

'It really is a matter of some urgency. I deeply regret this, but if you don't give me the address, I shall be forced to march up and down outside your house, weeping and wailing and proclaiming at the top of my voice that I am your jilted toy boy. Hardly an original ploy, I grant you, but it should cause a reasonable stir in a neighbourhood like this, don't you think?'

There was a moment of silence. Then the rattling of the security chain. Then the yanking open of the front door.

The sunlight did not favour the woman in the leopard-skin leotard. Cornelius noticed that she bore an uncanny resemblance to the gaunt woman who ran the kiosk on Edinburgh station. He wondered if perhaps they might be related.

'Now just you listen to me.' The leopard lady of The Laurels glared up at her tormentor. She drew back her bony shoulders, bringing a pair of soggy-looking breasts into undeserved prominence. 'I am going to say this only the one time.'

Cornelius observed that the visible area of bosom cleavage closely resembled the flood plain of the Indus Valley, during a period of severe drought, as viewed from an orbiting weather satellite.

'I told all those weirdos,' went the woman. 'I told the bearded guru in the pink Rolls Royce. I told the groupies and the good-time Charlies. I told the bongo players and the scrapers of washboards. I told the stiltwalkers, the dog-faced boys and the alligator girls. I even told Zippy the frigging pin head. And now I'm telling you. Jack London doesn't live here any more. He's moved. Gone away. Got it?'

'I see.' Cornelius nodded thoughtfully. His hair didn't bother. 'You get quite a lot of people asking then?'

'No!' said the woman.

'But you just said . . .'

'That was years ago.' The leopard lady counted on a freckled claw. 'Thirty years, to be precise. I have a very long memory.'

'Thirty years ago? Jack London moved thirty years ago?'

'That's what I just said. My memory is virtually photographic. And I never forget a face.' She stared into that of the Murphy. 'Especially when describing it to the police.'

'I am certain then that Mr London's new address will still be fresh in your mind. The sooner I could have it, the sooner I could be on my way. I am in such a hurry. You know how it is.'

The woman sighed and let down her bosoms. The Indus Valley became Utah Salt Flats. 'If I give you the address, do you promise to go away and never return?'

'I swear by all the gods of light and darkness.' Cornelius made an appropriately sacred sign.

The woman eyed him up and down. 'Another weirdo,' was her conclusion. 'Wait here. In silence. And I'll write it down for you.' The door crashed shut.

Cornelius turned once more to view the crowd. It was composed of fresh-faced young folk. The boys all slicked-back hair, blue jeans and campus jackets. The girls, dime-store pony-tails, tight sweaters, flared skirts and Bobby sox. And all about sweet little sixteen.

The front door of The Laurels opened for a final time and a slip of paper was thrust into the Murphy's hand. 'And don't come back.'

'Thank you.'

Cornelius studied the slip of paper. He studied his shoes. The closed front door. The sky. And then he stooped. Plucked up the karaoke crate. Tramped down the garden path. Through the sun-ray gateway. Across the pavement. And out into the road. The Cadillac's wireless was playing Chuck Berry and Cornelius had to force his way through the now jiving throng.

He flung the crate on to the back seat. Swung open the driver's door. Climbed in and switched off the wireless.

'Aw,' went the crowd. 'Dragsville' and 'unhip'.

Tuppe, who had been gaily popping his fingers and grooving with the chicks, caught sight of the Murphy visage. It wasn't grinning.

'Cornelius?' The weeny man tugged at his friend's sleeve. 'Something is troubling you. What might it be?'

'Jack London has moved. In fact he moved thirty years ago.'

'Thirty years? We've lost him then.'

'No, we haven't lost him. I have his new address.'

'That's good.'

'Not altogether.' Cornelius fished out the slip of paper and passed it to Tuppe.

Tuppe read it. 'Oh Gawd,' said he. 'It's . . .'

'My address.' Cornelius spoke in a low doomed voice. 'My own house.'

He thrust the key into the steering column, revved the engine and prepared to back through the crowd.

But the crowd had vanished. And but for two epic travellers and an electric-blue eyesore, Sunnyside Road was deserted.

19

INSTRUCTION MANUAL FOR THE TRAIN OF TRISMEGISTUS MODEL 4

You lucky person!

You are now the proud owner of a **Train of Trismegistus Model 4**. The very latest in **Deviant Extermination Systems**. Featuring:

1. Inner-zone to outer-world modes.
2. Fully armoured attack, search-and-destroy capabilities.
3. On-board tennis-ball-with-nail-stuck-in-the-top assisted memory.
4. Holographic Day-Glo decals.
5. Free stationmaster's cap.
6. And flag.

The Trismegistus Train Company hope that the *Model 4* will give you many happy hours of use. Our salesman (Wally) has no doubt informed you that this model is a **Last Resort Option**, and as such, the company can accept no responsibility for its bad language, unpredictable behaviour or radical course of action.

The *Model 4* replaces the *Model 3* (squirt flower and smiley face on front), whilst retaining the ever-popular exploding handbag, whoopie cushion and bad-boy Princey fake doggy-doo accessories.

To these have been added the **Total destruction of anything that stands in its way** facility and the **Scorched earth**

policy policy. Please note. *These come as standard and are* not *optional.*

 THE TRAIN OF TRISMEGISTUS WILL GET THE JOB DONE!

TO OPERATE

To get the very best from your *Model 4* please follow the following *to the letter.*

Please note. The *Model 4* comes fully assembled and does not take kindly to having unqualified persons tinkering about with it.

Do not engage it in conversation.

Do not attempt to open the little box on the side which has the words EXTREME HAZARD: DON'T EVEN THINK ABOUT OPENING printed in huge red letters on it.

1. Stoke up the boiler with the piece of coal and the match provided.

2. Place photograph of deviant in slot 'A'.

3. If you do not have a photograph, then jot down a few details on a postcard instead. Approximate height. Colour of eyes, skin and hair. Age, sex, clothing favoured. Things of that nature. Anything you feel might help the *Model 4* to get some idea of exactly who it's supposed to be wiping out. It will then systematically snuff anyone even vaguely resembling the subject sought.

4. Open door to outer world.

5. Don stationmaster's cap.

6. Press start button and retire to safe distance waving flag.

7. Close door to outer world upon train's departure and keep it shut if you know what's good for you.

Please note. If scale of ensuing carnage exceeds acceptable norm (ie: total extinction of dominant planetary species) contact **THE TRISMEGISTUS TRAIN COMPANY** at once!

We will be pleased to sympathize deeply, whilst stressing in no uncertain terms that it is **NO RESPONSIBILITY OF OURS!**

Arthur Kobold shuddered. He closed the instruction manual, wiped cream from its cover and consigned it to the waste-paper basket.

It was no responsibility of his either, he considered. All he had needed was a little more time and the whole operation could have been concluded in a civilized fashion. He didn't hold with the total extinction of a dominant planetary species. Especially when that species was his own.

Sucking ruefully upon a creamy thumb, Arthur Kobold began to pace up and down in his office.

In the front room of twenty-three Moby Dick Terrace the Campbell was doing some pacing of his own. He had listened, for what now seemed to him an eternity, whilst the mother spun tales which would have had Havelock Ellis, Krafft-Ebing, or even the now-legendary Magnus Hirschfield himself, wilting under the assault.

If there was any conceivable form of sexual deviation, gross depravity, or outlandish perversion abroad on this planet, then this woman had watched it, full frontal, red in tooth and claw, whilst stopping off somewhere for a small sweet sherry, during some charabanc outing, package tour, or trip around the bay.

And if there was any end to it, none seemed in sight.

'And then the headsman asked us if we'd ever

watched an elephant being circumcised,' the mother went on. 'Have you ever watched that, by the way?'

'No,' said the Campbell, continuing to pace. 'No no no.'

In the back garden, penned within the circular confines of the magic wall, the daddy also paced. The ARP helmet was off. The shirtsleeves were in the 'rolled' position. The pacing that the daddy went in for was made precarious by nature of the many blunt and discarded garden tools which lay scattered about him. Many a chum had been ground down, during an afternoon of fruitless assault on the magic wall. And many also were the words of profanity that the no longer merry fellow had offered up, to be taken as they came, by the deity of his choice. The daddy fumed as he paced. And paced as he cursed. But he didn't seem to be getting anywhere just at the moment.

Cornelius Murphy didn't seem to be getting anywhere either.

The Cadillac Eldorado was all snarled up in the rush hour.

There was a time when London had two rush hours. One in the morning and one in the evening. Then a very wise man, whom no-one can remember the name of, had a very wise idea. He invented *flexitime*, which meant that workers could stagger their working hours and avoid the rush hours if they wished to. And so they all did and now London has a rush hour all day long.

'Get out of the way!' Cornelius meeped the horn, rose from his seat and made fists at the car in front. It was a black cab. The driver ignored him.

'Have patience,' Tuppe advised.

'*Patience?*' Cornelius glared at his small companion. 'Patience, did you say?'

'Cornelius, sit down. You'll draw . . . a crowd.'

Cornelius sat down. 'This is bad, Tuppe. This is really bad.'

'Oh, I've seen worse. You should try passing through Paris with a packed pantechnicon of porcine prodigies. Or even saying it.'

'I am not referring to the traffic, as you well know.'

Tuppe made an encouraging face.

'Jack London! The daddy himself! It was so obvious. I should have seen it earlier.'

'Oh come on.' Tuppe dispensed with the encouraging face. He'd stick with the anxious one. 'It could have been anyone. London is a very large place.'

'But the world we inhabit is not. Everything so far has been a coincidence of one kind or another. We've been led along by coincidence. Coincidence and design. Give me the map. Let me show you.'

Tuppe fumbled in the glove compartment. 'Here you go.'

Cornelius took the map. 'Now give me a Biro.'

Tuppe fumbled in his pockets. 'I know I have one. I picked one up in the auction room. No, I lost that. But I found another in the Holiday Inn. Where did I put that? No, I don't seem to have one at the moment. Where ever do they all go to?'

Cornelius raised an eyebrow and dug in his own top pocket. Here he found his pencil. He licked the point. 'Now look at this.' He spread the map across the ample dashboard. 'Our epic journey takes us from my house, to King's Cross, up and around here to Edinburgh. Across to Sheila na gigh. Back to Edinburgh, for a visit to the police station. Back to Sheila na gigh. Down to

Milcom Moloch, which for some reason doesn't appear to be on this map, but must be about here.' Cornelius sketched in the route with his pencil. 'From there we go to Cromcruach, where we acquire this car. Then to the Holiday Inn, North Ameshet. You are following this?'

Tuppe nodded. 'I am.'

'Good.' Cornelius sketched on. 'Then, by a curious route we reach the monastery. Then we come all the way down here to Penge. And we are currently travelling, I use the word in its loosest sense, right across here and back home.' He held the map towards Tuppe. 'Now what does that look like to you?'

Tuppe studied the pencilwork. 'It looks somewhat like a deformed rocket ship. Or possibly a hunchbacked cigar.'

'Not quite.' Cornelius snatched back the map. 'We stopped at other places along the way. For food, petrol, visits to the toilet.'

'I only have a tiny bladder. It's not my fault.'

'Never mind. We stopped here, here, here.' Cornelius drew circles. 'Here. Here, I think. Here, I'm sure.'

'And there.' Tuppe pointed. 'You had to get out there, I remember.'

'All right. There too.' Cornelius circled it in. 'Now what do you see?'

Tuppe gave the map another looking over. 'It's a what'saname. One of those things you blow. Except it's got too many holes.'

'It's a reinvented ocarina,' said Cornelius Murphy. 'That's what it is. And its pointy end is sticking right into my house.'

'V marks the spot, as it were?'

'Precisely. And that's why I should have seen it earlier. It's what I *do*, Tuppe. See, *observe*.

273

The patterns. The cross-correspondences. The things written into other things. It's what I am, Tuppe.'

'Anyone ever tell you you're a weirdo?' Tuppe asked.

'Funnily enough . . .' Cornelius grinned.

'The traffic's moving,' said Tuppe.

It was a little after seven of the nice summery unsuspecting evening clock, when the Cadillac Eldorado finally stuttered to a halt before an area of wasteland, which had once been number one Moby Dick Terrace.

Cornelius shook the pockets of his jacket. 'Out of petrol. And out of money. Not one penny left.'

'It would seem, then, that the travelling part of our epic journey has come to an end.'

Cornelius agreed that it probably did.

'Which also means that the really exciting climax can not be far away.'

Cornelius agreed on this also.

'Which would be why I need the toilet rather badly.'

Cornelius thought this more than likely.

'You know *he's* probably already in there, don't you?'

'The Campbell?' Cornelius sniffed the air. Certain subtle odours drifted to him. Others steadfastly refused to do so. 'He's in there.'

'Then I'll have to find a bush to go behind, before we do anything else. That Campbell gives me the sh—'

'He doesn't exactly brighten up my day.' Cornelius wondered where lay the nearest and stoutest of sticks. He was very concerned for the safety of his parents. Murphys, Londons, or whatever they turned out to be.

'This Campbell. What is he, Cornelius?'

'A would-be student of the reinvented ocarina, would be my guess.'

'Do you have a plan, by any chance?'

'Do I have a plan?' Cornelius managed a nod and a wink. 'Do *I* have a plan.'

'Well, do you?'

'Well . . .'

The daddy had given up on the pacing. Now he sat, in the doorway of his shed, smoking his pipe and discussing the sad decline of popular music with his chums. The way one does.

'I can't help feeling responsible,' the old one told his tools. 'If I hadn't tampered with that karaoke machine, The Beatles would never have had to split up. I just took the front off to give it a clean and this small screw fell out . . .'

'I never dug The Beatles myself,' said the trowel. 'Dug 'em, geddit?'

The daddy didn't.

'Whatever happened to Reg Presley?' asked a couple of unemployed trugs.

The daddy shrugged.

'I'm more a Philip Glass man myself,' announced the shed window.

'Rap!' went the hammer.

'Soul,' sang three spades.

'Listen, I appreciate the gesture, chaps,' said the daddy, 'but I'm afraid it isn't helping matters.'

'I'll scrub around my fondness for Dean Martin then,' chuckled the screwdriver.

'Hang about,' cried the hosepipe, a Tom Jones fan. 'The day may yet be saved. Here comes the son.'

'Do-dn-do-do,' went a passing beetle. 'What about a reference to Pink Floyd then?'

Unaware of what lay in store for him, Cornelius Murphy shinned over . . . *The Wall*.

'Ah,' said he, viewing with interest the spectacle of

his father, seated in a kind of smokey-glass dome, at the bottom of the garden. 'Daddy?'

'Cornelius, my own dear boy.' Murphy Senior arose and smote the magical wall. The dull chime rang out once more.

'Mike Oldfield,' said the dibber.

'The secret is in knowing when to stop,' said the daddy. 'Cornelius, fruit of my passion for your sweet mother. Cornelius, release me from this devilish entrapment, if you have an ounce of common decency in your fine young body.'

Cornelius approached the man in the magical prison. 'I have a delivery outside for you, *Mr London*,' he said.

'Oh dear. Oh woe.' Arthur Kobold let up on the pacing.

He studied his pocket watch and glanced down at the telephone. Once the train was set in motion, there was no telling what might happen. But it was bound to be something terrible. If he, Arthur Kobold, was to do anything, then now was the time that he had better be doing it. Arthur gnawed upon his knuckle. He would dearly have preferred cake.

'Oh dear. Oh woe.' The mother ceased her latest fascinating monologue. 'Would you look at the time already? You must be craving for your supper, Mr Kobold. I'll just pop out to the kitchen and rustle you something up. Another cup of tea perhaps. I've a bag drying on the window sill. Still has a bit of life in it I'll bet.'

The Campbell dispensed with further pacing. 'Pop out to the kitchen? No, I don't think that would be a good idea. Tell me some more about how you learned head-shrinking from those natives in Papua.'

'Well, they slit open the back of the head, you see, from the nape of the neck to the crown and prise out the skull. There's a knack to it, but I soon got it right. You know you look a little off-colour, Mr Kobold. What with all those lumps beginning to sprout out of your head and everything. Are you sure you won't reconsider the tea?'

'Oh dear. Oh woe. Cornelius, release your daddy and find favour in his eyes for ever.'

Cornelius approached the trapped fellow and ran his fingers lightly across the invisible barrier. 'How is this done?' he asked.

'The powers of darkness, my boy.'

'Those demonic lads, eh? Well, it looks like you're done for then.' Cornelius turned to take his leave.

'No. Wait. Where do you think you're going?'

'To save the mother of course.'

'Then help me out. I'll give you a hand.'

Cornelius grinned at his father. 'There is one thing you could do.'

'Anything, thou chip off the old block.'

'Tell me where you've hidden the ocarina.'

'Oh no. Not that.' The daddy covered his face.

'That indeed. I want it and I want it now.'

'Cornelius, no. You don't have all the papers yet.'

'I expect the ones I lack are hidden with the ocarina. Where did you say that was, by the way?'

'I can't tell you.'

'Then I'll just have to leave you here. Sorry, *Mr London*.'

'No wait. Cornelius, I can explain everything. About the ocarina and "Jack London". Everything. Just apply yourself and get me out of here.'

'You promise?'

'I do. I do. Cross my aching heart.' The daddy did so.

'Don't trust the old bastard,' muttered the wheelbarrow.

'Shut up, you!' The daddy flapped his heart-crosser at the two-handled traitor.

'Who are you telling to shut up?'

'Not *you*, my boy. Perish the thought. Come on now, apply your ingenuity.'

Cornelius shook his head. 'I think not.'

'What? But the ocarina . . .'

'You'd best stay here. After all, if your own wheelbarrow doesn't trust you, I don't see why I should.'

'Cornelius, wait.' The daddy biffed upon the invisible wall.

'Bong bong bong,' it went.

And bing-bong went the front-door bell of twenty-three Moby Dick Terrace.

'A caller,' said the mother. 'Now I wonder who that can be. It's a bit early in the year for the dustmen.'

'Allow me to answer it, dear lady. It might be Cornelius. I'd like to surprise him.'

'Cornelius has his own key. Just sit down. I'll go.'

'Then I'll go with you.' The Campbell smiled sweetly.

'No. It's quite all right.' The mother smiled also.

'I really must insist.' The Campbell stopped smiling.

The mother didn't. She said, 'I expect it's little Tuppe come to use the toilet. Cornelius probably went around the back. He's not going to be very pleased when he sees what you've done to my husband.'

'What of this?' The Campbell stiffened. 'What do you mean?'

'You know exactly what I mean, Mr Deviant-lumpy-head.'

'Oh ho!' The lumpy-headed one took off his spectacles and tucked them into the sharp top pocket of his sharp grey suit. 'I thought I had the right address in more ways than one. This bodes ill for you I fear.' He snapped his fingers and fire branched once more between them.

The mother looked singularly unimpressed. 'That's nothing,' she said. 'I once took tea with a Ugandan obi-man called Katafeltro who could do that with his willy. And one evening he came with me to a do at the British Embassy in Kampala. Lady Windermere was there and you'll never guess what happened. She asked Katafeltro if he had a light for her cigarette and . . .'

'Shut up, woman!' The Campbell grew ever so lumpsome. 'I'll fix you.' He spread his fingers and the flames rose like an Olympic torch.

'Careful. You'll scorch my antimacassars.' The mother made a rather interesting mystical sort of a pass with her right hand. And uttered several magic syllables.

A sizeable pail-load of old fish guttings materialized. It swung forwards. Crossed the room. And caught the Campbell squarely in the gob. It extinguished the flames.

'What? How? Blurgh!' went the Campbell, floundering in foul-smelling confusion.

'Conjured forth, of course.' The mother blew on to her theurgical fingertips. 'Mr Katafeltro taught me. Bit like riding a bike really. Once you've tried it without the saddle you never forget how the bell works.'

The Campbell staggered to his feet. He didn't look altogether appetizing. But a fine kettle of fish. The unappealing lumpy head began to swell. And swell.

'You'll do yourself a mischief,' the mother remarked.

'Grrrrrrrrrrrrrrr!' and 'boiiiiiiiiiing!' The transformation was rapid and it was dramatic. And effective. And downright weird. The Campbell changed into a great spinning multicoloured ball. This hovered motionless in the air for a brief moment. And then began to bounce about the room. Rapidly. And violently.

The mother ducked nimbly, as the now-spherical deviant bowled over her head and slammed into the fireplace wall. Mincing the mantel clock, scattering Spanish dancer dolls and fracturing the framed photo of the Queen Mum (God bless her).

And then it was up and down and here and there and all about. Again and again and again and again. Floorboards gave, ceiling plaster showered, furniture pulverized. Crash, bang and wallop.

'Golly.' Tuppe peeped in through the letter flap.

'Golly indeed.' Cornelius, who had been creeping from the kitchen, suitably stout stick in hand, jumped back as the front parlour door burst from its hinges and splintered into the passage.

'Oh dear. Oh woe,' went the mother. 'Oh . . .'

And then suddenly there was silence.

Cornelius stood in the passage. Stout stick in an unsteady hand. Breath held. Tuppe scaled the front door and let himself in with the tall boy's key. Cornelius pressed a finger to his lips. And then took a furtive shufti into the front parlour. There wasn't anything he recognized. Although dust fogged up the air, the scale of the devastation was clear enough to see. The room was utterly destroyed. The plaster was gone from the walls and ceiling. A great hole yawned in the dividing wall to the back parlour. Every stick of furniture was now a shredded memory.

All that remained intact was the front windows.

Untouched. Their nets and chintzy curtains totally unscathed.

Cunning, thought Cornelius. 'Hello? Mum?' He stepped through the doorway and on to the rubble. Floorboards groaned ominously.

'I wouldn't if I were you;' they whispered.

Cornelius stepped back. 'Is anybody there?'

'I'm here.' The voice came softly at his ear.

Cornelius jerked around, wielding his stick.

'Put it down.' The Campbell emerged from the back parlour, looking like his old charming self once more. He hauled out a dust-besmirched woman and put the muzzle of his gun to her head, the way only really bad baddies do. 'Put it down or I'll shoot this loquacious harridan. And I'm not kidding around.'

'Hello, dear.' The mother waggled her fingers at Cornelius.

Cornelius let the stick fall from his fingers. 'Let her go, Campbell. I have what you want.'

'You haven't. But I'll wager your father does. Shall we call him in and find out, d'you think? Oi *you*!'

'Me?' Tuppe asked.

'You, y'wee bastard. Where do you think you're creeping off to?'

'Nowhere.' Tuppe smile crookedly. 'Nowhere at all.'

At a little after seven-thirty of the something-bad-is-going-to-happen early evening clock, the Murphy family, Jack, Bridie and their son, Cornelius, sat at their kitchen table. With them, on a cushion, sat young Murphy's best friend, Tuppe. And watching over them, gun in hand and wicked smile on the face thereof, stood evil Jim the Campbell.

'I do believe,' said this very body, 'that this is what they call the showdown.'

They again, thought Tuppe. But he said nothing.

The Campbell turned an evil eye upon the daddy. 'The ocarina. Give it to me at once.'

'What is so important about this frigging ocarina?' Tuppe whispered to Cornelius.

'Tell the wee bastard.' The Campbell waved his pistol at the daddy.

The daddy made surly grumbling sounds. 'I don't know what you're talking about.'

The Campbell cocked his pistol. 'Tell him.'

'Go on, Jack,' said the mother. 'Tell him.'

'Yes, *Jack*,' said Cornelius. 'Why don't you tell us both.'

'Oh, all right.' The daddy sighed dismally. 'The ocarina is the key. It unlocks the entrances to the Forbidden Zones.'

'Then these zones really exist?'

'Of course they do, son. Where did you think this plug-ugly spawn of the pit sprang from?'

'Watch it, you!' The Campbell made a face of surpassing plug-ugliness.

The daddy continued. 'The Master always suspected that mankind's progress was being purposely blocked. That vital information was being withheld. That truths were not being told. That there was in fact a great conspiracy. When he discovered the existence of the Forbidden Zones, everything fell into place. The powers that orchestrate the spontaneous generation of crowds, the small screw phenomenon, the vanishing Biros. These powers lurk within the Forbidden Zones. *His* lot,' the daddy gestured at the Campbell, 'have been screwing mankind up for centuries.'

'And then some,' smirked the Campbell.

'But why?' Cornelius asked. 'Why screw up mankind?'

'Because it's there! That's why.'

Cornelius scratched at his chin. Was that stubble he felt? Probably not.

'Hurry up now,' the Campbell demanded. 'Finish your little speech and hand over the instrument.'

'Rune conducted experiments,' the daddy went on, 'to discover what was being withheld. He found that there were other colours.'

'We met Rizla,' said Cornelius. 'He showed us one of those.'

'Brother Rizla. Does he still have the . . . ?' The daddy twirled his large fingers above his large head. Cornelius nodded.

'His lot did that.' The daddy offered the Campbell a glare.

The Campbell returned it without thanks. 'Get on with it,' he said.

The daddy did so. 'Rune also experimented with sound. He reasoned that the tonic sol-fa was only telling part of the story. That there were other notes. Notes between notes. Notes no man had ever heard before. Notes no man was intended to hear.'

'Hence the now legendary reinvented ocarina.'

'Exactly, son. The Master added new notes to it.'

'And to cut a dull story short,' the Campbell broke in, 'Rune also discovered why these particular notes were kept from mankind. Because of their vibrations. When the notes are played, their vibrations open the doors from this world to the one that lies within the Forbidden Zones. So now you know. Give me the ocarina, Mr Murphy.'

'Hold on,' said Cornelius. 'Not so fast. I'm missing something here. If you come from one of these Forbidden Zones, what do *you* need the ocarina for?'

'Because he can't get back in without it,' the daddy

explained. 'He's an escaped criminal. Escaped from the inside. A dangerous deviant.'

'That's me,' said the Campbell.

Cornelius was still baffled. 'But if you've escaped from captivity inside, what do you want to go back in for? To give yourself up?'

'Give myself up?' The Campbell shook with laughter. 'Shite no. I want to rob the bastards. There's a fortune in there. The crock at the end of the rainbow. A million mislaid diamonds. Ancient treasure. More Biros, umbrellas and yellow-handled screwdrivers than you could use in a hundred lifetimes. There's gold in them there Zones.'

'So whoever has the ocarina holds the key to boundless wealth?'

'That's it. All you have to do is whistle.'

'But surely the entrances are guarded.'

'Against who? Rune was the only man to believe that the Zones really exist. The only man to hold the key. And now he's . . .'

'Dead?' Cornelius asked. 'Or trapped inside perhaps.'

'Buggered if I know. And I surely don't care. But that's enough chat. The ocarina now, Mr Murphy, or I shoot your lovely wife and your fine tall lad.'

'You're bluffing.' The daddy folded his arms and stuck out his bottom lip. 'You wouldn't dare.'

Jaws dropped around the table.

The Campbell turned his gun upon Tuppe. 'Right then. I'll shoot the wee man first. To give you an idea of the noise the gun makes. And the mess, of course.'

'Hang about,' cried Tuppe. 'I'm not happy about this, me.'

'Only joking,' said the daddy. 'I'll fetch the ocarina.'

'I do think that would be for the best.'

*   *   *

Felix Henderson McMurdo, of whom nothing had been heard of late, was happy. He was hungry and he needed to go to the toilet. But he was happy nonetheless. He'd been having the most exciting day of his life. A definite improvement on the one previous, where he'd been duffed up by Wild Warriors and pie-faced by a monster. This day was in a class of its own.

It all really began for him after he ran away from the monastery. He hadn't managed to run far because his knees were shaking so badly. So when he came across the old car in the ditch, it seemed like the ideal place to hide, while he organized his thoughts and let his knees calm down.

After all. There it was. Doors unlocked, no tax disc, clearly abandoned. Anyone could have made the same mistake. Anyone could have said, here is a clapped-out old black VW all covered in spikes that no-one wants any more. Felix did. And in no time at all he had fallen asleep in the back of it.

He didn't half wake up with a start the next morning though.

Because at six o'clock on this day the VW had suddenly driven off. Felix jumped up in the back seat to apologize to the driver.

But found, to his amazement, that there wasn't one.

The car was driving itself!

At first Felix simply gazed dumbstruck as it changed gear, bumped back on to the road and made off for the motorway. Then he panicked. And he was about to open a door and fling himself from the speeding car when a wonderful thought struck him.

He recalled seeing an old Walt Disney film where this very thing happened. And the car in that film had been a VW, hadn't it? Yes, it had. Felix put one and one together. This had to be the same car. There could be no other explanation. It was obvious. He, Felix Henderson McMurdo, was actually being driven along by that world-famous sentient VW. What was its name?

He wracked his brains. It was right on the tip of his tongue.

Herpes. That was it!

'Brilliant,' said Felix. 'This is just brilliant.'

And so he began chatting. To be friendly, build up a rapport, things of that nature, he told Herpes all about himself, leaving out the more dismal parts, and asked what the car had been up to since it left Walt Disney.

But Herpes didn't answer. It was clear, though, that he'd fallen on hard times. Typical of Hollywood, thought Felix. One day you're up in lights. And the next, down in the gutter. He gave the empty driver's seat a comforting pat. He understood.

And Herpes rushed on. He was clearly on some important mission. Perhaps he had an audition or something. Whatever it was, he was not prepared to stop. For anything.

Felix broached the matter of breakfast and how he needed to visit the toilet. But Herpes just rushed on.

The first real shock of the day came when the VW suddenly swept up behind a very familiar-looking electric-blue Cadillac and tried to run it off the motorway.

The second came a little later. Felix had been crossing and recrossing his legs for an hour and found he could contain himself no longer. So he opened a rear window, unzipped and took careful aim through the gap.

Had he been less pressed he would probably have checked the driving-mirror first. But he wasn't so he did not. The police motor cyclist, who was coming up behind, caught Felix's outpourings full in the face.

And he wasn't pleased. He switched on his siren and made it quite clear that pulling over was the order of the day.

But Herpes just rushed on. Colleagues of the damp policeman soon fell into pursuit. But Herpes outran them all.

The first police roadblock was somewhere near Banbury.

Herpes ran through that as if it was nothing at all.

Felix was really impressed. He received only the barest minimum of brain-stem-snapping whiplash.

Somewhere north of Long Crendon, on the B4011, the Buckinghamshire Constabulary imaginatively employed the use of two bulldozers to close the road.

Felix recalled another film he'd once seen. It was called *Vanishing Point*. And he shut his eyes very tightly indeed.

But the big bang never came. Herpes simply leapt right over the bulldozers. And rushed on.

Felix clapped his hands. Then he rubbed his head. It was only minor concussion. The double vision would soon pass. But this really was exciting. Just like the movies.

London proved to be exciting too. Felix had never been there before and he saw a lot of the sights. And he had a good view, what with Herpes driving over the roofs of all those cars that were stuck in the rush hour.

The police helicopter had spotted that. Felix watched it swoop and hover. He was still watching it when Herpes suddenly screeched to a halt.

                        *   *   *

'*Come out with your hands up.*' The police-chief-through-loud-hailer voice echoed in the kitchen of twenty-three Moby Dick Terrace.

'Nice try.' The Campbell fixed Tuppe with a bitter eye.

'But I never . . . honest.'

'Would you like me to call you a cab?' Cornelius asked the Campbell.

'If you think it would get a laugh. It's a very old gag.'

'That's not what I meant.'

'I know what you meant.' The Campbell perused his combat watch.

'I came here under my own steam.' He made an obscene gliding motion with his gun-toting hand. 'Very fast. But tiring. I have summoned transport for my departure. It will be here now, so I shall say ta ta.' He patted a bulging pocket, which now contained the reinvented ocarina. 'I doubt if we'll meet again. But I'll be around. You probably won't recognize me, of course. But if you look out for that fabulously wealthy independent candidate, whose party sweeps to power in the next general election . . . You know the form. Today Westminster. Tomorrow the world.'

'Fiend,' said the daddy.

'Quite so. Bye now.' The Campbell backed from the kitchen. 'Don't forget to register your vote, by the way.'

And then he was gone.

'Well,' said Mrs Murphy. 'What a very unpleasant creature.'

The daddy sprang to his feet. 'Up and after him, Cornelius,' he cried. 'Do your stuff.'

'My stuff.' Cornelius gazed up at the big fellow. 'And exactly what sort of stuff would that be?'

The Campbell ran out of the front door and across the road towards the spikey VW. And suddenly found himself caught in the searchlight of the hovering helicopter. Which seemed a bit unnecessary, considering how it was still such a nice bright summer's evening.

The wail of sirens reached the Campbell's ears. Police cars were lurching over the wasteground from all directions.

'Shite!' said the Campbell. 'But no matter.' He patted his bulging pocket. 'Plenty of places to hide out.'

'Your stuff,' went the daddy once more. 'Your epic stuff.'

'Oh, *that* stuff.' Cornelius glanced down the passage and through the open front door. He saw the black VW and the scurrying hindquarters of the Campbell. He could hear the rest.

'There seems to be a considerable police presence. A helicopter and everything, by the sound of it. Best leave the Campbell to the boys in blue, I'm thinking.'

'No no.' The daddy flapped his big red hands about. 'They won't stop him. He'll get away. Come on, Cornelius. Come on.'

Cornelius shook his head, and his hair shook with it. 'I think not. I am no match for that thing. Whatever it is.'

'But you are. You have to be.'

'Why?'

'Because . . .' The daddy bit upon his lip. 'Because . . .'

'You'd better tell him, dear,' said the mother. 'All this is getting out of hand. He has to know.'

'I have to know what?' Cornelius looked from the

one to the other of them. They were both looking very sheepish indeed.

The daddy puffed out his cheeks. 'I was supposed to tell you on your next birthday. When you came of age, as it were.'

'Tell me what?'

'We're not your real parents,' the daddy blurted out. 'You were adopted.'

'*What?*' Every hair on the tall boy's head stood upon end. '*What?*'

The big fellow dabbed a tear from his big left eye. 'I'm sorry, Cornelius. I'm not your real daddy.'

'What? What?' Cornelius shook his head, filling the kitchen with hair. 'What are you saying? Not my real daddy? Then if you're not, who on earth is?'

'Hugo Rune,' said Jack Murphy. 'Although as to whether he's on Earth or not . . .'

Bad Jim Campbell ignored the sweeping searchlight and the advice to give himself up. He dragged open the door of the VW and jumped into the driving seat. 'We'd best be away,' he told the car.

'Brrrrrrrrm brrrrrrrrrm,' went the VW eagerly.

'Then let's do it.' The Campbell stuck the car into reverse and adjusted the driving-mirror. And in it he saw the face of Felix Henderson McMurdo.

'You!' cried the Campbell.

'You!' screamed Felix. 'Oh no!'

There is a persistent rumour, kept persistent by the rat men who work on the London Underground, that deep beneath the streets of the great metropolis, in a blocked-off tunnel, there stands a Victorian train. Full of skeletons, still clad in the costumes of that noble era.

Opinions vary regarding the disaster that befell it. Some speak of cave-in. Others suggest that Jack the Ripper ran amok on that train. And that the authorities dynamited the tunnel to seal the mass murderer in for ever with his victims.

There are others still, and these are wild-eyed fellows for the most part, who turn up around closing time and whisper words of warning into the ears of patrons who would rather not be hearing them, that the line the train travelled upon, passed through a certain area where two worlds meet. And that the train was literally swallowed up.

But who in their right mind would believe a thing like that?

Although.

Anything could happen.

Down there.

Because in the darkness, deep below the London streets, something stirred even now. In the Stygian blackness, a circle of light appeared. A light issuing from an ancient bull's-eye lantern.

It swept along a ruined platform. And danced momentarily in the glass eye of a Victorian doll.

And then the circle of light rose. Brought forth a coloured plaque. An unearthly coloured plaque.

On which were printed the words, THE TRAIN OF TRISMEGISTUS MODEL 4.

The circle of light bobbed about a bit and then illuminated a photograph, held in an unseen hand. It was a photograph of Jim Campbell, maniac, deviant and potential PM.

The light bobbed again and a little slot marked 'A' was seen. The photograph vanished into it.

And then there came a terrible sound. Echoing in that dark and eldritch place. The sound as of ancient gears grinding upon one another. Of cogs meshing. And a rumble of a mighty force, straining for release.

'My father?' Cornelius was shaking. He was also waving his fists and kicking the kitchen table.

'Cling on.' Tuppe clung on to the tall boy's left leg.

'Yes, I'll cling on.' Cornelius fought with his hair. 'I always knew there was something. That I was different.'

'You are,' said the adoptive daddy. 'You are the stuff of epics. Just like your father. You must continue with his work. You weren't supposed to know about it yet. But with the coming of the deviant and everything . . . You have to stop him, Cornelius. Only you can.'

'Only me?'

'Only you,' said Arthur Kobold from the kitchen door. 'Go after the deviant, Cornelius. Destroy him.'

'I can't.'

'Of course you can.'

'Oh no I can't.'

'Oh yes you can,' they all went.

'I can't. The Cadillac is out of petrol.'

'Cadillac?' the daddy asked.

'Nineteen fifty-eight,' said Tuppe. 'Electric-blue paint job, electric-blue upholstery . . .'

'Wireless set that always plays Max Bygraves?'

'That's the fellow. How did you know?'

'Because it's my car. I bought it for Cornelius. For his birthday. My pal Mike was restoring it for me. Well, trying to fix the wireless anyhow.'

'There goes your birthday surprise,' said Tuppe.

Cornelius had nothing to say.

'Are you sure it's out of petrol?' the daddy asked. 'You did try switching to the reserve tank, didn't you?'

The Campbell revved the engine of his particular motor car.

'I'm getting out of here,' he told Felix. 'And you're in big trouble by the way.'

Felix covered his face. 'Not the pie,' he begged. 'Anything but the pie.'

The Campbell considered all the police cars. They were now parked in nice neat rows at either end of the foreshortened terrace. Men in body armour were climbing out of vans. They were carrying guns.

'Fuck this!' said the Campbell.

There was almost as much activity going on inside number twenty-three as there was outside.

The daddy was rummaging through kitchen drawers, in search of something important. The mother was flattening down the tall boy's hair, so that he'd look his best for his epic confrontation. Tuppe was a bit stuck for something useful to do, so he just got in everyone's way.

'You'll need this.' Arthur Kobold pressed a velvet bag into the epic lad's hand.

'What is it?' Cornelius asked.

'A very special gun. It will kill him.'

Cornelius looked very doubtful indeed. 'I'm not an assassin, you know.'

'There'd be a very large bonus.'

'Nor a bounty-hunter.'

'But you are a human being. The Campbell isn't. Take the gun.'

Cornelius pocketed the bag.

'Found it!' cried Mr Murphy, hoisting a grubby old book into view. 'Come on.'

There followed a lot of rushing and getting stuck in the kitchen doorway and cursing and pushing and general bad behaviour.

'Hurry hurry,' went Arthur Kobold. 'He's getting away.'

And the Campbell was. Herpes meeped his horn. Tyres spun on the asphalt and he was off. Felix ducked his head once more as the VW shot towards the nearest police barricade, gave a mighty leap and plunged down the other side.

Policemen ducked their heads and shook their fists. Some of the men in the body armour fired their guns. And then there was a lot of rushing and getting stuck in the doors of cars and cursing and pushing and general bad behaviour.

Police cars swerved, bumped into one another, spun around and set off in hot pursuit of the Campbell.

Jack Murphy admired the Cadillac. 'The front bumper's scratched,' he observed.

'The deviant,' said Tuppe. 'Wait 'til you see what he's done to your front parlour.'

'Bastard.'

'My feelings entirely.'

Cornelius was climbing into the Eldorado. 'Where is the switch for the reserve tank?'

Jack reached in and gave it a flick. 'Just there. We'll bump start you. You'll need this.' He handed Cornelius the grubby old book.

'What is it?'

'Your real daddy's A–Z. All the locations of the Forbidden Zones in London are marked on it. The deviant will surely run to the nearest. He'll want to lose the police first, of course. Perhaps when he arrives at his destination, it might be nice if you were already there waiting for him.'

Cornelius grinned. 'What a good idea. Thanks . . . dad.'

Arthur Kobold lifted Tuppe into the car. Cornelius passed the A–Z to the weeny man. 'You are the navigator once more. Which way do we go?'

Tuppe leafed through the grubby old book. 'Blimey,' said he, 'there're entrances every which way. But not many in this neck of the woods by the look of it.'

Jack Murphy, his wife and Mr Arthur Kobold put their combined weight to the Cadillac and began to push.

'Aha!' went Tuppe, as the engine caught. 'Just the one. For miles. Right on the top of Star Hill.'

20

Mr Yarrow paid no heed to the racket. He was deaf to the screeching tyres, screaming sirens and grinding gears of the chase, as it passed by his front door.

The youth employment officer was taking a bath. And he was in a merry mood. He sang loudly, as he dewaxed his ears with the pointy end of his loofah.

The discordant strains that rose from his lips were somewhat difficult to identify. There were elements of Status Quo in there. But more than a hint of Max Bygraves. Whatever they were, they echoed loudly about the shabby bathroom, before burying themselves in the curious white silk robes that hung upon the door hook in the dry-cleaner's bag.

The ears done, Mr Yarrow set aside the now cerumen-encrusted fibrous interior of the fruit of the dishcloth gourd and applied pumice stone to his orange fingertips.

The light porous acid volcanic rock, with the composition of rhyolite, deftly removed the residues of tobacco's principal alkaloid ($C_{10}H_{14}N_2$) and presently Mr Yarrow set this aside also.

He was scrupulously clean. And no mistake about it. He sank into the scented suds and scrutinized the visible portions of his body. All spotless and nice to know. The contemplation of them caused Mr Yarrow to sigh not a little.

He had never been a particularly fragrant fellow.

Never a fop or a Dapper Dan. More a crusty-underpants merchant really.

But not any more.

Those evil days were good and gone. He was a re-formed character now. And why? Because Mr Yarrow was a man in love. That's why.

And why shouldn't he be? He was a man, after all. And she was a woman. And what a woman she was.

Oh Roellen.

Delilah of the double eggs, chips and peas.

Our lady of the lissom legs.

Roellen Ridout, café proprietress.

'Down boy,' Mr Yarrow told his well-scrubbed member, as it raised its head above the water. 'Not yet.'

Mr Yarrow sank lower and luxuriated. Tonight he would see her. And tonight he would declare his love. Tonight.

During the ceremony.

When he and all the other local Wiccans assembled before her.

Her, their high priestess.

This very night at the drawing down of the moon and the whipping off of the Y-fronts. At the bare scuddy dancing.

On the top of Star Hill.

On the top of Star Hill. On top of the copper map, on top of the concrete plinth, on top of the mortal remains of the Reverend Matthew Kemp, sat Tuppe.

The Cadillac Eldorado was parked two hundred feet below, well hidden on the edge of the golf course. Its driver was viewing the not too distant car chase and wearing a worried expression.

'Nice night for it,' said Tuppe. 'Splendid view also. We'll have the blighter dry-gulched before he even knows what hit him.'

'But what if he doesn't come here?'

'He'll come.' The small fellow flicked back and forwards through Rune's A–Z, but his eyes didn't stray too far from the excitement. 'I told you. This is the only entrance for miles. Once the Campbell's, er . . . disposed of the police, he'll make for here. Bound to. I think.'

Cornelius remained doubtful. 'I wonder how come all those policemen turned up in the nick of time like that anyway. I really did think it was you doing your voice again.'

'So did I.'

'Eh?'

'Well, after all that business of my shadow pulling you out from in front of those lorries, I'm beginning to wonder just what I might be capable of.'

Cornelius shrugged. 'Look at this gun Arthur Kobold gave me. I ask you.'

Tuppe examined the weapon. It was a 1950s-style pressed-tin Dan Dare sort of job. The words THE CAPTAIN TRISMEGISTUS DEVIANT DESTROYER were printed on the side.

'Doesn't look quite in the same league as Saint Sacco's firepower, does it?' Tuppe handed it back.

'Do you think I should test it out? Fire it at a tree or something?'

'Best not. If a little flag with ZAP written on it pops out of the end, you'll only get disheartened. Oh, look down there. The Campbell's turned into the high street. I wonder if he knows about the new one-way system.'

The Campbell didn't. But even if he had, he wouldn't

have cared. He curled his lip, Herpes meeped its horn and Felix clutched at his groin. A police car drew alongside.

'Pull over!' shouted its driver.

'Och away with you.' The Campbell tugged on the steering wheel. Herpes side-swiped the police car. The police car swerved. Mounted the pavement. And ploughed straight through the unwashed front window of Peter's Pets.

Cages tumbled. Broke open. Spilled out all manner of godless creations. Strange beasties rose in a flurry of beating wings, whacking wattles and quivering membrane. Flying lobsters barked and hissed. Scaley sheep clicked their mandibles. And things that went bump in the night went, sort of . . . bump.

Peter Polgar survived without even a scratch. Because he wasn't in his shop when the police car hit it. He was several streets away in a pub called The Flying Swan. Enjoying a drink and a chat. And looking forward, with some relish, to the uninhibited night of drawing down the moon and whipping off the Y-fronts, that lay ahead for him.

'It's a genuine religion, you know,' he told Jim Pooley, who was propping up the bar. 'The fact that we dance around in our bare scuddies tends to give some people the wrong idea.'

Jim thought it did anything but. He studied the empty bottom of his glass. 'Sounds like a clear case of religious intolerance to me,' he said.

'What's the time?' Tuppe asked.

Cornelius looked at his watch. 'Coming up to eight. Is it important?'

'Shouldn't think so. I'm just hungry, aren't you?'

The telephone on Arthur Kobold's desk began to

ring. Ring ring, it went. But there was no-one there to answer it.

Plenty of cake though.

The Campbell ran another police car off the road. Their numbers were definitely thinning. But there was still the matter of that helicopter.

That helicopter suddenly swept away and returned to base. It was nearly out of fuel. Which was pretty boring, considering how it could quite easily have done something really spectacular. Like crashing into power lines, or the side of a tall building. Or a hill. Or something.

But then helicopters do cost an awful lot of money. And the men who pilot them do tend towards the cautious. And this wasn't America. So, for anything like that to happen would have been a bit far fetched. Wouldn't it?

The Campbell smashed another police car off the road. This one slewed across the forecourt of a petrol station, knocking down one of the pumps. The policemen had just enough time to leap from their car and take cover, before the entire petrol station erupted in flame. There was a really spectacular explosion.

The boys on the hill watched the bowl of flame billow into the sky.

'I shall have no compunction about shooting the Campbell,' said Cornelius.

'Good for you,' said Tuppe.

Ten miles due east of Star Hill, or ten and a half from Peter's Pets, as the four-legged crow now flew, there stands a pub. And this pub hasn't changed one little bit since Hugo Rune played darts there back in 1931 and purchased a packet of pork scratchings for Max

Ernst, because there wasn't any bird seed on sale.

True, the pub had been blitzed out of existence in 1941. But it had been rebuilt in 1951. True, it had been thoroughly refurbished in 1961 and completely modernized in 1971. But in 1981 the establishment was purchased by the grandson of its 1931 landlord and painstakingly restored to its original grandeur, down to the smallest, tiniest, most minutest little detail.

Which meant, that if Max and Hugo were to stroll into this pub, this very night, they would find that, to every appearance, nothing whatsoever had changed.

There still wouldn't be any bird seed for sale. And Max would still have to settle for pork scratchings.

Well, just around the corner from this ageless, seedless establishment, there stands a row of hoardings. These hoardings carry huge expensively produced posters on them. And these posters display really clever and difficult-to-understand images. So really clever and difficult to understand are these images, in fact, that only the smug little prannies who thought them up have the slightest notion what they are supposed to mean.

Beneath these images, however, dire and terrible warnings shriek down at the passing populace. They don't beat around the bush. They say that EEC COUNCIL DIRECTIVE (89/622EEC) reckons TOBACCO SERIOUSLY DAMAGES YOUR HEALTH.

Well, just behind these hoardings there is a Forbidden Zone.

It's not a particularly big one. About a half a mile square. Well camouflaged though and it can't be seen from the air. To its mysterious denizens it's just another suburb. The only obvious difference being that this one has an old blocked-off tunnel entrance with a weed-grown track leading from it. A retired tom-cat sleeps upon this track. It is dreaming of Virginia Rappe.

And when the old blocked-off tunnel entrance suddenly bursts open, the retired tom gets one hell of a start.

Lightning arcs into the sky. Coloured lightning. Unearthly coloured lightning. And something quite horrendous rears into view. It's hard to describe because it's moving so fast. But it looks like some kind of train. And it's got a definite steam on and lots of sparks flying from its wheels. It rips right through the hoardings and out into the street. It looks like trouble.

And it is trouble.

It is The Train of Trismegistus.

'Yabba dabba do!' it goes.

'Did you see that?' Tuppe pointed away towards the eastern horizon. 'Lightning. Perhaps there's a storm coming.'

'Oh I do hope so.' Cornelius made a bitter face.

'Have you decided what you're going to buy yet?'

'Buy? With what?'

'With all the golden booty from the Forbidden Zones that you will be helping yourself to once you've disposed of the Campbell and got your old man's ocarina back.'

'I thought I'd start with Old Kent Road. Then Whitechapel Road, King's Cross Station and The Angel Islington.'

'Just sort of work your way around the board, eh?'

'That's it. On the way I'll house all the homeless, feed all the hungry and see to it that every aspiring writer gets a thousand Biros a week, for life. How does that sound?'

'Very generous. What a nice fellow you are.'

'Thank you very much.'

'Don't mention it.'

302

'What about you?'

'What about me what?'

'What are you going to do with your share? Naturally half of all the booty comes to you.'

'I thought I'd just waste mine on riotous living.'

'I thought you might. Of course, if the Campbell doesn't show up and I don't manage to dispose of him and get my daddy's ocarina back . . .'

'He'll come. Trust me, Cornelius, he has to come. He has to come here for the final big, dangerous, exciting epic confrontation. What time is it now, by the way?'

'Somewhat after eleven.'

'He's not coming. Let's go home.'

'Time gentlemen *please*.' Neville the part-time barman smote the saloon bar counter of The Flying Swan with his knobkerrie. 'Let's have your glasses.'

'I need my glasses,' said Peter Polgar. 'Buy some of your own.'

'I don't wear glasses any more,' said Mr Yarrow, who had just stopped in for a tot of 'Wiccans' warmer'. 'I have contact lenses.'

'I know you, don't I?' Jim Pooley waggled his glass at Mr Yarrow. 'You were my youth employment officer. You tried to fix me up as a professional potholer.'

'You too?' asked Peter Polgar.

'*Get out!*' The Campbell told Felix Henderson McMurdo.

The VW was now parked where the buses turn around at the foot of Star Hill. The police cars had all finally been outrun. And their wreckage towed away. The fire appliances had finished with the petrol station and their crews gone off watch. Most were now at their homes, preparing for a night of drawing down the moon and whipping off the Y-fronts.

Felix got out. 'Would it be all right if I just sort of drifted away into the night, never to be seen again?' he asked hopefully.

'No it wouldn't. What is that funky smell, by the way?'

Felix fingered his sodden trousers. 'I didn't do it.'

The Campbell lifted the VW's bonnet. '*Get in!*' he said.

On top of Star Hill. And now hidden in the top of a tall tree. Cornelius Murphy and his best friend Tuppe were sitting uncomfortably.

'It's getting really dark now, isn't it?' Tuppe clung miserably to a lofty branch. 'I think we should turn it in.'

'There's a nice full moon. We'll wait a bit longer.'

'But there haven't been any explosions for ages. And there's still no sign of the Campbell.'

'He'll come. You said he would.'

'What do I know? Let's go home.'

'No. Hold on. I hear something.'

And indeed Cornelius did. It was a distant sort of something. But it was growing closer. It sounded a bit like voices. It sounded a lot like chanting voices. It was chanting voices.

Tuppe strained a small and shell-like. 'Oh no,' said he.

'What is it?'

'Chanting voices.'

'Very amusing.'

'Wiccans!' said Tuppe.

'Up here? Tonight? Oh bugger.'

Tuppe's head bobbed about amidst the leaves. 'They

dance about in their bare scuddies, you know. I wonder who the high priestess is this week.'

'Tuppe. We can't have them here. Climb down and tell them to go away. Tell them the hill's closed for repairs, or something.'

'Not me.' Tuppe shook his head vigorously. 'Do you know how many Wiccans there are in this neighbourhood?'

'Couple of dozen?'

'Couple of hundred, more like.'

'*What*?' Cornelius took to chewing his fingernails.

'Well, it's a genuine religion, you know. The fact that we dance around in our bare scuddies tends to give some people the wrong idea.'

'We?' Cornelius spat out a mouthful of fingernails. '*We*?'

Hugo Rune wrote a long and erudite monograph on the subject of *shape shifting*. And it would appear, from accounts given by his various biographers, that the great thinker and mystic was not averse to a bit of it himself, every once in a while.

One tale, often repeated, is of how he once grew a pair of sideburns overnight, to win a bet with Herbie Wells. And there are numerous accounts of him actually shrinking to less than half his regular and prodigious size, at the approach of a waiter bearing the bill.

It was Rune's conviction that a lot more shape shifting went on in this world than folk cared to admit. And he claimed to have uncovered a Secret Society of Spontaneous Human Combustionists, responsible for The Great Fire of London, the destruction of The Crystal Palace and the R 101, the blitz and his garden shed.

One day the truth shall out, he wrote. And it was

yet possible that the day in question would shortly be in the dawning.

Down beside the VW, the Campbell's human form dissolved into a gooey, runny, slimey, ill-smelling variety of vegetable soup and began to flow up Star Hill.

Felix watched it occur through a crack in the bonnet and disgraced himself once more.

'Oh no,' whispered Cornelius. 'Would you look at all that lot?'

And what a lot of a lot there was. The chanting grew louder as the figures appeared. They moved up the tracks, passing between the trees. Each clad in robes of white silk. Each bearing a lighted torch.

Cornelius felt the hairs rise on the back of his neck. The cantillation and the robes and torches conspired to create an effect that was eerie and enchanting. Here, upon the top of this ancient hill. With the lights of the town far below and the full moon riding high in the star-scattered heavens.

And still they came, figures in white, drifting like wraiths on to the brow of the hill. And here they formed into a great circle around the concrete plinth. And a great cry rose up from them.

The circle broke and a tall imposing figure appeared. His robes were of gold, his hair and beard long and shining white. He carried a tall black staff, tipped with a five-pointed star. The white-robers bowed low as he passed them by.

'Who is *that*?' Cornelius asked.

'Oh, that's Merlin,' Tuppe replied.

'*Who*?'

'Keep your voice down. It's Merlin. If you'd ever bothered to attend any of the interviews Mr Yarrow sent you to, you'd recognize him.'

'Mr Yarrow never sent me off to take an apprentice-ship with Merlin the magician. I would have taken that job.'

'It's not Merlin the magician. It's Fred Merlin, the monumental mason.'

'Oh.'

Merlin of the golden robe stood before the concrete plinth.

'Give us a bloody leg up then,' said he.

Several figures leapt forward to offer assistance.

'And don't slide off. If I fall arse over tit, I want some bugger there to catch me.'

'He certainly enters into the spirit of the thing does Fred,' Cornelius muttered.

'Ssssh,' whispered Tuppe.

'Right,' said Fred. 'Now let's come to order. Before we kick off with the bare scuddying, a few notices.'

'Mumble mumble,' went the crowd.

'Give over,' went Fred. 'Firstly, I still have a few tickets left for the annual coach outing to Stonehenge. We've got permission this time, so you won't need to bring your stout sticks. Light refreshments will be provided and Mr O'Hagen from the off-licence is laying on six crates of brown ale.'

'Hooray,' went the crowd.

'Now, I've had yet another complaint from the Parks and Amenities bunch at the town hall about our little get-togethers up here.'

'Boo, boo,' went the crowd.

'Quite so,' Fred raised his staff. 'Apparently local residents have been moaning about the noise. And not without good cause. Certain of you, and you know who you are, have been slamming car doors and waking people up. So keep it down when you leave the car park. Oh, yes, and while we're on the subject, there's an Austin Allegro down there with its lights left on.'

'Mumble mumble,' went the crowd, shuffling its feet.

'Typical,' whispered Tuppe.

'What's that?'

'No-one wants to admit that they own an Austin Allegro.'

'Well, please yourself, it's your battery. Now, is there anything else before we kick off? No? Right . . .'

'Er, excuse me.' A lady stepped forward. She was whitely robed. She also wore a straw hat. 'About the tickets for the coach outing.'

'Yes, madam?'

'I bought a ticket last year, but I wasn't able to go. Can I come this year for free?'

'No, I'm sorry. Prices have gone up, I'm afraid.'

'Well, what if I paid the difference?'

'That would be all right, providing you have last year's ticket.'

'I do, it's here in my handbag.'

'Jolly good, then let the festivities commenc—'

'Er, just one more thing.' The lady in the straw hat put her hand up.

'What is it now, madam?'

'Well, I just wanted to know. If I wasn't able to go again this year, could I get a refund?'

'Yes, I'm sure that could be arranged. Now if you don't mind—'

'Would I get a refund on the full ticket price?'

'Yes, yes.'

'Well, would that be for both this year *and* last year?'

'But you didn't go last year.'

'Well, that wasn't *my* fault. The coach left without me.'

'Haven't we seen this woman somewhere before?' Tuppe asked Cornelius.

'Listen, madam!' Mr Merlin waved his staff, ugly murmurs broke out from the crowd. 'If you have last year's ticket and you are willing to pay the difference, you can have a ticket for this year. If you can't come this year, I will refund your money, for *this* year, do you understand?'

'What about my husband?'

'What *about* your husband?'

'Well, he bought a ticket last year and he couldn't go either. But he doesn't want to come this year.'

Grumblings and mumblings rolled around the circle of torch-bearers. Feet were beginning to stamp and there were cries of 'burn the witch' and 'bring out the wicker man'.

The lady in the straw hat clouted the nearest protester with her handbag. Someone threw a clod of earth.

It struck Fred Merlin.

Fred struggled to keep his balance. 'Who bloody chucked that?' he demanded.

'He did,' cried someone.

'I never,' cried someone else. 'Take that!'

'It's a genuine religion you know,' whispered Cornelius, as punches were exchanged beneath his tree and a decent-sized barney got on the go.

And then a most extraordinary thing happened. A kind of ripple flowed through the rowdy congregation, as of electricity borne in the air. The punching and pushing and general bad behaviour ceased. An embarrassed foot-shuffling uncomfortableness took its place.

Cornelius sensed that something important was about to occur and craned his neck to get a better look. His hair became intimately entangled with the branches above.

'What's happening?' he asked Tuppe.

'She comes,' the small fellow replied. 'Can't you feel her? She comes.'

And come she did. The circle broke once more. Mr Merlin stiffened to attention and whacked his staff on the copper map. 'All kneel,' he bawled. 'All kneel before the priestess.'

And kneel they did.

She strode into the circle. A tall and beautiful woman. Proud and erect. A billow of golden hair, a swish of silver robes.

Cornelius fought to free his tangled locks. His eyes bulged. 'It's *The Wife!*' he gasped.

'I wonder if she's doing suppers later.'

Mr Merlin biffed the nearest kneeler with his staff. 'Help me down, you wally.'

The high priestess approached the concrete plinth. There was no shortage of helping hands to give *her* a leg up.

And didn't she look something in the moonlight. All that golden hair. Those flashing green eyes. The full red lips. The generous helping of nipple-definition and the length of leg. Lovely.

She flung her hands wide. 'Blessed be,' she cried.

'Blessed be,' the circle agreed.

'Love is the law.'

'Love under will.'

The high priestess crossed her hands above her breast. 'I am the manifestation of Nuit. The continuous one of Heaven. I am the blue-lidded daughter of sunset. The naked brilliance of the voluptuous night sky. I am the queen of space.'

'Oh yes,' Cornelius agreed. 'You certainly are.'

'Ssssh,' whispered Tuppe.

'To me! To me! I call forth the flame of the hearts in my love-chant. Sing the rapturous love songs unto me! Burn to me incense! Wear to me jewels. Drink to me, for I love you. I love you.'

And with that said, she flung off her robe. And needless to say, she wasn't wearing a single stitch beneath it.

Cornelius Murphy all but fell out of his tree.

'Love is the law,' called the naked woman.

'Love under will,' the circle called back.

And then it was down with the torches, up robes all and Devil take the Y-fronts.

'It's bare-scuddy time,' said Tuppe.

And bare-scuddy time it was.

Cheers and shouts filled the night air, as drooping tums and dismal dangly-bits were shamelessly unfettered. And the dance began. The celebrants formed themselves into concentric circles and high-stepped it out for a knickerless Star Hill Ho-down.

Naturally most kept on their Wellington boots. Well, a lot of dog-walking goes on up there and . . .

There was no shortage of musical accompaniment. Many a weird and wonderful instrument was being struck or plucked or strummed or smitten. The local chapter of the Olde English Folk Music Society was out in full force. And going about it with a will.

This particular chapter, in keeping with most of the rest, was composed of earnest bearded fellows, who shared a love for an ancient instrument, an ethnic shoe, a cagoule, a pint of real ale and a girlfriend called Ros. Which kept Ros pretty busy when she wasn't running her encounter group.

Tuppe winced at the dedicated discord. 'Not exactly The Quo, are they?'

Cornelius shook his entangled head. 'Look at that

tall, bearded oaf plucking the hautboy.'

'Which one? Where?'

Cornelius pointed. 'Next to the slightly shorter bearded oaf who's strumming the gittern.'

'That's never a gittern, that's an archlute.'

'No. I didn't mean the oaf picking the archlute, I meant the oaf strumming the gittern. The oaf plucking the hautboy is next to him.'

'The bearded oaf?'

'That's the one.'

'Got him. That's never a hautboy though.'

'Of course it is.'

'No it's not. That's a heptachord. The bloke over there's plucking a hautboy.'

'Bloke with the beard?'

'No, next to him.'

'Oh yes. So he is. What's the bald bloke in the spectacles playing?'

'That's an ocarina. Oh shit!'

The Campbell, for it was indeed he, was not actually playing the ocarina. Not yet. He was just miming. But he was thoroughly enjoying himself, nonetheless. He pressed himself up against whatever naked flesh happened in his direction and jigged about merrily.

Tuppe tugged at the tall boy. 'Shoot the blighter, Cornelius.'

'I can't get a clear shot from up here. I might hit someone else.'

'Then we'll just have to go down. Quick, take off all your clothes.'

'I certainly will not.'

'Cornelius, you just can't go wading in amongst all that lot fully dressed. If the Wiccans don't duff you up, and they will, the Campbell will spot you, and then who knows what he'll do.'

'Oh God.' Cornelius held on to his hair and leapt from the tree. 'Jump, Tuppe. I'll catch you.'

Tuppe jumped. Cornelius caught him.

'Bare scuddies then.' Tuppe unfastened his dungarees and began to unbutton his shirt. 'Hurry or we might lose him.'

'Oh dear, oh dear.' Cornelius took off his jacket, neatly folded it and laid it on a bush.

The hautboys, archlutes and gitterns, not to mention the dulcimers, tabors, seraphinas, flageolets and union pipes, were all going at it hammer and tongs. The bombardons, polychords, shawms and timbrels were letting it all hang out. And the lady in the straw hat was playing the washboard. Freddie 'The Fingers' Merlin accompanied her on the tea chest bass. 'The Rock Island Line is a mighty fine line,' he sang.

Tuppe slipped out of his cut-down boxer shorts. Revealing a midnight growler of epic proportion.

'So it's true what they say about little men,' said Cornelius.

Tuppe looked up with a grin. 'But not what they say about thin ones, by the look of it.'

Cornelius took up Arthur Kobold's gun. 'Shall we dance?'

All across Star Hill there was a whole lotta shakin' going on.

Cornelius did a soft-shoe shuffle, and Tuppe, the Michael Jackson Moonwalk, and the two of them slipped in amongst the dancers.

Cornelius manoeuvred his way through the bacchanal. He ducked and dived and bobbed and bopped. And did his best to keep the Campbell's baldy head in sight.

Cornelius held the pressed-tin gun straight down at his side. His plan was simplicity itself. Circle around behind the Campbell, stick the gun in his back, dance him away to a nice quiet spot and execute him.

It was a quite appalling idea. And Cornelius knew it.

Dance him away to a nice quiet spot and *execute* him? What on Earth was he thinking about? He couldn't put a gun to the head of a naked man and squeeze the trigger. It was unthinkable. It was unspeakable. There had to be another way. And one that did not involve him in cold-blooded murder.

But then, was it really murder? After all, the Campbell was not actually a human being. Although he did look all too human now. But he wasn't and Cornelius knew it. The Campbell was a dangerous deviant. He was not a *he*. He was an *it*.

But that didn't make Cornelius feel any better. Because, when you got right down to it, what was the Campbell being executed for? What had he done to warrant the death penalty?

He'd done a bit of kidnapping. He'd done *a lot* of kidnapping. And there'd been a great deal of violence and mayhem. The Campbell was a regular berserker. But was he a murderer? Cornelius had no proof that he was. No real proof. And even if he had, would that make matters any easier?

'No,' Cornelius told himself. 'It would not. I have been manipulated throughout this entire affair and I will be manipulated no longer. I shall deal with the Campbell in my own way. Because, sod it, I am the stuff of epics after all.'

Tuppe had already managed to get himself lost amongst the dancers. He'd been admiring a tall girl's bottom and by the time she'd taken exception to this and cuffed him in the ear, Cornelius had gone. And so now Tuppe bumbled around between high-stepping

314

legs, dodging the Wellingtons and worrying after his friend.

And the dancing was gathering momentum. This wasn't just your average Wiccan bash. But then, this wasn't really a Wiccan bash at all. As Tuppe, who had attended several gatherings, would have known full well, had he listened to any of the sermons, rather than spent all his time gazing at bottoms. Because these weren't your genuine Wiccans.

Your genuine Wiccans do not form naked, dancing legions, two hundred strong, on moonlit hilltops. Much as they'd like to. Your genuine Wiccans form tiny, intimate, naked, dancing legionettes. Generally on the Axminster shag-pile in the front room of some bungalow in Ruislip. And there's usually only about six of them.

Traditionally, there is a fat girl who works in a bank and reads the tarot. A computer programmer who's into Black Sabbath. A retired chiropodist who claims he once met Gerald Gardner. A bearded hautboy player and his girlfriend called Ros. And one other, who can't come because he's got a cold.

No, this bunch were not your genuine Wiccans. They were something else entirely. This bunch danced to the off-beat of a very different drummer. They were members of an exclusive sect.

The Secret Church of Runeology.

This bunch were *The Runies*!

And they had all turned out tonight for a specific reason. To celebrate the centenary of their guru's birth. Their holy guru, the guru's guru. The greatest unsung genius of the twentieth century. The prophet. The Master. The man, the myth and the unpaid restaurant bill. The reinventor of the ocarina.

Mr Hugo Rune.

And they'd come with one shared purpose. To conjure forth the spirit of the Master, and hang upon its every word.

It was the way *he* would have wanted it.

Cornelius ducked and dived and bobbed and bopped. The Campbell's head came and went in the frenzy of waving hands and leaping bodies.

But Cornelius didn't seem to be making much progress. There were too many people. It was very frustrating. The Murphy set his jaw into an attitude of determination and pressed on.

The music, the instrumentation, the songs, howls and hoots, seemed now to be taking a definite form. A steady rhythm was growing. Though loose at first, it fell in upon itself from many disparate directions. The hand-clapping and foot-stomping drew a regular beat. One and two and one and two.

Cornelius found himself falling in step with it. As he followed the Campbell's bobbing head, he did it now in time to the beat.

This made it a little easier. But not much. And then not at all. Cornelius lost sight of the Campbell.

One and clap and
One and clap and
Chant and clap and
Chant and clap and
'Hu' and clap and
'Hu' and clap and
'Go' and clap and
'Go' and clap and

Tuppe hopped about. On one leg and the other. Where was Cornelius? The small fellow worried and worried. He knew he'd never forgive himself if something terrible happened to his bestest friend. He should never have been so irresponsible. Staring at a tall girl's bottom when Cornelius needed him. He should be ashamed of himself. He *was* ashamed of himself. 'I shall put tall girls' bottoms behind me for ever,' vowed Tuppe.

Smack! went a tall girl's hand. 'Stop staring at my bottom,' she said.

The dancers now took to leaping up and down. Pogoing like good'ns. And the chant now resounded across the moonlit hill.

'Hu-go,' it went. 'Hu-go. Hu-go. Hu-go.'

'Hugo?' went Cornelius.

'Hugo?' went Tuppe.

'Hugo!' cried the high priestess on the concrete plinth. The lady of the legs. 'Hugo!' She clapped her hands again and again. 'Hugo!'

Once more there came that electricity in the air. Something was about to happen.

A very distraught little Tuppe peered all about. He could see nothing but leaping legs.

'Cornelius, where are you?'

'I'm here.' A hand dived down and scooped up the Tuppe.

'Thank goodness,' sighed the small fellow. 'I thought I'd lost you.'

'Oh no.' The Campbell shook Tuppe vigorously by the throat. 'But I really thought I'd lost *you*. Y' wee bastard.'

'Hu-go,' went the crowd. 'Hu-go Hu-go.'

'Hugo Hugo?' mouthed Cornelius. 'What is going on here?'

'My children,' cried the high priestess. 'My children, hear my words.'

The music and the chanting and the leaping ceased. The celebrants panted and wheezed and coughed. Most of them really weren't up to this kind of lark anyway.

'Let go . . . mmmmmph.' The Campbell's hand clamped across Tuppe's mouth. 'Shut it,' whispered evil Jim. 'Or I'll snap your head off.'

'My children. Tonight is the night. *Our* night. *His* night.'

'*His* night,' intoned the celebrants.

'Although he is gone from us, he will return. His wisdom will open the way for us all. The scales will drop from our eyes. The hidden truths will be revealed. The Ultimate Truths.'

The Ultimate Truths? The tall boy gazed over the heads of the not so tall. The high priestess continued. She still had no clothes on.

'The Master must be returned to us. To we, his followers. Tonight he will speak from beyond and we will bear his wisdom to the four corners of the world. We shall be the voice of Rune. We shall carry his word. We shall reveal all.'

'Oh yes,' said Cornelius. 'Oh yes yes yes.'

'Oh no,' growled the Campbell. 'Oh no bloody no.'

'Oh grmmmph,' went Tuppe, which meant, 'Help!'

'Oh yes.' The naked lady on the concrete plinth raised her hands once more to the night sky. 'By the power of our collective will, so shall we conjure forth his spirit. We must concentrate our energies. Marshal our thoughts. Crystallize them into positive forces. Direct them and cast them to him. Cast these charged thoughts to the Master. Cast them. Right down our nostrils.

Like snot!'

'Oh no you bloody well won't.' A baldy-headed, bespectacled, shortish, beefy, naked kind of a body shouldered his way through the crowd and glared up at the high priestess. He wore an ocarina, strung on a piece of string around his neck. And carried a big gun in one hand and a small dwarf in the other. 'You'll do nothing. Get down from there.'

'Blasphemy!' cried the crowd. 'Beat the blasphemer with a big stout stick.'

The Campbell turned upon them. 'Vice squad!' he shouted. 'You're all under arrest.'

Now, this did catch the crowd with its proverbial trousers down. The celebrants took a step back. Then made a pause. Then took a menacing step forward. Then another back. They just weren't sure. Vice squad or blasphemer? Difficult decision. Several magistrates and a couple of genuine members of the vice squad eased their way from the crowd and made off quietly to their Austin Allegros.

The crowd took two paces forward. Then another one back.

'Stop that dancing,' the Campbell demanded. 'Stand still and put your hands up.'

'Er, excuse me.' A lady wearing nothing but a straw hat stuck her hand up and stepped forward.

'That's the way.' The Campbell gestured with his gun. 'Both hands now.'

'I wasn't putting my hands up. Well, I was putting one up. I just wanted to ask a question.'

'*Ask a question? What* question?'

'Are you really a policeman?'

'Plain clothes.' The Campbell sniggered. Nobody else did.

'Oh good. Then in that case I want to file a complaint. I bought a ticket for last year's coach trip, but I wasn't able to go. So I asked the organizer if I could go this year for free. But he said I'd have to pay the difference, because prices were up this year. Which was fair enough. But what I want to know is this . . .'

'What?'

'Well, if you're a policeman, why aren't you out catching real criminals, rather than harassing good decent folk, who only want to worship in the church of their choice. This is a genuine religion you know. Just because we dance about in our bare scuddies some people—'

'*Shut up!*' The Campbell fired his gun into the air. 'None of that was funny the first time round. The trouble with you people is you don't know what *is* funny. But *we* do. Me and my kind. We know a good joke. And you're it.'

'How dare you.' The lady in the straw hat made a fierce face.

The Campbell made a much fiercer one. 'You!' he shouted. 'All of you. This world of yours. Your so-called society. Your so-called history. Your arts and sciences. It's all a big joke. A big game. A big laugh. And it's on you.'

'Hold on there,' cried the fearless straw-hatter. 'You're not from the vice squad. I know what you are.'

'Oh no you don't.'

'Oh yes I do.'

'Oh no you don't.'

'Oh yes she does,' called the crowd. Glad to get a word or two in.

'Who is he, by the way?' asked Mr Yarrow.

'He's that bloke. You know. Britain's number-one practical joker. The merry prankster himself. He's Jeremy B—'

'Oh no I'm bloody well not.'

'Oh yes you bloody well are.'

'He is, it's him all right.' The lady pointed at the Campbell. 'See he's shaved his beard off. That's why

320

I didn't recognize him right away. Come on, own up. Where are the hidden TV cameras?'

Hidden TV cameras? Now that really did get the crowd on the bubble. Collectively it suffered the kind of crisis that Adam had suffered, when he tasted of the fruit of the Tree of Knowledge.

There was now a very concerted backing away. Faces and privy parts were being covered.

'Stay where you are,' ordered the Campbell.

'Could I do my tea-chest bass playing on the show?' Fred Merlin asked.

'Don't be daft, Fred.' The lady shook her hat. 'Novelty musical acts are Esther. Jeremy's home videos of people falling over and practical tricks.'

'Tricks, is it?' roared the Campbell. 'I'll give you tricks. Here's one for you. Notice what I'm holding in my hands. In this hand I have a big gun. And in this, a small struggling twat. I put the muzzle of the big gun to the head of the small twat, like so, and then I—'

'No you don't.' Cornelius Murphy stepped from the crowd. 'That's not what you do. What you do is this. Put down my friend. Give me the ocarina and go your way. I don't care where you go, it's not my affair. But that's what you do. And you do it now.'

'You . . . you . . .' The Campbell began to heave all about. There were strange comings and goings up and down his person.

The crowd shuffled feet, stepped forwards, backwards and sideways. It was a confused crowd. It didn't know what to do for the best.

'See that?' The lady in the straw hat pointed again. 'He's got a courgette instead of a willy. What a wag that Jeremy.'

'Now,' said Cornelius, raising his gun.

The Campbell shook his head. It was turning very

lumpy. A veritable vegetable garden was sprouting.

'Blurgh!' went the crowd. Agreeing that a step back was in order. But only the one.

'I'll shoot the wee twat!'

'Then *I'll* shoot *you*. I really don't want to. But if you hurt my friend, I'll have no choice.'

'Guns can't kill me,' crowed Jim.

'This one can.'

'Oh no it can't.'

'Oh yes it can,' went the crowd.

'*Shut up!*'

'It's a very special gun,' Cornelius explained. 'It's a Captain Trismegistus Deviant Destroyer. I don't think Airfix do it.'

'*Trismegistus?*' The Campbell's flowering head rose from his shoulders and turned several times in the air.

'Put down my friend and give me the ocarina.'

The Campbell's head whacked back on to his neck. Upside down.

'Blurgh!' went the crowd once more. 'And yuk!'

The Campbell turned his gun upon Cornelius. He let Tuppe tumble to the ground and gripped the ocarina with the free hand. 'You know I can't part with this,' said the mouth in the forehead.

'But you know I *must* have it.'

The crowd looked from one of them to the other. This was the good old Mexican stand-off.

Members of the Olde English Folk Music Society sought about in their repertoire for a bit of suitable 'Gunfight Background'.

'How about "All around my hat"?' a bearded fellow suggested.

'Give me the ocarina, or else.' Cornelius held his pistol in a steady hand.

'Or else what?' The Campbell held his in a likewise

fashion. 'If you use that gun at this range, you'll destroy the ocarina.'

'But you'll be dead, of course.'

The Campbell mused upon this regrettable eventuality. His head rotated slowly and righted itself. 'This is true,' he said slowly. 'But then, without my father's ocarina, it is just a matter of time before they catch up with me anyhow.'

'What did you say?'

'I said *they* will catch up with me.'

'Before that, you said *your father's* ocarina. What did you mean?'

'Hugo Rune was my father,' declared the Campbell.

'Whooooooooooooooah!' went the crowd. 'What?'

'*Your* father?' Cornelius was horrified. 'But Hugo Rune was *my* father.'

'Whooooooooooooooah and double *what*?' went the gob-smacked crowd.

'I don't think they're twins,' said the lady in the straw hat.

'You're lying.' The Murphy's gun hand was beginning to shake. 'You're no brother of mine.'

'Half-brother.' The Campbell's hand was as steady as the proverbial. 'Different mothers. Yours out here, in this world. Mine inside. Inside the Zones. That's why I am what I am. A deviant. Outcast. Neither one thing nor the other. But both. And hating all. I'm taking everything. It's my birthright. My legacy. And I'm not sharing, by the way. So it's goodbye to you, *brother*.'

The Campbell cocked his pistol.

Cornelius dithered. The goalposts had just moved again. He didn't know what to do.

The Campbell did, he squeezed the trigger.

And Tuppe did too. He took a mighty leap, knocked

the Campbell's gun aside. Tore the ocarina from his neck and ducked away.

'Shoot him, Cornelius,' he shouted.

'Y' wee sod ya.' The Campbell swung his pistol after the fleeing Tuppe and fired.

And Cornelius fired at the Campbell.

Something leapt from the barrel of the tin gun. It was a zig-zag of unearthly coloured lightning and it cracked through the air like a whip. It missed the Campbell though. It struck the Reverend Kemp's concrete plinth. Cleaving it from existence.

The high priestess, who hadn't had anything to say for ages, now at least had something to do. She fell down.

But there was no-one there to catch her. The Runies were running. Enough was enough after all. They'd come up here for the bare-scuddy dancing and a spot of centennial necromancy. Not to get caught in the crossfire of some family dispute.

Tuppe plunged between this leg, that leg and the other. He'd never been very fast on his feet, not until now, anyhow.

'Come back!' The Campbell fought his way after Tuppe.

'Stop or I fire.' Cornelius fought his way after the Campbell.

Tuppe ran. He didn't know where he was running to. But he knew what he was running from. And so he just kept going.

When the legs thinned out, he ducked for the trees. Made into them and ran on. The grass was high and he stumbled through it, panting deeply. But clutching the ocarina to his chest.

And he wasn't alone. There were still folk everywhere. Gathering up their clothes. Fighting over whose were whose. Dante would have been in his element.

The Campbell was possibly in his. He marched on, buffeting folk to the left and right of him.

The high priestess was lying dazed on the ground. Mr Yarrow hadn't been near enough to catch her when she fell and he felt very guilty about that. But he'd make it up to her with mouth-to-mouth resuscitation.

'Pucker up, my dear,' said the youth employment officer.

Tuppe struggled on. Ahead of him was a fence. Its cross bars would have blocked the way of a taller person. But not the Tuppe.

If he'd thought to look up, he would have spied the great big sign that was nailed above. This spelled out, in big red letters, a warning, thus:

DANGER
CLIFF EDGE
200-FT DROP

But he didn't. So he missed it.

And then a large dark cloud covered the moon, and it got very black indeed on the top of Star Hill.

'Oh bother,' went Tuppe, feeling his way forward.

'Oh damn,' went Cornelius, floundering blindly about.

'Oh perfect,' went the Campbell, thrusting a finger into his left ear and twisting it around. Cogs whirred, his eyes revolved like the drums of a fruit machine. A succession of different eyeballs blurred down, finally to stop at an evil-looking cat-like pair, with vertical pupils.

'That's better. But to make doubly sure.' He tinkered with his spectacles, adjusting them to *night vision mode*. 'Perfect.'

The Campbell gave the area a quick infra-red scan.

To the south, the flickering rainbow images of departing celebrants. To the west, beside the smouldering ruins of the concrete plinth, a courting couple locked in erotic embrace. To the north, and not twenty yards away, a single figure, tall and angular. The Murphy.

Evil Jim turned his gun in the tall boy's direction. It was an easy shot, he'd never know what hit him.

The single figure turned suddenly away, tripped, fell and vanished from sight.

'Later then,' the Campbell lowered his gun and set out towards the east.

'That was close.' The head of Cornelius Murphy rose in the darkness. Although he hadn't been able to see the Campbell, he'd smelt him, smelt the pistol. The iodine scent of cordite, as the barrel turned in his direction. Cornelius took another noseful, rose from his cover and loped after the Campbell. He knew the scent of Tuppe well enough, and he knew that the deviant was hot upon his trail.

The Campbell was very hot on the wee man's trail. He followed it with no difficulty at all. The residual heat-traces left on the ground by Tuppe's naked feet shone like rubies.

Tuppe backed away towards the cliff edge. The Campbell closed upon him. He pushed aside a tree branch and focused his vision.

There was the little multicoloured image. The clear silhouette of the ocarina obscuring the greater portion of its upper half.

And there was something else. The Campbell blinked

and squinted. Another heat image, long and low, snaking towards his quarry. Its contours were unclearly defined. It seemed to drag itself along on two front legs, but its overall shape appeared to be that of a great fish. A shark? Jim scratched at his baldy head. Whatever it was, it was closing fast on Tuppe. And suddenly there came a snap snap snapping.

And with equal suddenness the moon returned in all its splendour.

Cornelius caught sight of the Campbell's plump backside.

The Campbell spied out the Tuppe, inches from the cliff edge.

And Tuppe, turning at the snapping sound, found himself staring into the gnashing jaws of a large and furry fish.

'Hands up!' cried Cornelius.

'Don't move!' cried the Campbell. .

'Aaaaaagh!' cried Tuppe.

And snap snap snap, went the furry fish.

And then the moon vanished once more and chaos reigned supreme.

Tuppe took a leap in the dark as the furry fish sprang upon him.

The Campbell flung his gun aside and himself at the furry fish.

And Cornelius Murphy brought down the Campbell with a rugby tackle. All this accompanied by a great deal of shouting and snapping.

And presently the moonlight returned once more. This time to illuminate a frozen tableau that was not without passing interest.

Tuppe hung motionless in the air, approximately one hundred and ninety feet above the eighteenth green of the golf course below. He clung to the ocarina, that was now locked firmly in the jaws of the furry fish. The Campbell, hanging over the cliff edge, held the fish by the tail. And Cornelius Murphy clung to the Campbell's knees.

'Tuppe, are you there?' Cornelius struggled to support the combined weight.

'Cornelius, help me.'

'Can you climb up?'

'No. Can you pull me up?'

Cornelius tried. 'No,' he gasped. 'I don't think so.'

'That's a pity.'

'I think we'll have to let the wee twat go.' The voice came from the Campbell's left buttock, which now bore the features of his face. Specs and all.

Cornelius drew back in horror. But he clung on nevertheless.

'Let him go and I let you go,' he told the grinning face.

'I've still got the ocarina,' called Tuppe. 'Well, the fish and I are sharing it actually.'

'Best hold on tight then, *brother*,' said the horrid face.

Cornelius slipped nearer to the edge. He dug his toes into the ground and strained for all he was worth.

'Cornelius, help me.'

'I'm trying.'

'I can't hold on much longer. The fish is dribbling on me.'

'He's a gonna, bruv, let's try and save the fish.' The horrid face grinned evilly.

'Where is my father?' Cornelius could feel his toenails splitting.

'Our father, don't you mean?'

'Where is he?'

'Pull me up and I'll tell you.'

328

'Tuppe,' called Cornelius. 'Get ready to jump.'

'*What?*'

'That's the way,' whispered the face. 'Lighten the load.'

'Is my father still alive? Quickly.'

The face began to laugh.

'Jump, Tuppe. Trust me and jump.' And with that Cornelius let go of the Campbell's legs. The face took on a perplexed expression as the legs up-ended and the Campbell toppled over the cliff.

Cornelius clawed his way to the edge. 'Tuppe, come back. Now!'

Tuppe fell in a flurry of arms and legs. The great furry fish came after him and something bad and bloating on its tail.

'Heeeeelp!'

'Bring him to me *now*!' shouted Cornelius, reaching down his hands.

And something swept up, as all about it were sweeping down.

Something black and cold wrapped around the Murphy's wrists.

He gripped it and pulled with all his strength.

And Tuppe stopped falling. The fish and the ocarina and the swelling something flew by him and went down and down and down.

But Tuppe began to rise. Up the wall of the cliff.

It doesn't take long to fall two hundred feet. No more than a few short seconds. There is, however, just enough time to do either of the following; curse the name of Murphy, or, swallow an ocarina.

Then it's SPLAT!

The Campbell and the furry fish struck the eighteenth green of the municipal golf course. It was a hole in one. It was a very devastating SPLAT!

Cornelius hauled Tuppe back over the cliff edge. The small fellow's bewildered face gaped at him.

'How?' asked Tuppe

Cornelius lifted him to safety and set him down. 'That was close,' he said.

The grand full moon shone down upon Star Hill.

Cornelius sat in the thistles on his naked bottom, gasping and wheezing. 'I think we've finally seen the last of the Campbell,' he panted.

Tuppe glared up at his friend. 'I could have been killed. You let me fall.'

'It was a calculated risk.'

'A calculated what? You bas—'

'Tuppe, there was no other way. I couldn't have held on any longer.' Cornelius plucked a thistle from his bum. 'I had to rely on your magic shadow. It saved me. So it seemed reasonable to suppose it would do the same for you.'

'And what if it hadn't?'

'If it hadn't, I would have thrown myself over the cliff and let God sort it out.'

'You wouldn't?' Tuppe looked into the face of his friend.

There were tears in the tall boy's eyes. They told Tuppe all he needed to know.

They found their clothes and they dressed.

'I'm sorry about the ocarina,' said Tuppe. 'I did my best.'

'I know that you did. I'm just glad that you're safe.'

And they strolled down to the car. Cornelius stuffed Arthur Kobold's gun into his jacket pocket. 'I shall have many words to say to Mr Kobold and also to the daddy, when we get home.'

'I'm sure that you will.'

'We may still turn a handsome profit though. All is far from lost.'

'I'm very pleased to hear it.'

The Cadillac stood where they had left it, shining beautifully in the moonlight, on the edge of the golf course.

'Handsome car,' said Tuppe. 'Yours, is it?'

'Birthday present. I'd hoped for an Allegro, of course.'

'You could always trade it in.'

Cornelius grinned. 'Shall we go home?'

'Let's do. I've had quite enough for one night.'

A light wind drifted over the top of Star Hill. Rippling through the grass. It turned the hem of a discarded silk robe or two and lightly brushed the strings of a hautboy, or it might have been a gittern. It trickled a little dust over the rim of a small crater, where a concrete plinth had recently stood. And the dust fell on to the soles of a pair of ancient clerical boots.

'Hello,' called a muffled voice. 'Is it Judgement Day already? Hello? Hello?'

21

'Let's go.' Cornelius turned the ignition key.

Fut fut fut fut . . . fut . . . went the Cadillac Eldorado.

'Oh great.'

'Out of petrol?' Tuppe asked.

'Can't be. Unless the tank's been siphoned.' Cornelius shinned from the driving seat and ambled around to the back of the car.

'Aha!' He stooped down and plucked something up.

'What is it?'

'It's a sprout. Some joker stuck it on the exhaust pipe.' Cornelius threw the vegetable at Tuppe, who caught it.

'I hate sprouts.' Tuppe gave the thing a sniff. 'And this one's on the turn.' He flung it back at Cornelius, but it bounced on to the back seat.

'Let's go home.' Cornelius climbed back into his seat. Keyed the ignition. The engine caught and the Cadillac rolled from the golf course and down towards the road.

'I grieve for that ocarina,' sighed Tuppe, as they rolled along. 'All that booty, there for the taking.'

'We'll still make good, I told you. We have Rizla's papers and the adoptive daddy will yield up the remaining. Mr Kobold will pay handsomely. And I *will* be claiming the bounty he offered on the Campbell.'

'Quite right too. But what about your real daddy? Is he still alive, do you think?'

'Oh yes, he's alive. The Campbell knew it. I'll find Hugo Rune somehow.'

'*Oh no you won't!*'

'Oh yes I will.' Cornelius turned to Tuppe. 'How did you do *that* voice, by the way?'

Tuppe shrank down in his seat. 'I didn't. Oh, Cornelius . . .'

The Murphy saw it in the driving-mirror. A shiny green horror, rising in the back seat. Swelling from the discarded sprout. Forming once more into the shape of the Campbell.

'Oh no!' Cornelius slammed his foot down on the accelerator.

'Ha ha ha ha ha,' went the jolly green Jim. 'You're dead, by the way.'

'Not yet.' Cornelius kept his foot down and the Cadillac gathered speed. It swept from the golf course road to the place where the buses turn around. And there, parked all alone, was a spikey black VW. And through the crack in its bonnet, a pair of frightened eyes viewed the oncoming car.

'Oh no,' wailed Felix Henderson McMurdo.

The Campbell sprang forward and caught Cornelius by his hair.

Cornelius clung to the steering wheel. 'Get the gun, Tuppe. Shoot him.'

Tuppe rightly panicked. 'Where is it?'

'In my pocket. Oh ow.' The Campbell yanked back the tall boy's head. 'Hurry, Tuppe, I can't see.'

'Look out. We're going to crash.' Tuppe grabbed the steering wheel and dragged it to the right. The Cadillac swerved and raked along the side of the VW, overturning it in a fine cloud of sparks.

'My bloody car,' roared the Campbell. 'You vandal.'

'Let go of me.' Cornelius fought to free himself. 'Get off.'

'No chance.' The Campbell opened a cold yawning mouth. Evil pointy fish teeth snapped ferociously. Snap snap snap, they went.

'Get the gun, Tuppe.'

'And steer the car?'

'Use your initiative. Aaaagh!'

The Campbell tore out a great chunk of Murphy mane. 'Haircut, sir?' he sniggered. 'A little off the top?'

'Tuppe, help!'

The small fellow scrambled on to his friend's lap. He couldn't steer *and* search for the gun. And so he did a courageous thing. He swarmed on to the tall boy's shoulder and poked a finger into the Campbell's eye. 'Take that,' he said.

'Ouch!' The Campbell fell back. Lumps of big hair in each hand.

'Ouch!' Cornelius fell forward, dislodging Tuppe on to the floor. He flung the steering wheel this way and that. The Cadillac swung along the parade, narrowly avoiding the parked cars. It flew by The Wife's Legs Café. And onward.

The Campbell was up and at 'em once more. He raised a claw-like hand, which had more than a hint of furry fish about it and flung himself again at the driver.

'Find the gun, Tuppe. Hurry.'

'I'm trying.' Tuppe rooted from pocket to pocket. It wasn't exactly an easy task. 'Ah. I've got it.'

'Then use it. Ooooooh . . .' The Campbell's talons hooked into Murphy's hair again, dragging him up from his seat. His hands left the steering wheel and the car cannoned from one side of the road to the other.

'Shoot him, Tuppe.' Cornelius fought and twisted. He struggled and he kicked. 'Shoot him, Tuppe. Tuppe?'

But Tuppe did not reply.

Because Cornelius had kicked him right in the chin and Tuppe was now unconscious. He lay slumped on the floor.

On top of the accelerator pedal.

The Cadillac thundered through red lights and into the high street. It smashed along a row of parked cars, losing many precious parts and a lot of shiny paintwork. But it kept right on going.

The Campbell's claws locked around the throat of Cornelius Murphy. 'Goodbye, brother,' crowed evil Jim.

'Urgh,' went Cornelius, fighting for breath.

The claws tightened. Cornelius felt his ears popping. His eyes bulged as darkness began to close in. This was surely the end. This creature that called itself his half-brother was actually killing him. Killing *him*. The stuff of epics. That couldn't be right. Could it? He was only starting out on his epic career.

The claws closed upon his windpipe. And suddenly Cornelius Murphy saw the light.

And the Campbell saw it too.

A real Bobby-dazzler of a light. Sweeping towards them. It lit up the road and the sky and the shop fronts, flickering through a spectrum that was all its own.

The Campbell gaped in horror. 'Trismegistus!'

Yabba Dabba Doooo . . . The train dashed forwards. Systems clicking and clacking. Full steam ahead. Its smokestack rained fireflies of electricity. Within its swift smooth shape, tennis balls with nails in the

335

top modulated the flow of beta particles from the positronic generator. Transponders hissed through the anti-matter drive and the little clockwork mouse raced round and round in its wheel.

Identification circuits meshed. Cross-referenced the face in the rear of the oncoming car with the one on the photograph in the slot marked 'A'.

And came up with a match.

The Campbell's grip loosened momentarily. Cornelius tore himself from it. He scooped up the Tuppe and forced both feet on to the brake pedal. The Cadillac slewed, wheels locked, tyres burning. Cornelius threw an arm across his face. The Campbell flew forward. Passed over the cowering Murphy and continued on. Straight into the path of The Train of Trismegistus.

YABBA DABBA DOOOOO

22

'And then one night in Bangkok,' the mother continued, 'we were supposed to be going to this chess tournament. But the coach driver got lost and we ended up at this little night club on the north shore of the Chao Phraya. The star turn was a contortionist. His impression of The Worm Ouroboros was an absolute scream. More tea, Mr Kobold?'

'Is there a fresh pot going?'

'No, there's plenty left in this one.'

'I'll stay as I am then, thank you. Did you say there was cake?'

'No. Did you?'

Arthur Kobold didn't get to answer that one. Because the kitchen door burst open and two terrific figures stood framed in the portal.

There was a long one and a short one. Both appeared somewhat smoke-blackened. The long one seemed to be lacking most of his hair. The short one looked a bit dazed.

'Cornelius.' The mother blinked. 'What have you done with your big hair? And Tuppe, sit down, you look most poorly.'

'Cornelius.' The daddy rose from his chair. 'Is everything all right with you both?'

'We're still alive. Almost.'

'Let me help you.' Arthur Kobold stepped up to assist.

337

'Stay away from us.' Cornelius helped his friend on to a chair. The mother reached down two more tea cups.

'The Campbell . . .' Arthur Kobold asked. 'Is he . . . ?'

'He's dead.' Cornelius slumped into the chair the daddy held out for him. 'Very dead indeed.'

'Well done.'

'Don't thank me. The Campbell was hit by a train. In the high street.'

'The boy's delirious.' The mother put aside the cold teapot. 'Let me phone for Doctor Jameson.'

'Better tell him to bring lots of bandages. Mr Kobold is going to need them.'

'Oh no please.' Arthur tried to take a step back. But you just couldn't do that sort of thing in the Murphys' kitchen. So he wrung his hands pathetically. 'Please let me explain.'

'You'd better.'

'I've never lied to you, Cornelius. I didn't tell you all of the truth. But that was for your own sake. I didn't want any harm to come to you. I told you to quit, didn't I? When things began to get dangerous.'

'You did, that's true.'

'You see, *they* wanted the Campbell back. And *they* wanted the papers. *I* wanted them to have the Campbell back. But I had no intention of letting them get the papers. I never trusted them. And when they released The Train of Trismegistus, not caring who it might have killed, I knew that I had to expose them. Let the whole world know the truth.'

'The Ultimate Truth?'

'The very same. Look, see, this is for you.' Arthur Kobold pulled a slip of paper from his pocket and handed it to Cornelius.

Cornelius eyed it suspiciously. 'What is this?'

'It's a cheque. Read it.'

Cornelius read it. Then he handed it to Tuppe.

Tuppe read it and he whistled. 'One hundred thousand pounds. Made out for cash.'

'It's an advance. Against royalties.'

'Royalties?'

'Your father's work. I mean to publish it. In its entirety. You do still have it, don't you? The papers Brother Rizla gave you.'

'I wonder how you knew about that.'

'I phoned the abbot. He told me.'

'Oh.'

'But *do* you still have the papers?'

'I have them. And the "daddy" here, has the rest.'

The daddy smiled. So did Arthur Kobold. 'I've just bought his,' he said. 'Drives a hard bargain does Mr Murphy.'

The daddy smiled again. Cornelius shook his head.

'And the ocarina?' Arthur Kobold asked. 'What of that?'

'It got smashed to pieces.'

'That is regrettable. But no matter. We can work without it.'

'We?' Cornelius asked.

'We, my boy. I want you with me. I will publish your father's work at my own expense. But it won't be easy. *They* will do everything in their power to stop us. And power is something *they* have a great deal of. What do you say?'

'I don't know.' Cornelius stroked his chin. There was definite evidence of stubble.

'You would oversee the entire operation. Edit your father's work. Supervise its publication. Everything. By its nature it will become the best-selling book in the world. So, I hope you don't think the advance too meagrely. I am a man of not unlimited resources. I can't do it without your help.'

Cornelius looked at Tuppe.

And Tuppe looked at Cornelius.

'I will need to know everything you know about *them*,' Cornelius told Arthur Kobold.

'You certainly will if we are to succeed. Give me the papers now. Cash the cheque first thing in the morning and be in my office by ten. And then you and I will change the world for ever. What do you say?' Arthur Kobold stuck out his hand for a shake.

Cornelius rose and took it. 'I say we have a deal,' said he, grinning for all he was worth.

23

Cornelius and Tuppe took breakfast in The Wife's Legs Café.

The wife seemed a little off-hand with the tall boy. She served him cold tea and a broken egg, floating in grease.

'Never mind.' Tuppe scooped it on to his plate and mopped up the grease with a slice of toast. 'Cash the cheque and buy her out. That'll teach her.'

'The daddy did suggest I invest in some insurance for the Cadillac.'

'Well, after that then.' Tuppe wiped his mouth.

'After that we go and speak with Arthur Kobold. This is far from over.'

Jeffrey Barlow-Clowes the junior bank clerk (Mr Yarrow had been particularly pleased about getting him placed) looked up through the bullet-proof glass of his till window, as Cornelius swaggered towards it. He'd been in the same class as the tall boy, but they'd never been friends. Jeffrey considered Cornelius a no-mark. Cornelius thought Jeffrey something of a prat.

'I'd like to cash this please.' Cornelius pushed Mr Kobold's cheque beneath the armoured glass.

Jeffrey glanced down at the cheque and then up at the tall boy.

'Oh yes?'

'Oh yes indeed.' Cornelius smiled warmly.

'Cashed, you say?' Jeffrey did not return the smile.

'If you'll be so kind. Here is my library ticket, if you need identification.'

'I don't. How would you like this cashed exactly?'

'Fifty-pound notes please.'

'Fifty-pound notes.' The prat sat back in his chair. 'Not titters, perhaps? Or chortles? Or even guffaws?'

'Come again?'

'Piss off!' Jeffrey pushed the cheque back under the glass. 'You no-mark.'

'Eh what?' Cornelius took up the cheque. It appeared slightly different from the way it had looked only moments before. In fact it looked considerably different. For where it had just read, CASH £100,000, it now read BANK OF FUNLAND. I promise to pay the bearer 100 laughs.

'I'll start with the chuckles then, shall I?' asked Jeffrey Barlow-Clowes. 'Ha ha ha ha ha.'

Cornelius dashed back to the Cadillac. Mr Twaites, the traffic warden, was just tucking a ticket under the windscreen wiper.

'Move over, Tuppe.'

'I am over. What's going on? Where's the money?'

Cornelius leapt into the car. 'There is no money. Arthur Kobold tricked us.'

'The treacherous sod.'

'And then some. We've been had. He never intended to publish the papers. He's been working all along for the bogie men in the Forbidden Zones.' Cornelius brrmed the engine and pulled away without a glance in his mirror. Cars screeched to a halt. Austin Allegros shunted into one another. Cornelius put his foot hard down.

Tuppe clung on to his seat. 'What are we going to do now? Everything's lost. The ocarina, the papers, the money, most of your hair.'

'We're going round to Kobold's. We're not done for yet.'

They really shouldn't have expected otherwise. But they were desperate and so they did. It was very disappointing.

The offices of Arthur Kobold Publications were no more. And, by the look of the scaffolding and the shored-up façade, they had been no more for a very long time indeed.

'Are you sure this is the right place, Cornelius?'

'Damn and blast!' Cornelius smote the steering wheel with his fists. 'Damn damn damn.'

Tuppe struggled down from the car and gazed up at the ruination.

'And this was where he was?'

Cornelius sighed and joined his companion. 'This is it.'

'Looks like we missed him by about a century. How do they do these things?'

Cornelius shrugged. 'I don't know. But I mean to find out.' He took a step or two towards the crumbling premises. Brickdust fluttered down between scaffold boards. Its warning was loud and clear.

'Damn,' said Cornelius once more.

'Perhaps we just aren't meant to be rich and famous.'

Cornelius plucked up a half brick and weighed it in his hand.

'I'll beat this. Somehow, some way. I'll beat Kobold and the things in the Zones. I will find my true daddy and I will triumph. Somehow I'll do it. Somehow.'

'I'm sure that you will, Cornelius. I believe in you.'

'Thanks, Tuppe.' Cornelius patted his chum on the shoulder.

'But what do we do now? I spent my last pennies on breakfast. We're broke.'

'This does present certain difficulties I agree.'

'We could busk,' Tuppe suggested.

'Busk?'

'Certainly, why not? Sing for our supper.'

'Sing for our supper? Tuppe, you genius.' Cornelius Murphy began to laugh. 'That's it. That's it!'

'It is? What is?'

'That. That.' Cornelius was pointing.

'I can't see.'

Cornelius gave the Tuppe a leg-up. 'That,' he said.

'That.' Tuppe stared down at it. Jammed there behind the passenger seat and completely forgotten in all the excitement, was the nice, sturdy crate containing the magic karaoke machine. A now fully restored karaoke machine, all set to belt out the hits from the future.

'We're made.' Tuppe climbed on to the back seat and jumped up and down. 'You're made, I mean.'

'*We*'re made. This is a partnership. Murphy and Tuppe, songwriters to the stars. I shall have my hair professionally groomed.'

'And I will buy some platform shoes.'

Cornelius Murphy jumped back into the car. 'And Arthur Kobold will get what's coming to him.'

The tall boy hefted the half brick and slung it at the scaffolding.

'Let's go.'

Fut fut fut fut fut, went the Cadillac Eldorado.

'Not another sprout,' said Tuppe fearfully.

344

'No!' Cornelius thumped the wheel. 'It's really out of petrol this time.'

'What is that noise?' Tuppe turned towards the sound. It was a low rumbling. 'I don't like the sound of that.'

'Oh shit!' Cornelius climbed up in his seat. 'The front of the arch is coming away. I must have done it when I threw the brick.'

And indeed this was so. The scaffolding heaved and rocked. Timbers dropped away. Bricks began to bounce down. One struck the bonnet of the Cadillac.

'Grab the karaoke machine,' cried Tuppe.

Cornelius leaned over the passenger seat and struggled to free the crate. It was well and truly stuck. 'Give us a hand, Tuppe.'

Tuppe hastened to oblige. A scaffold pole smashed into the seat beside him.

'Get out, Tuppe. Leave it.'

'It's coming. I felt it give.'

'Leave it.' Cornelius grabbed Tuppe by the arm and hauled him from the car. And it wasn't a moment too soon. As they fled across the street, the whole kith and kaboodle and without any doubt, the kitchen sink, of Arthur Kobold Publications, descended upon the Cadillac Eldorado, in one God-awful soul-destroying karaoke-crunching skip-load. Crash and bang and wallop, it went.

And then some.

It was nearly two of the sunny afternoon clock, before the men from the council finished clearing away the rubble.

Tuppe and Cornelius sat at the roadside and watched sorrowfully, as Mark the mechanic (no relative of

Mike) winched the tragic remains of the once-proud Eldorado on to the back of his truck.

'I'm sorry, lads,' said he, wiping his fingers on the traditional oily rag. 'It's a total write-off. Best I can do you is a nifty for the scrap.'

'A nifty?' Tuppe asked.

'A nifty fifty. Fifty quid.'

Cornelius groaned.

'We'll take it,' said Tuppe.

'Oh no, you won't take it.' Mark laughed. 'My call-out fee for vehicle recovery is fifty quid. So I suppose that makes us even.'

Cornelius groaned again.

'Still, never mind,' Mark went on. 'Your insurance will pay up without a fuss.'

'Allow me, Cornelius.' Tuppe groaned for the tall boy.

'Ah,' said Mark. 'Like that, is it? Life's a bummer, eh? Well, I've your personal effects here. Not much I'm afraid, a route map and an A–Z from the glovey. And about thirty Biros, they were all stuck down the side of the driving seat. Funny how you come across them in places like that, but there's never one around when you need it. I wonder why that is, eh?'

'Search me,' said Cornelius, burying his face in his hands.

'Well, there you go then. See you, lads.'

'See you,' said Tuppe. 'Be lucky.'

'You too.' Mark returned to his truck and the erstwhile epic adventurers looked on as the Cadillac's wreckage was towed away.

'Damn,' said Cornelius. 'Damn damn damn.'

'Well, that would definitely be it.' Tuppe tossed the personal effects into the road. 'We've lost it all. The ocarina, the papers, the cheque, the karaoke machine and the Cadillac.'

'And most of my hair.' Cornelius ran his fingers over his numerous bald patches. 'Let's not forget my hair.'

'I hadn't. I just didn't like to mention it.'

'Perhaps there's a moral in it or something.' Cornelius stood up and stretched.

'Perhaps.' Tuppe stuffed a handful of Biros into his pocket. 'Waste not want not?' he suggested, dismally.

Cornelius Murphy began to laugh.

Tuppe rolled his eyes. 'I'm glad you can see the funny side.'

'Oh, I can. I really can.' Cornelius reached down and took up the route map and the dog-eared A–Z. Rune's London A–Z Street Directory. In which the great man had marked the precise location of every secret entrance into the Forbidden Zones. All clearly marked and just waiting for some epic personage to take up a reinvented ocarina, play the magic notes, open up each one in turn and claim the hidden wealth within.

And, of course, the map. The tall boy's map of the British Isles. On which Cornelius had pencilled the route and stopping points of his and Tuppe's epic journey. A dot-to-dot pencil picture which formed the perfect blueprint for the reinvented ocarina.

Cornelius looked at Tuppe.

And Tuppe looked at Cornelius.

And then they both began to laugh.

THE END

SPROUT⟨P⟩LŌRE

The Now Official
RŌBERT RANKIN
Fan Club

Members Will Receive:

Four Fabulous Issues of *The Brentford Mercury,* featuring previously unpublished stories by Robert Rankin. Also containing News, Reviews, Fiction and Fun.

A Coveted Sproutlore Badge.

'Amazing Stuff!' – *Robert Rankin*.

THE BRENTFORD TRIANGLE
by Robert Rankin

'A born writer . . . Robert Rankin is to Brentford what William Faulkner was to Yoknapatawpha County'
Time Out

'Omally groaned. "It is the end of mankind as we know it. I should never have got up so early today" and all over Brentford electrical appliances were beginning to fail . . .'

Could it be that Pooley and Omally, whilst engaged on a round of allotment golf, mistook laser-operated gravitational landing beams for the malignant work of Brentford Council?

Does the Captain Laser Alien Attack machine in the bar of the Swan possess more sinister force than its magnetic appeal for youths with green hair?

Is Brentford the first base in an alien onslaught on planet Earth?

The second novel in the now legendary *Brentford Trilogy*

0 552 13842 8

ARMAGEDDON THE MUSICAL
by Robert Rankin

From the point of view of 2050, you're history.

Theological warfare. Elvis on an epic time-travel journey – the Presilad. Buddhavision – a network bigger than God (and more powerful, too). Nasty nuclear leftovers. Naughty sex habits. Dalai Dan (the 153rd reincarnation of the Lama of that ilk) and Barry, the talkative Time Sprout. Even with all this excitement, you wouldn't think a backwater planet like Earth makes much of a splash in the galactic pond.

But the soap opera called *The Earthers* is making big video bucks in the intergalactic ratings race. And alien TV execs know exactly what the old earth drama needs to make the off-world audience sit up and stare: a spectacular Armageddon-type finale. With a cast of millions – including you! Don't touch that dial – it's gonna be a helluva show!

'To the top-selling ranks of humorists such as Douglas Adams and Terry Pratchett, let us welcome Mr Rankin'
Tom Hutchinson, *The Times*

'He crams enough gags into *Armageddon The Musical* to last anyone else for a trilogy. And nothing's sacred. So buy this quick, before he ends up sleeping in Salman Rushdie's spare bedroom'
Terry Pratchett

0 552 13681 6

SNUFF FICTION
by Robert Rankin

'He does for England what Spike Milligan does for Ireland. There can be no higher praise'
John Clute, *Mail on Sunday*

Society's plug is about to be pulled, big time. At the stroke of midnight on 31 December 1999, computer systems all over the world will crash and plunge us into chaos.

But so what if it's the downfall of civilization? These things happen. We'll just have to take it on the chin. Or at least up the nose. Because rejoice and give thanks, snuff is making a comeback. And who do we thank for this? Who is the man who brings joy to the nostrils of the nation? The tender blender with the blinder grinder? The master blaster with the louder powder? The geezer with the sneezer that's a real crowd pleaser? Mr Doveston, that's who, and this is his story.

So forget about impending doom and enter the glamorous world of snuff-snorting. Oh, and don't forget to bring a hankie. Things could get a little messy later.

0 552 14590 4

A SELECTED LIST OF FANTASY TITLES
AVAILABLE FROM CORGI AND BLACK SWAN

THE PRICES SHOWN BELOW WERE CORRECT AT THE TIME OF
GOING TO PRESS. HOWEVER TRANSWORLD PUBLISHERS RESERVE
THE RIGHT TO SHOW NEW RETAIL PRICES ON COVERS WHICH MAY
DIFFER FROM THOSE PREVIOUSLY ADVERTISED IN THE TEXT OR
ELSEWHERE.

☐	14802 4	MALLOREON 1: GUARDIANS OF THE WEST	David Eddings	£5.99
☐	14807 5	BELGARIAD 1: PAWN OF PROPHECY	David Eddings	£5.99
☐	14256 5	SWORD IN THE STORM	David Gemmell	£5.99
☐	14257 3	MIDNIGHT FALCON	David Gemmell	£5.99
☐	14274 3	THE MASTERHARPER OF PERN	Anne McCaffrey	£5.99
☐	13763 4	THE ROWAN	Anne McCaffrey	£5.99
☐	14478 9	AUTOMATED ALICE	Jeff Noon	£6.99
☐	14479 7	NYMPHOMATION	Jeff Noon	£6.99
☐	14614 5	THE LAST CONTINENT	Terry Pratchett	£5.99
☐	14615 3	CARPE JUGULUM	Terry Pratchett	£5.99
☐	13681 6	ARMAGEDDON THE MUSICAL	Robert Rankin	£5.99
☐	13832 0	THEY CAME AND ATE US, ARMAGEDDON II: THE B-MOVIE	Robert Rankin	£5.99
☐	13923 8	THE SUBURBAN BOOK OF THE DEAD ARMAGEDDON III: THE REMAKE:	Robert Rankin	£5.99
☐	13841 X	THE ANTIPOPE	Robert Rankin	£5.99
☐	13842 8	THE BRENTFORD TRIANGLE	Robert Rankin	£5.99
☐	13843 6	EAST OF EALING	Robert Rankin	£5.99
☐	13844 4	THE SPROUTS OF WRATH	Robert Rankin	£5.99
☐	14357 X	THE BRENTFORD CHAINSTORE MASSACRE	Robert Rankin	£5.99
☐	13833 9	RAIDERS OF THE LOST CAR PARK	Robert Rankin	£5.99
☐	13924 6	THE GREATEST SHOW OFF EARTH	Robert Rankin	£5.99
☐	14211 5	THE MOST AMAZING MAN WHO EVER LIVED	Robert Rankin	£5.99
☐	14212 3	THE GARDEN OF UNEARTHLY DELIGHTS	Robert Rankin	£5.99
☐	14213 1	A DOG CALLED DEMOLITION	Robert Rankin	£5.99
☐	14355 3	NOSTRADAMUS ATE MY HAMSTER	Robert Rankin	£5.99
☐	14356 1	SPROUT MASK REPLICA	Robert Rankin	£5.99
☐	14580 7	THE DANCE OF THE VOODOO HANDBAG	Robert Rankin	£5.99
☐	14589 0	APOCALYPSO	Robert Rankin	£5.99
☐	14590 4	SNUFF FICTION	Robert Rankin	£5.99
☐	99777 3	THE SPARROW	Mary Doria Russell	£6.99
☐	99811 7	CHILDREN OF GOD	Mary Doria Russell	£6.99

All Transworld titles are available by post from:

Bookpost, P.O. Box 29, Douglas, Isle of Man IM99 1BQ

Credit cards accepted. Please telephone 01624 836000,
fax 01624 837033, Internet http://www.bookpost.co.uk or
e-mail: bookshop@enterprise.net for details.

Free postage and packing in the UK. Overseas customers allow
£1 per book (paperbacks) and £3 per book (hardbacks).